POISON KISSED

ERICA HAYES

St. Martin's Paperbacks

This is a work of fiction. All of the characters, organizations, and events portrayed in this novel are either products of the author's imagination or are used fictitiously.

POISON KISSED

Copyright © 2010 by Erica Hayes.
Excerpt from *Blood Cursed* copyright © 2010 by Erica Hayes.

For information address St. Martin's Press, 175 Fifth Avenue, New York, NY 10010.

ISBN: 978-0-312-62470-5

Printed in the United States of America

St. Martin's Paperbacks edition / October 2010

St. Martin's Paperbacks are published by St. Martin's Press, 175 Fifth Avenue, New York, NY 10010.

10 9 8 7 6 5 4 3 2 1

1

They say that when a banshee sings, someone dies.

It's true. But only if we mean to kill.

I pulled my knifeblade tighter against the gangster's throat and jammed his heavy body harder into the rainbow-sprayed brick wall with my hip. Tall shadows stabbed into the grimy alley beneath a hot moonlit sky, and the evil scent of his blood watered my mouth.

Unluckily for him, I meant it all right.

Sweet poison music swelled in my lungs, dripping with enspelled emotion and blood. I crooned a withering curse, and his dark-stubbled cheek blistered under my breath. "You murdered three of my friends, Sonny Valenti. All I have to do is sing."

Summer heat tingled my hypersensitive ears like a distant symphony, the dry air murmuring below distant traffic noise and soft breeze. Beside me, moonlight glinted silver in Joey's hellgreen eyes, his blond hair gleaming white. He slipped closer, a lean black shadow in his dark suit, and his voice slid like a needle, bright and easy under my skin, where it belonged. "Easy, Mina. Let him talk."

My name in his mouth made me shiver. Joey DiLuca is my boss—he pays, I fight—and I know he doesn't deal death lightly. If Joey says Sonny deserves to die, that's fine with me. Joey's the thinker in this outfit. I just do.

I yanked Sonny's black curls back in my fist, easing the

knife off a little to let the blood run. He's a big tough guy—he's not the Valenti family's chief headkicker for nothing—but I held him no problem. With my spellsparked reflexes, I'm stronger than I look. "Tell us who helped you, and this'll hurt a whole lot less."

"I never had nothin' to do with it." Sonny struggled, his face scraping bloody streaks on the jagged bricks. "I never even knew what they done. Get the fuck offa me."

Joey tapped his shiny black cane impatiently on the concrete. "Persuade him, Mina."

I inhaled, tingling. Summer warmth soaked my tight leather vest, safe and comforting. The music of midnight in Melbourne: sparking neon, stifling heat, a storm's sharp ozone tang, and the throbbing roll of thunder. My ears exulted at the delicious vibration. To a banshee, everything is music.

Melody wrapped around my tongue like a fairy lover's kiss, and I sang sweet terror.

Sonny gurgled, spit bubbling. His hard muscles jerked against mine, splashing me with the dirtybright scents of cold sweat and fear. He shuddered, but hatred twisted his lip. "I ain't telling you shit. Fuckin' snakewhore."

I didn't pity him. An evil man, this Sonny—killer, armed robber, beater-up of girls, and torturer of minions for money. He and his Valenti friends had murdered our boss and his closest cousins in a spiteful preemptive strike. Which dumped the responsibility for leading our gang squarely and unexpectedly on Joey. We'd moved up in the world, like it or not. Joey didn't ask for it, or want it. He just dealt with it, calm and unruffled as always.

So here we were, getting our own back. And I had extra reason to hate Sonny. When I was a mouthy teenage brat who did any dirty thing for cash, he spat on me, kicked me, laughed at me along with the rest. Maybe I slept with him. I don't remember a lot of things I did back then.

Besides, we DiLucas didn't start this gang war. That happened before my time, when we were all just small-time gangsters, running illegal games and protection rackets, selling the latest psychotic fairy drugs, and minding our own business. But the demon court brought their eternal bickering to town—imagine a cross between *Gossip Girl* and a pack of soulthirsty hyenas—and the old ways of tolerance and sharing erupted in blood and bullets. The demon prince, Kane, wanted the city for himself, and he chose Angelo Valenti, a crafty old vampire gang boss, to rule his turf. So Ange and his crazy-ass cousins systematically crushed their opposition, killing and maiming and damning souls to hell, until Joey and our little gang were all that remained.

We have our demon patron, too, or rather, patroness—I don't trust Delilah's sultry lies, but Joey says we can't do without demon backing, not with Kane and the Valenti gang gunning for us—so I guess we're all hellbound. But who cares? They'd forced us into a corner, these vicious Valentis, and like any cornered beasties, we fight back.

That didn't make killing easy, or mean I'd enjoy it. But it had to be done. It was my job. Let's just get on with it.

I yowled, imminent death a rich thrill in my mouth. "You done, boss?"

Joey shrugged, fluid. "Last chance, Santino. Anything intelligent to say?"

Sonny spat, spit and blood splashing Joey's shirt. "Angelo's gonna rip your heart out and drink your shitstained blood—"

"Didn't think so. Thank you, Mina."

My magical melody swelled and twisted in my chest like a snake, longing to sing free. She's a cruel deathwish mistress, my song, and she'd warp the world to her capricious will if I let her. She makes me strong, but her hunger shivers ice in my blood. I don't want to be a killer.

Sometimes fate doesn't give a fuck what you want.

I closed my eyes, the better to hear my racing heart, and imagined Sonny was the man who murdered my mother.

Memory chilled my skin, trailing goose bumps and the dark scent of flowers in its wake. I inhaled, and with a rush of blood, I was fourteen again, huddling behind the dusty velvet sofa with fear freezing my muscles solid.

The lights are broken. I can't see much, but even if it were daylight, I couldn't drag myself out. I'm so scared, I can't move. My untrained song is dry and jagged like crackers in my throat. I whimper, and no sound comes out.

The footsteps come closer, soft and unstoppable like a vile ticking clock. My mother howls and thrashes on the floor, and the window behind me shatters as her wild harmonics rend the air. The smell of her blood rips my stomach raw.

My heart judders. My bowels run like hot honey, and I wrap shaking arms around myself so tightly, my gut aches. I'm gonna piss myself, and he'll smell it and when he's killed her, he'll kill me, too, only he'll do things to me first, the kind of things that have only ever meant hell to me and are about to get a whole lot worse.

The footsteps stop. My mother's nails scrape the floor, razors on a blackboard, her beautiful magical voice shredded like tinfoil: Please. Help me.

Tears carve hot channels down my face. I want to scramble up, leap on him, and chew his throat out, but terror washes my will to water. Shame savages my heart. Oiled metal clicks, and my mother screams no, and then the sound of a gunshot rips my head apart.

I opened my eyes. Moonlight slashed through cold tears, scratching in my ears like sandpaper. Weak, terrified little girl, hiding while her mother died screaming.

Black lust for revenge bubbled inside me like tar, and the olive-shaped poison sacs under my tongue swelled hard, threatening to burst.

Sonny didn't kill my mother. His death wouldn't give me revenge. But sure as the devil lived in Toorak, it'd make me feel better for now.

Bloody deathsong swelled hot and delicious in my lungs, and the promise of release built like a dam in my fevered veins. I yanked Sonny's head back, forcing his bleeding ear closer to my lips, and opened my mouth to kill.

The air whistled, and flashing glass wings scythed from the sky.

My neck whiplashed, my skull forced at right angles. Pain exploded like a firework and poured molten down my spine. I tumbled, dragged aside by cold grasping hands. My knife clattered to the pavement, lost.

Sonny staggered and fell, blood streaming from his skull, and his pistol bounced away.

Body weight crunched me into the ground, ultrasmooth limbs flexing around mine, cold claws grasping for my throat. My neonblue hair tumbled in my face, blinding me. A fresh crystal chuckle tinkled. "Sing for me, bluebell. I dare ya."

I wriggled beneath him, drenched in the smell of roses and rainwet glass, and my pulse skipped over a thin squirt of fear. I knew this glassfairy asshole better than I should—a Valenti minion, swift and dangerous with a conscience as brittle as his element—and they didn't call him Diamond for nothing. Word was, Sonny and Diamond hated each other. It didn't matter. They hated us DiLucas more.

And in the tall shadows, cold silver eyes glinted that weren't there a moment ago. A spriggan snorted and snuffled, the wet leather stink giving him away, and I heard a rush of wings and a dirty fairy snigger that didn't come from Diamond.

Sneaky fucker hadn't come alone. Ambush.

Joey hissed. Shiny black webs crackled out from under the skin between his knuckles, and blood-tipped talons stretched from new, glossy black fingers. He braced his cane in front of him like a staff, and a green venomdrop plinked from one claw and sizzled on the asphalt. Shiny snakefangs flickered out, threatening. "Let it be, Diamond. Not your fight. Don't piss me off."

Diamond just cracked that mad fairy giggle and yanked my hair tighter.

I scrabbled for my jacket, my other knives. My nails ripped on rough ground, but my hand was pinned. I dragged my face up, only to have it jammed down again. Pebbles scraped my cheek raw. My teeth sliced into my tongue, and honeysweet poison popped and splashed. My mouth was stuffed with hair and poisoned blood and dirt. I choked, my throat parched, and only a weak gurgle came out.

Diamond giggled and licked my cheek, his smooth hot tongue lingering at the corner of my mouth. "What you gonna do, pretty? Sweat me off you?"

My skin recoiled, and fury iced my blood. *Don't squirm. Never let them see you're afraid. Never show weakness.* Joey taught me well.

I dragged in a breath and hummed deep in my larynx, letting the song grow and fester. Music warmed my blood and my belly, harmony vibrating sweetly in my lungs, and I stretched my torn lips in the dirt and let it burst out.

Shrill chimes tore the air ragged.

Glass cracked. Diamond yelped and flitted off me, shattered wingtip fragments tinkling rosy on the ground. He leapt onto the wall and hung there on shining claws like a glowing pink harpy, long glassfibered hair tangling over ruby eyes, jagged glitterwings swept back. Pity the broken bits would grow back.

He snarled like a roseglass panther, crystalline fangs glinting. "That all you got?"

In the dark, Sonny hulked to his feet in a spray of blood and curses. Diamond's flunkies slithered and giggled, sugar-fragrant wing glitter puffing from the shadows.

Beside me, Joey hissed dangerously in his throat and flexed poison-tipped fingers. "Back it off, Mina."

Frustration buzzed in my ears like a maddened wasp. The Valenti clan and their arrogant demon lord had it over us, so we DiLucas had to be careful who we killed and who found out. This was meant to be a safe, secret ambush, not a fight stacked against us. How in hell did Diamond find us?

I scrambled up, cold hatred warbling in my throat. Heat haze twisted, ghostly, the air vibrating to my magic.

Diamond unsnicked one hand from the wall and beckoned to me with two fingers and a lascivious glassfae grin. Crimson veins glowed in his thick-muscled arms, translucent skin shining. "Dare you, scaredy-banshee. Show us what-cha got."

Four against two. I'd run from better odds. But Diamond's taunts scratched my skin raw and reckless. I flipped out a spare blade, slid into a fighting crouch, and snarled, my mouth wet with blood and the toxic melody of disorientation. "C'mon, then, jewelboy. I'll smash off a few more important bits. Not that anyone'd miss 'em."

"Shut it, songwitch." Sonny staggered, my spell dizzying him. He swiped blood from his face and charged at Joey like an angry, drunken bull. Quick, for such a big guy.

But Joey's faeborn blood made him resistant to my spells, and he snaked aside and swung his cane hard, clubbing Sonny right in the balls. No one said this game was fair.

Sonny retched and clutched himself, and quick as a moonlit cat, Joey dropped the cane, whipped up Sonny's pistol from the asphalt, and leveled it at Sonny's temple. His fingers reshifted, black webs sliding away under white human skin as he snapped back the slide.

He stared at Diamond, unblinking. Joey rarely blinks. Snakes don't need to. "Back off."

He was right. We couldn't win. Goddamn it. "Boss—"

"I said back. The fuck. Off." Joey's jaw set tight, crisp blond hair tumbling across his cheek. "Both of you."

Frustrated obedience curdled my song in my chest. I sheathed my knife and sprang backwards, lighting beside Joey with a crack of sharp heels, my palms flat on the pavement.

Sonny stumbled away against the wall, blood splattering from his hair, his face, his nose. He laughed scarlet bubbles. "You're chickenshit, DiLuca."

"And you're a corpse. Just not tonight." Joey's aim didn't waver as he reached down for my hand and pulled me away with him, and carefully we retreated, broken pavement scraping under my heels.

Diamond swooped into the air like a glassy dragonfly. Behind him an albino firefairy slunk from the shadows, his white hair rippled with scarlet flame, sharp black teeth gleaming wet. The snot-nosed spriggan scuttled out on all fours, claws tapping like a spider's legs. His squat green body rippled with muscle, a sawed-off shotgun strapped to his brawny shoulder. We'd done the right thing, but it itched me like a rash.

Diamond winked at me, rainglitter lashes flashing. "Run and hide, little banshee. It's what you're good at."

My hand trembled, flashes of that petrified little girl clawing shame and fury into my heart. Damn him. I didn't want Joey to see me weak. We'd screwed this up because of me.

But Joey squeezed my fingers, effortlessly strong and comforting, and whispered low for my ears alone. "Peace, Mina. Walk away."

Retreat hardened like a rock in my stomach, and frustration shook my muscles sore. At the last minute, I flexed down and fetched the boss's cane from rainslick asphalt. My fingers slid on wet black lacquer, and I held on tight as we turned the corner. I liked the feel of it, so smooth and light—like both of us, more potent than it looked.

I liked Joey's hand in mine more.

I flushed, my pulse still racing from the fight. *Don't even think it, Mina. No good can come of it, his smooth palm on yours, the slick slide of his reptile skin retreating, the tantalizing roughness of that ridge below his knuckles where the spines hide. You're just a tool, and not a very useful one. You just screwed up his night's work. You're nothing to him.*

But tingles crept up my arm, a hot teasing melody I couldn't shake off. His pulse, the tension in his wrist, the whisper of hair on his cheek, the smooth moist sound of his breath. Sometimes, when he touched me, his skin stung cold, his blood slow and sluggish like the creature he hid inside him.

Tonight, he was warm.

I snatched my hand away as we rounded the corner, my face burning for more reasons than one. Diamond's triumphant voice floated after me, singsong and taunting. "Be seeing you, bluebell."

Retort bubbled to my lips in a wash of bile so banal, I forced a swallow to keep it down so I wouldn't make an ass of myself.

You sure will, you slimy silicon-ass son of a worm.

But not if I see you first.

2

Crashing nightclub metal wound sinuous tentacles into my ears, vibrating my body with sweet longing until the club's dark humidity caressed me like a lover's fingers. You'd think a nightclub would be deafening for a banshee's heightened senses, but I could hear everything: the warm rainbow whisper of wingbeats, sharp teeth clinking on glass, claws scraping skin, the silky slide of kisses, and the tantalizing friction of bodies shifting and swaying as they dance and drink and fuck.

Unseelie Court, the dirtiest, sexiest club in town. The hottest action, the coolest drugs, the wildest party. In here, fairies hid themselves from human eyes with glamour, that shadowy, look-away, don't-see-me magic that makes them look normal. Vampires dazzled their prey, that mesmerizing glint in their eyes, and humans blink and sigh and forget they saw anything out of place. We all did it, glassy and effortless, and the air sizzled and clashed with spells, sparks alight, the magical stink of ozone faint but definite.

Beside me, Vincent DiLuca offered me a cigarette, his jagged dark hair damp with sweat. Lasers flashed off the red jewel in his earlobe to light his cocoa brown eyes with crafty come-hither. "What happened to your face, darlin'? Did Sonny kiss you, before you let him go?"

I ignored him, my scraped cheek stinging sweetly. Vincent is Joey's cousin—we're all cousins in gangland, even if we aren't related, and family is everything—and he's the guy who gets things. Untraceable handguns, blackjewel sparkle, an elephant-ear sandwich—if it's out there, Vincent will find you one. Crafty like a rat, but just a human, not tough or intimidating enough ever to make it in gangland. Still, Joey didn't trust the conniving little fucker, so neither did I. Vincent's one of those few gifted humans who aren't fooled by glamour, and for all I knew, Vincent had told Diamond about our ambush for some petty advantage of his own.

I crossed my arms in the dim reflection of flashing strobe lights and shifted my weight onto the other leg, flexing my leatherwrapped thighs to show how tough I was. I had an appointment with my therapist later—if you could call getting your memory chewed to magical shreds in an effort to remember the face of your mother's killer *therapy*—and my belly tickled warm with impatience, but I suppressed it. I had work to do first, and work was just fine with me.

Vincent lit his own cigarette, smoke curling between his golden rings. No smoking allowed in Melbourne nightclubs anymore, but no one tells DiLucas what to do, and anyway, they'd have a pretty slim leg to stand on, what with the sparkled-up idiots screwing their brain cells into mush six feet away.

He slipped his silver case and lighter away into the ripped pocket of his jeans. "You could at least pretend you know I'm here."

I sent him a sharp poison smile. "Hello, Vinny. Shut the fuck up," I said, and turned back to the boss, scanning the crowd for threats. No gang fighting allowed at Unseelie Court either, and generally that rule got followed, but that didn't mean some hormone-drunk dickhead wouldn't decide it was his lucky night.

"I hate it when you call me Vinny." Vincent dragged in a nicotine lungful and scanned the crowd, too, more likely for talent than for danger.

"There you go again. Mistaking me for someone who gives a shit."

"Bitch. You know you want me." He winked at me, dark eyelashes dipping.

I couldn't help but smile. He already had a girlfriend, and he knew I was on ice, so to speak. You could see the sweet tanned curve of his ass through the fluffy tear in those perfect-fitting jeans, and he knew that, too. How the hell did he get a suntanned butt? "Tear you in half, pretty boy."

"Any time." He laughed, not quite convincing to my sensitive ear. What was he up to?

The tense vibration of his nervousness shivered my spine, but his tart tobaccosweat scent and the soft rustle of his hair invigorated me. Sparkle's sugartoxic tang licked the air, tempting me, and I couldn't help wanting, that snide and hungry addictworm chewing in my guts. Fairy drugs are the ultimate mindfuck, exquisite and dangerous, sucked like sparkling juice from stray memories and heartache by crafty fairy dealers with malicious spells on their candysweet breath.

They don't always ask, and you won't know until it's too late. It pays to be careful about who you hook up with around here. A breathless clinch in the dark, a few careless kisses with a pretty fairy boy, and before you know it, you've forgotten your name or fallen out of love, or you curl up in the corner sobbing, with all your happiness drained away.

And then they pour your stolen emotions into a sparkling glass bottle and sell it. Anger, jealousy, sweet delight, lust's dark oblivion. You can buy it all, if you've got something they want, and let's just say the average fairy doesn't care too much about money.

My palms itched. I was trying to quit. It wasn't easy.

I surveyed my domain, my nerves on a shatterglass edge. The mezzanine, dim and fragrant with smoke and sweat, the ribbed metal floor vibrating and flashing in rippling lights. Some tasty boy candy had turned up at the Court tonight, and not all my frustration was sparklefever or memory itch.

Off to my left, a long-haired vampire in leather and rusted chains pressed his half-naked boyfriend up against the wall, hands sliding inside tight jeans in search of hot flesh. Helljuice-tainted blood dripped satinblack in their kiss.

To the right, a drunken fairy girl sprawled on the floor, giggling, her wet mauve wings splayed wide, while a muscly green troll licked his way up her purple thigh, sweat glistening on his massive chest. Trolls rarely wear shirts. Must be a rule.

I eyed his curving muscles appreciatively, and squirmed a little as his girl moaned and shuddered. Damn good rule. Pity about the pants.

I scanned behind me, my thighs twitching. A skinny blond human girl in a red satin party dress knelt on bruised kneecaps, and left off swallowing some gorgeous firefairy's hard-on for just long enough to snort a shimmering blue line from a broken mirror. He took the glass from her, tossed his sweaty scarlet hair back, and inhaled the leftovers while she got on with it. Beautiful, he was, tight pale body and sultry black eyes and rubyglass wings licked with flame.

His pleasured groan and the wet squelch of his veins expanding tormented me. My mouth crackled dry with envy. I hadn't had a hit all week, and I hadn't had what he was getting for a whole lot longer.

I sighed, sultry harmonics humming, and warded off Vincent's snicker with a glare. Two in the morning at Unseelie Court, situation normal. Everyone having a good time except me.

But I couldn't complain. Being gang muscle is easy, so long as no one's shooting at you or scraping your face into concrete. All you have to do is stay awake and look mean, and I had that last one down to my own unsettling brand of art.

First, I wore high stiletto-heeled boots—being on my toes was surprisingly practical in a fight—and black leather pants I squeezed into by a minor feat of quantum physics every night. My leather corset showed a few inches of my belly and pushed my breasts up into provocative shapes, and my black velvet choker was rimmed with silver studs.

I'd checked my jacket and knives outside the metal

detectors—this was Melbourne, not Texas, and even DiLucas got arrested for flashing weapons around, especially now that those Valenti assholes had offed our best crooked cop—but still, leather's smooth embrace buckled tight around my body made me feel safe somehow. Protected. No one could get in.

And I did look mean. I'm tall and lean, and this outfit showed every muscle and curve. Men liked my body. They ought to, after the work I'd put into it, but it also made them nervous. I was probably stronger than them, and they knew it.

Next, the Mad Banshee Aura. I tried dyeing my hair to look tougher, but it's sky blue, and the black wouldn't take, so I slashed the ends in sharp zigzags and let it spill over my shoulders, dead straight. I painted my eyelids a different rainbow shade each night, and sparkled my lashes silver. Sharp painted nails, strange spicy perfume. My teeth are cute and sharp, my lips improbably scarlet.

And lastly, I glower like a champion. I don't smile or flirt or get distracted. I just scowl and pace up and down, quivering. Banshees are notoriously crazy, and it's not an unwarranted reputation. I could be a yowling psychobitch. No one in their right mind messed with me, not anymore.

All part of the plan, see. One day, my mother's murderer and I would come face-to-face, and I'd be ready.

Besides, looking dangerous was my job. It's what the boss paid me for.

And there he sat, a couple of yards away, on a couch on the warm metal mezzanine. My boss, doing the business cool and unruffled, as if we didn't escape by a buttwhisker from getting our asses thrashed to hell only an hour ago.

A glass of golden fairy wine glimmered untouched on the metal table before him. His cane leaned against the table's edge, brass glittering, my fingerprints polished clean.

I watched him, pride mixing darkly with passion in my blood. Joey had built a fearsome reputation with guile and a few carefully chosen demonstrations of sheer ruthlessness, and what he is underneath freaks people out. All faeborn creatures are weird—not human, not fairy, a kind of in-between genetic accident—and most are crippled, deformed, their unhumanity in plain view. But Joey's weirdness is invisible until he shows it, and that makes it all the more threatening. People sidle away, break eye contact, avoid him if they can.

But they didn't see what I saw.

Call me crazy—I'm a banshee, after all—but I couldn't tear my eyes away.

He reclined with his long legs crossed in denim, one ankle over the other. White shirt, sleeves turned up to show strong wrists and lithe forearms, one draped across the couch's back. Hard, lean, muscled body, not a mote of wasted flesh. Just a beguiling flush of darkness showing beneath that taut skin, luminous sweat caressing the tantalizing glimpse of his chest with a faint green glow. He moved, lazy, and his thighs didn't so much ripple as *slide*—like all his movements—serpentine, erotic.

I sighed. Fantasy cheekbones I longed to trail my mouth over, crisp whiteblond hair just made to sift through my fingers. Top lip fine and bow-shaped, the lower one sinful and ripe for kissing. He didn't wear jewels or gold. He didn't need any. His eyes shone brighter than any gemstone, piercing and relentless and greener than envy.

Joey's faeborn glamour is transparent enough to be useless, so he covers himself, and usually he looked sleek and dangerous in his suit and hat. But these last few nights, summer had closed in, dry and relentless, parching the city to a crackle, and it'd just been too damn hot, even for him. It's hell, this crisp dry heat, scratching your eyeballs and scorching your face raw, and you sweat and sweat until your skin swells clammy and your head aches like poison from dehydration, but the air just sucks it up like a hungry sponge.

But I wasn't complaining. Not if it meant I could see him like this, the sensual nightclub light caressing his skin, underwater shadows pouring, sultry air sticking that crushable hair to his cheek.

Beside him, a skinny metal fairy hunched, his deformed spine twisting like his jagged-toothed smile. Rust rotted his stubby ironfeathered wings. His skin gleamed dusty pewter, his hair lank and bronze, his long limbs emaciated like muscled wire. Metal bracelets decorated his wrists, the rusty barbs drawing dark hematite blood.

Silvery drool slipped from his misshapen lips, and he wiped it away with deft crooked fingers. He caught my gaze, one eye blue, the other muddy green, and dropped me a sly golden-lashed wink.

I scowled, my stomach rich with disgust. Iridium, another of our dead boss's leftovers, assassin and threatmonger, an unsettling metal monster who liked watching people hurt. With the Valentis gunning for us, we needed all the friends we could get, but for me, Iridium took far too much pleasure in his work.

Some say Iridium's an artist. Joey doesn't trust him, but says he's necessary.

If you ask me, Iridium's a fucking psychopath.

The willowy bronze earthfae girl Joey spoke to slid a chunk of cash onto the table—her drug trade, it's either us or Sonny Valenti, and we don't smash your knuckles to a bloody mess with quite so much relish. Joey cut her share back to her and made the rest disappear.

She blushed and stammered something in reply, her dusky golden wings flushing dark.

Iridium giggled, rusty, and I resisted a jealous yowl. The boss's charm was hard-earned. I didn't want it wasted on her.

I tried to concentrate on the crowd, but invisible magnets constantly yanked my eyeballs back to Joey. I liked watching him, watching him move his body, now touching hands briefly with a wild-haired waterfae courier. Talented hands, fluid like a pianist's, his voice's soft timbres sliding between the music's dark frequencies like a velvet caress. The eeriest thing about the boss is his flawless skin. Every time he shifted, it remade itself.

Not that I've ever seen him, beyond the fingerwebs and the fangs and that one time a few weeks ago when we needed to sniff out a bunch of murdering fairies and he . . .

I squirmed, the memory of that smooth black skin hot and arousing. *Never mind that. Brain on the job, please.* If they got to him because my mind wallowed in the gutter, he'd be just as dead.

I scraped sweaty hair from my neck and reefed my gaze back to the crowd. The band started another set, and the screeching melody of frenetic cymbals and pissed-off guitars vibrated sweetly in my flesh. A shifty green spriggan eyed me off, leathery skin gleaming, black hair sticking up like a wire-brush between pointed ears heavy with golden rings. His dirty jeans were tight and torn over one scrawnymuscled thigh. His black T-shirt read I'M MEAN BECAUSE YOU'RE *STUPID,* and his round belly stretched the letters out of shape.

I scowled at him until he looked away. I don't like sprig-gans. Too many bad memories, bad breath and wicked teeth and horny yellow claws. Call me racist, but I never met a spriggan I didn't want to murder.

At my elbow, Vincent tossed his cigarette away, pulled out his glass-rimmed phone, and rattled off a quick mes-sage. He had his keytones set to silent so I couldn't hear, and he shot me an unnerving little smile as he tapped SEND.

On the table, Joey's phone buzzed.

My skin prickled. I didn't like secrets. I'm used to hear-ing everything.

Joey picked up and glanced at the screen. No reaction showed on his face, but he dismissed the dripping blue fairy and snaked up from his chair, slipping his phone away.

He moved fluidly, nothing wasted, his gaze on Vincent until he leaned to whisper in my ear. We're almost the same height, Joey and me, and his hair slid softly on my bruised cheek. "Go get us a drink. I need to talk to you."

He smelled of fresh mint, burning cool and invigorating. My nerves jangled. To Vincent, he meant. He was getting rid of me. Damn it. I forced a weak smile. "Margarita, right? Extra salt?"

"Funny. Scotch, of course. Make it a double, and what-ever you're having."

"Your shout."

"Naturally. Otherwise they'll think you're bribing me." He breathed in, scenting me, the tiny inward rush of air a hot tease on my neck, and under his skin, something invisible writhed, the groan of hidden serpent muscle a temptation in my oversharp ears.

Heat pooled deep in my belly. I wanted to bury my mouth in his hair and inhale. My mind stuttered for something to say, some way I could promise him that whatever the slur on my character was that Vincent didn't want me to hear, it wasn't true.

He could trust me. I'd die for him. I died for him every night, when he wouldn't touch me or smile for me or treat me as his equal.

But he swallowed and leaned away, and the moment fled.

And all I could do was walk away in a cloud of desire and frustrated sweat, imagining the million and one ways Vincent could steal my master from me.

Joey watches her walk away, and for too long a moment, the room fades from view, leaving only her swaying hips, that sharp-cut satiny blue hair swinging hypnotically around shapely shoulders, nightclub lights licking rainbows over her delicious female skin.

Beautiful Mina, strong but frightened and delicate under her gangster-hard shell. That athletic body, so inviting. Sober for once, no sparkle ripping her nerves tight or splashing wild words from her pretty red mouth. So desperately sad and vulnerable, she makes him ache in places he does his best to forget about.

A laugh twists in Joey's throat, aimed at himself. He's known her since she was a teenager, when they all teased him about her schoolgirl crush on him, a wide-eyed puppydog thing he always discounted for gratitude. Now, she's a quivering whipcord of intoxicating, sensual woman, and when she looks at him like that—eats him alive with those haunting ruby eyes, both predator and quivering prey—he can't help but imagine what it'd be like *if*.

If she didn't work for him. If he weren't a monster. If his

enemies weren't stalking in shadow, waiting for the first tiny crack in his ice-walled façade.

But she does, and he is, and they are.

She lifts her chin to glance back at him, those seductive crimson eyes tilted under glitterpainted lashes. Strobes flash on her scraped cheek, and Joey's tongue forks, pushing at his lips, longing to search the air for her vibration. Her lost bloodscent makes him warm and twitchy, the snake jealous and quivering inside. He tasted her once, foolish kisses he couldn't resist, and ever since, the memory of her succulent flesh and her hot, supple mouth has taunted him at the most inopportune moments.

Strong, yet so delicate. Feminine. Impossible. Always he fights the weird urge to shelter her, leap between her and danger with a swipe of venombright talons and a fanged snarl, protect her even though he pays her for that, not the other way around, and she'd rip his skin off five times out of ten if it came to a fight.

Already she distracts him too much, and to show an ounce of weakness in gangland is death.

She turns away, and he bites his tongue, his own tart blood a sharp taste of reality. The room slams back into view, dazzling.

As if she'd ever want more than his money.

Her disgust is too apparent, in the way she freezes and stammers whenever he's near, afraid of losing his confidence and her job if she shows just how much she loathes what he is.

Always different. Always weird, disgusting, evil, even when he was small, the sick little boy with snake eyes and forked tongue and venom-splashed fangs he couldn't control. Even in this faeweird world of wings and rainbow skin, Joey's a freak.

Shapeshifter. It's ironic. The word reeks of enchantment, simplicity. Switching from one to the other in a puff of smoke. Not crackling bone and stretching flesh and the agony of displaced nerves. He's freakish, a grotesque faeborn aberration. A long time ago, he tried to be normal. It took only so many flinches and retches and averted eyes to figure that was impossible.

And now Mina's doing it, too.

He cracks shifting knuckles and spins away, his human body hot and aching. *Fuck it. Can't concentrate with a hard-on.* And concentrate he must, if he wants to stay alive. Vincent is a weaselly little scumbag, but he's not stupid or harmless. And always hunchbacked Iridium watches with mismatched eyes, twisted and compelled, waiting for a glimpse of weakness. Only strength and ruthlessness keep Iridium in check.

But even the thought of warming his smooth black snake skin on Mina's magnificent body, sliding over her sweet curves, slicking his tongue into her hot wet crevices, wrapping it around her hard little bit of flesh and making her squirm and moan and come, her body heat glowing like fever and her every sigh and shudder a snakebright glory . . .

It'll never happen. Joey doesn't have lovers. He's taught himself to do without, and it's better that way. Too difficult to lock the snake inside, so deeply unsatisfying, it only frustrates him. And it took only one accident—one nameless girl long ago, with shock-wide eyes and sick green toxin choking her breath away—to prove that letting the monster out is unthinkable.

Joey's fingers twitch for his absent cigarette, webs crackling out as his nerves stretch and search for chemical stimulation. He sweeps up his cane and rakes his nails on the lacquer, agitation an ants' nest on his skin. He's quitting, and it fucking sucks.

Vincent offers him one. Joey waves it away, his mouth parched. He beckons, and Vincent follows him over to the wall where it's dark, away from sly metalfae eyes and clever, sweetpointy magical ears.

Beside him, a green fairy girl in denim shorts and torn fishnets kisses her scarlet-haired banshee deep and slow. Their sugary lips melt together, a dim neon halo shining from lustswollen wings. Eyes closed, breasts molding on breasts, slim green hands sliding between satiny thighs, the sweet melodyspelled moan of desire.

The fairy drops to her knees, easing up the redhead's skirt to slide her long tongue in. No underwear, and the hair there is scarlet, too, neatly trimmed. The fairy sucks, drawing out swollen pink flesh and licking it lovingly.

Joey rips his gaze away, his own tongueforks slithering hungry. She doesn't even look like Mina. "You'd better mean what you just sent me."

"It's a no-brainer, boss." Vincent lights up, ash flaring. "She's guilty as a fairy in a sugar factory. Think about it. Who else knew about that ambush?"

"You did."

Vincent laughs and puffs artful smoke away. "I'm not the one picking asphalt grit outta my face. Do I look dumb enough to sell you out without taking a hit to cover it up?"

Joey cuts a sharp laugh. If he knows one thing about Vincent, it's that looks mean nothing. "And she does?"

"Just watch her, boss, that's all I'm asking. See where she goes tonight. Who she goes with. That Diamond's got a lot to offer that we don't, you know what I'm saying."

Spines press against Joey's scalp from the inside, threatening to burst out. He itches to slam his brass-topped cane into Vincent's smug face. Diamond's reputation with the girls is legend. Rumor is, Mina and Diamond knew each other once. It's all too believable, a stunning, hot-blooded woman like her. Nothing less would satisfy her. But the image of glassy fairy hands—anyone's hands—caressing his woman's naked skin lights Joey's blood with pure reptile envy.

His vertebrae crackle, ready to slide apart. He grits sharpening teeth, his forking tongue alive with malice. "Choose your words, kid."

Vincent drags on his cigarette, infuriating, that tempting smoke drenching Joey's senses like a succubus's rapture, irresistible. "Hey, I'm just a realist. Whatever you're doing to her in bed better be g— Jesus fucking Christ, Joey."

Joey's neck stretches and snaps tight like rubber, and his

nose quivers to a stop an inch from Vincent's tobacco-fragrant mouth. Burning fangs snap from his gums, rich snakevenom sparkling like fury on his tongue. "Accuse her again without proof, and I'll rot your filthy skin off."

Vincent backs off, his cigarette tumbling to the floor in a tiny rain of sparks. "Sure, boss. No offense. If I find anything, you'll be the first to know. Just forget I said anything." And he rakes sleek fingers through his hair and slinks away.

But too late. The accusation's made.

Sick suspicion burns deep in Joey's veins, where the snake's blood runs cold.

He reshifts his spine with a crunch, his mouth sour as he jerks those hungry fangs back into aching gums. He doesn't want it to be true. But he can't afford to ignore his instincts.

Beside him, the scarlet banshee shrieks and shudders, clutching her fairy lover's hair. Spellsong dulls the fairy's eyes and blanches her apple skin white, but she doesn't care, and as her girlfriend sighs in aftershock, she presses her cheek against that shivering white thigh and whispers, *"I love you."*

Mina could be the traitor. Her shy smile sheltering rank deceit. Her hypnotic redjewel eyes masking poisoned lies. Swallowing her revulsion like acid and using her body and her face and her quivering jasmine scent against him, after everything he's done for her.

Sick self-disgust prickles his guts. He didn't drag her out of drugsmeared oblivion for reward's sake. He never wanted gratitude for saving her life.

Just not to have her spit on his compassion by betraying him to his enemies.

Stupid to trust her for a moment.

Snakemuscle roils in his limbs, stabbing his bones with a deep yearning ache he knows won't fade, not tonight. The heat torments him, luring the snake out. His human body perspires under his clothes, itching at him to rip them off, breathe, stretch, change.

He forces himself to move slowly, calmly, only a tiny

quiver ratcheting his hands as he lights a cigarette and drags deep. The chemicals spread in his blood like shivers from a hot shower, stroking his nerves just a little looser.

Fuck.

He inhales once again. Lets the tranquil smoke out. Slides calmly to the table, stubs the half-smoked cigarette out with a jerk of his wrist. He flips up his cane and walks to the steel mezzanine rail, where below, bodies crush and mingle in pale nightclub smoke crisscrossed with green lasers. Leather and lace and hot bare skin, shining limbs, fresh rainbow wings, the strobelight flash of eyes.

He scans the neonwhite bar for a glimpse of sky blue hair. There she is, one long leg hooked into her stool's rung, that luscious blue waterfall streaming over her shoulders, her long throat gleaming as she kicks back a beer. Her breasts swell against her tight leather, so soft and feminine, glistening damp in the heat. If he shifted, he'd smell her sweat.

His heart stings bitter, and distantly he wonders why. He's usually clinical. Practical. In gangland, life is simple. On any given day, either someone's your friend or they aren't, and his venomsharp instincts have never failed him before.

But even the suggestion of her betrayal hurts.

All the more reason he must distance himself from her.

He never wanted to be in charge. Liked it better lurking in the background, cleaning up messes, whispering calculated advice to cool his vampire prince's hot temper. But now the boss is dead, and there's no one else left. Joey has no choice. And it was a lot easier to be cold and objective when someone else was making the decisions.

He can't trust her. She's charming him, using his weakness to lure him astray. But he can't trust Vincent, either. He'll watch them both, test them, feed them different lies and see where they resurface.

Joey taps curling claws on the railing, conviction hardening like ice. Pretty Mina can't hide, not from him. If she's seeing Diamond on the sly, he'll know about it. If she's a traitor, he'll find her out. And when he does, he'll pin her down, let the snake burst cold and hungry from his skin, and eat her heart.

Even if it breaks his own.

Iridium hunches sore and shivering at the table, his fractured metalsense painting harsh glowing edges along the iron railing, the gritty steel floor, the smooth globe of the snakething's brass-topped cane.

As Joey retreats, Iridium grates a rusty giggle at the freshmint stain of frustrated need. Vincent's tricks, so blunt and jealous. So easy to trick cold, calculating Joeysnake into dumbthinking chaos.

Iridium likes chaos. It counterpoints the screaming zoo inside his head, voices and whispers and horrid groans that never cease. Not unless he blots them out with realer, more urgent sounds, screams, whimpers, the warm splash of blood.

Harsh nicotine smoke drifts, shimmering with heavy metal glitter, and Iridium coughs bloody iron shards and stubs Joey's half-lit cigarette out harder. Pain lances up his crippled arm, deformed bones burning. Always, the pain, his bent spine crackling, the torture of misshapen muscles and overstressed joints popping gristle and blood, the excruciating rot of rust in his aching wings.

He can't fly. Never could. Crooked metalfairy, always spoiling the fun.

He eases back, vertebrae grating like acid on gravel. His barbed wire bracelets pierce his wrists, the ooze of steely blood calming. At least he can control that pain.

Speaking of fun, there's Vincent's girl, Flora, dancing, flaunting her slim green thighs, her perky little breasts jiggling under falling rosepink curls. Behind her, two vampires kiss, a pale black-haired gothic girl and a musclebound blond. Bright crimson splashes over their chins.

Virusrich bloodstink sweetens Iridium's coppersour tongue. His cock twitches and aches. His rusty iron flesh burns, and inside the hunger grows, festers, boiling alive like an angry black fungus.

Joey doesn't get it. Doesn't understand what hunger's

like. He thinks his monster is hateful, relentless, eating him up without remorse.

He should try rusting to death, one screeching muscle fiber at a time.

The pain starves Iridium, makes him so hellspitting hungry, for pleasure or sweet numbness or anything other than screaming agony, that nothing satisfies him. He's fought the snarling painbeast every interminable hour of his life.

Doesn't make the sadistic fucker hurt any less.

Flora blows him a kiss, and he scowls, silvery drool licking his lips. Gangland used to be such a lovely façade. Under the old leadership, he could murder and torture and destroy without need for reasons or restraint. But Joey is different. Joey disa-fucking-proves.

Well, Joey can keep his own monster locked up if he wants to. Not this angry ironfairy.

Iridium wrenches aching wingjoints, and rusty shards crumble onto the floor, but he's still got a hard-on. Yes. He'll let the painbeast roam and shatter and kill, and if Joey doesn't like it, Iridium will just have to find another stupid gang puke to shelter behind. Someone fresher, more pliable. Pity Vincent is such a weakling. He'd do fine.

Flora sashays up, little ass cute and chewable in a flimsy miniskirt, fluttering long glowpink wings. Her drugged eyes sparkle cruelly. "Wanna dance?"

Taunting the cripple. Classy.

He watches those hungry vampires circlesucking, fangs buried in each other's throats. The girl moans, pleasured, and an idea rusts solid in his mind.

"Bite me," he says absently, giving Flora the finger.

Flora laughs, a sharp stab in his ears. "Want me to? You look tense, poor baby." And she actually reaches for him, her palm grazing his hard twisted flesh through his jeans.

His tortured nerves spasm, and his pulse throbs, dangerous. Unused to being touched voluntarily. Unwilled, he imagines her scream vibrating his teeth. Excruciating. Exquisite.

Tension burns his balls, and he yanks Flora's hand away

before he explodes. It hurts to come. Better make sure it's worth it.

Sour metalgrit scrapes his tongue. "No. But you can play a tricky trick on Vincent for me. He won't mind," he adds when she pouts. "Promise. Make him horny as hell."

Flora's eyes glint magenta with mischief. "Okay. But rain check on the blow job, sweetie. You've got a real big cock."

Whore. Iridium smiles, disgust and broken iron teeth stinging his lips, and beckons. "See those vampires? Go on over there, and tell them . . ."

3

From the bar, I glimpsed Joey at the rail, searching the crowd for me with that cold, empty look in his eyes, and helplessness flooded my limbs, sluggish like treacle. Damn that sneaky Vincent-rat, always trying to insinuate himself with the boss at my expense. If I lost this job, I had nothing.

Worse than nothing—once the Valentis discovered Joey wouldn't protect me, I'd be a red smear on some back-alley sidewalk. I'd kicked too much Valenti butt to be allowed to walk away.

His scotch sat waiting on the bar, ice slowly melting, an itching reminder he was working without me. I drank my beer, but the bubbles frothed weakly in my throat, the sweating lemon's bitter tang too gentle. I needed my therapy. I wanted to get on with hunting my mother's killer. But I wanted to wait for Joey, too, for him to melt my heart with that secret crazysmile and show me everything was okay.

I slammed the bottle down in frustration, that nagging little sparklefreak voice gnawing harder at my guts. *Feed me, Mina. I'm so hungry. You know where to get what we need. It's easy. Feed me, and I'll love you and stroke you and lick you, slide deep inside you and make you feel good, and we can forget everything. I'll make tomorrow better, I promise. . . .*

A scratchy giggle beside me grabbed my attention. A skinny yellow airfae girl blinked up at me with a split-lipped smile, her ragged wings brittle and undernourished. "Hey, Mina. How's it shinin'?"

"Hey, Violet." I tried a smile, but it didn't work. Once, Violet was my friend, sort of, if you call scrapping through garbage for food together friendship. We'd starved, fought, and hustled side by side, and the first time I ever swallowed some guy's sweaty hard-on for cash, she was right there with me. Far as I knew, she still turned tricks for a living.

She tugged moth-eaten sage hair in a tiny swirl of fairy breeze, her knobbly fingers scabbed with bruises or scurvy. "You got nice clothes."

"Thanks." I drained my beer, my stomach twisting in protest. She wore a faded blue halter top over a frilly skirt and cute heels that blistered her yellow feet blue. Her scratched legs looked scrawny and underfed, and unpleasant memory squirmed rotten in my soul. The only difference between her and me was Joey. I really didn't need that reminder tonight.

"Workin' out strawberries for you, then. That job."

"Yeah. Umm . . . how you doing?" Fucking lame question. Bruises mottled her skinny arms, and her pale blue eyes gleamed tired and dull. She looked like a corpse, and a poorly used one at that. The weak magical breeze stirring from her ripped wings smelled foul.

But her pretty smile flashed, game as ever. "Okay, y'know. Same old. I was wond'rin, maybe if ya had some spare cash—" Her face fell. "Oh. Never mind."

A tall black spriggan in jeans and no shirt loped up, long wiry hair swept forward and springing in front of his pointed chin. Multiple body piercings shone golden on his coarse skin. He grabbed her elbow with sharp shiny fingers, his lean muscles hard and unforgiving, and planted a rough, possessive kiss on her mouth.

She didn't respond, and he grinned cruelly around broken black teeth. "There y'are, sweet thing. Gotta run. Sorry." He flashed me a warning glare beneath spike-pierced eyebrows. *Mine. Don't touch without paying. You want a job, pretty? You want something to eat? We got work for ya. Easy money.*

The golden rings in his sharp ears made me shiver. I didn't recognize him. But I knew him too well, and I wanted to scrape his face off with my nails, rip those haughty piercings from his body, and feel him scream. I swallowed on angry scarlet chords. "You okay, Vi? Call me if you need anything, huh?"

She sniffled. "Yeah. See ya, Min. You look great." And the spriggan dragged her away, his black limbs shining like a crab's.

Guilt spilled bitter into my mouth, and I swallowed it. None of my business. For all I knew, the bastard paid us protection. Not my fault I got lucky and she didn't. Right?

I waved at the handsome blond barboy, my heart aching. "Gimme a double bloodfever, ice, no cherry."

He winked, muscles shining beneath his leather vest as he poured, bourbon shots over ice first, then the splash of sparkling cola, then the rich scarlet dash from a clotted squeeze bottle and a sprinkle of crushed chili. Deep old scars showed white on his shoulder blades as he slid the short glass over to me and popped in a pink straw, his oceanblue eyes glinting merry. "Shitty night?"

"Ain't over yet. Gimme another one." I tossed the straw away and swallowed half the drink in one gulp. Chili stung my tongue, and bourbon and rich vampire blood slid like boiling honey down my throat. It hit my stomach and frothed like a witches' brew, and right away that rich slinky darkness spread in my veins.

I sighed, deep, relaxing. The stuff felt good, caressing my nerves like a slow, deep kiss. Drinking infected blood was supposed to be like kissing someone with HIV—you'd have to be very unlucky. If you wanted the virus, you really had to persist, and most people didn't live long enough. Good thing for us, or there'd be fucking vampires everywhere.

So yeah, it was safe, so long as you didn't overindulge. Right?

Live music tonight, the crowd packed and warm, thundering guitars over a frenetic panic of drums and bass. The skinny singer tossed long ink-dyed hair over her jewel-pierced face and screamed of tunnels in the dark and the black canker in the depths of her heart.

Automatically my ears filtered harmonics, nuances, spikes in amplitude and wavelength, flaying the melody to bare emotional truth. Flashes of hard flesh piercing her body as she screams, laughter, a metal pistol butt smacking into her face. The air swelled tight with her raw-skinned pain, and sweet agony stretched my eardrums rigid.

I gulped my drink, and my belly heated. *Right on, sister. Share the hurt. Make them feel as you feel. That's the only way you'll ever live again.*

A glass rang sweetly against mine. "Cheers."

I jerked, fumbling. I hadn't heard him approach, and the deep smooth frequencies of his voice vibrated to my core. I flushed, and cursed under my breath, hoping he hadn't noticed my concentration wandering. "Um, yeah. Yourself."

Joey sipped and offered me a shattering smile, green lights flashing on his pale hair.

His smile was hard to take, cold and perfect like an evil djinn's, inviting but sinister. He used it to scare people away. But it made me think of flesh, warmth, a sweet poison kiss, the shiver of hot lips caressing my spine.

Tall-blond-and-scarred slid me my second drink. I drank, alcohol and virusflesh sharp on my tongue. Sounds swelled and faded, the music swirling like ocean water. "Finished talking about me?"

"It's business." Joey sucked an ice cube into his mouth and crunched, leaning his elbow on the bar and glancing around like I bored him, his gaze lingering on a busty blond vampire slut with her tight black skirt up around her butt. Immediately, I wanted to punch her.

His attitude rubbed acid into my hurt. God, I hated how my confidence relied on him, how desperately I needed him to make me feel safe and important. I hated that I wanted things from him I had no chance he'd ever give, that the only man I ever respected had no respect at all for me.

Vampire blood whispered hot distraction inside my skull, staining my vision scarlet, dizzying me and dragging words onto my tongue that would never otherwise have made it. "Yeah, it's business. Everything's business to you, right?"

I tilted my glass again, my bloodseduced mouth already watering for more.

He grabbed my arm, stopping the glass an inch from my mouth. Sweat shone on his lean-muscled wrist, his grip light but steely. "You shouldn't drink that shit."

"Why not? Afraid I'll embarrass you?" I yanked my hand away, half-hoping he'd hang on and drag me closer. But he let go, and I shook my wrist and downed the rest of my drink, defiance scorching my veins.

"It fucks up your brain, Mina."

"What do you care?" I wanted to provoke him into revealing something, anything, even disgust.

"I care because I need you first thing tomorrow. Breakfast with Delilah down at Southbank, the usual."

I swallowed. Delilah, our demon patron, probably with some helltwisted scheme to annoy the Valentis and score points against Kane. Demons always bicker amongst themselves, and Delilah has it in her head that Kane's got it coming, because he's arrogant and in charge and scary as shit.

Maybe she was right, but her last effort at pissing him off nearly got us killed. We were just game pieces to her. But even pawns get to party when the enemy king dies.

I shouldn't miss this breakfast. Joey might need me. "Um . . ."

"Don't be late. Unless you wanna let some glassfae maggot kick your ass and get away with it."

Challenge stirred embers in his eyes, and my heart tumbled like it always did. He knew what I liked, how I thought, where my darkest desires led me when I thought no one watched. I fiddled with my bodice's low neckline, my temper fizzling out in a warm wash of blood-sharpened need. "Look, I didn't . . . I'd never lie to you. You know that, right?"

He just looked at me and finished his drink.

My stomach tightened. No matter how I fought to hang on, my life was slipping away from me. I needed this job. I didn't know how to do anything else. Poor Violet wasn't just my past. She was my future, if I didn't hold on to this, now, here, until my fingers bled.

The vampire blood burned under my skin, swelling my flesh, nagging at me to consume, touch, swallow. I stabbed my courage to reluctant attention and tried one more time. "Can I get you another? It's kinda loud in here. We can . . . y'know. Go somewhere, if you want."

Yesss, whispered the blood, its lust an unpleasant echo in my sex. *Somewhere like your place, where it's warm and dim and I can slip my fingers beneath your clothes, kiss you until I ache, tempt your hands onto my body, wrap my legs around you and warm that cold blood of yours with my pleasure.*

My face burned, and I held my breath. Waited for him to smile coldly, embarrass me, pretend I wasn't there.

Joey took my hand and kissed it.

Just a light brush of ice-cooled lips, his fingers warm under my palm. And a tiny flicker of his tongue, hot and exciting on the back of my hand like a flashburn.

My gaze dragged to the place where his lips touched me, and my blood-drunk optic nerves set off a sizzle that stabbed all the way down to my breasts. I wanted to touch his cheek, hear my fingertips brushing his skin, slide my finger past his tempting lips into his mouth. I remembered how that mouth sprang alive on mine, that night a few weeks ago when he kissed me, wired and feverish from a fight. So fresh and dangerous, his forking tongue demanding, the hot snaky shift of his flesh and the urgency of his lips on mine showing me how much he wanted . . . something.

Maybe not me.

But he was alone. I was alone. We're both old enough. Even if he just wanted to forget all this macho gang bullshit for a few hours and make himself feel good, I'd do it if it meant he believed me.

He leaned closer and inhaled. His lips inched apart, and my breath caught. I knew he examined me with those enhanced reptile senses, tasted my sweat, smelled my blood. Did he like it?

He cupped my bruised cheek and raked his thumb over my lips, only a few inches from kissing me. "You'd have killed him tonight, wouldn't you? Sonny Valenti, I mean."

"Yeah." My voice withered to a whisper, and my body ached with helpless longing. So much for toughness. He'd disarmed me with a glance and a rough caress. If he slipped his thumb into my mouth, I'd suck it.

"Because I asked?" He grazed his teeth over my chin, possessive. Bit me softly.

Oh, god. I shivered, terrified. "Uh-huh."

"Would it feel good, do you think? Would you *like* it?"

His whisper sizzled down my spine, and the way his tongue tasted those words made my belly melt inside. I felt it in my breasts, between my legs, all the way to my toes. Daring, I slid my hand on his chest, his taut muscles warm under my palm. My fingertips brushed bare skin, and beneath them something dark and hungry shifted and groaned. "I'd have liked it if you told me to."

"Mmm. And what else, if I told you to?" The briefest kiss, just a faint brush of his lips on the corner of my mouth, so soft, I might have imagined it. Helpless, I followed, but he pulled back, just an inch from my reach.

"Anything." Desire throbbed tight and wet between my legs, so hard, it made my head swim. I pressed closer and gasped at the steely pressure of his hardness against my belly. He liked it when I surrendered. Liked the power.

I liked giving it to him.

Now I ached for his body, hard and shifting against mine, his teeth on my nipples, the scorching pleasure-pain of him entering me, his bitter venom seeping in my mouth. I didn't care if it was sick. Whatever it was, this weird lust-hate-punish-me attraction sizzling between us, it was past time we purged it. *Take me. I'm empty without you. I'll beg for it if you want. I don't care. Fuck me, and let's get it over with.*

His grip tightened on my chin. "Anything?"

I grabbed his hair and pulled myself up to him, thirsty for contact. My mouth hovered so close to his, I could taste delicious scotch and mint. My mind swirled, drunk, and my whisper cracked with desire too long denied. "Everything."

His fingers closed light and steely around my throat.

Shock flickered my eyes open. His hot green gaze hardened like glass, and he twisted from my grip and softly pushed me aside. "Sounds expensive."

My bowels heated, and an angry flush rushed straight to the top of my head. Always he tempted me. Always, once he'd won, he rejected me. Like there was never any question I'd submit.

I swallowed, burning, trying to halt the stupid tremble in my lip. He was just my boss. I shouldn't care what he thought of me, so long as I did my job.

But I did care.

His gaze met mine, cold, impassive, and too-familiar shame crunched in my guts. His arrogant little games hurt me. And he didn't care. Wouldn't be kind to me. I'd cry afterwards, in the bathroom where he couldn't see or hear me. I'd done that before. And Joey paid me more to guard him than the assholes who sold my body ever did.

Once a whore, always a whore.

I yanked my hand from his and scrambled away, my cheeks scorching like poison.

Deep in the shadowy mezzanine, where fairies tumble and bite and pleasure each other and vampires lick thick scarlet rivulets from bleeding skin, a willowy golden lady named Ivy tumbles a vial of sparkling green liquid over long-jointed fingers, a satisfied smile creeping over her long scarred face. She glides forward to the rail on ragged icewhite membranes, her wingjoints warm and alive with the pleasure of watching the snakeman squirm.

It's him, no doubt about it. Joseph the fat black serpent, wriggling like a fish on the barbed hook of his own stubbornness.

Ivy laughs, and humid breeze flutters her long silver dress, teasing her smooth gold-dusted brown skin. The prickly blue banshee yearns for more than the slim regard he shows her. She's pretty like a doll, smooth young cheeks and perfect red lips, and sour jealousy ripples Ivy's skin. She can smell the girl's desire, sliding like oil on the warm updrafts that tease her wings and stretch her silvermetal hair away from her face. And she longs to whisk the poor girl away from the evil snakything before it's too late.

Ivy understands desire. She's hidden in darkness for years, too ashamed of her scars to come out into the light, but her yearning never ceased in all that time. So many nights of sleepless tears, her mind screaming for help and her body afire. Her memory isn't what it once was. Always struggling to remember what she's lost, always an ache between her legs and a hollow, empty place in her heart.

But she remembers Joey.

Her blood bubbles with sick yellow malice, flushing her torn white wings golden. Oh, yes indeedy, she remembers that foul black serpent thing, all shinysmooth and prickly with razor fins and a sharp spiked tail.

Absently, Ivy's fingers flutter to her ruined cheek, tracing the horrid lumpy ridges that make her so ugly, no one can ever bear to touch her. Glamour covers her well enough for humans, but everyone else can see how she really is, scarred and horrible and disgusting. Once, she was so pretty, they all worshipped her, especially . . . and here her treacherous memory fades again, lost, a fleeting glimpse of beautiful smooth hands adoring her body, lips so gentle and fresh on hers, a whisper of fragrant golden hair . . .

What? Yes, they all worshipped her. She's sure of that. All except the nasty snake man, too evil even to offer her mercy. And now they all avert their eyes in disgust.

Hot tears spring to her eyes, and her heart hurts. She can still feel those venomstung claws gashing her face, the horrid acidhiss of his snakeforked tongue in her eyes. A cold and ruthless man, delighting in the vicious beast trapped inside

him. Letting it rip from his pale human skin with a wet pleasured sigh, the slide of human into snakeflesh a bloody ecstasy.

He's older now, colder, the reptile prince of a black-jeweled
thieves' court drunk on blood and hurt. But the serpent still
rules him. She wonders how many more he's tortured for his
pleasure.

Ivy rakes furious claws across her scalp, drawing berry
blood. The sting whets her desire sharp. He did this to her.
And it's time he suffered for it.

She flitters downstairs to the bar, where Joey glowers in
solitude. A pretty, unsuspecting human girl sidles up to him
with a smile and a few shy words, but he flashes her a smile
in return, a thing of menace and pure threat, and the girl
backs off faster than Joey can say, *Fuck off, sister, I swallow
rats whole.*

Such an elegant façade, hiding a monster so foul. Ivy
leans long dusky arms on the glowing white glass beside
him, spinning her bright green vial in her palm. "Sparkle,
honeychild?"

It isn't good sparkle. It's a vampire boy's bitter hatred, stolen with a kiss while he slept, mixed with vengeance and
sweet fairy psychosis. Ivy likes to make pretty cocktails.
Should be fun on an unsuspecting victim.

Joey turns, irritation creasing fine brows, ready to give
her the same treatment he gave the girl.

His fingers crackle into shiny black flippers, and his glass
slips, shattering on the metal floor in a wash of ice and whiskey glitter.

Ivy giggles, malice roasting her heart. "Watch it, snake-
head. Might show what you really are."

Joey sucks his fins back in, but his serpentgreen eyes
glimmer golden with threat. "I said I'd kill you if I saw you
again. Consider this your one and only lucky break."

Ivy cackles, delight crowing. "Kill a poor defenseless girl
in a crowded nightclub? You won't get away with it, not even
an ego-mad lizard ganglord like you. Packed in like little
silver fishies, we are. See if you can."

His hands quiver. "Don't let me see you anywhere it's dark and lonely, then, you sick harpy. Crawl back to whatever rock you've been hiding under. I've no quarrel with you anymore. Don't change my mind."

He spins away, dismissing her, and Ivy's throat burns. Angry glitter bursts from her wings. "Oh, you won't. See me, I mean. You'll just see your lovely banshee doll's face, once I've made her like you made me. See how you threaten me th—ogg!"

The brass head of Joey's cane crunches hard into her belly. She yelps, the precious spellvial slipping in her fingers. Breath squeezes from her narrow fairy lungs, and black fingers stretch cold around her throat.

His serpent breath scorches her cheek, sparking horrid memory, and his cold green gaze traps her, inescapable from inches away. "If you lay one spellblack claw on her, I'll finish what I started, Ivy, and I won't care who watches."

Ivy wriggles, but she can't escape. Tears flood her eyes, helpless. Her voice gurgles. "You ripped up my face, snake-thing, all claws and smells and itchy poison—"

"Your *face*? Spare me. You deserved every cursed scratch." He shoves her away.

She stumbles, knocking over a stool with flailing wings. She screeches, and jumps into a crouch, hissing her sharp teeth bare.

Around them, people start to notice, flirty girls in satin and lace sidling away, their boys alert for trouble. A heavy-set green troll stalks forward, growling deep in his chest, and Joey lifts his hands in peace and backs off, spearing her one last menacing green stare before slipping into the crowd and away.

The troll helps Ivy up, sticky black hair trailing over his leatherclad shoulder. Purple ink decorates his massive green arms, and clean white tusks curl up over his lip. The leather buckled around his huge wrist would fit around her thigh. "You okay, lady?"

She sniffles, fury and shame burning her blood. He's nice. Gentle. Not evil. His rich fleshscent sparks her nose alive, his glamour warm and inviting. Her skin shimmers silver, thirsting for a kind caress. A boy hasn't touched her for so very long, and it hurts, deep inside her where she's still a girl, no matter her ruined face and torn wings, no matter the spells and tricks and nasty thoughts that plague her, asleep and awake. "Butterflies. You're very kind. Can I . . . umm . . . charm you a gift? Something unusual?" She tries to smile, but his hot black gaze slips away, and he mutters something, drops her hand, and leaves her alone.

Ivy's bright heart extinguishes like a doused flame. She wants to scream and hide her horrid ugly face in her hands. It's the scars. Always the scars.

Black hate festers in her heart, crusting like old blood clots she's waited seven years to excise. Joey will suffer for what he's done, and his sad banshee, too. No doubt he's screwing the poor little thing, writhing his disgusting snake body over hers, flickering his long wet tongue over her skin, those slick black fingers sliding inside her . . .

For a moment, Ivy's heart softens, but she chews the compassion up and spits it out in a wet crunch of bone. A beautiful ingénue like that can have any man she desires. If she wants to let an evil serpent take his sickening pleasure, that's her own can of rocks.

Ivy lifts her chin, her bruised dignity aching. She exhales, and honeyed poison blackens the air. No, Joey will suffer, and damn the consequences. But Joey already hates himself. No point in scarring him. If she hurts the banshee, though, he'll feel the pain Ivy's felt. And when she's swallowed enough of his agony, she'll kill them both.

She brushes smeared floorgrime from her bruised elbow, and scans the crowd with hungry senses for a pretty blue-haired banshee with the stink of scales ruining her lovely white skin.

4

Outside, beneath a burning moonlit sky, black pavement crackles in dry summer heat. The air hangs still and stifling, sucking every drop of moisture from breath and skin and gritty eyes. In the dark alleys behind Unseelie Court, a greasy green spriggan in a shiny trench coat waddles and curses, poking in the garbage with a stick, his wiry black hair crinkled in the heat. Glamour stings the air around him like static, fooling the casual eye that he's just a dirty old wino.

A rat sniffles in strewn black garbage, nose twitching in the stink of rotten cheese. The spriggan mutters and shakes his stick, flicking the squeaking thing away and stuffing the rancid cheese into his mouth. On the bin's rusty lip, skeletal white goblin fingers stretch and curl in a smear of black blood, and from inside a croaking black cackle gurgles into silence. Still the spriggan waddles on, chewing contentedly with moldy cheese crumbling on his chin, sorting in the junk with fat green fingers.

Tiny footsteps clatter closer. The spriggan glances up, his yellow eyes narrowing

A squawking manikin scuttles by on long white legs, dry insectoid wings flapping, his little elfin body shining white. He dives for cover behind the rusty blue bin, scrawny knees knocking in terror.

The spriggan growls around broken black teeth, waving his stick. "Fuggoff, skinny. My garbage."

The thing stares at him, chewing little pink nails, shimmering blue eyes wide. Like a little angel with no feathers. But before the spriggan can whack him again, the air splits apart, and the alley shakes with hellripped thunder.

A gruesome black creature thumps to the ground on all fours, shining blue hair dragging over its long hellscorched body. The ground quakes. Smoking black claws rip the asphalt. Long needle teeth gleam and run with hungry spit, and yellow eyes swivel in dark burnt eye sockets to fix on the creature.

The manny shrieks, tears splashing. His wings clatter together, and he dives in scattering garbage, desperate to crawl under the bin and away. But the black hellthing strikes like a screeching vulture, and long charred fingers wrap around the creature's tiny waist and pluck him effortlessly away.

The manny screams and kicks and flails his wings, but the demon just jerks his bony chin forward to stare the little creature in the eyes. Hellish malice sears the manny's skin to bubbles. The demon laughs, hollow like a drum, and the air rains ash. "I warned you, minion. This is my city." And he stretches his jaws wide, and with a swift crunch of razor teeth tears the screeching thing in half.

Scarlet blood froths down the demon's chin. Wingbones crunch and split. Flesh stretches, tearing as he shakes his long jaws, and soon there's nothing left.

He swallows, blood dripping, and gives a bone-shattering screech of triumph. And then his birdlike limbs contract and turn pale, his cobalt hair shrinks to blond, his needle teeth slip away behind soft red lips, his blazing eyes fade to cold sparkling black. One moment, a monster. The next, a handsome blond man in a black suit.

And Kane, demon lord of Melbourne and eater of souls, picks a shred of meat from his teeth and turns his empty gaze on the spriggan.

The spriggan gulps, and scrambles away as fast as his fat green body will go.

* * *

Kane gnashes fresh white teeth, fury burning rich like lust in his veins. The creature's foul blood stings in his mouth. He sizzles the stains on his hands and face to nothing with a fresh burst of demon wrath that stirs a sharp whirlwind in the scattered paper at his feet. His clipped fingernails flush violet with rage, and he cracks his neck stiffly, resisting the impulse to change again and howl his indignation to the sky.

Angry blue flames spurt between his clenched fingers. Dirty angel spies. Slinking about where they're not wanted. Scuttling about on vile spider feet, the flowery stink of heaven's intruders thick like rotten body fluid.

Kane knows that smell. He scrubbed the city clean of it long ago. It's Shadow, the feathered freak. Honey-sucking angel scum.

Tossing back clean blond hair, Kane stalks away, his shadow a lean black insect on the spraypainted wall. The battle with heaven was won a long time ago, the territory claimed, the casualties burned and eaten. And the people like it here, living their wild, godless lives without remorse or regret. The city prospers under hell's rule. Soulfood is plentiful and ripe. Shadow's nectar-lickers should know when they're beaten.

He sucks the last bloody remnant from his teeth, his stomach pleasantly full of cherub meat. It's fun to chase the ugly little fuckers down. Still, he can't let them do as they please. He's in a good mood. He'll talk to Shadow, give them one last chance. No one can call him unfair.

He veers around the corner, malice shimmering around him in a hellbright halo. Outside the club, blue neon shines darkly on colored skin, jeweled piercings, the waft of glitterbright wings. Queuing nightclubbers in denim and lace and stiletto heels move aside unconsciously to let Kane pass. He glares coolly at the troll guarding the door, and the big green thing swallows and steps aside.

Inside, darkness enfolds him like hot velvet. The noise swells his lungs, rich bass thudding in his guts. Salty flesh-scent pleasures his nose, and he inhales deep. Colored strobes fire like rockets in smoke, gloating over sweating limbs, painted eyes, glitter lips wet with spit, the shiny glint of fangs.

His hunger stirs again, emptiness roiling in his stomach like a snake. So many souls, ripe and bursting like pomegranates with lust, greed, gluttony. All for the taking. Begging him to ravage, rape, swallow, drink their souljuice like blood and lure them gasping home to hell.

Curse the fucking angels. No one here is on their side. It's too late for them.

Kane's nails sprout into hungry claws. A long time since he indulged. Willing flesh presses around him, whetting his desire hard. A soulful fairy child with smudged blue skin and a dark fall of wet inky hair blinks at him, desire hypnotic in his rubylashed eyes, and Kane's limbs shake. Later. Once he's finished his work. He resists the need to grab the sherbety sugarplum thing and lick the sweat from its skin, whisper its darkest desires in its ear, and savor its surrender in a bloody kiss.

Instead he blinks, and a wave of hellblack compulsion splits the air, spreading the crowd apart like a spellwarped ocean.

He stalks up to the bar, his mouth watering over sharpening teeth. His fingers smear charcoal on the glowing white glass, and the bargirl with the glitterpink ponytail glances at his sparking blond hair and reaches behind her to tug the scarred boy's vest.

Rainbow turns, and his oceanblue gaze falters. He swallows and walks up, wriggling his shoulders, no doubt in nervous memory of the day Kane chewed his wings to bleeding shreds. The scars are still there, raw across his back like burns.

Some angels chose to surrender rather than vanish into the void. Like Rainbow, who begged Kane to eat his soul, that last beautiful day when the city fell. For now, Kane lets Rainbow stay. He did promise, after all. Sometimes that's worth something.

Kane flashes a ravenous grin. Rainbow's skin still stinks

like flowers after all these years, though the smell's faded. "Bring me Shadow."

Rainbow laughs, sunflower hair jittering with nerves. "He doesn't talk to me anymore, you know th—"

"And don't give me crap about meeting him halfway. He comes here."

"He doesn't like it h—"

Kane leans forward, and above the bar, glasses shatter. "I want Shadow. Bring him to me."

Rainbow's perfect face pales, and a tiny trickle of blood leaks from his nose. He fumbles for a cloth to clean the bar. "Okay. I'll do what I can. Don't break anything else."

The scent of rich angel blood waters Kane's mouth. He licks parched lips. "Get me a vodka and lime while you're at it."

"Make that on me." Low purring voice, female. Charcoal. Burnt hair. Ash. Demon.

Irritation sandpapers his skin. His nails blush scarlet, and he tinkles broken glass from his hair, tense. "Don't even talk to me, minion."

Delilah smiles and stretches lithe brown arms, jewels dripping yellow and blue from delicate wrists. Pale silk shimmers over her bronzed body, mirroring the sparkles in her champagne glass, the split in her dress sliding up one dusky thigh. Her sultry green gaze drapes over him, inviting. "Oh, come on, Kane. We can at least be civil to each other."

His mouth sours. She dares to align with his enemies, that cringing DiLuca clan. She's wasting her time. He's almost finished them off.

But Delilah's persistent. Last time, she even tried to seduce him. Pathetic little temptress, desperate to make her mark in the demon court. Just another wriggling worm who thinks she can challenge his rule. He should crush her skin under his nails, make her whimper, sweat, beg. But . . . she does remind him of home. "What do you want?"

Delilah eyes him slyly, painted lashes long around thistlegreen eyes. "To make peace."

"Were we at war?" He sips his drink through the straw, tart lime pleasuring his tongue, and flicks her a glacial glance of warning.

Ice crystals crinkle her long wine-red curls. She cracks them off in a white puff with a hellbright smile, but dented confidence flickers violet in her eyes. "Don't posture. We got off to a bad start, you and I. I wanted to ap—"

"You're not sorry, Delilah. Just get out of my place before you get hurt."

"I thought we could spend some time. Get to know each other." She strokes a curl from his cheek with one long purple nail, the caress lingering slyly in a rain of golden sparks. "You know. Make friends?"

Her touch warms his blood sweetly. She's lovely. Strong. Not vulnerable or breakable like humans, her immortal demon blood insatiable and irreducible. Inviting. Submissive. Starved, like a puppy dog eager to please.

Delilah's fingers creep to Kane's shoulder, twining in the hair over his collar. His groin heats. She's also a disobedient worm who should grovel at his feet. Who should know better than to touch him without asking.

He slurps his green drink to ice, and blasts her finger from his shoulder with a rude electric shock. "I could drag you before the demon court and flay you raw just for showing your face in my city. Imagine how long I can make that agony last."

She heals her wounded finger, a hiss of steam and a sweet careless smile, but angry ash gusts like snowflakes from her hair. "And I could tell the court how you won this city in the first place. How d'you think they'll like that?"

"They answer to me. I don't need to justify myself. You do."

Delilah smiles tautly. "That so? Your brother Phoebus would say different. . . . Oh, wait. You got rid of him, didn't you? The rightful prince, out of the way forever. What would the court make of that, if they knew the whole sordid tale?"

Angry red flame licks Kane's hair. *How does she know that?* Phoebus is gone forever. He made sure of it. Sometimes he still dreams of his brother's accusing eyes, the blinding brassy flash as the shackles gripped tight, hungry gulls squawking, the deafening crunch as the stone ground into place. He clamps his teeth tight. "Phoebus isn't your concern."

Delilah grins, flicking a stray lump of ash from his lapel. "We'll see, handsome. Remember, you could just be nice to me, and it'd all go away." She bends closer, and his hair springs alive in her breath, the hot slickness of her tongue a temptation on his ear. "I'm not so bad, once you get to know me." She nips his earlobe lightly and stalks away, curving hips swaying in translucent silk.

Kane cracks angry knuckles, sparks showering. He could chase her. Drag her down to hell, like the old days before the court took hold. Strip her naked on burning crimson rocks, pin her down with barbed chains and a bloody dagger through each wrist. Taste her blood, her salty juice, her flesh, thrust himself inside her and teach her a lesson. Make her writhe and scream, hurt her, pleasure her until she begs for death or mercy or more.

Hunger rips through his body like razors, and he slams the glass down lest he crush it. The court has rules. He's broken enough of them already to get here. Best leave it lie. She's no threat, not really, no matter her taunts. She can't know anything about Phoebus. Phoebus is dead, or as good as.

Beside him, a clean-faced mortal in an expensive suit shakes his head in sympathy over a glass of goldenbrown spirit. "Women. They're all the fucking same, mate. They'll tear your heart out just to watch you bleed."

Kane inhales, the raw steak scent of the boy's unrequited need stirring dark desire in his veins. Soulfood. Timely. He clinks glasses. "She can try."

"You're tougher than I am, then. Good for you." The boy's intoxicated blood smells like plumjuice, sweet and heady, and his tone scrapes with bitterness and loss.

Kane follows the boy's covetous gaze to a shapely blond girl in a slim red dress. "Is that your girlfriend?"

"Not anymore." The boy drains his drink, dark auburn hair brushing his shoulders.

"She's very beautiful." Kane licks his lips, soullust rich like hot honey in his blood. He wants to squirm, shift, devour.

"Beautiful. Smart. Going places. Fucks like a goddess. I shoulda known better."

The boy laughs, and Kane smells heartbreak, obsession, cold liaisons with other, faceless girls that end in silence. Desperation. He nods slowly, teeth sharpening. "I imagine a man might trade his soul for a woman like that."

"Heh. If only, mate. If only."

Images of bloody shreds, gnashing teeth, the ripe deliciousness of soulflesh. Kane glides to his feet, uncomfortable heat swelling his veins, and leans over to whisper as he passes. "I shouldn't give up, Joshua, if I were you. I believe it's your lucky night."

The boy stares. Kane glides onto the floor. Red-dress girl jumps as he approaches, and flinches when he trails his fingers over her hand.

She stares, curious and wary, but doesn't pull away. "I know you, don't I?"

He leans closer, her oriental scent lighting tiny flames along his skin. "You've always known me, Lucy."

Blood rushes from her shoulders to her face, and she gasps, the same raw, throaty sound they give when he pleasures them. He inhales deeper, and her secrets flower, limp like weak-stemmed roses for him to taste.

Bruises in the bathroom mirror, concealer makeup cold and sticky on her fingers. A man's harsh fists across her face, the sick punch in the guts that made her body bleed dark crimson lumps onto the shower floor, bigger than any clot had the right to be.

Kane's muscles twitch. Taste that fertile blood, drink that wasted life from her body and make her shudder, lick her soft folds clean and lull her to peaceful sleep in his arms. Drag her and her lovesick auburn pet to hell.

He brushes his cheekbone against hers, just a tiny gesture of dominance, and she shivers. His throat stings raw. She's already there, her own private hell of despair and emptiness.

Such a small step into the abyss. He whispers warm in her ear, curling a demonic wisp of longing into her despair like sly smoke. "That boy's dying for love. He'll never hurt you like the other one did. Why don't you go to him?"

"But he lied." She stares, her lush lip trembling. "He slept with her."

"Because you left him. Without you he's lost."

She swallows, her eyes glazing bright with desperate hope. "Really?"

"I believe there's magic in the air tonight. He can give you that child you yearn for. Wouldn't you trade everything for that?" He sears his lips across her cheek, like a mark.

She trembles beneath his kiss. Her gaze meets his, wide and raw with longing, and she's lost.

Kane shudders, breathless. It's like love, this luxuriant warmth in his blood, so rich and rare and intoxicating. Better, because no one ever says no, not in the end.

A tear slips down her face, unwilling. She blinks it away. "Thank you," she whispers.

Maybe he'll let her live long enough to enjoy it. "No, child. Thank *you*."

And as she walks shyly across the floor to meet her lover, Kane smiles, content.

Behind the bar, below gleaming rows of colored bottles that prism strobe lights to shards, Rainbow mixes an angry vodka tonic without looking, his gaze fixed on Kane's retreating back. The sight of the demon's ash-strewn hair spikes phantom pain through Rainbow's shoulder blades. He accepts the girl's money and fumbles the change, not really paying attention, the cold longing for flight withering his composure.

A sharp-eyed troll with a shaven green skull orders a cocktail and a whiskey soda. Rainbow spills the ice, and his shaking fingers slip on the glass. It smashes at his feet, and angrily he scoops up another one and jams the ice in hard. After so many years, the memory of the demon's cruel teeth slicing his flesh and ripping his precious wingjoints apart is fading. Some days, he even forgets completely.

A rotting pox on Kane for reminding him.

He pours the milk and chocolate sauce over berry liqueur, and this time he gets the change right.

He ducks, pretending to clean up the mess so no one can ask for anything else, and peeks out to see if Kane's still there. After more than a hundred years, his balance without the counterweight of heavy feathered wings is perfect.

But the demon's moved away, chatting up some tall blond girl with one elegant, persuasive hand laid casually on her arm. The worst breed of monster, the kind who looks exactly like everyone else.

Rainbow's stomach folds, images of bloody soulflesh splashing his mind scarlet. Once, he'd have protected her, under Shadow's orders. Pulled the hungry demon away from her, snarling and biting with righteous wrath flashing like lightning from snow white wings.

Now, he's just another hellslave, helpless as a succubus or a revenant. Worse, because no demoncursed spells cramp his spirit. No magical compulsion sucks his will away.

No. Rainbow just knows when he's beaten, and on his good days, he has the grace to feel ashamed of himself.

The rest of the time, he just works the bar, goes shopping, hangs out. And life is fine, an honest, simple, human life. Kane let him keep his body, and he looks good. No one cares about his fading scars. He's not in pain, and he's even learning to feel pleasure sometimes. He's got money, a girlfriend who adores him, a nice apartment with a view. Who cares if the world's going to hell? Most of these creeps fucking belong there.

He folds his cloth and sidles away, lifting the tiny hinge to let himself out into the pulsating crowd. Sugary sweatscent, adrenaline-soaked breath. Music tingles over him, raw and sultry. The cruel sensations still make him shiver.

He pushes through toward the back, and people smile at him, clap his shoulder. A sultry-eyed blue fairy slides inviting fingers over his thigh, and he presses a kiss to her shining lips with his fingertips and throws her a smile as he moves on. He's got friends here. Where he comes from, they do masters, colleagues, minions. Not friends.

Beneath the mezzanine, his reflection slinks beside him in the mirrored wall, tall, graceful, muscles shining, straight blond hair pulled back in a metal clip. Against the glass, that pretty blue banshee crouches, warbling low and threatening. She of the double bloodfevers, scared ruby eyes stark in her pale face.

Rain's sense of mischief sparkles. She's a DiLuca minion, Kane's enemy. Perhaps he should tell her what Kane unwittingly revealed—that Shadow's plotting something— just to piss Kane off.

Maybe that'd wreak some pleasing havoc.

But she doesn't look in the mood for confidences, and after an indecisive moment, Rainbow shrugs and walks on by unnoticed. Whatever.

Out the back, stars twinkle feebly through city smog and heat haze, and the black alley is quiet. Heat soaks through his jeans, into his skin. He wipes damp hands, pops out his phone, and speed-dials. Lets it ring, just once. Hangs up.

A minute of silence. Then another. Overhead, a crow calls. Rainbow kicks irritably at the dust, scattering ripped paper. He's not a fucking voice mail service. Screw it. Maybe he'll give work the flick, call Melanie—

His ringtone buzzes, a bouncy hip-hop tune.

Rainbow's spine crawls. He swallows, and picks up. "Umm . . . yeah?"

"Keep it short." Shadow's voice is musical, eerie like echoing wind chimes.

It reminds Rainbow of snowflakes, and he wonders if he once sounded like that, too, instead of whiskey-roughened, tired, old. He grits his teeth. "Kane wants to see you. Here."

A chuckle, like ice. "Of course he does. Tell him I'll be by Saint Patrick's tomorrow afternoon."

And Shadow hangs up. Just like that.

Rainbow flicks the call screen away, confusion wrapping cotton wool around his thoughts. No argument. Shadow didn't sound surprised. Or scared. Maybe he really is up to something. Plotting, scheming. Planning another war . . .

Whatever. Rainbow doesn't want to know. Doesn't want to answer the question festering in his soul, the horrid uncertainty about whose side he'd be on if it came to another fight.

Sweat trickles in his hair, the heat scorching his breath a dark reminder that he's only one step away from hell. He lifts his face to the heavens, searching, but the demonblack sky offers no answer.

Frustration cracks his knuckles. He's happy here—isn't he?—and before, Shadow gave him nothing but crisp orders and an inferiority complex. But still, somehow, he longs for home.

He taps a quick text to Kane, not expecting a reply, and hits another speed-dial. "Mel, hi. Yeah, sorry it's so late. . . . Well, thanks, I miss you, too. . . . No, I've got the night off. . . . Sure, I'll come to yours. . . . Huh? No, everything's fine. See ya soon. . . . Yeah. I like you, too, darlin'."

Beneath an endless, mind-twistingly blue sky, Shadow kneels in warm sunlight on a broad green lawn, his frosted white wings stretched out behind him. Before him, a deep blue pond lies still, its grassy edges neatly trimmed. The water's surface shows Rainbow, reflected perfectly as if he stood before a mirror, a blond strand falling in his eyes as he talks on his phone. His voice rings through clearly—*like you, too, darlin'*—and as he hangs up, Shadow sets off a ripple with the tip of his finger, and the image shimmers and pops away.

Shadow chuckles, and lights to his feet with a sweep of snowy feathers. "It worked."

His breeze swirls Whisper's simple white dress around her ankles. She stands back from the pool's edge, wary, nervous hands folded in front of her. She smiles, and the radiance glints in her golden braid, wrapped thick and hanging over one shoulder. "Of course it worked, Seraph."

Inwardly, Shadow rolls his eyes. The way she worships him is appropriate, but irritating. "Don't flatter."

Whisper's face falls, and her oceanblue gaze slips away under modest golden lashes. "I only meant—"

"It's all right." He smiles coldly. No need to let minions get comfortable. He slips his hand into hers, and they walk together across the leafy garden, their wingfeathers almost but not quite touching. Pale flowers grow in neat rows, the gardens tended to a minute perfection that pleases his eyes. Bees buzz and dart, orderly. The sun is warm and bright, its very sameness a comfort. A child treads past with neatly folded wings and nods respectfully, a book open in clean white hands.

Whisper clears her throat nervously. "So what now?"

Shadow plucks a mauve daisy and hands it to her with a smile. "I'll talk to Kane. Put him off the scent. He's too arrogant to figure out it's the dissent in his own ranks that's breaking his barriers."

She takes the flower, solemnly sniffing its perfume, and her shy gaze tilts upward. "You are . . . most courageous, Seraph."

He stops beneath a weeping willow, examining the small pale female hand in his. It feels cool, smooth. Neither pleasant nor unpleasant. How it should be. Coldly, he imagines kissing it, touching her, taking her in his arms and pressing his lips to her skin. Not a hair of arousal in his blood. Nothing. No reaction.

Kane tried to tempt Shadow, last time they met on the field of battle. Lured him with pain and pleasure and secret desires, the way he tempts them all. It didn't work. Shadow has no desires, except power and amusement.

But not all Shadow's children are as strong as Shadow.

His grip tightens around Whisper's fingers. "Courage is irrelevant. Kane is weak. I can feel it, Whisper, in my blood. Do you know what that means?"

Whisper's eyes brighten, curious and empty blue. "No."

"Never mind. We must strike while Kane is distracted.

The cherubs are amusing, but they're not enough. We need a spy. Someone who knows the place, who can watch Kane and discover his weaknesses." A golden butterfly flutters onto her wrist, and he brushes it away with one finger, leaving an ocher dust trail.

Whisper blushes, endearing. "But . . . Seraph, we already have Rainbow."

"Rainbow is lost." Shadow's tone whets harsh, and somewhere on earth, a gale blows. "Kane has poisoned him. We need new blood."

"But Kane can smell us. How will we hide someone new?"

Shadow gazes into the shimmering water, abstracted, remembering Rainbow's dirt-smeared reflection, the scars on his shoulders where his wings used to be. A real angel's body, not the ugly human-suit Kane's dominance usually forces on Shadow's kind. A strong, useful body. A body Kane is used to, and never inspects too closely.

Pity there's not someone else in it.

Someone eager and clever, who isn't afraid to immerse himself in Kane's sordid world.

Someone Shadow can control, and dispose of when he's finished.

He smiles, and below in a desolate desert, flowers bloom. "Let me worry about that. I have just the man."

Whisper smiles back, and dares to cover his hand with hers, and this time Shadow lets her.

5

I slouched against the mirrored wall deep beneath the mezzanine, shame still stinging my blood. Glass slicked cool on my bare shoulder, my hair sticking like wet paper. Flashing lights cast me in bloodstained colors, blue and green and crimson, and my mirror-banshee stared at me with reproachful garnet eyes. Fresh scarlet bruises already turned blue on her delicate cheek. She looked gaunt, pale, her blue hair frightful.

I turned away, sick. I didn't want to see myself.

White dry ice drifted low and fragrant, hissing over metal and suede, mixing with tart pot smoke and the fleshy scent of sex. On the couch beside me a skinny vampire girl with white dreadlocks and angry scars laddering her forearms ravished a half-insensible bloodfae boy. Tiny holes bled freely in his dark-skinned throat, and she lapped at the plumrich blood. His wet caramel hair dripped sanguine sweat onto the suede, his half-lidded eyes rolling white. She had her hand stuffed down his bloodstained jeans, and his sprawled limbs twitched limp, his breath ragged.

He didn't look fully conscious to me. I kicked at her starved ankles. "You paying for that, missy?"

She snarled at me, blood and spit dripping, and the kid groaned and clawed at her dreads to drag her back down.

I grunted, flushing. One girl's disgusting is another boy's wet dream. I didn't get it. Any bloodsucker who tried that with me got a swift stiletto heel somewhere hard and pain-ful. But that kid's throaty need crawled under my skin like a worm, slithering over my muscles and carving my nerves to a jittery mess.

The singer's raw-ripped voice slid drunkenly inside my head, that vampire blood I'd drunk still coating my guts with desire and velvet compliance. I could see Joey at the bar, coolly polishing off another scotch, and the humiliating temptation to creep back up to him and apologize tickled my skin like fairy flame. His lips still burned on my cheek, the tiny touch of his tongue a stab of sweet torture I couldn't forget. What was he thinking? What the fuck was I thinking?

Frustration seared into my guts like a hot iron rod, and I banged angry fists back against the glass, the mirror's cool slam only aggravating my unease. Lately I'd become ob-sessed with touching him, some dark empty place inside me longing for his presence. Every glance, every scrap of his regard, I played over and over in my mind, searching, won-dering, cursing my cowardice.

Those few precious seconds a few weeks ago when he'd kissed me reverberated in my daydreams, and soaked my nights with feversweat. I was high when it happened, my nerves strung tight on fight and sparkle, my blood afire with stolen fae adrenaline. Maybe it wasn't real. Maybe I'd hal-lucinated the whole thing.

Maybe I just needed to get laid.

God, I was so pathetic. I couldn't even wish myself back to the days before I'd noticed him like this. I'd noticed him that very first night in the spriggan gang's squat, when he lifted me up by my shackle-scabbed hand. My knees had buckled, my feet slipping on the greasy floor, but he helped me stand, his hands cool and reassuring on my waist. He'd touched my bleeding lip with a single gentle fingertip, his eyes for once warm and compassionate, and said, *Are they hurting you, miss?*

I'd never forgotten that shy, shivering melt in my heart when I realized he meant they shouldn't.

He'd paid the spriggan off on the spot by smacking the

bastard's grinning head against the wall until it bled and stopped wriggling. Vicious justice, maybe, but it impressed the hell out of me, and from that day, it was Joey for me.

He cleaned me up, gave me a fresh start. It wasn't easy, shivering and screaming and choking on nosebleeds, and a dozen times I wanted to give up. But I wanted Joey's approval more. He found me a place to stay, a real house where they didn't use my body or stuff drugs up my nose, and if sometimes I couldn't pay the rent, no one ever came looking. He even found me jobs, off and on, basic stuff but clean, and sometimes he'd drop by to check on me unannounced.

I lived for those days, his quiet questions, the heart-stopping flash of his smile.

He wasn't like anyone else I knew. He never lied, or apologized. Never patronized me. Never touched me. Like a dark knight from a fairy tale, cold and distant but ever-present, and people soon learned not to make my life difficult. Not unless they wanted trouble.

Gifts are suspicious when you're alone and vulnerable, and for a long time I waited and hoped to see what he wanted in return. But he'd already gotten it: loyalty, blind and absolute. I'd have done anything for him, and though he asked little at first—some spying here, a little spine-tingling thieving there, the occasional con trick or streetfight mayhem—I wanted more. I learned to fight so I could impress him, and soon no one gave me shit anymore.

Safety, shelter, a decent living. He gave me all those things. But what he really gave me was a reason to live.

When he kept his distance, I told myself I was only sixteen, and he was too old for me. Besides, he was an up-and-coming friend of important friends, a cousin of Salvatore DiLuca himself, and me just a cheap sparkleblind whore.

I wasn't sixteen anymore.

I banged my head and clawed the mirrors with screeching nails, but my body wouldn't relax, my blood boiling with empty hunger. Even now that I finally had this job, and got to see him every night, he still pushed me away. Like he went out of his way to prove he didn't trust me, when the very fact that I still worked for him proved that he did.

My hands shook, my magicspiced reflexes jerking to leap, strike, kill. Fuck it. I couldn't function like this. It'd get me killed. I needed distance. I needed to get my mind back on the job. Where the fuck was Cobalt? He should've called by now.

Seven years had passed, and I was no closer to finding my mother's murderer and the healing I craved, that I'd get only when the bastard lay dead at my hands. But recently I'd found something that might help. Something dangerous and edgy, painful like razor oblivion and as compelling.

I gritted my teeth, remembering last time, how the mind-scrape had hurt me, how I'd woken weeping and covered in scratches from my own ripped nails. Digging through your own suppressed memories was a ragged road to insanity. But it might help. It had to help. I didn't know what else to do. If I didn't find my mother's killer, all this death would be for nothing.

I yanked my phone from the slim pocket at my thigh and typed a terse text. *U holding?????* It took me three goes to get it right. I jerked through the address book for my trader's number and jammed my thumb on SEND. I leaned my head back on the cool glass and clutched the phone in sweaty fingers, waiting for the comforting buzz that meant Cobalt was here, and had what I needed.

Music screeched in my ears, scraping like thorns, the distorted chorus bass vibrating my guts to nausea. Before me, dreadlock bitch was fucking her snack now, riding him with her torn black skirt rolled up on her thighs, peeling back his shirt to lick blood from his fangslashed nipple. Wet flesh slicked and tore. He whimpered, pain and longing gnashing sharp teeth in my ears. I closed my eyes. I couldn't block out the sound of his violation, but I damn well didn't have to watch.

"Looking for some light, pretty girl?"

I jerked, and the phone slipped from my fingers as I went for knives that weren't there.

A lissome golden fairy smiled down at me, her wings frosted silver like a spider's web in the rain.

My fingers shook, scarily empty. I scrabbled on the ground for my phone, begging it not to be broken, not now. The screen lit, and relief slashed my nerves. Still no reply. I clutched it tight, like a lifeline. "No, thanks."

"Smell like you are. All broken glass and blood. Sure you're not hungry?" The fairy gave a toothy white smile, her sweet musical voice like warm lotion on my tortured ears. A light scar caressed her gold-brushed cheek, like she'd been burned long ago, and she held her head self-consciously askance, hiding the mark with her long silver hair like she didn't want anyone to see.

But she was still beautiful, her forestgreen scent an enticement. She looked interesting, intriguing, experienced. Not just a disposable china doll like me. I swallowed. Hungry? I was ravenous. "Really, I'm fine. Thanks anyway."

Silvery silk flowed as she reached out a long dusky arm. Her three-knuckled fingers unfolded, claws glinting silver. In her narrow palm sat a long glass vial. Inside, emerald liquid sparkled, twinkles of gold and silver winking at me like a demon's tempting eyes, colored shadows dancing over her palm.

My gaze locked on that shimmering green prize, and a hot ache flowered deep in my belly.

My mouth stung dry. I had to wait for Cobalt. If I sparkled out now, I'd miss his message, and only Cobalt knew for sure how to help me. But . . . "I'm . . . I've got my score coming. I can't—"

Her eyes glinted. She darted forward, her cool arm sliding around my neck, her smile hot and conspiratorial on my ear. "But mine's special, snaky girl. So bright and angry. I made it just for you. Drop of agony, splash of bitterness, bloom of rosy revenge. Make you feel special. Send you dreams. Give you what you need."

Her honey breath danced on my tongue, ripe with weird fairy insight. She slid long delicate fingers over my collarbone, trailing golden dust down to where my pale breast swelled. Goose bumps stung, and my nipple reacted, twist-ing tight.

Desperate chemical need crooned deep in my throat. I could have thrown her off me easily enough. I wanted to shove her off me, to slap her lovely face and stalk away. But I wanted what she was selling more.

She swept the vial up under my nose, where I could smell the cursed stuff as it dampened the cork, rich and citrusy like preserved lemon. I could hear it, the tempting effervescence tinkling like tiny demon bells, and my body ripped and tore inside with an addict's helpless yearning. My breasts ached. Glands swelled to painful hardness between my legs, and poison throbbed full and threatening in the sacs under my tongue. I wanted it that bad.

The fairy's long tongue curled along the top of my bodice to the soft crevice between my breasts, and dipped inside. Slick, warm, inviting, the maddening scent of oranges drift-ing from her hair. I slammed my palms into the glass so I wouldn't rip her limbs off and snatch the vial from her bleeding hand. I was no better than that sorry bloodfae boy. If she wanted money, she could have it. A poignant memory or two? No problem. If she wanted to fuck, I'd do that, too. Just feed me.

"Whoa, easy on, lady." Smoke-cracked voice, dark and familiar, the fleeting scent of bourbon and expensive men's perfume. Strong hands grabbed the fairy's soft silver hair and yanked her away from me.

The fairy snarled, golden spit flecking, and Vincent shoul-dered between us, though her height outstripped his and probably her strength, too. Pretty boy acted tough enough when it suited him. "Whatever you're selling, she ain't pay-ing like that."

"Want your own, candy child? Ask her yourself." She ran that long brown tongue over her teeth in a lascivious wet grin and scampered away.

My body screamed, thwarted. I wanted to scream, too, chase her and make her give me what I wanted. I whirled and shoved Vincent in the chest, wrath sparking from my fingers and welling deep in my lungs. "What the fuck did you do that for?"

"Thought you needed help." He turned his wounded hot-chocolate eyes on me, that wishful-yet-sultry *you might be out of my league, princess, but I can show you one helluva good time* gaze. No doubt that sexy let-me-make-you-moan glance wheedled him into more girls' beds than he deserved.

But not this angry blue banshee. My fingers itched for a weapon, to gut the sneaky little fucker. I didn't for a moment mistake his effort for gallantry. Whatever he'd secretly texted Joey about me, it wasn't good. He was undermining me, yet he was supposed to be on my side. "Like you give a toss about helping me, Vinny. I don't need help from a lying little weasel like you. What sick shit did you tell the boss about me, huh?"

"Calm down, Minwah, okay? I didn't say nothing." He sidled back up to me, scraping his elaborate hair even more elaborately messy and endearing. Had to give him points for guts. He stuffed his hands into his faded jeans pockets, and pulled them out again, nervous. "Look, are you, uh . . . are you needing?"

Like it wasn't obvious. I resisted niggling sympathy. He was my friend, and he was just a human. It wasn't his fault he had to lie and connive to get what he wanted. But he still had no right. I averted my face, my skin still running with sweat. "That's none of your goddamn business."

"I can help you."

"I told you. I don't want your help." I jammed my still-silent phone away and walked off. If Cobalt wasn't here, I'd have to go home and sweat it off. Terrific.

But Vincent grabbed my elbow, fingers warm and tight in the joint, and pulled me back against him. His warm whisper shivered my hair. "Ain't you sick of following him?"

"What?" I tried to shake him off, but I didn't try very hard, distracted by his body, hard and fragrant against my back, his pulse feeding my hungry ears. "Are you high or something? Get off me before I hurt you."

"The boss. He's never gonna make you his equal. Don't that hurt?"

"Dunno what you're talking about." I tried to ignore his fingers, gliding dulcet on my wrist. A moment ago, he forced me still. Now he invited me to stay, and temptation prickled nerves deep inside me that hungered for stimulation, any sensation to make me feel alive.

"You and me, Mina." His words slid deftly into my vampire-addled blood, caressing me to warm desire. He slipped his arm around my waist with uncanny seducer's instinct. "We're both strong, smart, tough. We've both got . . . talents. We'd make a good team. No rule says Joey's gotta be the boss." He caressed my bare midriff, lingering on the belt of my low-cut pants, his thumb teasing inside.

I turned to face him, letting his hand slip over my hip. His thighs felt strong and warm against mine, his arousal slow but definite in the way he pressed against me, slid his body slowly across mine. Hot body, for a human, strong and male, hard-muscled in all the right places. Not too gay to have a hard-on. They said he was careful and considerate in bed. I even liked him, sort of.

I hadn't been with a man in a long time, and my sparkle-parched body itched at me to act. I wasn't taken, not really. In my dreams, maybe. But Vincent had a girlfriend, a pretty blue water fairy named Flora. She was my friend, too. Did I care? "Vincent—"

"You're so beautiful, Mina." He dipped to tease warm lips along my jaw. "Bet he never tells you that."

Curiosity and temptation chewed through my reason, and I sighed and sank my fingers into his fragrant hair, drawing him gently on. It felt so good to be touched. He nuzzled me, kissing just below my ear, where my pulse thudded. Sparks danced over my scalp, forcing pleasured melody from my lips. My eyelids flickered and threatened to close.

I crept my hand to his chest, where his heartbeat beckoned. The tense, steady thump of his pulse spread over my palm, sank through my flesh into my bones, teasing me like hot spicy music. I murmured, and I felt him smile, his whisper tempting. "You like that. I knew it. We're meant to be, Mina. We don't need Joey tellin' us what to do."

Lightly he caressed the sensitive place at the small of my back. I shivered under those delicate fingertips. I crushed his hair in my fist as he kissed his way back along my jaw. His lips lingered at the corner of my mouth, his sweet bourbon flavor a rich lure, the shy bitter taste of his loneliness drawing me closer than rash seduction ever could have.

My lips parted, anticipating his kiss, a deep satisfied purr ready in my throat. I should go with him. Forget sparkle, memory, revenge. Just go with him, taste him, feel his desire rise with mine, pin his hot male body down beneath me and share some meaningless warmth and pleasure, before we had to wake up and remember how insignificant our sad little lives were.

No one'd ever know. Joey didn't have to find out.

His lips hovered an inch from mine, a final question laced with bourbon and intoxicating hope. But it wasn't right. I wanted those lips to taste of venom, wanted to feel shifting flesh roil under my hands, inhale the hot melting scent of mint. I wanted the hair wrapped around my fists to be blond.

I yanked Vincent's head back to glare into his eyes. "Stop right there and I won't kick your skanky ass into next week."

He groaned and tugged away, scowling. "Dunno what you think you're saving yourself for."

"And you can leave that right alone, smart-ass. I should tell the boss everything you just said." My body still ached, and I dragged my hair straight, my face hot. Infuriating, that he'd crept under my skin so effortlessly.

"Think he'll believe you after tonight?" A sly glint ignited in his eyes, and the truth nagged at me, irritatingly transparent.

All part of Vincent's plan. Seduce me while I was weak and needy. Blackmail me into helping him. Fix it so I couldn't tell without seeming like I was to blame all along.

Icy anger spiked, and a deep furious hum built in my lungs. "You cunning little shit. I don't want any part of it. Fuck off."

That wounded look again. "Think about it, Min. He's using both of us. We're worth more than that."

Laughter sputtered, it was so ridiculous. "Vincent, you're just a human! You're not even faeborn. No one takes you seriously. What you gonna do against Diamond? Ange Valenti, the toughest vampire son of a bitch in town? Kane, for fucksake? You start playing with the big kids, and they'll tear your eyeballs out—"

"Joey's never gonna want you!" Bitterness splintered Vincent's tone flintsharp, his handsome face tight. "You think you're special 'cause you're a girl? Because once he took pity on you? You're just a resource. You'll fight for him till you bleed dry, and one day they'll kill you and he'll just shrug and scowl and get himself another slave."

My heart stung. "Yeah? Guess that's how he picked you up, then."

"It's what he does, Mina! Jesus, can't you see how he leads you on? You really think he'll lower himself to fuck a needy sparkled-up whore like you?"

We stared at each other, tension stretching the air between us like hellblack glamour. We'd been friends since I was eighteen. We'd known each other too long to pull punches, and we knew exactly where it hurt the most. My throat ached. This time, we might really be over.

Against my thigh, my phone shrieked.

I pulled it out, my ears ringing sourly. *Cy@ back. ru sure??? xxC.*

I swallowed on sticky virusblood residue, and my body burned. I was sure, all right. I just wanted it all to go away.

Vincent sucked in a breath, dragging shaking fingers through his hair. "Fuck. I'm s—"

"Forget it." I shoved past him, banging into his shoulder with mine. He didn't follow me, and after a few seconds, icy consonants rippled my skin as he cursed.

I stalked along beside the mirrored wall, past a gaggle of twirling drunk fairy girls in stiletto heels and satin party dresses, a redheaded vampire girl in black vinyl and industrial ear piercings jabbing a helljuice syringe in her arm, three fat spriggans in drag playing drinking games with a bottle of blood.

In a dim smoke-wreathed corner, Iridium hunched one misshapen shoulder against the glass, ironsharp claws glinting as he stroked a pretty young girl's bleached hair. His glamour flickered sweet lies, a clean slim blond boy with pale mismatched eyes. The girl smiled and leaned closer, and over her shoulder, Iridium winked slyly at me beneath a fall of dirtybronze hair.

My stomach churned. None of my business, right? But Iridium's sense of fun was grotesque and dangerous. He wore barbed wire wrapped around his wrists, for fucksake. I walked up and tapped her on one satin-strapped shoulder, giving my best crazybanshee glare. "You making moves on my boyfriend, bitch? Clear off or I'll scratch your eyeballs out."

She stared at him, twisting long green nails in her dress. "What? You never . . . goddamn it." And she flounced away with a pained scowl.

Iridium twitched, some deformed muscle in his back spasming. He couldn't stand upright, and he had to twist his crooked hips and cock his head to look me in the eyes. He grimaced in pain. "Wasn't very nice. Cripple can't get laid in peace?"

The stink of his rust-rotted wings slicked my tongue with salt. "Since when did you ever just get laid, you sick freak?"

"Do what I have to." Coppery teeth glinted, a shark's inviting grin. "Should try it. Might like."

"Screw you." I spun and stalked away.

His grit-on-iron laugh followed me, taunting. "Some girls just die, Mina. You and Joey can't save them all."

An angry yowl trembled my lungs. But he was right. I couldn't.

Forget Vincent and Iridium. Forget Joey, like he'd surely forgotten me until he needed me again. There was only vengeance.

Echoes of the pain I'd suffered last time I tried this stung deep in my temples like wasps, only a dim reflection of the blinding agony of memoryslash. I'd learned nothing, only the same images I'd always seen, over and over until I screamed and clawed and begged Cobalt to stop, my ears bleeding scarlet into his dirty hair.

Why did I do it? Why was I so convinced that somewhere in the hellscraped cavern of my soul, I'd repressed some clue that'd lead me to the killer?

Maybe there was no answer. My mother died, screeching for help, and I'd never find out who or why. I'd spent years forging my body into a weapon. But until I found my target, no kill could satisfy me.

My heart twisted tight like a wrung-out rag. Stupid tears flooded my eyes, and my ears popped like a wet thunderclap. My nose swelled and ached inside as if I'd stuffed it with sparkle hours ago. I tried to picture her face in my mind, her kind pewter eyes, her smile, but the image kept blurring, washed out like a watercolor as if I couldn't remember what she looked like.

Fingers slimed my wrist, and I whirled, my nails striking out.

Yellow limbs recoiled, long fingers hiding a pointy face. A wet sniffle, a sob.

I backed off, shaking. Violet. It was just Violet, lank green fairy hair tumbling over skinny shoulders. Her ragged wings trembled. Bruises shone with tears under her tired eyes, matching the new one on her chin, where fresh teethmarks gleamed wet. "Please, Min. I got nowhere to go. Can you just spot me—?"

"I can't right now, okay? I'll call you." Remorse twitched, but I shook it off and walked away. I didn't want to see Violet, the ugly, pitiful ghost of Mina-past. She wasn't my problem. We make our own luck. Right?

Besides, I needed all my cash for Cobalt. Without it, he wouldn't help me.

I strode down a metal ramp that shuddered to the band's cruel beat, the music thudding up my calves, resonating in my bones. My metal heels cracked loud on the steel floor, a harsh, comforting rhythm of my own making, a quantifiable cosmic reaction to my presence that proved I was alive, and not just swept-together fragments of some ghastly memory.

A couple of drunk faeborn kids smoking a ragged joint slouched on the floor against the wall, misshapen legs sprawled in grimy jeans, half-formed wingstubs stretching beneath ripped T-shirts. Not all the faeborn were as well-camouflaged as Joey.

One looked up as I passed and winked at me, eyes slitted like a cat's and glazed bright. The tart pot smoke galvanized me, and determination clenched my fists like steel as I approached the dim vestibule that led to the fire exit. If I achieved anything tonight, at the very least I'd remember my mother's face for a few more weeks.

I rounded the corner too fast, and blundered into warm, pliable glass.

Rose scent pinched my nostrils, and alarm ripped through my reflexes like electric shock. My pulse bolted, a scared rabbit. I jumped backwards, agile, and landed with a metallic snap on my toes, my knees bent, balancing tight on quivering ankle tendons and luck.

Diamond laughed, a deep crystal tinkle that hacked at my nerves. His long glass-spun hair glinted, crackling over translucent skin. "Surprisify you again, bluebell?"

I sneaked a slow deep breath, stroking my jittering nerves calm. My cheek still stung where he'd rubbed it into the ground earlier, but his insults stabbed my pride deeper. Swiftly I checked left, right, behind him. He was alone, and my palms itched. I wanted to rip his pretty transparent face off. But the rule said no fighting at the Court, and if Joey caught me breaking the peace, he'd have my skin.

I sucked in another breath, damping down the earsplitting yowl that threatened to burst from my throat. "Let it be. No fight."

"If you say so. Actu-mally, I was looking for you." He fluttered closer, quartz wings glittering, and his shadow rippled dim on the floor like a watery reflection. He wore tight dark jeans and a slashed black shirt with no sleeves, typical fairy show-off, and glimpses of his glassy skin shone violet and green in the nightclub lights over faint scarlet veins like webs. Shorter than the average fairy, bulked up instead of slender, the outlines of his hard muscles defined. Long straight hair like optic fiber, perfect face, his sculptured fairy weirdness doing nothing to disguise long rainbow lashes and liquidberry eyes and ripe sulky lips.

Yeah, okay, so he was fuckable. Strip-him-naked, chain-him-to-the-bed-and-play material. If I wasn't his sworn enemy and up to my eyeballs in unrequited fuck-me for another man, that is. And it was a pity such a magnificent body belonged to Melbourne's most magnificent asshole. Them's the breaks, I guess.

Diamond settled on the metal in front of me, uncannily silent. Too close. The warm rosy wind from his wings teased my hair back, and my gaze drew to the pulse that throbbed scarlet in his tight faemuscled arm, and I wanted to duck away. But Diamond was Ange Valenti's new golden boy, going places like a rocket. If he wasn't merely taunting me, this could be an opportunity to deal.

I swallowed, and stood straighter. "What you want?"

"Same-same thing your musky friend Vincent wanted, of course." He sniffed at me like a cat, showing that wicked smash-me grin, and his wind chime voice clattered cold down my spine.

I forced a laugh, though my guts crunched tight and hot that I'd let him trick me again, and speared him on a sharp smile. "Fuck you."

I tried to shoulder past him, but he planted his hand on the wall beside me, trapping me close to him with that shiny arm. "Not that. You're wastified at DiLuca, Mina."

Was he watching me? Following me? Cold glassfae insight stroked my face, seductive and ugly at the same time. A misty memory flashed, the two of us kissing, hot and breathless, his hands on my ass and sugarbright sparkle shining in my blood like starlight, and I couldn't be sure it wasn't real.

My face flushed, and I snarled and cracked his mindtouch off with a sizzling soprano chord, swatting his arm away. "Was it the *fuck* or the *you* that you didn't understand?"

"Do the snake and his wormatrons ever let you think? Or

do you just obey?" Diamond's garnet eyes glinted under goldsparked lashes, studying my face, coolly analyzing me with prickly faespell.

"You don't know anything about me, okay? Give it up."

"Like to know about you, Mina. Really would." He slipped me another dark rosy grin, his wings twitching.

I caught his meaning, and angry spit filled my mouth. "The day I rat on him to you is the d—"

"No rats, little mouse. Just tastyliciousness for you." He tilted his head, seductive silver sparkling in his eyes. "I'll give you more money. More responsibility. More respectimacality. It's a brave new world down at Valentino's these days. Come see for yourself." And he actually dared to touch me, his claws a dark caress of promise on my cheek.

A hot poisoned warble vibrated my larynx, and I slapped his fingers away. "You're lucky I don't shatter your lying face off. I'm not having this conversation, okay? I never saw you." And I spun to shoulder past him.

"I'll tell you who murdered your mother."

Melody jammed in my throat like a stuck gumball, and my skin shrank cold. I halted.

Diamond's lips twisted in rosedark amusement. "Them's expensive whisperings, though. Might involve a pinch more rat-icality."

My heart somersaulted. How could he know anything? How did he even know she died? This was my secret mission, my hidden heart's desire. Diamond was guessing. Had to be.

I tried to breathe, but my lungs cramped tight and brittle like glass, and I gasped, my eyes stinging wet. "You're lying."

He folded flexible fairy fingers over my bare shoulder to steady me. A stray laser caught his hair, lighting it up like hellish rainbows. "Find out."

His flowery scent sickened me, but longing churned my guts harder. Diamond was a liar, an enemy and a lover of sweet fae chaos. Surely he played with me, lured me to betray my boss with promises he couldn't possibly keep.

But what if he wasn't lying?

Raw need thinned my blood like a drug, boiling in my veins. He asked for the one thing I could never give. I'd never sink that low. I should go to Joey right now and tell him everything Diamond said, only Vincent had already made Joey suspicious about me with that stupid text message. Vincent probably watched us right now. Spied on me. Was already telling Joey what a dirty lowdown traitor I was.

I swallowed a spelldrenched scream, twisted my arm from Diamond's grip and strode away.

He let me go, and the sound of his giggle as he swept away slid over my skin like hot slime. I stalked along the wide corridor, my heels crunching as the pitted metal floor gave way to concrete. My ankle twisted as I hopped too fast down the steps, and I righted myself with a curse and a vicious swipe of hair over my shoulder.

Cobalt lounged against the steelbarred fire door, texting rapidly with one pale hand while he knotted three feet of dusty nightblue hair at the base of his neck with the other. There was always something chalky and earthbound about Cobalt, and sweat bled his earthfae colors, his white skin stained gothblue like inky paper. He twirled his phone away as he heard me coming, and flitted up the steps to meet me on wings like torn black velvet.

I attempted a casual smile, though my blood still stung like poison from Diamond's insolence. "Hey, C. You on?"

Cobalt sniffed, his long curled nose twitching, dark remnants of a sparkle hit showering wild glitter deep into his indigo eyes. He blinked feathery black lashes, focusing. "What did he want?"

"Who?"

"Diamond. Asked me about you. He said, where's the flexy blue songstress? I said, fuck off, glitterboy, heh heh." He wiped multiknuckled white fingers on his jeans, smearing them black. He wore a stained white shirt with no sleeves, a silver belt buckle and dusty boots the color of rain. All he was missing was a cowboy hat and a guitar. He shrugged loose shoulders, that lazy movement I liked, and the dust springing from his wings smelled of warm earth and sunlight. "So what did he want?"

I liked his smell, too, even if it came laden with the memory of pain. Once, Cobalt was my friend, sort of, and we got drunk together, shared greasy hamburgers at four in the morning, called each other *bitch* and *skankface* and pretended we didn't like each other as awkward sort-of-friends do. Now, he was my dealer, and I avoided him whenever I could. Except on nights like tonight, when Joey broke my heart and scraped my composure raw, when the old need blinded me and the heart-ripping quest for vengeance became my solace.

My palms itched, ready. "Nothing. He didn't say much. You good?"

He chewed one inkstained claw, his pointy white chin bobbing. "You look like shit, Min-bin. You sure this is a good idea?"

Did I spy a twitch of guilt in his narrow face? Caution plucked tinfoil melody from my nerves, but I ignored it. I didn't care what he meant. I didn't care if it hurt. I just wanted tonight to be over, and for once I didn't want to be alone.

I stuffed my hand in my pocket, pulled out a wad of bright plastic cash and rustled it in front of his face. No mystery about Cobalt. Only two things he wanted from me anymore, and money was one. "I'm fine. Let's go."

Unease shone violet in Cobalt's eyes, but he took both the cash and my hand.

6

Dim and almost invisible like a glassy shade against the metal wall, Diamond stretches out a long ghostly finger and caresses her hair as she walks by. So soft, that ultrablue cascade. So vulnerable. Just like the girl behind the façade.

Glamour crackles his fingertips, and she tosses her head, like she's shrugging off a fly, but doesn't turn. When she and her dustified blue friend disappear into the crowd, Diamond giggles and snaps back into sight, and static shatters a few glassy fragments off his wings to tinkle on the floor.

The wiry, muscled feel of her shoulder still stings his palm, and black covetousness warms his shining blood. She's easy prey, her secrets transparent to his fickle faesight. Too easy to tease her, tempt her, plant treachery's tasty seed deep in her belly.

A slim finger of bloodscent traces down his cheek. He looks up, spearing his pierceglass gaze into the crowd. Images merge and shimmer, vanishing to show him what's behind, and he glimpses short dark curls and golden chains, shining teeth and the flat glint of slategrey vampire eyes.

Diamond's mouth crunches sour, and he snaps his faesight off with an electric zap. Angelo Valenti is here, vampire lord of the family, surrounded by sycophants and wannabes vying for his attention. Just like his opposite number, Joey, holding his rustified little court like it glittered with gold and jewels and wasn't about to explode around him in a hail of hellflame.

Diamond's guts squirm, hatred and jealousy fighting like scorpions. He should be there, with the other minions, fighting for a few seconds in the sun. Ange will like his plan to trick Joey. Bold subterfuge appeals to a 350-year-old schemer. That's the sharp bit, the pointificality of the whole thing. Raise his profile in the family. Get Ange's attention. Make Ange trust him.

And then, the fun can really begin. One day, Diamond will snatch that tainted crown from Ange's failing hands. And then he'll see just how long it takes for a tough-as-shit Sicilian vampire to bleed to death.

Molten glass hardens in Diamond's bones like steel. He scrapes his hair straight in a shimmer of fiberoptic rainbows and heads for the bar, but Flora, Vincent DiLuca's alleged girlfriend, floats up, her pretty green skin glowing in the warmth. She lights beside him, her face neutral under a nest of rosy curls. "What was that about?"

Her vinegar jealousy stings his skin. Gratifying. Diamond smiles, because he knows she can't take his smile. She's half in love with him, this little plaything. Too bad for her. "Patience, flower. Waitification. You'll see."

She pouts soft apple lips and snakes slender arms around his neck, her little waterfae body soft and wet. "Don't see why you need her when you've got me."

"But I don't have you, flower. Vincent has you most of the time." He tweaks Flora's sharp nose with his teeth, careless of being seen.

She gasps and giggles. "And I already tell you everything he says."

"Pity he never says anything interesting, then." He's had Flora too many times. The freshaliciousness is lost. But it pleases him to steal from DiLucas. Especially from Joey, if it comes to that. Slide secretive, illicit hands on that pretty blue banshee, hmm-mmm. Make Joey squirm.

Hot blood forces down to his loins, and glowing red veins pulse and swell beneath his skin. Flora murmurs and presses against him, imagining his reaction is for her. Flora is still succulent, her slim body inviting, the tastylicious flavor of her devotion a bleak distraction from lies and black treachery.

Once, the world was always like that, clear and shiny like sunshine on a windowpane, and to kiss a girl and mean it was its own delight. Now, Diamond doesn't know who his friends are, or if he's even got any, and a kiss means less than nothing.

He doesn't think about *her* anymore. The girl he lost. She might hear him with those new virus-sharp ears, and hate him forever for what he's become.

He tugs Flora back into the dark corner where no one can see, and she sighs and snakes one lissome leg around his hips. Her dress sticks to her small body, the fabric transparent with moisture, showing sweet green breasts, straining nipples, the druglike curve of her hip. Her dripping wings glow with desire, lighting his glassy skin like neon.

Diamond flares his wings for balance and lifts her, bruising her softness against him, and bites down hard on memory's sharp spritz. No, don't think about *her*. Never imagine how soft and wonderful she felt, her swelling red lips, those long dark lashes, her besotted eyes when she leaned in for a kiss.

Instead, imagine it's Joey's girl, surrendering to him so he'll talk. His chest tightens. Crack Mina open like an oyster, peel that hard leather shell from her skin, expose the tender flesh beneath. Excitement grips his balls tight, and he nuzzles Flora's dress aside and fastens hungry teeth on her eager nipple.

Flora murmurs in pleasure, wet waterfae desire soaking his shirt, his jeans, his arms. "Mmm. More." Her nipple springs hot against his tongue, the flesh around it so taut and soft. He curls his tongue around her, sucking, and she pulls his hand down under her skirt where she's naked, slick and delicious.

Her apple scent both irritates and inflames him. He squeezes claws into her thigh, drawing out a gasp, and his palm slides sticky over torn skin and blood, the crusted shape of fangholes where the vein pulses.

Vampire marks. Just like Rosa.

Diamond squeezes his eyes shut on glassy memory, his stomach hot and sore. He hit her, that first night, dark hair cascading over her bleeding face, and he still remembers the shocked disbelief brimming in her eyes, that heart-wrenching distance he never quite closed again. He's never forgotten that sick rush of power.

Never forgiven himself.

His cock swells harder, and he sinks his cruel teeth into Flora's collarbone, marking her. He prods the fangmarks in her thigh, accusing. "What's them, flower? You spreading yourself again?"

A delighted whimper of pain. "Just now. I set a little trap for Vincent. Iridium gave me the idea. You'll like it, I pr—"

"I don't share with a vampire." Her blood stings his tongue, fresh and fruitified, and he lets go before he can really hurt her, even though she likes it, the little vipercat. It doesn't make him feel good, that urge. As rotten as those he despises. Instead, he slides his hand up to where she's swollen, pressing his fingers just where she likes it, letting her shudders feed slow desire into his body, clean like it should be. "Not ever. Understandify?"

"But Vincent—"

"Because I tell you so. Not because you feel like it. Get it?"

She nods, panting through a wicked smile. "Guess that makes me a bad girl, then."

He pins her against the wall with his chest and a powerful pump of wings. She helps him, wet fae fingers fumbling together to get his cock out. He parts her flesh with hungry claws and pushes deep and hard into her, forcing her breath away.

Her hot flesh squeezes him, still slick with what she's done. He can smell the feversick creature on her, blood and sweat and strange male flesh. He can see the thing's fingerprints on her arms, shining ultraviolet in his eldritch faesight. Hot vampire come burns his cock, sliding down over him in a delicious caress. The mixture of fluids inflames him, and he grips her hips and thrusts harder, breathless.

Her wings flatten green against the rippled metal wall, and she arches and grips tighter with her thighs, murmuring tiny cries of delight. She's not faking it. He can smell that, too, the rich fleshscent of tension rising inside her, the pleasure chemicals leaching golden into her veins. Fucking like this ignites her. His anger turns her on, and her breathless excitement is sweet poison.

Memories of Rosa's betrayal boil into his blood, and guilt only fires his rage. He burns to kill the creature who ravished her. Scour and scratch and chew its foul touch from her skin. Reclaim her for his own, any dark and desperate way he can.

Don't. Share. With. Vampires.

Flora's muscles stroke him, squeezing as he thrusts, delicious friction but not enough. She squirms, her gasps coming faster. "Yes. Now. Hurt me."

Toxified fucking relationship, Diamond. Dump her while you can.

To blot Rosa from his mind, he imagines Mina like this, jerking ever closer to the edge, that slutty blue hair falling in her face, her sweet sharp song caressing his skin, vibrating his throat as he swallows.

Scorching heat spears his balls. He grits his teeth and flits swelling wings, banging Flora roughly against the wall. "Mine, Flora. Say it."

Candysweet pink hair tumbles over her quivering mouth. "Yes. Yours. All yours."

Liar.

Acid untruth scorches Diamond's mouth, and it whets his orgasm sharp like razors. Throbbing release drags from him on a curse, brief and hard and painful. She shrieks and sighs, and the instant she's finished, he pushes away from her to clean himself up.

Flora wobbles on her feet, wings limp and glowing pink. Her swollen lips twinkle into a rosy giggle. "Naughty boy."

"Bitch." He dresses himself, spitting as his fingers slide in fluid not his own. Her fruity scent drenches his clothes, her clawmarks on his shoulders stinging like guilt.

She's not Rosa. None of them ever will be. Rosa's gone.

All that's left is vengeance. Trickify the DiLucas, seduce Mina away so Joey's weak and ripe for a killing. Get rid of Ange. And then Diamond will own the world and nothing will ever hurt him again.

To be untouchable, he has to win. It's the only way.

Disgust clenches his guts to obsidian, and he sweeps his hair over his shoulder in a shining rainbow and stalks away to lie to Angelo.

Vincent slouches against the glass wall in scarlet-drenched shadow, sourness festering in his mouth, and watches his girlfriend fuck another guy.

Diamond's doing her against the mirrors, her long green legs folded around him, her glowing wings splayed behind her. His massive arms bunch and relax as he grips her bare bottom, and he flexes those powerful thighs, thrusting deep and hard. She comes, her luscious mouth shuddering open, and a second or two later, Diamond's right there with her.

Humiliation scrapes like potato chips in Vincent's throat, and he cracks his head back against the mirror, his heart raw and bleeding and his cock aching hard.

Music rips his ears, some skinny blond waif screaming jagged melody. The hatred in the singer's voice crackles painfully along his spine, a side effect of his accidental faetalent, and he knows he deserves the discomfort. He'd only slipped back here to spy on Mina. But if you slink around in corners, you might see something you don't like. No mystery where Diamond's getting his sneaky information now.

Diamond lets Flora slide to the floor and jerks away on impatient glass wings. No kiss. No caresses. Not even a thank-you. Vincent slams sticky palms hard against the mirror. Fucking prick.

Flora straightens her dress with a wicked smile and walks off, her skin flushed and damp, her guilty wings swelling pink. She's even wincing as she moves, her step awkward like it hurts. Vincent's throat swells. He's been tempted by others. Almost succumbed a few times. Flirts like a whore, always has. But he's never actually cheated, not on Flora, and she looks far too pleased with herself for this to be the first time.

Not that it's a fucking surprise, or anything.

After all, she's a fairy, dazzling and magical, sweetly crazy under that tricksy glamour, and Diamond is a fairy god, hot and male and stunningly, unapproachably beautiful.

Vincent's just a pale, ordinary, boring human, stumbling starry-eyed through a seductive shadow world where he neither belongs nor measures up.

He swallows bitter inevitability and turns away, shouldering through the faebright crowd toward the bar. A gift, they reckon, the trick of seeing past fairy glamour, and he should be grateful because not many pathetic humans can.

Gift. That's a good one. More like a curse, this constant acidscratch reminder of his own mediocrity.

He flings himself onto a stool and slouches his elbows on the glowing white bar. The cute blond guy pours him a bourbon and Coke, and the alcohol glitters warm and dangerous on his tongue. Bitterness twists his heart, and to amuse himself he flicks through his phone for the sneaky photo he took of Mina and Diamond and texts it to Joey's number.

That'll learn the snarky glass-ass fucker. They're only talking, but Joey won't know that, and Diamond's long knuckles on her cheek look intimate enough.

It doesn't. Amuse him, that is. Remorse scrapes him raw, but too late. He can't unsend it. And he can't stop seeing them together, his apparently ex-girlfriend and Diamond. Glowing glass hair tangled damp on her shoulder, her petal-pink lips swollen open, her bared nipples hard and wet with sharp-toothed fairy kisses. Glistening male muscle, pulsing veins, the smell of sex. Glassy hands on her skin, under her skirt, those slender green thighs spread around the bastard's hips.

Fucking her. Biting those lovely breasts. Making her squeal, first that light breathy cry Vincent knows so well, and then a deeper, more throaty sound that made him shiver and ache. Last time they were together, he almost told her he loved her.

His eyeballs burn, and swiftly he blinks so he won't embarrass himself any more. Hell, for all he knows, she faked it all along.

"Oh, dear. Is that fresh-cut grass I smell?" Delilah saunters up, tossing crisp winedark curls over an elegant brown shoulder. Her slinky dress glitters in rainbow lights, showing off her curvaceous hips, the deep cleft between her breasts glistening like warm chocolate.

Joey's demon princess. Beautiful, cunning, a royal pain in the ass. Vincent tilts his glass to finish his bourbon, ice stabbing cold on his teeth. The liquid aches as it goes down, and burns in his stomach like guilt. He throws her a sarcastic smile. "Never liked her that much anyway."

Delilah purses sexy brown lips and strokes his hair, sultry. "Obviously. But you can hardly blame her, I suppose. He's richer than you, right?"

He never knows if she's teasing him or pulling moves. Her ashen scent angers him, and his hard-on isn't helping. He adjusts himself, aching, trying not to stare at that stunning cleavage. "Wouldn't know."

"More powerful. Girls like power, d'you think?"

"I guess." He clenches his fingers around the glass, itching to punch her annoying face. If he doesn't react, she'll get bored and walk away.

"Better looking?"

"If you say so." His pulse aches. He doesn't give a fuck what Delilah thinks of him. Her meaningless taunts shouldn't hurt. But they do.

"Oh, I say so." Delilah eyes him slyly, and leans in to whisper. "Doesn't he make you want to touch? I mean, those sweet glassy muscles? That tight ass? Hell, he makes me wet just looking at him. Don't those narrow hipbones just beg you to peel off those jeans and lick your way down? Ever wonder what that barely-there skin feels like? You can't blame her, spreading her legs for a hottie like that, can you?"

Vincent flushes, hotter than the alcohol. He isn't gay. Not

really. Maybe he's experimented, but a few—okay, more than a few, but who's counting?—a few breathless blow jobs in the dark don't count. And until the day he's sober when he lets some gorgeous hard-muscled fae boy fuck him, that doesn't count either.

He fingers sticky hair off his neck. Diamond's probably straight anyway. Straight enough to bang Flora, that's for sure.

Delilah laughs softly, her seductive breath warm on his cheek, and she flicks her tongue out to taste the jewel in his ear. "Mmm. Fae, as well, and glassfae at that. Kinky. Much more intriguing than a human. No doubt he's a shit-hot screw, too. That big hot hard fairy cock probably fits pretty good up your girlfriend's—"

Vincent slams the glass down on the bar, his fingers shaking. "Why don't you go fuck him yourself, you nasty hellbitch? He's obviously got a hard-on for low-down lying whores. You two'll really hit it off."

His stomach shivers, sick. She could chew his throat out if she wanted to. Right now, he doesn't give a damn.

But Delilah just chuckles and slings a smooth brown arm around his shoulder. Up close, her perfume is dark and fleshy like a woman's sex. "I like you, Vincent DiLuca. Your pathetic pondscum antics make me laugh." She glides hot ashen lips across his cheek. "I saw you sniffing after Joey's leavings tonight. Brave boy. If you ever get sick of wriggling through snakeshit, give me a call."

Vincent's bones jolt cold, but by the time he can react, ask her what the hell she means, she's gone.

He slides his glass across the bar, disgust and embarrassment twitching his nerves in tandem. Demon bitch is teasing him again. Like she'd ever do business with a stupid human. Like any of them ever would.

Not even Mina. Guilt still stings his lips as he thinks about her, her smooth belly tingling his palm, those lush breasts pressed against his chest, her toxic breath tempting his lips. He didn't exactly set out to deceive Flora with another woman, not that it fucking matters now.

He'd just wanted what Joey had. Mina, strong, pretty, and resourceful, and fixated on Joey like an infatuated puppy dog.

Bad idea.

Sourness twists Vincent's bourbon-rich stomach. Joey has everything. Respect, power, minions, Mina's attention, Delilah's favoritism. Vincent has nothing. Not even a girlfriend who'll stay true to him for five minutes.

He waves at the long-lashed barboy for another, his gaze sliding easily over the kid's hard-muscled arms. But a narrow white hand slides a glass along to him, rustbrown liquid tilting on ice, and a husky female voice tingles his nerves taut. "That one's on me, beautiful."

Deathburnt goth hair, long and straight to her breasts, which swell out of a black lacy corset crisscrossed with white ribbons. Pearly skin under inkblack makeup. Legs slender and sexy in tall black boots, frothy white miniskirt frilling around her ass. She smiles around glinting vampire teeth, charcoal lips full and soft like velvet.

Vincent glances at the drink and back again. Her painted eyes glint scarlet, inviting. He's just the fang-girls' type, he knows that from experience. And some of them like drug-poisoned blood. It helps them get high. Short odds she's slipping him a mickey.

He sends her a flippant grin he doesn't feel. "No thanks, petal. Nice try."

"Dance with me, then." Her sexy voice darkens. She crushes her cold hand over his and pulls him away from the bar, the satinblack bow on the back of her skirt bobbing in a froth of white lace.

Alcohol and sorrow mix a warm whiskey sour in Vincent's heart, and he follows, already regretting that lost bourbon.

She wraps her arms around his neck, her breasts crushing on his chest in the warm rainbow riot of the dancefloor. Reluctantly, Vincent slides light fingertips on her hips, feeling her muscles move, watching the moisture glimmer as she wets her swelling lips.

Her body's sinuous slide feels good. He swallows, aching. She's kinda hot. He's getting hard again. Maybe he could just . . .

Perfumed female sweat and flesh tantalize his nostrils, the music's dark beat drowning him, and he grips her hips tighter, closes his eyes to feel her body dance. He could pretend she's Flora. It wouldn't help. He sighs, lost. "You feel good."

She molds her hands over his ass, pulling him into her, and her whisper thrills his ear warm. "We've been watching you. My friend and me. We'd like to play with you."

Vincent chuckles. He has no issue with being used for sex. At least he's good at that. And so long as he's conscious, he can stop her before she gets too fanghappy. Danger thrills darkly down his spine. "Sure, darlin'. Maybe I'm up for a little game. Where's your friend, then?"

"Here." Another, deeper whisper shivers his skin. Hot male scent dizzies him, and a hard body slides against his back.

"Whoa." Vincent's eyes snap open, and he tries to squirm away, but the guy sighs hot breath along his neck, the brush of burning lips and sharp teeth spiking anticipation deep inside him. Strong dark hands grip his hips, a massive cock pressing like hot stone against his ass. Vincent's blood burns, and his balls ache for real this time.

The old learned self-hatred spews inside him like hot oil. He won't, he shouldn't, it's evil, hellcursed, all that bullshit. But he can't help wanting it. Can't deny it, the aching need deep inside, and it doesn't even matter that this guy's a stranger. Hot male flesh makes him horny, and it feels so fucking right, he wants to laugh. *Hear that, Dad? Your son's a fag. I suck cock and swallow. I take it up the ass and love it. Fuck you, you hate-twisted moron.*

The girl stings her fang along his earlobe and laps at the blood. Her chuckle resonates deep. "I'm Jessie. That's my friend Rafe. He's new. Always hungry. Don't be shy, pretty. Wanna play with us?"

"Yeah." Breathless. Hot. Horny as hell. Vincent twists his

head to chase Jessie's mouth with his, catching her in an openmouthed kiss that spills warm lust into his guts. Her hungry tongue slides around his. His own blood zings like salt on his lips, and he gasps, his veins swelling with longing.

Her boyfriend, Rafe, groans, hot, long blond hair falling over Vincent's shoulder. Rafe mouths his throat, ravenous, tongue flicking hard over his pulse. He rubs himself harder, like they're fucking, a hot rhythm that sends Vincent's imagination to dark and forbidden places.

Vincent can't help but groan, too, the stranger's kiss and the hard, lithe bodies surrounding his so deeply arousing, he's afraid of what he might do. Take the girl, rip her panties away, and fuck her while she bites his throat. Get naked and wrap his legs around this hot guy's hips and let him do the same. His cock strains harder, stretching his jeans.

Jessie slinks against him, grinding her hips into his erection. "More like it," she purrs. "Look at me."

Golden seduction glimmers deep in her irises, and Vincent's conviction slips away like wet plastic. He blinks rapidly, forcing himself conscious. "You don't need to do that."

Her growl vibrates his chest, and she snarls softly. "Look at me, pretty."

Alarm spices his blood. Vincent tries to wrench his head back, tear his gaze away, the man's hot kiss on the tense muscle between his neck and shoulder a feral distraction. He wriggles, tries to squeeze his eyelids shut. But Rafe yanks his head back by the hair, growling as he grazes stinging fangs over Vincent's throat, and Vincent can't help but stare into her eyes, his breath stolen away and his body bursting with confused lust.

His skin burns. His pulse deafens him. Her eyes swirl crimson, sucking his will away. The room fades, only her eyes and her fleshy lips on his, the sharp meaty taste of her tongue wrapping around his and the hot slide of Rafe's dark-skinned hands over his belly and down between his thighs, he's working those long hard fingers into the ragged rips in Vincent's jeans and Christ, it's the biggest fucking hard-on he's ever had.

The world tumbles, disoriented, colors flashing behind his eyelids. He grabs Jessie's long black hair and forces her mouth open wider, and next thing he's on his back, soft suede rubbing on his skin when they tear his shirt off, Rafe's burning mouth sucking his bar-pierced nipple.

Jessie's lips slide on his throat, her tongue pressing hard, sucking sharp bruises into his flesh. The threat of razor fangs spears dark desire deep into his guts. She grabs his hand and forces it under her skirt. She's not wearing panties, and his fingers slide easily between her burning wet folds. Hot, slick, delicious, her tiny clit already swollen hard. She sighs and rubs against him, her breath coming faster.

But forget that. Rafe's rough kisses inflame his belly, sharp nips leading downward. Strong male hands on the buttons of his jeans, tearing them open, sliding them down, sweet relief. A crushing bite on his thigh, the pain creeping delicious in his balls, strong tongue sliding where the veins throb. And at last, that hot wet mouth on his cock, enfolding him deep, sucking, the pleasure so deep and cruel that he barely notices when Jessie's acid fangs sink deep into his throat.

His muscles jerk and shiver, pleasured and ravaged at the same time. She purrs and slides her mouth in the sticky mess, tongue lapping. She pops his skin again, sharp fangs sliding in, and god, it hurts, a dagger through his vein, the vile backpressure of her sucking ripping a blaze of agony right down to his heart. His skin rips open wider into her mouth, and she swoons, gulping the hot splashing blood faster and faster. If he doesn't get her off him, this could be very bad.

But Rafe swallows Vincent's cock again, deeper, clever fingers slipping between his legs, feeling for his ass, seeking his pleasure. Sensation tears up from his balls, so hot and bright and shocking that Vincent groans and lets go, jetting desperate heat into that talented mouth while Jessie feasts on his blood, sick delight throbbing over and over until he's got nothing left.

He chokes, bile and his own blood mixing in his mouth. His pulse hammers. Jessie rips hot fangs from his neck with a cry of triumph, and blood splashes like hot oil. Agony and afterglow swamp him, bitter and sweet. Lights glow faintly, sounds fade, dimmed by dizziness and pain.

Not enough, he registers distantly. He won't die. They'll probably just leave him here now they're finished. Sickness fights a raging battle in his guts, and he lifts a weakened hand in a lost effort to get up, to cover the wound and stop the bleeding.

But strong arms pin him down. Hands clench in his hair, and the blond crawls over him, levering his thighs apart. Rafe's naked brown muscles glide on Vincent's chest, so hard and smooth and rich with hot male scent. Sharp fangs nip at his lips in a cascade of musky blond hair. "Not finished with you yet, pretty. You ready?"

Their kiss slides in a sickening smear of vampire blood. It drips into his mouth, burning like ironrich honey, delicious and disgusting. Blood crawls over his tongue, coating his teeth, sliding down his throat, hungry hellvirus cells mingling with clean. It trickles down his cheek, and Jessie licks it up, smearing it, sliding her hungry tongue into a three-way kiss. She slashes Rafe's throat with hungry fangs, and Vincent can't help but follow her, the syrupy taste intoxicating him, the deathrich pulse of Rafe's blood in his mouth making him groan.

Somewhere deep and distant in his lustdrunk mind, Vincent knows this is very bad indeed. Dangerous. Flirting with darkness.

But he gulps, and swallows, and swallows some more, his ragged nerves afire. Mouths mingling, tongues sparring, suction and heat and salty bliss.

Jessie snarls and wraps a hungry thigh around him. Her nails scratch his chest, she's lithe and hot and slick and he's inside her before he can remember the word for *wait*. So smooth, so tight. He's hard again so soon, the friction unprecedented, and when she sinks her teeth into his throat again, he can't help but thrust into her, searching for her groans to match his. God, it feels good, tension ebbing and flowing like a slow-cooking orgasm, the faintness of shock and the fevered lust of touching, and Vincent wonders dimly if this is what dying should be like.

Rafe covers them, his body hard and light. White-blond hair smothers his face again, drowning him with stolen fruity scent. There's something familiar in that smell— something he should recognize—but too late. Rafe's fangs rip deep into Jessie's shoulder, blood splashing hot into Vincent's mouth, over his face. Jessie moans and writhes between them, her nipples rubbing hard and wet against his chest, and he feels the other man's hardness slide against his as Rafe pushes into her.

Flora. Rafe smells of Flora. It's a trick. They're killing him. Or worse.

Vincent's heart gallops weakly, and he wants to scream *no*—or *god, please, yes*—but his head swims deeper with confusion and blood loss, and Jessie's hot flesh drags pleasure like burning wire from his balls, and his throat fills with glorious spelldrunk vampire blood and his vision swirls to black.

7

I perched on my sofa in flickering candlelight, nerves trembling. My bare toes clenched in the pale carpet, cold despite the heat.

Cobalt laid a bony white hand upon my heart, his hot fingers sticking to the leather. "You ready?"

I shivered. The hot summer night soaked through my open windows like blood. No breeze lifted the lace curtains. The moon set fat and swollen behind jagged apartment blocks, lighting my sparse cream furniture in hellish orange. Tree branches reached gnarled shadows through the window to grasp the bare blue walls like skeletal fingers.

The candle flickered, making the fingers stretch and twist. The ripe patchouli scent sickened me. "Do we have to have that? It smells weird."

"You know it helps sometimes."

"Sure you're not just trying to get laid?" I smiled weakly, but it wasn't funny.

Cobalt thumbed the clotted cork from a long glass tube, his feathery blue gaze hesitant on mine. "Drink up."

I took it, my guts rippling at the sight of the dirty khaki sludge inside. It wasn't sparkle. I didn't want to know where he got it, or how it was made. I only knew it worked. I closed my eyes, tilted my chin back, and swallowed the lot.

It scratched my throat, thick and gritty like burnt custard. I choked on the salty flavor of bad seawater, my stomach

twisting. My eyes watered. Already my head swam and
ached, my mind stretching like rubber, dragged in too many
directions at once. Colors flashed, and strange music whirled,
snatches of half-remembered songs.

Cobalt stroked my hair, mesmeric. "S'okay. Close your
eyes. Don't think. Just let it take you there."

"Hurts," I protested, my voice already slurred. Slashes of
bright memory already ripped the real world to bleeding. Images splintered in, a madman's axe through a balsawood door.
But it wasn't just vague memory. More like being there, the
magic brew lashing every twitch and sting and breath to
harsh-lit life.

*This afternoon, the sun stabbing my eyes as I woke in a
sweat with a poisoned screech ripping from my throat.
Dreams of Joey again, aching and feverdrenched.*

*The other night, glinting knives in the moonlight, warm
and soothing in my hands. Cool breeze lifting my hair, my
breath's hot catch, the burn of my thigh muscles as I ran, a
salty red groan of pain.*

*A few weeks ago, a fight with angry fairies, my body hur-
tling backwards, crunching into the ground, the breath
ripped from my lungs. Joey's hands on my face, safe and
warm, my bones hurt like a motherfucker but I want to stay
there, he's gazing into my eyes and just for an instant I
see . . . and then the blistering taste of our kiss, the delicious shift of his tongue on mine before he shoves me away.*

I groaned and swiped the image away, colors slashing my
vision like clawmarks. Cobalt shuddered. It hurt him, too,
this memoryscrape. His faetalent dragged my thoughts like
barbed wire through his mind, and I got them back tainted
with his flesh, his blood, the dusty sweetness of his sweat.

He pressed his fevered cheek to mine, shivering with
need. "More. Further. You can do it."

The memorysauce stabbed deeper into my veins, a hot
shock of compulsion. I yowled, helpless, cold fear springing threat into my song, and Cobalt covered my mouth, his
fingers hot and wet. "Shh. Not that. No poisonsong. Let it
come."

Confusion muddied my vision. I wanted it. I didn't want it. But too late. My limbs jerked, my slimy sweat bitter on the air. We were going whether we liked it or not.

I closed my eyes, and my memories hurtled back.

But not far enough.

Sultry midnight in the spriggan's den, the reek of stale sweat, humidity stinging like salt water on my bitten skin.

I squirmed on the sofa, dread chilling me, but I couldn't shake it off, and the vile memories slid into me like bad heroin, warm and delicious for a few seconds until the fucker bares its teeth and chews you ragged.

Metal floor, gritty and damp on my back. Bare lightbulb buzzing, flickering yellow shadows. A rusty shackle scars my ankle raw. I'm so hungry, my stomach hurts, and a smelly black spriggan fucks me, his cock long and barbed, his clawed hands cruel on my thighs. Rotten meat stinks. My flesh stings again and again. I squeeze my eyes shut and think of dinner, old Chinese food, cold salty fries, my next hit, anything but the stink and the stabbing pain.

Serrated teeth slash at my naked breasts. I scream, my song lost and broken in a thorny scrape of sparkle and the weak acid they force down my throat every night. So many more days like this, on and again and forever before Joey finally comes for me.

In my lounge, I yelled and wriggled, my guts afire. The magic sauce gripped me like the spriggan's horny claws, not letting me free. I'd stay there forever, trapped in a hall of evil mirrors, unable to wake up.

Cobalt whimpered and pressed his forehead on mine, thumbing my wet hair from my cheeks, his dusty scent sweet solace. "Don't, Min. It's over. Let it go."

"I can't!" A sob tore my chest raw. *Cold hard flesh, crushing my guts from inside. Sick vomit spewing into my mouth.* I clawed at Cobalt's hair, wild.

"You can." Cobalt kissed me, once, again, a swift crush of lips and tongue and sharp fairy teeth intended to distract and shock, and at last the horrid sensory violation ripped free, images and sensations spinning off into some blacker void.

I gasped for blessed, untainted air. Dim patchouli smoke filtered in, comforting. My racing heartbeat calmed, little by little. My body ached, and I swam in space, weightless, in neither present nor past. Distantly, I saw Cobalt rocking me in shaking arms, the earthy smell of his hair, his lips hovering hot on the corner of my mouth. Like he held some other helpless girl, and I was just watching.

Dimly I felt him speak, his chest vibrating on mine, his addict's need still raw and unsated in the way his body trembled and shivered, feverneedy. "S'okay. Enough. Try 'nother time—"

"Nononono . . ." My syllables slurred, but black determination poured into me like sticky tar. I'd see that killer's face tonight if it tore my heart out. I twisted my neck, sliding my sweaty cheek on his, searching for his mouth. "Moremoremore. Gimme . . ."

His lips tasted fresh, like pine. He gasped into my mouth, the memories flowing between us like water. Glimpses of his mind, a black alley, his phone's neon shine, a dark fairy kiss, guilt, a throbbing headache, a sweeter ache flowering in his groin.

He whined like a puppy, his sharp teeth grazing my tongue. "You hurt so much. You want more? I got a special one. Help you see."

Anticipation burned, even as the stupidity of it all washed my muscles to water. Trust a guy who's already up to his eyeballs in glitter, rubbing his hard-on against your thigh and whispering about pain. Good move.

I knew he didn't do it for my sake. He was a junkie, just like me, only for a darker, more lethal drug.

But Cobalt shared my pain. He took my money when he knew it'd hurt him. He held me when otherwise I'd be alone.

I summoned my voice, groggy with confusion. "Yeah. Hit it."

He uncorked another shimmering indigo vial and pressed it under my nose. Faint alarm pinged, somewhere in the minute part of my brain that didn't slaver like a rabid beast at the sight of that sparkling temptation. That dark blue looked menacing, evil silver glitter winking at me like demon eyes. Something wasn't right.

But the dribbling beast chewed my common sense to mush. I didn't pause or think. I just inhaled.

Brightness rained, shiny and delicious. Drugspell burned my nose, my sinuses, my throat. My eyes stung fresh and watery. My limbs swelled with starry warmth, and a slow jitter of desperate relief jerked my spine. So soft and shiny, floating weightless on fruity nectar. Bliss, this stolen emotion, some other creature's happiness bottled just for me.

Pleasure rippled softly through me, warming me, like someone licked slow and gentle between my legs. My thoughts twinkled like glitterbright stars, distant and clear. I groaned. I'd do unconscionable things to feel like this. I already had.

Cobalt gasped a smile and finished the sparkle off with a wet sniff. He sighed, raw and rough, his eyes glimmering. I relaxed in his arms, dimly aware that he laid me back on the sofa, sniffed at my throat, buried his nose in my hair. "Come on, pretty. Remember for me. Let me in."

I gripped his knotted blue locks and pulled him down to me. We connected with a crunch, our minds slamming together like cosmic jigsaw pieces. Flashes of his guilty desire, stabbing pain, a rabid thirst for mental contact.

And then, it was all me.

Whirling back through black oblivion, evil-smelling wind dragging my hair over my face. A thousand dark images, smells, sounds, swirling in jagged fragments like a smashed mirror. The night the giggling spriggans caught me, stupid drunk little girl stumbling alone in the dark around scarlet-topped flametrees in Fitzroy Gardens, my dress smeared with beer and lipstick, my best and only weapon lost to cheap wine and laryngitis I caught on my knees in some dark sweaty corner.

Backwards in time, a riot of intoxicated brawling and faceless un-friends, falling into gutters with blood in my eyes. My first knife fight, flashes of steel and reflexes jerking tight, the shock of blood and my skin splitting open, glass shattering as I scream.

Back again, to shoplifting, purse-snatching, grifting for cash, picking horny old men's pockets and stealing plastic chips at the blackjack tables beneath glittering casino chandeliers, crafty fingers and a flutter of painted lashes while the dirty sods fingered my ass. Stolen cocktail dresses that never fit properly, black bruises on my thighs, my limp blue hair pinned up to make me prettier. Always hungry, always broke, always scraping for a score.

Further back, fevered, breathless, broken bricks against my back and delicious fairy flesh yearning against mine, smooth clawed fingers teasing up my miniskirt, the dark-eyed fairy devil who fed me my first bloodlaced sparkle hit just so he could get laid.

Before that, nights spent crouching in freezing shadows under the rainbowsprayed Jolimont railbridge with greasy drunks and hookers. Stealing a blanket from a mad old bag lady. Sallow skin and pimples and digging in the garbage for junk food, scratching another girl's face when she grabbed the half-eaten burger first.

And then, there I am, crouched in terror behind that dusty sofa, those horrid footsteps crashing in my ears like helldrums.

"That it? We there?" Cobalt fisted my hair tightly, trembling, his sharp fairy teeth clattering with my terror. Fragrant black glitter shivered from his wings, warm like butterfly dust on my skin.

My throat corked. I nodded, and squeezed my eyes shut. I forged my concentration like steel, filtering out everything, the candlelight piercing my lids, the pain. Cobalt's fevered body on mine, his palms seeking my warmth, crafty fairy fingers dragging my zipped corset open. The strange drug glittered darkly along my optic nerves, skewing my vision with silver like a moonlit ocean, ringing a jerky carillon in my ears.

This time, it'd be different. This time, I'd remember.

My head split with agony as time ground forward, inexorable slow motion, moment by tortured moment.

My mother wails and thrashes weak limbs. The footsteps

*click softly forward. Click. Click. I wrap my arms around
my knees, and my elbows crack, one by one.*

Click.

*A tear runs down my nose. Plink. It hits the floor like glass,
so loud, I cower. My guts ache like hell. If I lose my bladder,
he'll find me, kill me, rape me. I squeeze my eyes shut.*

On the sofa, I groaned and sweated, my pulse aflame.
Cobalt whimpered and pressed his face into my naked chest.
His inkblue tears smeared dark on my breasts. I didn't care. I
willed that terrified me to swivel her eyeballs north, just for a
moment. My breath ripped shorter, faster, and . . .

Click.

*My teeth rattle together. I clamp down hard. My tongue
slices, salt and sting.*

Click.

*He stops. Mother's nails screech and rend the wooden
floor apart.*

"Please. Stop it. I can't." Cobalt sniffled, hot and wet on
my breast. His face slid clammy with my pain, and in the
depths of sweet sparkle psychosis, I felt his hooktaloned
memoryspell withdraw, stinging like a wicked knife curving
from flesh.

The images dimmed, sounds vanishing like smoke.

Horrorworms rippled my skin. I could see them, dirty
brown worms, wriggling under there, cheap effects from a
sparklebright horror movie. Desperately I dragged Cobalt's
hands to my hips, making him work my buckle loose. He
needed contact. So did I. My voice trembled. "Help me. Just
a little longer."

Cobalt sobbed, but let me wriggle my pants down, let me
guide his hand between my legs. His cool fingers quivered
on my bare skin, warming me. He sighed, and gradually the
scene sprang alive once more, melting back into my mind
like burning film rewound.

*My spine crackles cold. Sweat dribbles down my temple.
A moth darts under the darkened lightbulb, lost.*

*My mother moans, her pretty voice shattered, and her
words stretch into a ghostly howl.*

Pleaassee. Heeellp meeeee.

The sound skewered deep into my ears. Long fairy fingers eased inside me, comforting, that gentle palm pressing against my flesh, drawing pleasure from my belly that I didn't want. I writhed, warmth sliding against cold disgust.

Clothing whispers aside. Iron scrapes on leather, and soft fingertips swipe steel as the killer pulls his pistol.

Clunk.

The slide springs back.

My body quivered with urgency. Please, little innocent girl. Open your eyes. You must have opened your eyes. Just for a second. Let me see.

Clink. Crunch.

Bullet in the chamber.

Slap, hiss, smack, as my mother struggles, her hair dragging on the floor.

I muttered, flinging my head from side to side, rusted chains bursting from my skull and growing into the sofa like weeds to hold me down. "Harder. Show me more."

Cobalt's tongue licked around my nipple, hardening it. He sucked it into his mouth, and as he groaned and swallowed, relishing the taste of my sweat, that shiny steel memoryspell sliced deeper.

I lift my head, and my eyelids flick open.

Shock riveted my nerves. My nails clawed at his jeans. I spluttered, "Fuck. It's working. Don't let go."

I knew it. I did see. I'd just hidden it away, all this time.

Light burns sepia, shapes odd and twisted like watermirrors. The shadows stretch and flow, ink puddling on glass, the air twinging sweet with strange flowers. My body feels light and free. I stretch, my thighs cramping sweetly, and suddenly I see her.

I can see my mother. Sprawled on the floor in a heap of bruised limbs and tears, that lovely silver hair torn.

My heartbeat thunders. I swivel my blurred gaze upward, and the killer's dark silhouette scorches my eyeballs black.

Dread and hunger shoved hot wires through my veins,

searing them raw. There you are, you murderous son of a goblin. Show me your face.

The images wavered and faded, the memoryspell blunting again. I screamed in frustration, and tiny sawtoothed insectmen leapt down my throat, yelling and ripping it to shreds. My head throbbed. Cobalt shuddered against me in a fever, his pollen-sweet hair caressing my face. "There's more. I can't reach. Please, let me go. . . ."

Swiftly I dragged our clothes aside. Damp leather peeled from my legs like paper. I wriggled to get him between my naked thighs. He felt strange there, his body lean and slim, twisted fae muscles shifting in his chest as he flexed velvety black wings to keep his weight off me.

Above my head, the dead lightbulb swings. My mother moans, and as the image shimmers again, the killer leans over her, his head turning to one side.

I wriggled, fumbling to touch him, make him touch me, get that connection back. My words slurred. "C'mon, C. Don' . . . flakeonmenowww . . ."

He squeezed his eyes shut. "Sorry. I didn't mean—"

The images ripple and fade like heat haze. Dimming. Dying.

"Now, C." My voice scraped raw. In my haste to undress him, my nails on his narrow fairy hips scratched up blood.

His dark eyes glowed silver. He wriggled like a worm from his jeans and slid his warm white body onto mine. After a moment, he even looked into my eyes. Edgy, remorseful, sweet. I wrapped my leg around his thigh to show him where, and he pushed his twisted length into me with an urgent sigh.

His cock was long and thick, and it stung, I'd been alone so long. He felt strange and good inside me, his hot fairy flesh alien but so familiar. My sex-starved muscles stretched around him, stroking him, warming my insides with sweet friction. He moved, and I groaned and parted my thighs to let him in, the sensation exciting yet soothing. He wasn't the man I wanted, or how I'd wanted it to be. But I didn't care, not when he slid his open mouth on mine and thrust harder into me, and in my mind he clenched a pale fist around his spell's wickedshiny blade and rammed the twinkling point deep into my skull.

Bone cracked as he twisted it. Flesh sliced. My ravaged brain screamed, and the memory came scorching back on his breath, a flash brighter than the sun.

My sofa lurches into view, the broken table, the torn rug beneath. Black silhouettes merge and sever, rippling like hot ghosts at first. The shimmer-killer crouches over the cowering shimmer-woman. His back's to me, dark coat dragging in the dust, his pistol's evil glimmer a sharp slash of clarity in muddled shapes. He's saying something to her that even I can't hear. She writhes, her voice torn, and now I can see her face, she's sobbing, tears streaking like dirt. "Nooo . . ."

Horror iced my blood, sharpening my slow pleasure to razors. Cobalt licked hotly at my nipple, his teeth scraping sharp delight. The knife wrenched sideways, slicing my brain to mush, and pain clawed my nerves, mixing with the growing tension, making it hurt and pleasure me in equal measure.

My drugthick sinuses ached. I'd never seen this before. Never had to watch the killer loom over her, see her last word ripped from her mouth. A greasy black hatebeast spat vile curses in my heart, and I strained against Cobalt's body, searching, begging.

Images waver and solidify. I can see her face again, her streaming eyes pleading for mercy. She stretches her ripped hand out weakly, fingers straining, fending him off. The killer stands, cocks his head to sight along a steady arm, and fires.

Slam.

Blood splashes. The empty cartridge clinks on the floor and rolls away. She slumps, still.

I sought Cobalt's mouth in a fevered kiss, drinking his rainy taste, willing him to work himself farther into my body, that wicked spell an inch or two deeper into my mind. He kissed me back, his tongue alive on mine, letting me use him, fuck him, claim his fairy tricks as my own. I tilted my hips, searching. His breath hitched short, an addict glutting himself on my agony.

I couldn't blame him.

The killer stands motionless, coolly studying her corpse.

Strange emotion washes my blood warm, parches my throat. Not hate. Not fear. I try to swallow, and an insane cracking sound erupts from my throat.

He tilts his head, alerted. The image tightens, focuses, rippling edges sharpening. His fingers twitch on that glimmering pistol. Slowly, he turns, and a hot fist of anticipation squeezes all the blood from my heart.

Tension racked my nerves, chewing like rats. Cobalt groaned, his cock swelling inside me and his skin flushing dark like he was about to come, and in my mind he peeled his lips back from gleaming eelsharp teeth and ripped a bloody chunk from my chest.

I see his pale chin, bruised and bloody. The marble line of his cheekbone. A soft fall of hair, shining like a halo in the dim light.

Hot blood sprayed. I screamed, the phantom pain wrenching deeper feeling from my guts, a rich anti-orgasm that chewed all the way to my toes. I wailed, magical vibrations shattering the fragile glass walls of my consciousness. My dreamself came crashing through into the present like a burning petrol bomb, and in the mangled black corridor of my memory, the killer's razor gaze fixed on mine.

Brilliant green eyes, unblinking—so beautiful, my heart spikes.

Blood shining on sensuous lips I'd kissed in a hundred feversoaked dreams.

That gleaming pistol, gripped in slender white hands that crackle and split with glossy black webs. As I watch, a green venomdrop slides down the glossy steel barrel and plinks onto the floor,

A scream hollows my stomach sick, but it won't come out.

My jaw works. Silence.

He blinks. Just once. Soft snowblond hair tumbles in his eyes.

And then he flexes those clever fingers to squelch the webs away, and walks out.

Hellbirds screeched and clawed in my ears. Blood gushed from my wounded chest, my heart exposed and throbbing. Cobalt ripped the knife from my skull and flung it away in a hail of blood, but the image stayed, scorched into my retinae forever.

Joey. My mother. The gunshot's evil crack.

He'd rescued me. Taught me, protected me when I was weak, earned my respect and my loyalty. Caressed my hair, kissed me, made me burn for him in ways no man ever had.

All false. All done knowing he'd destroyed my life.

Everything he'd ever done for me was a putrid lie.

A raw shriek of agony exploded in my throat, and died.

Sickness ripped me. I scrambled to get up, to push Cobalt's fevered body away from mine so I could sprint away into the night, huddle in some hot dry gutter and swallow my tears, scream ragged melody to the darkness and pretend this hadn't happened.

But wings descended like hot black velvet to enclose me, clog my ears, smother me. I struggled, but suddenly Cobalt's lithe fairy weight was enormous, his hands like shackles on my wrists, his flesh inside me strong and immovable like steel.

Panic tore my blood. I couldn't hear. I couldn't breathe. Terror dragged my lips apart, but I had no air to sing. My vision bled scarlet. My body thrashed one last weakened protest, and the light died.

She whimpers, fighting, but it's too late to pull away. With one final shudder and clench, Cobalt empties himself into her, guilt and desperate need spurting through his memory-drenched blood. The sting of her horror drags deep pleasure over his nerves, better than the orgasm, and he gasps and swallows and drowns in it, letting the fix consume him, already fearing it'll be too long before he gets another.

Her body jerks, dragging one last hot draft from his balls, and he groans at the delight of it. He fumbles long fingers in her hair, belatedly trying to quiet her as the last shocks rack his muscles. "Sorry," he whispers through gritting teeth, "sorry sorry sorry," and he means it, he didn't intend for it to be like this, kissing and touching and sweet girlsmell on his skin but he wanted her and she needed him and now she's not moving, she's limp and flushed and her pretty red eyes have rolled back and she's not moving, not one little bit.

Guilty spider feet track into his aching wingjoints. He'd known that supercharged blue sparkle on top of the memory-juice would be too much. But she wanted it, and he had a job to do, oh yes, jobs and secrets and tasties, oh my.

Her girlflesh still fits hot and perfect around him, slick with the mess he's made. She feels nice. Surreptitiously, he slides a little, enjoying her on him. He's clean. She needn't worry about that. He nuzzles her breast, seeking reaction, any reaction. "Min-bin?"

No movement. Still, frozen, pale and perfect like a broken china doll.

Fright stings him scary. He eases himself out of her and scrambles up, wiping his running nose, his long hair cascading undone around his waist. Her body lies limp, slim and white, her pretty head thrown back, sugary blue hair tossed wild on the couch. Her corset still drapes open at the front, and candlelight carves shadows under her naked breasts, her skin still wet from his mouth and smeared blue with his fingerprints and his tears. Her chest heaves suddenly, air screaming past her parted lips, and after a few gasps her breath relaxes into normal rhythm.

His wings flood cold, and he turns away, guilty. The taste of music ripples on his tongue like water. He scrabbles on the floor for his jeans, the pocket, his glassware, a clean one in here especially for her, and he pops the cork from a long glass tube and breathes over the lip like he's playing a little magic flute. The glass vibrates, singing, a tiny echo of her beautiful banshee melody, and fresh golden sparkle tumbles from his lips into the glass.

He presses the cork in tight and holds the filled vial to the moon, admiring the swirling glints of light. Tasties. Fresh ones. Just as the customer ordered. He holds it to his ear, and inside a faint song floats, bewildered. Stolen. Lost.

A glassy belltone shrills, and his wings jerk in fright, the vial tumbling in his fingers. He clutches at it, his heart thumping. The bells ring again. Her phone, the screen flashing blue shadows onto the kitchen bench. After a few seconds, it stops.

Cobalt slips the vial away and dresses himself with shaking fingers, claws catching in the cloth, silly things always in the way. He drags his messy blue hair into a knot and fumbles in his pocket for his phone.

After two rings, it picks up.

Cobalt swallows, parched. "I got it."

Diamond chuckles, a chandelier in summer breeze. "Of course you did. Good dog. Have a chocolate drop."

"Where can I meet you?"

"I'll find you. Oh, and the rate just dipped. Three hundred. Sorry 'bout that."

"What? You said—"

"I'm thinking you already got paid, puppy. Sweet, was she?"

Cobalt's wings jerk back guiltily, fluttering the curtains. "That wasn't wh—"

"You just fucked Joey DiLuca's best girl. Congratumalations. Try selling it and see how many people conveniently forgettify who you are."

"But—"

"I told you fetch. You fetched. Your job's done. Spit or swallow."

Clunk. Silence. Hung up on.

Fuck.

Cobalt rubs damp hands on his jeans, baffled. Moonlight glares harsh accusation in his eyes. He steals a guilty glance at Mina, who still sprawls senseless on the couch, her pretty breasts heaving gently up and down with her breath. It's warm in here. She won't freeze. Must get rid of the evidence, before she realizes what he's done and comes after him.

His greedy sinuses tempt him to just snort the thing and

forget about it, but he can't. Not her. Not after what he did with her. He'll just have to deal with Diamond, the lousy glassnose thief.

He tucks the vial deeper into his pocket, safe and hidden, and dives out the door on a swoop of black velvet wings.

8

In a deserted city street, dawn shatters the darkness. Shadows fall from silent tenements. Somewhere, a police siren wails and disappears. No trams run at this hour, and the lines hang silent and still. A car wobbles slowly past, headlights veering, the unsteady care of a driver stoned out of his mind.

Vincent staggers, shielding his eyes, the warm press of a streetlight pole against his shoulder agonizing. It's so damn bright. Every sound's piercing, like nails on a blackboard. A lost gull screeches, and he moans, his head clanging in agony.

He doesn't know where the fuck he is, how he got here. Dark stains crust his clothes. His skin stings all over, and he drags back his sleeve to see angry scratches, cuts, bites, crusted scabs already half-healed.

A hungry shiver racks his limbs. Fever roasts his body. Sickness pours off him in waves, and he doubles over, retching. Clotted scarlet mess splashes the pavement.

He wipes his mouth, and the meaty stink of blood and vomit makes him retch again.

The night just gone scorches in his memory. Sex, that luscious girl torturing him. Fingers, tongues, kisses rich with blood, her secret flesh throbbing in his mouth as she came. And that hot, sinful vampire boy, Christ on a barbecued cross. Burning teeth stabbing Vincent's flesh, the searing pressure of a hard cock deep in his body while the girl's wet warmth suckled on his own, the pleasure so deep and raw, it hurt. Taking, drinking, swallowing, bleeding, feasting, over and again and forever until his head swam, his body strained limp in agony and delight, his ripped veins screamed at him to stop before he died.

Vincent pushes himself upright, his balance swimming. Well, he's not dead. Not yet.

But fever liquefies his muscles, and he staggers, tripping on scattered newspaper. His breath sears his throat. Sweat drips into his collar, down his legs, over his chest. The empty pit in his stomach swells, gnawing at him like a beast, and he's hungry, so fucking starving, like he's not eaten in a week.

His vision swirls, a crimson waterfall of blood and flesh and pain. He chokes, his mouth parched like sandpaper, and his tongue slices on strangely sharp teeth.

The sting invigorates him. Blood seeps into his mouth, and nerves drain hot sensation all the way to his bruised balls.

His spine tingles. Fuck. What was that?

Carefully, he licks his teeth again.

Sting. Slice. Cruelly, impossibly sharp, his gums split and tender at the front where a pair of new canine teeth erupt.

He presses his tongue against the sore spot, and his old tooth squelches loose, letting the new one in.

He spits, and the bloody tooth bounces away across the concrete.

Double fuck.

He scrapes clotted hair from his eyes and lets them water in the sunrise's red glare. Buildings veer into focus, their outlines sharp and black, too sharp. A bird flits on distant roof tiles, and he can see feathers, a scratch on its beak, its dull glinting eyes. He stretches his head back, and deep in the sunlit sky, stars shine.

Another sick flush dizzies him, and hunger and denial war in his guts. It can't be. He's just caught some dirty flu. Better go home, sleep it off.

An engine growls to a halt, and a girl wobbles out of a taxi, fumbling drunkenly in her bag for cash.

Vincent's ears prick. He can feel it. The scent of perfume and female skin tantalizes him. He can see her legs under her shiny golden skirt, long and tanned, the faint blue pulse inside her thigh as she bends over.

She pays the driver cash, and her heels click as she stumbles onto the pavement. Her back is bare, her party dress's strings sliding over smooth beachtanned skin. Blond hair swings, a glimpse of pale throat. She slings her bag over her shoulder, flashing delicate wrists where veins darken and throb.

Hunger rips holes in Vincent's guts, and his cock fills with a rush of fevered blood. Black compulsion chews at him, strange and exciting. His own pulse thuds in his head, surely a mirror of her own. What would that feel like, under his lips? Her heartbeat's sweet throb on his tongue? Her honeywet flesh swelling in his mouth as the skin splits?

He can't tear his gaze away. Saliva spills hard and painful into his mouth, and crazy laughter grips his guts with dismay.

He'd heard that bloodfever was quick. But not like this. For some stupid reason, he'd imagined it more civilized. Not fevered, thirsty, rapacious like a starving beast.

The truth hardens black and unyielding in his heart. Somewhere deep and secret inside him, his conscience thrashes like a dying beast, drowning in scarlet dread.

But the damage is done. There's no cure. It's this, or die.

The girl stumbles around him, muttering, "Pizzoff."

He grabs her elbow, and his fingers crush effortlessly tight. "That's no way to talk to a lady."

"Huh?" Fear lights her glazed eyes. She wriggles, but he pulls her fast into his arms, and they stumble back off the street into a barred café doorway. She gurgles a scream, but the street's deserted and he's already scrabbling for her skin, her collarbone, her throat, anywhere he can find. Her dress rips, and her breasts spill into his hands, so soft and warm. She fights, but he's got her in the corner and in fever's scarlet rage, he's easily too strong, the force in his fingers alone enough to hold her. Stronger than he's ever been before.

His pulse thunders, the power intoxicating. Her sweet fleshscent tortures him. His growing teeth ache and swell. His cock hurts like fury, so very hard and ready, but he doesn't care about forcing it up into her, fucking her, releasing inside her, skin on fresh wet skin. He cares only about feeding this raging hunger.

He tears the last strap away, baring her, and lust for the kill roasts his body alive. He shudders, spit washing his lips.

She sobs, clawing weakly at his shirt with ripped nails. "Please don't hurt me. You seem like a decent guy. I've got condoms. We can fuck. Just don't hurt me."

Her words mean nothing, the whining of a cornered animal. His gaze fixes on the pulse at her throat. His senses home in like laserbombs, and all he can see or hear or smell is blood.

He thuds the heel of his hand under her chin, cracking her head back into the wall and exposing that luscious meal. His jaws stretch, and he sinks his teeth in deep.

Crunch.

Blood explodes into his mouth. Hot, salty, metallic, delicious with life's magical shimmer. He swallows, wet warmth gushing over his chin, and he can't help but groan in delight.

The girl gulps and thrashes, incoherent. His balls ache, pleasure swelling deep and raw. God, it's better than fucking her. He bites harder, clumsy, and his infant teeth scrape on gristle. Torn flesh slops between his lips. He sucks hard and hungry, and blood shoots into the back of his throat.

It splashes, and he swallows, and rapidfire orgasm spears raw fever through his cock, along his limbs, deep into his body.

Her nails scrape the wall as he gasps, spasms grinding his muscles tight. She's bleeding on her own now. Hot crimson delight streams down her neck, over her breasts. He gulps and slavers and licks it up, ravenous. He adores her coppery taste, her skin rasping on his tongue, the way his teeth graze her soaked nipple. His hard-on won't relax. The pleasure won't fade. The hunger won't die, and he dives for her neck again, sucking out more.

The pressure eases on his tongue, and he whimpers. But her body weakens, and she slumps in his arms, the blood flowing listless. Her head falls back, bloody blond hair dripping.

Empty. Dead. The spark gone. Already, the blood cools.

Panting, Vincent releases her, lets her crumple. Her limbs fold, her sightless eyes still. He gasps for breath. His mouth is already sticky. He spits, and clots splat the pavement.

His hunger growls, only partly sated.

He looks down at himself. Drenched in crimson and sweat, hardly a spot of white left on his shirt. The goresoaked fabric plastered to his chest. Blood streaking the come stain on his jeans. Charming.

But not boring. Not mediocre. Not just a weak human, not anymore.

A twisted metal hand clamps his shoulder.

He jerks around, cracking his skull into the wall.

Iridium grins, his lank bronze hair shining, and his crippled shoulder convulses with gritty laughter. "That, my friend, was fucking brilliant. Wanna come over and play?"

Vincent licks bloody lips, his pulse pounding with guilt and hungry fear. "Jesus. Don't tell. I didn't mean it, okay? I didn't mean to—oh, fuck. Fuckfuckfuck . . ."

Tears blot his eyes scarlet, and he grinds his palms into his cheeks. He killed that girl. Ate her. Drank her fucking blood. And the cursed hunger still won't fade. He'll do it again and again, until . . .

Iridium drags his hands away, insistent. "Listen to me. Different to them now. Rules don't apply. Vincent, look at me." Hot iron claws tilt Vincent's chin up. He blinks, and Iridium's mismatched eyes shine with crazy sympathy. "Understand, okay? Know how you feel."

"How the fuck can you know how I feel?" The words tear from him on a scream. It's not real. Not true. If he closes his eyes, it'll go away.

"'Cause you're like me now. Always in pain. Always wanting. So hungry, it hurts."

Vincent swallows, bloodrich. *It's not going away. Ever.*

Iridium licks silvery lips. "Can teach you to manage it. Trust me."

Desperation cracks Vincent's bloodstained heart, and he nods. Hesitant. Inevitable.

Iridium crunches a crooked arm around his shoulders, his twisted metal body's warmth a strange, compelling comfort. "There. Don't cry. Got so much to talk about." And he turns Vincent's back on the dead girl, and leads him away with a soft metallic giggle.

Noon sun burns hellish on the dry concrete riverbank, the shadows of the row of cafés and expensive flats short and dense. Gulls swarm and squawk in water-fragrant heat haze, fighting over dropped french fries. The river's hot brown glint dazzles. On the far side, high-rise buildings stab the flawless blue sky, their outlines hazy in superheated air.

Joey fidgets at the café table, his phone sticky in his hand. Normally, the heat curls his creature lazy and content. Today, he's twitchy, unsettled. He knows exactly why, and it only makes him twitch harder.

Aluminum chairs clatter and scrape, the rich smells of garlic and tomato mixing with sour riverwater. Fairies giggle and slurp frozen cola. People chatter, drink, laugh over their lunch beneath the canopy's warm shade. Across the table, Iridium slurps raw oysters from their pearly shells, slicking his blackened tongue over misshapen pewter lips, and the salty stink twists Joey's guts raw.

For the fourth time that morning, he hits Mina's speed dial and presses CALL.

It rings, and rings.

He hangs up, itching. She's still not there. Isn't like her not to call. He knows what she's been doing—mindscrape, with that dirtyfingered blue fairy—and deep under his skin, serpentine rage bubbles. He should never have let her go. Should've taken her home, made sure she was okay.

Disgust salts his mouth. Like she'd let him take her anywhere.

Beside him, Delilah slants teasing lashes at him as she

licks hot chocolate fudge from her spoon. Her skimpy white sundress shows off athletic limbs, her dark skin glistening in the sun. "Can't find your girlfriend? Too bad."

Iridium snickers, and sucks up another oyster, the barbed wire wrapped around his wrist glinting bloody in the sun. "Figured you were too pissy to have gotten laid last night. Should keep that banshee on a leash."

Joey drops him a sharp snaky grin. "Better pissy than overcompensating with comfort food."

Delilah laughs and attacks her banana split with relish. She's already polished off bacon and eggs, hash browns, mushrooms, grilled tomatoes, fried cheese balls, a latte, and a strawberry milk shake. Demons. Always hungry, never satisfied.

At the next table, a skinny brown spriggan glamoured up as a teenage girl swipes a woman's handbag from beneath her seat, snuffling in delight. Joey pushes aside his salad, swallowing a darker craving for raw meat still warm. Sometimes the snake needs feeding, too.

His fingers twitch for a cigarette, for his phone to call Mina again. Something's not right. She should've called by now. "You gonna tell me what this is about?"

"I told you, Kane brushed me off. I'm in the mood to irritate him." Delilah licks fudge-coated lips and pokes one long purple nail at his plate. "You gonna eat that?"

"Be my guest."

She grabs it and tucks in hungrily, her voice muffled by lettuce and red onion. "Is there no dressing on this? What kind of fucking puritan are you? And where's Vincent? I told him to get his fluffy gay ass down here."

"Don't twist your G-string. I'm here." The empty chair grates aside, and Vincent flops into it. He's flushed, chocolate hair dripping with sweat, dark shades covering his eyes. He shoves his hands into his pockets, shivering. "I'm starving. What's to eat?"

Iridium sniffs, and licks the scent from wet pewter lips. His glamour fractures for an instant, and he grins, knowing. "Big night?"

"Screw you, metalboy. Caught the flu off some skanky whore." Vincent wipes a dark smear from his nose, grabs two of Iridium's oysters, and swallows them whole, sweat trickling over his throat.

Joey's senses sparkle with danger, his tongue twitching in two in his mouth. Vincent stinks of blood and fear and fever. Either the world's nastiest sparkle hangover, or . . .

But his thoughts drag back to Mina, the image of her with her shifty fairy dealer—touching, kissing, his hands on her skin, it's how that shit is done—the thought of them together ripples cold reptile blood into his veins. What if the grotty little insect took advantage of her while she was distracted? Worse, what if he hurt her?

Joey's fingers crackle. *He'll be a dead fucking insect, that's what.*

Delilah pokes his shoulder with a sharp purple nail, and he starts back to reality. "What?"

A green-eyed demon scowl. "You listening?"

Joey scrapes his hair back, irritation spiking his scalp. "Sure. Whatever."

Vincent's saying something about Diamond. ". . . at the docks, midnight. They've got some kinda cargo coming in, all secret-like."

Delilah frowns. "How d'you know that?"

"I just know." Vincent reaches for more oysters, and Iridium snatches them away, greedy eyes glinting.

Joey licks the air, suspicious. He's heard the same rumor—that dusky bronze earthfae girl last night sold him a lot of gossip—but Vincent is up to something. "What's the score?"

"Who knows? One way to find out."

"Sounds fair." Delilah slurps up one last piece of tomato. "We owe Diamond a surprise or two. Let's crash their party."

Diamond's insults to Mina still sting bitter in Joey's mouth. Screw it. He nods. "Agree. Let's do it. Midnight. Come set for a scrap. If there's score in it, we take it. If they snark us, we fight. Otherwise, it's watch and wait. Anyone got a problem with that?"

"I say we kill 'em all." Iridium shrugs, crooked and

matter-of-fact, and licks oyster juice from rusty claws. "Diamond, Sonny, whoever. They started it; we finish it."

Joey hisses a snaky laugh. "Are you fucking crazy? You think that's all Ange's got? Kane will come down on you so hard, your sick fairy ass'll be tinfoil."

"Maybe. And maybe if you'd let me in on last night instead of thinking with your hard-on, Sonny'd be dead already, instead of just pissed off and chasing your ass." Iridium's mismatched gaze is mild, but Joey's reptile senses can taste sour, desperate rebellion on the fairy's rusty breath.

Anger flushes him, dark and rich with disgust, not because Iridium's lust for blood sickens him, but because he understands Iridium's pain.

Sometimes the beast inside just gets too much for you.

Black snakemuscle clenches rigid beneath his skin, and he inhales sharply. *Don't shift. Too many people. Just keep it quiet.* He slides out a lazy half inch of claw, deceptively calm. "This is my outfit, last I looked. We do things my way."

Delilah's eyebrows arch in amusement. Vincent scowls. And Iridium just grins, lopsided metal teeth shining, and shrugs rusty wings, defiant. "Maybe your way ain't working so well anymore."

Joey flashes to his feet and crushes blackened fingers into Iridium's scrawny gray collarbone, snapping his teeth within an inch of the fairy's razor-pointed ear. He whispers so the whole café won't hear, but venomgreen spit flecks the fairy's cheek from his hiss. "You work for me, understand? You do what I want, when I want it. Slaughter at random, and Kane'll come after us all."

"You afraid?" Iridium's voice slides husky and thick with challenge, and the pulse in his crippled shoulder quickens under Joey's palm.

Relish for the fight washes cool snakeblood into Joey's veins, and he grins. "Just happy to be alive. You will not indulge your twisted metal-ass urges on my watch, get me? Keep a fucking lid on it, Iridium, or I'll jam one on it for you." Joey shoves away and glares a challenge at Vincent, who eyes him sullenly in a froth of sweat. "Midnight, the docks. Don't be late." And Joey spins around before he can sprout angry fangs and fill Iridium's hellcrossed eyeballs with venom.

Furniture clatters aside as he stalks out, sun glaring in his eyes. He strides along the riverbank, crowds melting around him, and reaches for his phone. Gulls screech overhead as it rings. Still no answer.

Sun flashes on the screen as he checks the time. It isn't far to her place, down by Albert Park where the sun shines on greener water and the wide grass shoulder at the lake's edge withers in the heat. It won't hurt to check on her. Maybe the grubby little memoryscrape maggot has hurt her.

Best to be sure.

Of course, it's possible she's just in bed with said maggot. Sliding her sweet body over his. Enjoying a lazy morning of sparkle and screwing.

Venom drenches his mouth, and he wants to spit it out, but he swallows, hard, acid burning his throat. Or maybe she's finally split on him. Deserted. Defected to the other side. Not coming back.

Joey flips his phone away and heads westward toward her place, tossing his cane from hand to twitching hand. Either way, better to see the fuckover coming.

9

"Mina, wake up."

Hands fumbled with my hair. Gentle warm lips caressed mine, menthol and spice, and in fevered darkness I jerked away, whimpering. *No more monsters. I'll be a good girl. I promise.*

Strong hands on my shoulders forced me still. I struggled, fear stiffening my joints. Trapping or protecting me?

"Peace. You're okay. Wake up." Urgency roughened that familiar voice.

Limbs warm and hard beneath me, the air a cool sigh on my fevered skin. I inhaled, and comforting mint freshness pierced the fog.

My pulse calmed, and I buried my face in his shirt, inhaling safety and warmth. Fabric slid cool and smooth on my cheek. Nightmares still blotted my vision, black and stung with scarlet halos. Pain throbbed deep in my skull, a ragged knifewound.

God, what a horrible dream.

Random sensation scattered in my mind like smashed glass, spinning out of sight too soon. Vincent, trying to kiss me, his musky male perfume. Diamond's icy laughter, his fingers sliding smooth and alien on my shoulder. Cobalt, black wings like velvet on the dim back stairs at the Court, his long white hand warm in mine as we sprinted laughing across a traffic-bright street.

Nothing after that. *Did it work? Did we see anything?*

"Open your eyes. Come on. Stay with me." Joey's voice sounded muffled, dull, like I'd stuffed my ears with mud. His cool hands slid around my aching head, lifting me, unsticking the hair from my cheek. It felt so nice. I wanted to curl up on his lap and purr. I licked my parched lips, and his taste lingered, burning cold.

God, how embarrassing. Better get up, before he sees how weak I am.

But weird liquid confusion sloshed in my brain, mixing up with down, right with left until the world spun dizzy. My guts hurt, and someone had attacked my sinuses with red-hot sandpaper. Christ, we must have hit it hard last night.

I swallowed on crumpled razors, and my voice struggled out in a croak. "Where are we?"

"Your place. It's late. I wondered about you." His voice relaxed, a release of tension. A sigh. Like he'd really worried if I'd be alive.

"Why? Did I . . . oh." Now I remembered Cobalt, dragging through my memories, the dusty midnight scent of his hair, his body lithe and hot against me. . . .

Shit.

My cheeks scorched as I remembered undressing him, kissing, easing his twisted fairy cock inside me so he could dig deeper. I remembered him begging me not to, dragging his mouth away from mine, his inky blue tears staining my chest. Cobalt was my friend, and I'd used him like a whore.

I shoved the horrid images away. Did we make it as far as the murder scene? I couldn't remember. I didn't care. I just wanted to sleep. In Joey's lap. Forever, while he stroked my hair and kissed me and whispered gentle words in my ear.

Sharp, hateful memory niggled at the edges of my mind, but I ignored it. Joey didn't like me memoryscraping. Soon I'd get a vile piece of his mind, but I didn't want the nice part to end, no matter how my head hurt and my stomach ripped and my muscles ran to water.

I forced gritty eyes open. Harsh late afternoon sun spilled in my windows. I'd slept all day. Shit. My guts coiled slick like a worm, and I rolled onto my side, groaning and clutching myself. Sparkle hangover. Something else he could scold me for.

"Sorry," I rasped. "I must've . . . um . . . passed out. Did I miss breakfast? I'll—"

"You're okay. Never mind that." Joey's palm slipped down my spine, soothing, enticing on my bare back, his clawtip's secret sting faint and pleasant.

I sighed, shivering at the care in his touch, but strange unease twinged, too. My stomach bloated warm under my hands, my skin clammy with fever. . . .

Holy fuck-a-peacock. I'm naked.

My skin sprang tight.

Was he watching me? Examining my body with those secretive, give-away-nothing eyes? Did he like it?

A shudder pleasured me despite my headache. My nipples hurt, and it wasn't only embarrassment that swelled hot and hard in my belly. I felt every little intake of his breath, each sweep of his gaze like warmed honey running over my skin.

Naked, in Joey's arms. Days had started a lot worse than this.

Melting contentment drowned me, dizzy, and erotic images flowed hot. I wanted to slide my hands under his clothes, feel his skin on mine. I wanted him to ease my thighs apart and lick me, slide his tongue over me, into me, tease my pleasure deep. See if he couldn't make my sickness go away.

My skin burned afresh. His touch drifted to my hip, and with a tiny thrill, I felt his hand *shift*. Muscles straining, bones moving, skin shivering and stretching. His touch heated with the effort, and now his slick webs glided on my skin, warm and wet and delicious.

Sensation scorched deeper, dangerous, and my desire responded, spreading delight over my pain. What would he feel like, if he changed? Those sinuous muscles, that tempting black skin on mine?

Warm and amorous like a cat in the sun, I arched my spine with a pleasured sigh and gazed sleepily up into his eyes. So beautiful, so hot, absinthe green with a dark sparkle of desire. That crushable blond hair tumbling softly on his cheek.

In my mind, wet black webs wrapped around a pistol grip. Shock squeezed my heart cold.

My reflexes jerked, and I scrambled to my feet.

I backed away, stumbling, swamped by a landslide of jagged images that scraped my tender skull raw.

Joey killed my mother. I saw it. And he just touched me. Caressed me hot. Kissed my lips while I slept. Chased away my nightmare, only to take its place.

My mind screamed, the echo lost down a bottomless well of despair.

My pulse raced. It couldn't be. Cobalt made it up, his twisted fairy brain plotting against me. Or I dreamed of Joey while I fucked him, his touch and his wicked spell unearthing my deepest fantasies to mingle with those blood-scraped memories.

It couldn't be true.

Could it?

Joey stared back at me, a dark blot on my pale suede.

For an instant, pain swirled amberlight in his eyes.

And then he swallowed, and softly folded his fingerwebs away, and his composure crystallized once more. His jaw firmed, his face perfect and unyielding. Not a hair or a spine out of place. Distant. Icy. Unbreakable.

I clutched shaking arms around my waist, my gaze flitting, anywhere but on his. My hair spilled crisp and blue over my breasts, and I was desperately glad for the covering. My nipples still scrunched tight, my skin flushed and damp as if I'd wanted what he was doing.

As if I liked him staring at me like that.

But he could still see the rest of me, the bruises on my hips, my thighs, the hair between my legs sticky and unwashed from sex.

I didn't know where to put my hands. I wanted the air to swallow me, make me invisible, get his unrelenting gaze off me.

"You okay?" Cold, disinterested, like he didn't give a shit.

"Umm . . . yeah. I'm fine." I gulped, and scrambled on the floor for my clothes. My inner ears sloshed, confused, and I teetered in my haste, carpet scraping my knees.

"You sure? You were out cold."

"Uh-huh." I found my crumpled pants, but I didn't know which way to face so he wouldn't cop an eyeful. In the end, I gave up and just dragged them on. My flesh still burned under his gaze, and I tripped, my damp feet catching in the leather. He still hadn't looked away. God knew what the bastard was thinking, why he thought I'd jumped away like that. He'd no reason to suspect I'd found him out.

Urgency nipped at my toes like vicious crabs. I needed to call Cobalt, ask him what the fuck happened. Maybe he had a simple answer, an explanation that made everything okay.

Maybe my life hadn't just exploded in a screaming bonfire.

At last Joey dropped his gaze, reached to the floor for his cane, and held it before him in both hands, a shield. His fingertips silently tapped the lacquer, my blocked ears unable to detect the minute sound. "I need you tonight, then. Wanna get some snark back on your glassfae pal?"

"Sure." I buckled my pants, and even that fat metal click was dull, the leathery slide muffled.

My toes curled tight. Where were my ears? My music? My rippling harmonics, always shifting and warping with the tiniest movement? His voice chimed dull and distant. My ears felt stuffed with clay, and the loudest sound was my own skipping heartbeat.

Nerves chewed under my skin like ants. How was I supposed to fight if I couldn't hear them coming?

"Diamond and Sonny are running a show at the docks, midnight."

"Uh-huh." I scrabbled for my bodice, ripping my hair and hacking my fingers bloody on the zipper as I tried to pull it up. At last the black leather encased my aching body, tight and supportive, but I felt no safety in it anymore. Instead, it threatened, menaced, squeezed my breath away.

Joey's gaze stayed fixed on the floor a few inches from my feet. "Some cargo they don't want us to see. I want it, and I want you there." His fingers drummed on the cane, silent. Tap, tap, tap, tap, empty like a muted television. Over and over. No sound.

I yanked my boots on. "Sure. Uh-huh. No problem."

"Okay, then." He hesitated. "Business down at South-bank first. Have to make an appearance for an old family friend. Paella or tapas or some fucking Spanish thing. Want to come?"

Unwilling, my head snapped up, right into the arc of his lasergreen gaze. He never asked me what I wanted. What the hell kind of question was that?

He stared back, composed as ever. Like I hadn't just lain naked in his arms.

Bitter bile crawled up my throat at the memory of his caress, his hand's tempting heat on my spine. The way he'd touched me, comforted me, hesitant like he'd wanted to touch me more but didn't dare. I swallowed. Was he asking me out?

Warmth spread in my belly, but this time it smelled ripe and bloody of vengeance, and deep inside me some hot, salty creature squirmed and bit.

I could go to him. Push him back on the sofa, climb onto him and tease him with my body. Drug him half-senseless with my poisoned kiss, toy with him until he was weak, breathless, helpless as he'd made me after so many years of lies. And then I'd grab my knife and slit his lying throat, and it'd be done.

Spiky melodic magic fought like hacking goblins in my chest, longing to escape.

But it wouldn't come out.

My larynx wheezed, sticky and swollen with some rabid infection. My precious song, ripped to ribbons on sparkle and memoryscrape.

My voice was ruined, my ears shot. My reflexes dull and distant. My limbs reluctant. And my knives sat harmless on the kitchen table in my jacket, where I'd left them last night. Joey was cautious, but he wasn't clumsy or slow. He'd have me bleeding on my back beneath him before I got within six feet of them.

Cold granite reality ground ragged holes in my spirit. I'd failed. After seven long years, I finally faced the man who killed my mother, and I was weaponless. Weak.

Scared, like a little girl.

Not how I'd imagined this moment.

I tried to swallow, but choked on bitter phlegm. If I didn't go with him, he'd surely be convinced I was the traitor, off to tell Diamond everything. He'd come after me, and kill me, and in this state I couldn't take him on.

But I couldn't face another second of that relentless reptile gaze.

I hitched in a painful shallow breath and backed off toward the door. "Um, no, look, I've got stuff to do. Won't take a few min—I mean, an hour or two. I'll see you down at the pier. Really. I promise." Words tumbled, and I bit my tongue before I could ramble any more.

Joey shrugged. "Tomorrow night, then."

Fuck. I stumbled on my heels. My feet tangled together, and I clutched the doorframe behind my back for balance. "Sure. Okay. Um . . . bye."

And I bolted into the corridor on unsteady legs, my heartbeat deafening me.

Her sharp footsteps fade. Joey wraps tense fingers around his cane, his knuckles stinging. It's done. The lies sown, the trick set in motion. What happens tonight will show him if she's true. She's probably on her way to Diamond already, to plot a countermove.

But already guilt sours his mouth, the sickening stink of his own unspoken lies. He can't abide treachery. Not telling her everything tastes foul.

And already the room is duller without her, the sunlight harsher, her jasmine scent fainter until he can barely smell her at all. Still her jewelbright skin tingles his fingertips, the bitter sparkle taste of her lips a ghost he can't exorcise.

For a moment, when he first saw her lying there, he thought her dead, her beauty undiminished, and jagged dread slashed his heart.

Such a lovely, hot-blooded, sensual woman. His cold snakeskin writhes inside, pleading for her glorious warmth, and he jerks to his feet and paces the carpeted floor in hot sunlit streaks. That inkblue fairy's dusty skinscent reeked from her, his glitterspiked fluid still bright between her thighs, and even the memory splits angry fangs through Joey's gums, itching to kill.

It makes him want to laugh. Envy is such a pitiful emotion.

But her reaction still burns him, the way she shuddered and sprang away at the touch of his webbed fingers. His black reptile skin disgusts her. He disgusts her. There's no other explanation.

He should never have touched her. But he couldn't help it, couldn't resist the lure of her scent, the sweet vibration of her movement, the taste of her breath on the ultrasensitive tips of his reptile tongue.

Not to mention she was naked.

Unexpectedly, gloriously naked, tangled blue hair trailing over her skin, long limbs shining, breasts pure and beautiful in dappled sunlight. Soft sapphire hair between her legs, short and neat and so faint, barely covering the luscious fragrant shapes of her sex, just begging for the invasion of his tongue. A hot-blooded goddess, sultry and seductive in her sleep. Sweet death, he'd wanted to taste her, lick her, inhale the maddening jasmine scent of her, all sweat and sex and soft feminine flesh and fuck it all, if he keeps thinking like this, he'll be dead by week's end.

He can't live like this, not with her name always on his lips and her fascinating female scent forever on his tongue. Already he's left Vincent and Iridium alone with Delilah to be with her, and no doubt they've cooked up some vile treacherous stew in his absence.

Decision stings like rust in his mouth. He can't do this anymore. If she's false, she should die.

To let her live is weakness. He should relish her death. The cruel snap of her neck in his fingers, her last desperate gasp as the blood drains from her pretty lips . . .

His guts squirm tight. He can't. Not her. Can he?

Whatever. He'll deal with that when the time comes. Even if she's true, he'll have to get rid of her. She's a dangerous distraction. He's obsessed with her, and he can afford only one obsession at a time.

He snaps black spines flat against his skull and rearranges his hair with a toss of his head. If tempting him is her game, he's tougher than she thinks. He'll resist her. Make her work for it, humiliate herself, twist herself inside out for his attention. Make her beg for a glance, a caress, just one more kiss.

And then, he'll be rid of her, one way or the other.

In the stairwell, I squeezed my eyes shut, my pulse a mess. From the landing, his footsteps rang gluggy in my ears, the click of his cane on the marble as he stepped into the elevator muffled and soft. I waited, shivering, until I knew he was gone, and then I slumped in the corner, hugging my knees tight to my sweating breasts.

My stomach hurt. Hot tears hacked at my eyelids, but I didn't let them flow.

It couldn't be true.

But it must be.

Cobalt had no reason to lie. He'd never shown me false before. And the images felt so real, stabbing in my memory like the nightmare you have over and over again until it comes true and you see it while you're awake. The figures stalking you. The smells and screams and gunshots following you everywhere.

Joey killed my mother. Shot her coldly and without mercy as she lay screaming on the floor, begging for help. No one else there. No reason he couldn't just leave her there alone.

I never knew who'd beaten her. I didn't see who'd left her lying there, bleeding and broken, driven half-mad by the things they did to her.

Now, I didn't want to know. I didn't care. All I cared was that he'd betrayed me.

Black hatred spilled into my heart, overflowing, running down my body like evil helljuice, scorching me forever with pitted scars.

Joey, who despised treachery above all else. I'd looked up to him. Imitated him. Respected him for being the only one of us who never took an unnecessary shot, never loved violence for its own sake or raised a needless hand in anger.

I hugged myself tighter, taking refuge once more in my black leather carapace, letting it shield me, mold me, temper me sharp. My stupid girlish attraction had blinded me. I saw that now. I'd mistaken his taunts for encouragement. His tricks for praise. His sick humor for compassion. He'd known me all along for who I was, and it amused him to watch me scramble for his affection. He'd laughed at me, despised me for five ugly years, while the whole time I'd wanted to be just like him.

Liar. Hypocrite. Evil fucking prick.

To think I'd wanted to be his lover.

Resolution hardened in my bones like molten steel. I had a choice. I could run, skittle off into the night like a spooked rabbit to hide and lick my wounds.

Or I could fight. Stay close to him, so he'd get no chance to hear me creeping up. Use all my beauty and wits to charm him, beguile him into trusting me. Seduce him, my body and my song and my sweet poison kiss. Tempt him into showing weakness. And then, I'd unsheathe my knives and cut out his heart.

But not before he knew. Not before I dragged his head back and forced him to look into my eyes and said, *This is for my mother, you evil snake-hearted liar.*

Cruel anticipation caressed me. His little protégé, turning on him. Darkly, I imagined his surprise, the dumbfounded look on his face, and warm anticipation spilled into my belly. He'd shift, I'd sing him immobile. He'd fight me, but I'd be faster, tougher, stronger, everything he said he wanted me to be.

Revenge. At last. And all the sweeter for stabbing him right through his treacherous black heart.

My blood burned. I snarled, unfolded my arms, and whip-snapped to my feet.

My reflexes didn't respond, and I stumbled, my ankle twisting in a stab of agony.

I gripped the wall and gritted my teeth, determined to ignore the ripple of worry in my blood. My pulse throbbed sickly in my ears, deafening me. I was hungover, that was all. It'd pass.

I should call Cobalt, tell him I was okay, say sorry for what I'd done. Thank him for showing me the truth. Ask if he'd forgive me. He wasn't a bad shag, after all that, and I sorta liked him. Maybe when this was over, we could hook up, do some lines, have a party.

Might as well. Nothing to save myself for anymore.

I limped into my flat, where the setting sun glared ruby accusation through dusty windows. Joey's lingering minty scent lit a raging flame beneath my anger, and I slammed the door so hard, it rattled.

I'd shower. Eat. Rest. Gather my strength. And tonight, down at the docks, I'd have him.

10

Kane hops up smooth slate steps in summer heat, late afternoon sunlight glaring off the dark bluestone walls towering above him. The bronzecast figures in the stone archway groan in protest as he passes beneath. The massive oak door swings open at his flame-wreathed touch, and he wanders into church.

Shadow's too afraid to meet him anywhere else, and Kane's lips twitch in a hellhappy smile, remembering the night the city fell, the crosses burning, the tearing sound of feathers ripped away, the tortured screams of heaven's children.

The satisfying crunch of bloody godflesh between his teeth.

If Shadow thinks sacred ground will save him, he's been away too long.

Shafts of sunlight painted yellow and orange slant tall into the nave from dusty arched windows. Black and white floor tiles alternate in patterns. Pews lie silent and straight, only a few hunched figures marring the symmetry.

Kane's nose itches in the thick stink of pollen. He sniffs and stalks up the aisle, and candles in the nave gutter at his passing. He gives the altar a cursory nod, in case anyone's watching up there, and in the soapstone font, holy water boils and evaporates in a hiss of steam.

In the front pew, striped in shadows, a bruised-eyed girl

stares at him, her hands still clenched in prayer. Her skinny knees smear on the tiles. A crucifix glints around her neck, the chain tangled in neglected brown wisps. Beside her, a green shopping bag overflows with colored clothing, a plastic bag of jelly beans, a yellow teddy bear.

Death tingles Kane's tongue, salty and delicious. He inhales, desperation and grief and endless days spent crouched beside a starched white hospital bed, the crucifix on the wall, the shadow of that skinny dead god falling on the heart monitor's weak green blips. His nails blush an angry blue. So many lies. At least he's honest.

He smiles at her as gently as he can, ice crackling in his golden hair. "Twenty-six hours."

Her throat bobs. "What?"

"Your little girl will die. The doctors can't help her." He points at the altar and leans over to whisper. "They don't listen, you know. Too busy hiding. They can't even hear you."

"That's a horrid thing to say." Her voice cracks. Tears shine her eyes silver, and she tugs at her dress with desperate, tired hands.

"Twenty-six hours, Joanna. Don't waste them here." Kane shrugs, and flips out a card between two fingers. "When you're done believing? Call me."

She stares, her mouth quivering, and finally she snatches the card and her bag and hurries away.

"That was cruel." The flat voice slithers in his ear, wormlike, and Kane turns, imagined soulblood still stickyrich in his throat.

Shadow lounges in the opposite pew, fluffy whiteblond hair glowing orange in the hot sun. His big body is relaxed, the same nondescript human-suit they all wear when they come here. White suit, white skin, white hair, his mouth easy in a bland half smile. Shadow's real appearance is even more cringeworthy, feathers and baby curls and shimmer-bright glory shining all over the fucking place like a bad smell. But angels can't come here whole, not since Kane won the war.

Shadow's shockblue eyes are calm, unblinking. But his fingers twitch in his lap, barely perceptible, and satisfaction blackens Kane's heart. Shadow doesn't like it here.

Here doesn't like Shadow, either.

Kane resists a feral snarl, and instead plonks down on the cool hard seat next to Shadow, arranging his suit so it won't crush. "No crueler than promising the impossible. I'm not here to play nice with you. Call off your maggoty little spies. They're not welcome."

Shadow lifts blond eyebrows, a perfect facsimile of innocence. "I'm not sure I know what you mean."

Kane's nails blacken, gouging holes in the cedarwood pew, and obsidian shards spit from his teeth. "I eat the screeching little fuckers, angeldirt. I know where they come from."

Calmly, Shadow brushes charcoal from his pale sleeve. "Surely there's some mistake—"

"Don't gamble with me. You'll lose. This city's mine. The war's over."

Shadow laughs, a dull echo. "My dear hellminion, you mistake me. I've no intention—"

Kane hisses, flames licking his hair, needle teeth snapping an inch from Shadow's flowerstinking ear.

Shadow doesn't flinch. Just stares at him, heavenblue.

Kane's stomach growls for flesh, and his mouth springs full of greedy spit. "Swallow your rotting lies before I cram them down your throat. Last chance, shitworm. Get rid of your garbage, or I'll get rid of it for you." He whirls to his feet and stalks down the aisle, and as he passes, the prayer books tucked into the backs of the pews burst into flame. Petty. Beneath him. He doesn't care.

Fury still whets his teeth sharp as the door slams behind him. Sun glares in his eyes, the soothing scarlet shade of home. He strides into the leafy church park to escape the righteous stench, and his footsteps sear brown patches into the verdant lawn. He paces beneath creaking plane trees, traffic's buzz and the greasy city smells calming him. With an effort, he shrinks springing blue hair back to blond and swallows his rage to let his thoughts flow unchecked.

He doesn't believe Shadow for a moment. But the gut-worm is audacious. Cheeky. Unafraid. Not his usual scum-sucking minion act. Something's changed since last they quarreled.

Almost like Shadow's got top cover. Help. An accomplice, even.

Kane's nails sharpen again, and he yanks out his phone and dials.

A fashionably long time before she answers. "Yes?" Delilah's voice purrs, like she's luxuriating in a warm bath.

Even down the phone line, he can smell her, charcoal and delicious demon flesh. "I've changed my mind."

She laughs, crystal. "Extraordinary. I'll call the press immediately. What in hell are you on about?"

"About getting to know you. Meet me tonight."

No answer. But excitement clicks in her throat.

She didn't expect that. Kane smiles. "Not busy, are you?"

"Of course not. I'd be delighted. The Court?" Tension shines in her voice.

"No. Somewhere private. For dinner. The Crystal Club. Wear something I'll like."

She laughs again, faking a dismissal. "Are you teasing me? They don't do dinner at the Crystal, last I heard."

"They do when I tell them to. Midnight."

Her anticipation shimmers. "Whatever you say, darling."

"You're learning." He hangs up, his own anticipation a dark and cunning flame in his guts. Delilah can't hide her schemes from him, not in person. If she's in on Shadow's deception, he'll find out, and the fun he'll have teasing the truth from her will be worth spending the evening listening to her arrogant little lies and putting up with her bilious efforts to earn his favor.

Besides, he's hungry. For more than food, or soulflesh. It could be her lucky night.

A child totters on unsteady legs along the pebbled path in front of him, reaching up a fat little hand for the sun. The mother calls a warning, but the baby tumbles onto its nappy-wrapped bottom at Kane's ankles.

Kane picks it up and sets it gently on its feet. "Not yet," he whispers. "Grow first. Then we'll talk."

Its belly feels warm and soft, and for a moment Kane's hungry claws dig in. The baby gazes at him with wide gray eyes and giggles, blowing bubbles. Kane's sluggish heart warms. Pretty little thing.

The mother runs up and swings the child into her skinny arms, suspicion welling deep in her eyes.

"He'll be an engineer, Alice." Kane offers his best smile. "And good at sports. Just don't let him near his grandfather."

Her mouth twists, but guilt fractures her gaze. She clenches her teeth and backs off with a hiss. "Get away from him, you freak!"

Kane straightens his tie, winks at the little boy over her shoulder, and walks away.

Deep in the abandoned train tunnel, where rats scuttle in the dark and the echoes of darker monsters long dead ring and fade with the seasons, a tiny draft lifts the stifling air. Drops of water plink like clockwork. Rockworks long left half-finished, tools discarded, rusted track segments lying unused in the rubble-strewn ditch.

Grimy white wall laid in cracked tiles, black curves spelling a name long unreadable. On the half-built platform, sick yellow light wafts like mustard gas, sugary sweat and fluid gone stale, listless campfires and buzzing electric light gloating over prostrate bodies.

All fae. All limp, listless, wings drooping, skin sickly pale in shades of green and blue and scarlet. A pile of sleeping fairies, limbs entwined, wings fluttering limply in nightmares that boil the air black above them. A few of them fondle each other, blind and numb, their bodies famished for sensation.

A starved blue spriggan snuffles giggling at the wall's base for ants, his limbs blistered with sores. A skinny glass fairy slumps in a crooked archway, his orange eyes glowing dully, fixated on deep cracks that spread slowly up his arms, crackle, crunch. At his feet a white-haired banshee howls weakly and claws the concrete, blood oozing from ripped nails.

Litter scatters the floor, torn clothing, empty plastic take-out containers, charred cardboard, a cockroach-chewed hamburger fragment still dangling limp lettuce.

Silence, split only by moans. Stink, rotten food, and stale bodies. Rank humidity.

At a rusted folding table, Ivy mutters and pokes at her collection, long golden fingers flittering in a fairyglow halo. Glasses, bowls, vials lined up in moldering spice racks, row upon row of stolen essences, thoughts, memories, magic. Liquid sparkles in each, one emerald green, the next silver, the next raspberry like blood.

All emotions, sucked with magic-laced kisses from those willing fairy victims, like wickedbright soup through a straw. Sometimes memories, sweet or sad, a lover, a sunset, the nicest day of their life. Often they'll sell for cash, a trick, or another tastier drug. These fairies are too hopeless to care.

Myriad scents swirl and combine, sour jealousy, spicy rage, love bitter like daisies. A kerosene lamp reeks at her side, casting rainbow shadows through the glass.

"Christ's bleeding ass, it stinks like a trollwhore's crack in here." Delilah pushes a limp body from her path with one pointed toe and picks her way onto the platform, her pretty white dress silly and strange in the squalor. Her heels click, echoing along with her nasty demon voice, down the tunnel and back again like it's been to hell. "You got what I asked for?"

"Mmm." Ivy swallows from a rusty bowl, glittering red spelljuice salty on her tongue. Her blood stirs, and she sighs, lost. This one's a memory. A fairy boy's meaty lust, warm wet flesh on his cock, muscles straining, lips melting together, the iron flashburst of orgasm. How glorious, to be desired. Pleasure warms her belly. But too soon the feeling fades, and with a forlorn ache in her guts, she chooses a smeared drinking glass at random and samples that one, too.

Violet sourness stings her tongue. Oh, yes. Her bones shudder, and she groans, her fingers curling to hungry talons. Rage, pure and burning, the reckless need to destroy, flashes of a thwarted troll boy screaming in fury, fists bursting tight, his vision misting crimson.

Lust and anger. A heady mixture. Ripe for crime and rampage.

She pops the cork from an empty glass vial and puffs a gentle breath across the opening. Sparkles rain like wingglitter, deep cabernet red, angry violet swirling within. A fine cocktail for destruction. Should be a big seller.

She grins and stuffs the cork back in, leaning back to admire her spellcraft. The sparkling magic seethes, longing to escape. She clicks her tongue. "Nonono. You stay in there, tastysauce."

"I said, you got it?"

Ivy's wings jerk back, her heart racing. She thought she was alone. Wasn't she?

Delilah stalks up, one hand on her hip, her winedark hair tossed over one slim brown shoulder. She's wearing a long white dress, and the hem's getting dirty. A scowl mars her face.

Pretty things shouldn't scowl. If Ivy were pretty like she used to be, she'd never frown again.

Ivy plops the spell in the spice rack and wafts torn white wings, disturbed. What did Delilah ask for? She wriggles sly fingers, pretending she hasn't forgotten. "Didn't say what you wanted it for."

"Cheeky, aren't you? Since you ask, I have a date. An adversary who needs . . . softening up. And I can't use demonspells on him. I want something strong. Persuasive. Seductive. And I want it now. You got me?"

A memory glimmers, and relief washes Ivy warm. She's got just the thing. But no need to give it away for nothing. She rubs crafty palms together, claws shining, and lifts her chin airily. "None left. I'm right out. Come back tomorrow."

"Oh, no. Today. Now. No less."

Ivy clicks her tongue in mock concern. "Well, that'd be some extra work, now, wouldn't it? Only so many creatures to torture." She waves her hand at the listless bodies on the floor, already drained of their emotions to make her toys. Suck out too much in one day, and they'll wear out. But never mind. Diamond can always bring her more.

Rich demon laughter. "Oh, I like you, Ivy. You're a lady after my own heart."

Ivy folds a multiknuckled finger under her chin, pretending to consider. "So . . . say I could make an exception. What would be in it for me? Hmmm?"

Delilah glides closer, swaying those curving hips, and avarice glitters in her smile. "Whatever you like." She leans in and sniffs Ivy's mouth, and exhales deliberately, charcoal and crafty hellmagic. "Mmm. I taste some deep longing there. Tell me what you want, and maybe we can come to some . . . arrangement?"

Ivy's stomach hollows. She's miserable, empty, and forlorn, and she knows that once, she had it all. Mist clouds her vision, and she tries to swipe it away, but it hangs, white and shimmering, just out of reach. Desperately she digs in the slashed remnants of her memory, trying to see.

Delilah kisses her softly, hot demon lips tasting of ash. "Is it Joey? Hmm? The snake who hurt you? I can drag him here by his skinny black flippers so you can rip them off one by one. Would you like that?"

Ivy licks her scorched lips. "Mmm. That would be tasty. But . . ."

"Or is there something else you'd rather do with him, mmm? Some red-hot serpent action? That tongue of his certainly has potential. And he's a strong little brute, determined, too. I imagine he'd last quite a while with the proper . . . encouragement." Delilah traces a warm finger up Ivy's thigh, and lets it linger.

Warmth floods beneath Ivy's skin. She remembers making love, not to the nasty black serpent man but another one, so beautiful, he hurt her eyes. She gasps as she recalls the golden hardness of her man's body, his skin's stormy scent, his strong mouth pleasuring her, the wonderful sensation spreading beneath his fingers as he strokes her.

She squints teary eyes, trying to see his face, but it's blurred, distant, featureless like a ghost's.

Delilah chuckles. "Bingo. So it's love you're after. Lost your confidence? You're still a beautiful woman. No spring chicken, I suppose, but what's life without disappointment?"

Ivy fingers her ruined cheek, lost in despair.

Delilah frowns. "It's that, is it? We can be rid of that no problem. Sure there isn't something more difficult? I'd hate to think you were selling me cheap goods."

"You can make me pretty again?" Suddenly, Ivy's world glows.

A wily glint sauces the demon's glance. "Of course. So long as you get me what I want. Do we have a deal?"

Ivy jumps and claps, delighted. Peel his skin off, drip, slurp. Stuff that nasty black snakehiss in a bottle and drink it down. Oh, yes. "And the snake man. I want the snake man, too."

She holds limefresh breath, and waits. If Delilah wants her sparklies that badly, she'll have to agree.

But Delilah just shrugs. "Whatever you say."

"Oh, yes! A deal. Most definitely a deal." Ivy rubs her hands in glee and dives for her workbench. She's got just the thing. She fingers through the tubes, searching for the new one. Just this afternoon, from the dirtyhandsome glassfae boy.

Ah, there. She fishes out a golden vial with a cork and holds it sparkling to the light, the liquid inside sweet and bubbly like champagne. "Perfect. A pretty little song. Needy. Hopeful. A splash of desperation. And wait . . . yes." She rummages through and comes up with a glittering violet dropper. She flips back the cork and adds a single sparkling drop that dissolves instantly, swallowed by the hungry golden melody. "Just a dribble of unexpected. Surprise! Hah. Just what you need." She presses the cork back in tight and displays it with a cheeky flourish.

Delilah eyes it dubiously. "You sure it's powerful?"

A sly giggle. "Oh, yes. Some hardcore do-as-I-say here.

Concentrated, you know. Not a drop wasted. Washed passionate with unrequited love and a dusty fairy boy's pain. This'll do you sweetly." She twirls it in long-jointed golden fingers, shadows glittering. The subtle jasmine taint wafts, gratifying. Serpent man's lover, stuffed in a glass tube. Happy.

Delilah sniffs at it, frowning. "Doesn't seem like much."

Ivy wobbles it close to Delilah's ear, stirring the contents. A mournful tune drifts in minor mode, almost too faint to hear, and invisible strings of compulsion tug at Ivy's heart. Magic in this one, all right.

A savage grin spreads Delilah's rich brown lips. "Well, now. I smell banshee leather-fetish. Where did you get this?"

Ivy taps a claw to the side of her nose, grinning. "Couldn't say. Couldn't possibly tell. You like?"

"Oh, yes. Give." Delilah snatches at it, greedy.

But Ivy yanks the tube away, her pointed chin lifting haughtily. Dirt drifts pewterbright from her hair. "Pretty. And the snake man, too. Promise?"

"Darling, if this works on Kane, you'll be the prettiest girl alive and Joey will beg you to have your way with him. Now give it to me."

Curiosity itches Ivy's palms. Kane. The name feels delicious and textured in her mouth like a soft-centered chocolate. Who is he? She inhales, searching for the truth on drifting demon breath, and for a heart-stopping instant, she tastes her long-lost thunderstorm.

Her skin warms, and desperate longing uncurls like lace in her mind.

She rubs slinky fingers together, eager. "Now. I want the pretty now. Snake man can wait."

"Oh, ouch, stop. You're twisting my arm." Delilah smiles indulgently and tweaks Ivy's nose with an affectionate claw. "Greedy little fairyslut, aren't you? Did no one ever warn you not to deal with demons? Very well. For all the good it'll do you." She exhales, dark and fragrant on Ivy's face.

For an instant, pain tears along the twisted scar like fire. And then it's gone.

Ivy blinks, and her hand flies to her cheek. Her fingertips glide on silky skin. Nothing. She dives into the clutter on her desk and comes up clutching a shard of mirror. Her eager gaze devours her reflection. Smooth. Perfect.

Beautiful again.

Her blood thrums in swift delight. Who cares about silly spells? She won't need them to captivate her lover now. Charmed glitter puffs from her wings, and eagerly she holds out the vial.

"Good girl." Delilah smiles sharply, swipes up the vial, and stalks away into the gloom.

Holding her breath, Ivy waits until Delilah's footsteps fade. Then she hops into the sultry green air on sly white wings and drifts after her, love's lost echo a seductive black whisper in her heart.

Later that night, in a dark city street, where heat scorches the pavement and the air stings sweet with grime, Shadow's spy falls to earth.

Burning air rushes through the angel's feathers, dragging his wings back. The world snaps dark. Faster, falling through warm midnight sky. Stars dazzle, and below, a sterile tunnel of light rushes up, blinding him.

Concrete smashes his face, hard. Knocks his breath away. The impact thuds like agony in his bones, but they don't break. The lightbeam flickers, and zaps out.

His cheekbone scrapes rough pebbles. Dirt, filling his nails, his fingers rasping on uneven ground. Hot dry air caresses his skin. Velvety summer darkness. The grotty earthen smell of fumes, flesh, and fire.

Akash crawls to his feet, delighted. Midnight heat scours his skin, an orange-lit city street. The stink of blood and dirt works fresh seduction in his starved nostrils. Streetlights burn sunlike overhead. Trees, still in the stagnant air beside a rusted wrought-iron fence. Houses, jammed close and crawling with ivy.

Grateful tears sting Akash's eyes, and his mouth waters at that dirty taste. He inhales, and that delicious raw air fills his lungs, tainted sharp with emotion and human violence. Already, his starved senses glut themselves.

Shadow sent him to spy on Kane. That should be fun. But in truth, Akash has been longing for this rich rush of sensation. Pleasure, pain, the sultry lick of music in his ears, taste's sweet assault on his tongue.

And now here he is. Home is silence, the sterile smell of flowers, always the same. Not a scrap of stimulation. Earth is always so much more interesting.

His wings are gone, his body changed into a nondescript pale human-suit. Neat blond hair, white skin, plain white clothing. It doesn't matter. He'll get a better one soon enough.

He surveys the empty street, cunning. No time to lose. He's tried to hide here before, and he knows that time is short. Last time, Kane smelled Akash out and sent him back, even though he hid inside a fresh human body. This time, he needs a better disguise. Somewhere Kane will never think of looking, where flowery skyscent won't give Akash away.

This time, Shadow's already shown him just where to go. An angel lives here, goldenblond with brutal scars on his back, Kane's tame prisoner of war. In Rainbow's body, Akash will be safe to revel in the city's hellish delights.

Oh, and spy on Kane for Shadow. If he can find the time. Who knows? Maybe he'll steal a few souls back for himself. Shadow doesn't need to know.

Stealthy, he unlatches the rusted iron gate, metal sharp in his fingers. Soft light burns behind the pebbled glass front door, and he creeps up the path and onto the wooden landing. His footsteps brush softly, his muscles tense, every movement a frisson of anticipation. Soon, he'll have a real body, and all this wasted sensation will be wasted no more.

Dust crisps his mouth. He tries the knob. Click. Unlocked.

Silently, he opens the door. Creeps inside onto dark carpet. Clicks the door closed.

Inside, the living room is plush and neat, the tall lamp shining pastel over cushions and darkwood furniture. On the pale chaise longue, a woman stirs sleepy limbs, her pale silken robe dropping off one slim shoulder. Burgundy hair spills as she scrapes it from crusted eyes. "Rain? That you?"

"No," Akash whispers, and before she can jump or scream, he's on her.

Warm flesh in his hands. Soft breasts against his chest. Her succulent lips under his, her mouth forcing open. She struggles, her cries muffling to gurgles and whimpers.

Akash closes his eyes, sucks in one last mouthful of her fearsweet breath, and dives down her throat.

Her slim body jerks and shudders. He thrashes and coils inside her chest like a snake, chews her up and swallows her, hot soulblood running down his chin.

The empty white human-suit crumples, bereft of life, its blue eyes already washed clear.

Akash pushes it aside and slowly rises from the couch, his skin afire.

So good, to be alive again.

And now, the man-angel won't see him coming until it's too late.

Her heartbeat still thrums, pumping chemical excitement through his veins. The warm silk robe slides dark seduction over his skin. The short hem brushes his beautiful new thighs, and he watches her long slim legs as he moves them, muscles rippling gently under such delicate white skin. His new red hair whispers over his shoulders, a trail of pleasure, and something delightful happens in the area of his chest. He looks down, and her heavy breasts tremble, the nipples tight under thin silk.

He stretches, and laughs her husky female laugh. Her lips curl, her tongue sensitive and warm. He's never been a woman before. It feels different inside, all that tight prickly male rage gone and replaced with something . . . warmer. Slicker. More malleable. He wants to breathe, taste, touch.

Already, at his feet, the dead human-suit sags and crumbles, caustic white dust puffing.

Images of the man-angel kissing this woman—deep, wet, delicious, tongues sliding together, soft flesh warm in his hands, the silken tangle of her hair—slide hot currents of desire into his blood. Last time, he didn't get to. Maybe, when naughty-man-angel-Rain comes, he'll pretend for a while.

Shadow would disapprove. But Shadow need never know. Shadow doesn't know a lot of things Akash gets up to.

Behind him, the unlocked door creaks open, and a deep male voice caresses his ears. "Mel? Door's open. You okay?"

Akash smiles, clasps damp quivering hands behind his back, and turns.

11

The shipping container's metal ridges pressed warm into my back, the close space making me sweat. We'd been hiding here a few minutes now, the moon painting greedy white fingers over the deserted dockyard. Shadows poured ink on asphalt between the rows of steel containers, stacked two high, rust splashing dark through peeling paintwork.

A sweatdrop wormed between my breasts. The smell of corroded metal and water itched my nose. I glanced at my watch, sweating. Ten minutes to midnight. No sign of anyone. Didn't mean they weren't here.

To my left leaned Joey, a slim shadow among shadows, his minty scent an unwelcome distraction that sprang my skin alive. Once, I'd loved that smell. Now, it made me shiver. Beyond him, Iridium crouched, a dim bronze glimmer.

To my right, Vincent hunched over, sweat beading feverbright, and retched, muffling it with the back of his hand. Dark raspberry clots spewed onto the pavement, stinking of meat. He choked, and leaned against the wall, panting and covering his mouth. At least he was trying to be quiet.

I poked him irritably in the thigh with my foot. His bloodshot brown eyes glinted up at me, his face clammy and shining. Blood stained his shirt. Sweat dripped from his hair onto his bare arms, and he sent me a hungry red-tinged grin that shimmered discomfort through my veins. What the fuck was wrong with him?

Joey's eyes narrowed, but he said nothing, only slipped his warm hand over mine, that maddening mintgreen scent fresh on my tongue. In the dark, I felt the sweet prickle of claws on my knuckles as he tugged, letting me know I should follow him. He snaked out into the moonlight, silent and swift, his cane's glinting brass top the only hint of color. He'd covered himself again, black suit jacket neat and lean, dark hat tilted over his eyes. Distancing himself. It wouldn't do him any good.

My skin rippled hot. I wanted to leap on him, pin his squirming body to the ground, and tear his throat out with my nails.

But not yet.

Not until he'd admitted what he'd done, and pleaded with me not to end his deceitful little life.

I didn't just want to kill him. I burned to tear down his goddamn impregnable façade, humiliate him as he'd done to me. Make him beg, whimper, lose that precious dignity.

I took a deep calming breath and followed him. Behind me, Vincent and Iridium slipped off in the opposite direction to find their own hide. We'd done this before. No instructions required.

My boots clicked softly on the concrete as we slipped out across the train tracks into the docks proper. Damp hair stuck to my shoulders, and my muscles still ached. I'd left my jacket at home, my knives strapped tight to my ribs instead. No need to conceal weapons here. I swallowed, my throat thick and sore, my ears hot and sticky like some scarlet infection festered there. My headache had faded, but weakness still vibrated my limbs. If Cobalt gave me something, I'd kill the diseased little worm.

If I could get hold of him, which I couldn't.

I'd called him all evening—no answer. His number kept ringing out to voicemail. Memories of that evil blue sparkle taunted me, and I swallowed dark sapphire unease.

We slipped between container rows only a few feet apart, sheltering in the shadow of the first one, then the next as we crept closer to the dock. Heat haze rippled under golden floodlights, the concrete still overheated from the harsh summer sun, and sweat stuck my hair to my neck. Joey moved silently, slipping fluidly in and out of silhouette, his careful steps making no sound.

My pulse hammered, and I felt as though I clambered like a sweaty elephant, my feet clumsy and my boots echoing, though I knew from experience that they didn't.

Noises drifted closer, truck engines, the groan of hydraulics, voices shouting, the tide's dull slap against the bluestone breakwater. My ears ached, and dockwater's greasy stink fouled my mouth.

Finally, we ducked in beside the last row. Hot floodlights shone above the road along the water's concrete edge, and the crane's sharp metal shadows crisscrossed the pavement at our feet.

Joey crept to the end, and I followed. He sniffed around the corner, testing the scents, and motioned for me to take a look.

I listened, but my clogged ears revealed nothing. I slipped past him, close to stay out of the light, and my nerves twitched I could feel him breathing, his freshmint scent warm. So near. My knives so warm and ready against my ribs.

I swallowed and moved on.

I peered around the edge, my breath aching my throat. Grinding motors screeched. The crane groaned and shook as a heavy red container inched along the conveyor. A few wharfies wearing hard hats milled beneath in steel-capped boots, bright orange vests glowing under the lights. Melbourne dockworkers were universally corrupt one way or the other, and these guys looked no exception. Chains creaked and swung, and the container settled to the oily tarmac with a thud that vibrated deep in my lungs.

I checked my watch again, sweat glistening on my wrist. Midnight.

Chains rattled away, and Diamond lighted on the container's roof with a sharp crack, glassy wings dazzling. "Thanks, ladies. We'll take it from here."

I tensed. Joey gripped my wrist, holding me back, and I wanted to shake him off, scream, *Get off me!*

The wharf guys looked at each other, and one darted his hand behind his back for a weapon.

Diamond leapt to the ground like a glowing pink insect and kept running, waggling his finger in mock warning. "Uh-uh."

The guy fumbled his pistol. Diamond hurtled up to him, wings drawn back like blades, and crashed him onto his back with a rippling glass punch under the chin. And like black velvet ghosts, the Valenti gang materialized from the shadows.

Sonny, huge and hulking in a dark suit but silent on his feet when he wanted to be. Fabian, his cousin's image, only shorter and angrier, an ugly black automatic weapon clutched in both stubby hands. Three or four others, surrounding the wharfies in a ring of muscle and guns and slick vampire teeth. Everyone but Angelo himself, and I hadn't heard a damn thing.

The guy on the ground didn't move, his head stuck at a crazy angle, blood dribbling from his slack mouth. Diamond cracked his bruised knuckles, blood spattering, and gave the wharfies a psychotic grin. "Anyone else in a mood?"

Unwilled, my fingers clenched around Joey's. Sweat slicked his palm onto mine. My heart thumped. We had our guys hidden in the container park. Numbers were no problem. But this was a serious fight with serious consequences. We'd be lucky if anyone came out alive, and if they did, it wouldn't be for long once the repercussions started.

Adrenaline spiked in my veins, and my pulse rippled. I breathed hard, the metal hot against my bare shoulders. My heartbeat thudded, and blood coursed through my body, awakening my muscles, aching my flesh alive for action. This was what we did best, and I loved it.

Joey pushed his hat back, blond hair glowing white in the

floodlights, and skewered me on that wicked, unsettling smile. My heart fluttered, drawn and repulsed. He'd always gotten off on danger. One thing we had in common.

With a deft, sexy flick of his fingers, he sent a terse message and flipped his phone away. He plucked up his cane from where he'd leaned it against the steel, and dragged my hand to his lips in a rough, burning kiss. "Find out what's in that container," he murmured, and darted away.

Shock riveted my tendons tight. The container? What about the fight? Why was he keeping me out of it? I bit back a curse. Wormshit Vincent and his lies. If Joey didn't trust me, it'd make killing him that much harder.

Not to mention nowhere near as satisfying.

But I'd no time to think about it now. A gunshot ricocheted, the decibels jolting my head back. Shouts and curses stung my ears, scraping footsteps, slashing wings, and the harsh thud of metal on bone. My heart pumping, I risked a peek. Fabian on the ground, struggling under a cloud of thrashing nightblue wings and limbs, his weapon lying useless on the concrete. A body, limp and bleeding. Two vampires locked in struggle, fangs flashing. Diamond snarling, at bay, facing off Iridium's scything blades. Vincent on his knees astride another guy, slamming his head into the ground over and over again in a rich scarlet spatter. No Sonny. No Joey. Must have taken their personal fight elsewhere.

I sucked in a deep breath and sprinted for the container.

My calves screamed as I ran, my tendons not flexing as they should. I felt slow and sluggish, my muscles creaking. It took an age to reach the container, and when I leapt, I barely made it to the top, my boot heels clanging dangerously on the edge.

My heart tilted, my arms wheeling for balance. My inner ears sloshed, and only inertia kept me upright.

A human could almost do better than that. Christ, I'm never sniffing sparkle again. That stuff really fucks you.

I leapt down the other side, heels crunching as I landed. No one interrupted me. Another gunshot, a screech and a wet sigh, Diamond's crystalmad laugh.

The container was locked, a vertical metal pole sprouting horizontal bars. I grabbed the rusted handle and yanked it open with a screech.

Putrid fleshstink curdled my nose, and I choked. I peered into the darkness, my hand clutched over my mouth.

Pairs of glinting eyes blinked back. Dozens of them. From ceiling to floor.

Diamond's cargo wasn't drugs. It was people. Fae.

My brain clogged, and I stared.

Inside in the dark, the eyes moved. Wet wings flapped, and something snorted, deep and hungry.

Warning clanged dull in my skull. I tripped backwards, but too late. Giggles tore the stinking air apart, and the creatures rushed out.

I stumbled, bodies pushing me over. I whipped my thighs taut and backflipped, but I didn't make it all the way over and slammed into the concrete on one shoulder, the breath smashing from my lungs. Wet bare feet swarmed past me, over me, thudding into my chest, smearing me with blood and piss and slime. I choked and squirmed away.

A steely hand grabbed my hair and yanked so tight, my scalp tore.

I struggled. Flat brown eyes, a hard unforgiving face. "Glad you could make it," growled Sonny Valenti, and dragged me to my feet.

I wriggled, and yowled bloody aneurysm, but my voice broke and his grip held fast. His elbow rammed into my bruised ribs, a crackling maze of pain.

Confusion and the floodlights bloodied my vision. That cry should have blown his ears out. Swiftly, I whipped out a knife and slashed backhanded. Blood splashed. Sonny snarled and grabbed my forearm, mashing the bones together.

Agony ripped up my arm. I screamed, rich with hate and rage and bloody torture, but he just laughed, and the knife clanged from my numb fingers, lost. Panic tore at my pulse. Why couldn't I hurt him?

I didn't get time to think about it. He hurled me headfirst, and I tumbled sprawling onto the wet metal container floor.

Grimy. Stinking. Disgusting. My skin crawled. Dark walls loomed in on me, a smothering cacophony of memory, and my spine tickled from fear that the door would slam shut and I'd be alone in the dark. But I had more pressing things to worry about than my stupid phobia of small spaces. I scrabbled for another knife, trying to get my clumsy legs under me, but Sonny kicked me hard in the guts and I slumped like a wet sack, retching, my weapon spinning away.

His shadow loomed over me, and the stink of shit and vomit made me retch again. He grabbed my hair and yanked my head back, leering. "Payback, bitch. Shoulda done me when ya had the chance. What, no singing pretty songs for me this time?"

"Fuck you." Spit and blood splashed from my mouth. First words that came to me. No time for eloquent comebacks.

He yanked out his pistol and jammed it against my temple, bruising me. "Pity we don't have time."

My pulse jibbered. He cocked the weapon, and the clunk echoed deep in my skull. Mad melody scrambled like panicked rats in my chest, chords building, and I sucked in a deep breath and sang ghastly murder.

Sound erupted from my lips, and died.

Low. Breathy. Useless. My rippling soprano ruined. No force, no shrill operatic vibrato. No magic in that weak human sound.

For the first time, real fear leached ice deep into my heart.

Sonny laughed, evil. "Then again, maybe I got a few minutes. Won't take long, ya horny bitch."

He kicked me in the small of my back. Ache exploded across my kidneys. My face smacked into the soiled metal. My hair dragged in the muck. I struggled to stand, to get away, but my treacherous magicstarved muscles wouldn't work properly.

He pinned me down, and no matter how I flexed and screeched, I couldn't dislodge him. My blood chilled. I'd kicked a big dent in Sonny's pride the other night. It had humiliated him to the core to get beaten by a girl. I could feel his simmering rage from here, in the burning sweat on his palm as he grabbed the back of my neck and forced me down, brutish strength in his movements as he jammed my thighs apart.

I struggled, my limbs weak and useless. Outside, creatures screeched and giggled and moaned in mayhem, fairy feet dancing around like madmen. No one would hear me. We'd started the fight. Everyone was fair game, but like always, girls were the fairest game of all. He'd rape me. Fuck me. Rub my face in the shit. Get off on my powerlessness.

My heart quailed, but I steeled myself. I'd endured worse, right? I forced a laugh. "See if y'can get it up, cocksucker."

"Shut it, skank." His thick fingers dragged at my leather pants.

Perverse satisfaction giggled in my throat. Those pants were tough, the buckles tight. He'd not get them off me easily. I cackled, phlegm spewing from my lips. "Can't even get into a girl's pants. You're a joke."

Metal scratched, and suddenly my belt popped apart. My lost knife clattered as he tossed it aside. He wrenched at my waistband, and my buttons ripped open at the front. Warm air caressed my bare skin at the top of my bottom.

Sweat dribbled cold on my belly.

Fuck.

He laughed and jammed the pistol into the back of my neck again. I wriggled, but only worked my pants down farther. I kicked, lashing out with my steel-cored heels, but I couldn't connect. Sickness gripped my stomach tight. My heart galloped. This was going to happen, and there wasn't a damn thing I could do. He'd rape me, and then he'd probably kill me. Bullet in the skull. Bang, you're dead.

Just as things were looking up.

He forced his hand between us, and now his hot bare skin pressed against my butt. He was hard, all right, short and stubby and thick, his sweat and slick liquid sliming my skin. I struggled and yelled and wrenched my muscles tight, but he worked himself between my cheeks, pushing, searching roughly. "This gonna hurt? That snakeass prick's cock so small, you don't even feel it? Feel this, you uppity whore."

He shoved, spearing a sharp ache through my guts. I screamed. My muscles didn't give. He tried again, and I struggled to concentrate, plan, think how to get away, get him off me, anything but what he was doing.

Knife. Had to be here somewhere. His hot breath dampened my shoulder. Dimly I felt the pressure at my neck release a little, the pistol not scraping my vertebrae quite so hard. He was having too much fun humiliating me.

Don't close your eyes, fuckhead. Not for a moment.

Surreptitiously I twisted, wriggled, squirmed my palms along the floor, searching for my discarded weapon.

A sweet sting greeted my fingertips, and relief swamped me cold. I pawed it nearer, and at last my bloody fingers tightened around the handle.

He squirmed, working his way in, and groaned in triumph as he finally found the place he was looking for. "Oh, yeah. You're gonna feel g—owf!"

I slashed backwards with all my depleted strength, and the blade connected.

Flesh caught, and tore, my sweet steel edge slicing effortlessly.

Sonny howled and tumbled off me. The knife yanked from my hand. Gunshot thundered, ripping my ears raw.

My bladder clenched, stabbing heat into my belly, but I didn't die. If you hear the shot, you're safe. That's what they say. The one you don't hear has already killed you.

I scrambled up, wet leather twisting around my thighs. My hair hung stinking, smeared with blood and excrement.

Sonny staggered, clutching his neck, blood spurting between his fingers. He gurgled a curse, and more blood spilled, thick and bright. I'd stabbed him right in the throat. He'd probably bleed out, but the tough son of a bitch was still clawing with crimson hands for his dropped pistol.

Fury burned cool in my throat like mint, and I wanted to jam my steelspiked heel into his face and crush him. But now that I was free, fear crashed in like stormwaves, and my legs trembled though I tried to hold still. He'd nearly fucked me. Nearly killed me.

I bit my lip bloody, but the fleshy crunch between my teeth only made me shudder more, and all I could do was stand there and shake.

Frantically, I tried repeating it, over and again like I used to. Shouldn't care. Should be tougher than that. My body's just flesh. It's not me. Not me.

But this wasn't like surrendering my body for cash or food or drugs or shelter. At least then I was trading it for something. There was nothing in this for me. Just him, making himself feel good with my body.

Some proud female creature deep inside me curled up and wailed, its spirit burned raw. And hatred scorched me black inside like helldirt.

I fumbled to dress, my fingers numb. Rip his face off with my nails. Scrub myself raw. Crawl away and hide. My body shuddered, and hot tears streaked my face. *I should finish the fucker off.* But I couldn't move, couldn't scrabble up my knife and slit his throat, and my weakness ripped my guts raw. Had I gone soft, without my cruel songlady crooning murder in my heart?

A scream burst in my lungs, my voice a ragged ghost. "Just die, you fucking animal, get your—!"

A serpentine black shape scythed the air before me, and hot flesh ripped and splattered.

Sonny choked and crumpled, his throat a swelling scarlet mess, dripping emerald with venom.

"Filthy fucking hands off her," finished Joey, and kicked him in the balls.

Blood and flesh sizzled, and Sonny convulsed, spluttered, and died, his face turning slowly purple. Poisoned blood the color of rotting flesh soaked into his shirt, smoking. Froth spilled from his lips. The fresh stink of his bowels letting go mixed with the stale creature stench, sickening.

I stared, shock still riveting me cold.

Joey was breathing hard, like he'd been running, blond hair stuck to his cheek with sweat. Somewhere, he'd lost his jacket, and his shirt stuck wet to his chest, showing me more of the way his tense muscles moved than I needed to see. His sleeve hung torn around one bloodstained wrist, and venom dripped sparkling emeralds from his curled black claws. Glossy black webs stretched tight between his knuckles, the bones long and elegant like a fairy's, his skin dark and sleek and beautiful.

He whirled, and the momentum shifted his hand back with a wet snap. The snakeskin slid away beneath pale human flesh, the webs folded and crackled away into his fingers, his claws retracted into soft pale fingertips. His eyes glittered like icy jewels. "Can you run?"

"Yeah." My reply was automatic. Never let him see me hurting. I fumbled up my remaining knife—great, I'd lost another one, those things cost me a fortune—and dragged my disgusting hair back, shivering.

He stretched out his hand—his strong, pale human hand—to me. "Come on."

I stared, mesmerized by the pulse in his wrist. Just a smear of pungent venom on his knuckles, a tiny bloodcrust under his nails. That creature, writhing just beneath his skin. What would it look like? What would it feel like? Warm needles of sensation slid into my belly. Wonder. Excitement. Fear. I didn't know which.

My mouth dried. I swallowed, and he grabbed my hand and dragged me out.

12

We ran. Floodlights glared. Bodies scattered the bloodspattered tarmac, weapons and clothes discarded. I didn't see Vincent or Iridium. I recognized Fabian Valenti, slumped in his dark suit on the concrete with blood pooling from his skull, eyes rolled back, face even more vacant than usual. A cackle of baby fairies, escapees from that mysterious crate, licked giggling at the scarlet spill, their little wings flitting in delight.

Go to hell, asshole. You and your rapist cousin. Hope it hurt.

I didn't have time to see who else. Somewhere, I heard Diamond's wind chime chuckle coming closer. A few dirty fairies still hung giggling like monkeys on the crane, spitting and flinging debris at us. Joey tugged me around a corner, and we sprinted up a dark alley between container stacks.

My hand slipped from his, the better to run, and as I stretched my legs, the panicked shudder in my muscles at last began to ease, replaced by the warm thrill of fight and flight. My tall heels felt good under my feet, their strength pressing up into my calves. Warm clean air filled my nostrils, swelled in my lungs, fingered through my dirty hair. Blood pumped sweet chemical excitement through my body. My sweat ran, cleansing, fresh, ridding me at last of Sonny's vile smell and hot clammy hands and disgusting words.

Diamond's insane giggle lilted after us, and his tinkling

light step echoed in the metal corridors. "Run, shitlickers, 'cause ya can't hide."

Shadows thudded like hammers. My loose pants flapped on my belly, and strange weakness shrank my muscles. Struggle as I might, I couldn't run fast enough to keep up with him. My eyes struggled to adjust, blackness hemming me in. Joey's night senses were far superior to mine. I faltered, panting, the hungry air both a comfort and a threat in my lungs. "Wait. I can't see."

"Peace." He dragged me into a shadowy crevice to hide. Tall containers, rust stinging my nose, soft green venom luminescent on his sleeve. He was breathing hard. So was I. Our bodies pressed together, warm and alive, and I jerked back, but metal clanged my skull and scraped my shoulder blades.

Only half a step I could move. Only an inch or two keeping us apart. Nowhere to run.

My pulse clattered, too swift. Small dark space. Alone, in the dark, with him. My song ruptured, my reflexes sick and sore.

And now I owed him a goddamn favor.

He touched a light finger to my lips, warning me to keep quiet.

Inside, I squirmed. I tried to control my breathing, banish that bewitching minty scent from my mouth, but my lungs ached for air and I couldn't help gulping it in. My thoughts tumbled. Sonny was probably already a goner, but Joey didn't know that when he attacked. He'd protected my tarnished honor, killed to save me pain and degradation. Probably saved my life. Again.

And Sonny was Ange Valenti's favorite cousin. Joey had just made both of us fair game to save me.

Anger welled up like acid in my blood. Why did the bastard do it? Why keep up the façade? Why put his precious family business in danger just to trick me?

And what if he found out I was sick and couldn't fight? Surely he'd cut me loose, and I'd never get near him again.

Not that it mattered. If Diamond found us, we were both

surely dead, and then I'd never get breakfast tomorrow, let alone my revenge.

Ordinarily, I could sing blackness to hide us. I didn't dare try.

Glassy feet clanged on metal as Diamond landed atop a container nearby. Shadows flitted over us as his wings caught the light. "Fine," he called. "Piss off, if you're too scaredified to fight. I got drinking to do. Next time I see you, you're rat meat. Both of ya." Wind whistled as he flew away.

Silence. Just Joey breathing, my heartbeat, the sticky sound as I swallowed.

A trick? Maybe. Hot dry shadows closed in like smoke. Sweat stung my skin, and my throat parched. *Now what?*

"You okay? He hurt you?" Joey still gripped my arm tight, claws quivering. His murmur caressed my face, minty and warm, barely audible but strained with tension.

Automatically I shook my head, though my bruises still stung and the horrid slide of Sonny's skin on mine stirred my guts sick.

Joey banged his forehead on the metal next to my ear, his jaw quivering tight. I could tell he wanted to slam it harder. His body shuddered with stress, barely controlled, and his sibilants hissed. "Christ, I'd kill the fucker again if I could. You sure?"

His whisper slid warm into my hair, and bumps stung my scalp. I swallowed and forced myself to relax, though my hands trembled. My knife beckoned warm, tight against my ribs where my heartbeat thudded.

This was my chance. Jammed between two metal walls, nowhere for him to hide. Distract him, get him just a little closer. He drops his guard for a second too long, and . . .

My stomach wriggled. I licked my lips to make them shine, and flickered my gaze shyly to his and away again. "Umm. I'm a little shook up. C-can you just hold me?"

He ran his teeth over his bottom lip. Let my wrist go. "Look. You know I don't expect you to put up with . . . that kind of thing. Right?"

Scorn blackened my heart. Coward. I knew he wanted to

touch me, just to prove I belonged to him, even if he pretended otherwise. He didn't care what happened to me, but what Sonny did really chewed at Joey's pride. He wanted to kiss me raw, strip me naked, lick me clean inside and out and wipe off all trace of another man's touch so he could own me again.

I shivered, hot and icy at the same time. *Well, come on, then, you lying bastard. See what happens.*

Deliberately, I caressed his cheek, a seductive suggestion, tilting his face toward mine. God, his hair smelled fantastic, warm and minty, fresh like pine. Fucking prick. "You pretending you didn't hear, or what?"

He closed his eyes and let me bring him nearer. His cheek brushed mine, and he drew in a soft gasp. "What are you doing?"

I pressed closer, brushing my breasts seductively against him, finding his hands and sliding them onto my bare midriff. "You mean this?"

Unease licked me cold. I'd tried to inject some sly magical persuasion into my voice, but all that came out was a husky whisper. But it didn't matter. It did the job.

Green flame ignited deep in his eyes. His muscles jerked tight, and his hands quivered on my waist, barely daring to move. Like he couldn't help it, his lips crept into my hair, and his breath caressed my bare shoulder, hot and strained with temptation. "Mina, don't—"

"And this?" I traced tempting fingertips over his collarbone, down over hard shifting skin, inside his shirt. Dark muscle roiled under my touch, and he jumped. Christ, he was on edge tonight. Good for me. Bad for him.

His grip tightened on my waist, and he shuddered. "Jesus. Don't do th . . . Oh, fuck it." And he crushed me hard against the metal wall, wrapped his fingers in my hair, and brought his mouth down on mine.

Triumph spread warm on my heart, and I wanted to laugh, but his kiss tore the breath from my throat.

Dizzy. Intoxicating. Dangerous. I tried to hold my breath, pull away, change my mind, but I gasped, and inhaled him, and my treacherous senses exploded.

His hot mintleaf taste, not sweet but burning, venom's bright tang on my tongue. My wits shattered under an onslaught of frustrated desire. Diamond might hear us. I didn't care. I forgot my weapon. I forgot thinking. There was only this long-buried need, erupting inside me like a trembling volcano. "Oh. Fuck. Umm . . ."

"Don't talk. Just kiss me." He cupped my cheek and pushed my mouth open with his thumb, and his kiss was like sex, thrusting deep and hard with nothing left to the imagination. Heat splashed through my belly, scorching deep inside with delight and anticipation and five long years of shivering denial.

No time. No options. Every sensible shred in my brain screamed at me to run.

But my body growled with hunger, and my heart trembled, and I grabbed his hair and kissed him back.

Our mouths met, molded, hot and wet and ravenous with every simmering impulse we'd ever denied. He pressed into me, lithe and warm, serpentine muscles alive just beneath his skin. My breasts swelled against his chest, and desperate shivers pleasured my skin like a hot shower, rippling deep between my legs. My pulse threatened to burst my veins. I had shit in my hair, greasy fingerprints on my skin, the echo of a violent man's breath on the back of my neck, and all I cared about was Joey's mouth on mine, his hard-muscled body tempting me to touch.

He didn't tease me or test me or wait to see what I liked. He ravished me, more than I'd ever felt from him before, and the hot demanding scent of his pulse made me drunk.

My knees shimmied, weak. With no magic, how could I fight this? I clutched at his shirt, trying to keep some distance, but he fought for my wrists and pinned them to the wall at my sides, too strong for me to escape even if I'd wanted to. His lips tortured mine, his tongue demanding my surrender.

And I gave it, overcome by some twisted compulsion for belonging that melted my resolve. I swallowed, letting him fill me, his rich taste and thrilling sensation thrashing hot exhilaration in my blood. I was starving, and at last he fed me, every movement of his body and rough caress of his lips a feast.

Stupid, to imagine I could control this. That I could lead him only where I wanted to go and no further.

I kissed him harder, desperate. His soft groan filled my mouth, and his tongue shifted, wrapping long and sensitive on mine, teasing tingling pleasure from me that spread all the way to my nipples. The dangerous sensation of that muscle *changing* spiked moist desire deep into my sex, and I couldn't help but groan, too.

He nudged my chin up to spread hot kisses on my throat, and it felt so good, I gasped. Shivering danger sparked in my belly. Too tense. Too ready to break. The flesh throbbed between my legs, making me wet and swollen. If he touched me there, or sucked my nipple into his mouth, I'd probably come.

Fuck.

He'd spotted my attack from a mile away. And now I'd lost control. So very hard, not to revel in this fever-rich desire. Not to moan and shiver and beg for more.

Truth burned ragged holes in my conviction, and I wanted to scream. I couldn't deny this, no matter how my shredded wits screeched at me to fumble for my weapon and slit his lying throat. He made me feel alive. Special. Needed. Worth something, in this dirty world that despised me.

Anger mixed a scorching cocktail in my already heated blood. Just for that deception, he deserved to die.

"Mina." God, I loved it when he whispered my name. His words bruised my lips between kissing, like he couldn't stop. I didn't want him to stop. The risk he took even to make a sound exhilarated me. "I can't get you out of my head. I dream about doing dirty things to you. I feel you under my skin, every moment of every night, and it's not enough. I can't have you. I can't ignore you. I only want you more."

Shock and hot emotion swelled my heart sore. Finally, an admission that he wanted me, too, that I affected him beyond business concerns, that he cared when I got hurt. Those words I'd waited so long to hear him say dripped over my skin like warm poison.

So tempting, to swallow that dangerous nectar. Surrender my senses to that sweet opium lie, and die happy.

But I couldn't. I daren't. Wrong, wrong, wrong. My mind scrabbled for reason, and I made some incoherent sound into his mouth.

He pulled my hand between us, pressing my palm against his swollen sex. My skin scorched, and by themselves my fingers curled and stroked, caressing him. Not weird and twisted like a fairy. Just long and straight and perfect. How hard he was for me, a demanding desire that couldn't lie. His hot menthol scent maddened me, and all I could remember was how much I wanted him naked, so I could open myself beneath him and make us one, slide this tight hard cock deep into me where it belonged, lure that sleek beautiful creature from inside him and let him pleasure me until we died.

He shuddered and caught my bottom lip between his teeth, teasing me. His claws grew and dug sweetly into my wrists, and venomsting pierced my skin. My pulse throbbed, the tiny cuts swelling tight and hot, and I groaned at rawblind sensation, a whole lot similar to what was happening between my legs, where he pressed his thigh so wonderfully tight, teasing dark and forbidden pleasure deep into my sex.

I groaned, helpless, my breath lost. God, he knew exactly what he was doing. How did any woman ever resist him? "Don't. Don't tease me."

"Not this time. No more pretending. Tell me you want this. I'll give it to you." He eased my palm against him, stealing another mintscorched kiss, and his hand shifted. His slick fingerwebs enveloped my hand in delicious heat, and need shivered through me like bloodfever. Me and him. Naked. Sex. Now.

He didn't feel like a lying, thieving murderer without conscience. He didn't even feel like an ice-hearted ganglord who cared only for power. He felt like a man, hot and hard and barely controlled. A man who knew what he wanted and took it. And I still burned for him.

Hot steel denial pierced my heart.

No way. This wasn't happening. It couldn't be.

A cry warbled in my throat, but my magical voice still eluded me. I fought him, twisting my wrists, and tore my mouth away though nothing would have pleased my body more than to let him have his way. My muscles shuddered weakly. I couldn't break free. Fear wrenched an impotent gasp from my throat. "No. Stop it. Let me go!"

His body stiffened. He closed his eyes, and slowly his grip on my wrists relaxed.

I wriggled away, my burning skin suddenly cold and bereft.

He struggled to regulate his breath, and with a grimace he slammed his forehead against the metal where I'd been, wet blond hair sticking. Weird neon sweat glowed on his face, and along his cheekbones and in his throat, darkness writhed beneath his skin. He didn't lift his head, but his hot gaze followed me, unblinking, and slowly, with an effort that gritted his teeth, he folded his fingerwebs away.

My limbs still ached with desire, and sick remorse clutched my heart.

Even after all he'd done to me, I still cared that I'd hurt him.

Rabid self-disgust ripped my stomach like claws, and before he could speak—or I could change my mind—I ran.

13

Joey smacks his head into the metal, and the bright agony slithers his black skin away. She's too much. Too close. Far too mesmerizing, like a poison that tunnels his vision and warps his senses so they seek only her.

And now she's gone.

Fleeing the monster.

Memory of her breathless surrender maddens him. He crunches green-stained claws hard on the steel, but the bright pain does nothing to cool his desire. For just a moment, she felt it, too. He's sure of it. She wants him, sure as her mouth opened eagerly under his and her touch molded to him and her breath sighed helpless and needy onto his tongue.

And with a careless shift, he killed her desire, as swiftly and efficiently as if he'd sliced open her throat.

He bangs his head again, fighting the black reptile craving to slither and spit and splash the walls with venom. The serpent inside him roils in fury, stretching his human skin until it stings. Cold and hot streams mix hissing in his blood, so infuriating, he itches to tear his skin off in ragged strips and let the horrid stuff pour out.

Sickness chews his guts. He's rarely felt the hatred like this. Never burned so badly to hack his own poisoned flesh apart. She's at least curious about his human shape, if not attracted. Girls like power. But as soon as the serpent gets too close, she runs.

He disgusts her, and no doubt her desire turns her disgust on herself. Perfect.

If she'd wanted to kill him, she'd had her chance and wasted it. Did she rat on him? He doesn't care. All he knows is that seeing her bruised and bloody at Sonny's hands ran white-hot human fury through his cold snake veins, that her courage makes him weak, that kissing her warm full lips makes him feel alive.

Makes him care for something other than victory.

Where's the fucking sense in that? Only victory lasts. Everything else fades. Even the heat of her kiss, now just a toxic memory.

He scrapes shaking claws through his hair, over and over, willing the desperate ache in his cock to fade. There's something wrong with her magic, something that left her vulnerable to Sonny's crude violence and would have done the same for him, let him take her, hurt her, break her.

But the thought of hurting her jabs cold needles into his lust, ruining it. He remembers Ivy's cruel threat—*make her like you made me*—and iceblack rage thins his blood. If Ivy's hurt her . . .

His sinuses buzz. He whirls, snapping out one elongating black hand, and his forearm smacks hard into hot damp flesh. His claws spring longer, and his wet black flipper rakes a fevered throat.

Vincent chokes, sharp teeth snapping in fury.

Joey rams him back into the metal wall. "What the fuck's wrong with you?"

Vincent snarls, and blood shines on his lips, running over his chin and onto his unshaven throat. It's not just vomit. It's in his hair, under his nails, crusted on the golden chains around his neck.

Joey's blood slides cold. He doesn't have time for this in-fighting shit. If Ivy's put a curse on Mina, he has to stop her before Mina walks into a trap. Any danger she's in is his fault.

He should be after her, watching her, making sure she's safe. . . .

He gnashes cold teeth and jams his knee into Vincent's guts, making him retch bloody spit. *That's fucking stupid.*

It's backwards.

Forget her.

The old determination calms him like a soft breeze. Family is everything. Power—and hence safety—is the only thing that matters. Mina is nothing. Just a brave, talented, compassionate girl who'll never love a monster.

And where the fuck did that word come from?

Anger makes him hard all over again, and everything seems right once more.

He gives a twisted grin and slams Vincent's skull back into the metal once more for emphasis. "Don't ever try to creep up on me, kid. I can taste your grotty little thoughts from across the street."

Vincent squirms, his nose frothing crimson. "Get your scaly mitts off me."

Joey's serpent senses swell. Fleshy stink tainted with sharp virusfever, the bloody taste of lust. He grimaces. "Charming. What the fuck you doing, getting yourself infected? Trying to impress me?"

He tightens glossy webs around Vincent's throat, sliding venomtipped claws out another inch. The smell of shift tweaks in his mouth, dry and reptilian and disgusting, and seductive images flash of Mina, shrinking away from him, her pretty red lips quivering. But Vincent stinks worse, of stale meat and blood. "Think you can challenge me? You're lucky the bloodsuckers didn't kill you."

"You'd like that, wouldn't ya?" Vincent grabs at Joey's arm, trying to wrestle him off, but his infant vampire strength isn't enough.

Joey springs out his own fangs, and snakes like a whip to within an inch of Vincent's nose. His vision dims, serpent-sense taking over, his body suddenly awash with taste and vibration and hunger. "I'm telling you nice, just this once. Don't piss me off. We can be friends. Just let it lie."

But his forked tongue rasps with Vincent's diseased breath, the blood-engorged virus particles hitting the atmosphere and thrashing themselves to death. His sinuses vibrate with the stink of bloody vampire sweat, and he knows this isn't over. If Vincent lives long enough to gain his full strength, Joey's got a problem.

Vincent snarls. "I've let it lie long enough. Time we had this out."

"Don't be a fuckwad. Come back when you're grown up." Consonants lisp in Joey's distorted mouth. Evilcold snake strength washes dark delight into his roiling muscles, and he wrenches Vincent away from the wall and throws him to the ground.

Blood splashes crimson and blue on the concrete, remnants of Vincent's last bite. He crawls to all fours, snarling, and his bloodshot brown eyes gleam like jewels, artificially bright. "You don't do that to me anymore. I got special. Iridium said so. No one ignores me now."

Joey shifts his other hand with a hot squelch, and venom splatters the pavement. Toxin burns inside him, a vile hate-want cocktail, and his tongue flickers greedily in hot night air. Taste. Drink. Explore.

Delicious sensory pleasure slides over him, rich with guilt and disgust, and the desire to change grips him tight like a dead lover's flesh, beautiful and loathsome at the same time. "I'll do whatever the fuck I want. You're not stronger than me yet."

"But I will be." Vincent grins, cunning, and the rampant virus crunches his fangs a fraction longer, slicing his bottom lip bloody. "And I'm gonna rip your paranoid fucking honor out and chew it up."

Joey's blood shimmers bright. It's true. If he doesn't polish Vincent off now, he'll be sorry. But he fights the urge to snap to serpent and strike. Vincent is a cocky little asshole, but he's tough, and Joey needs all the friends he can get. "Don't belittle my honor, you ungrateful shitworm. It's my honor that keeps us alive."

"Whatever."

Joey spits, venom and bile. "Think you can survive without me? Sonny and Fabian are dead. Ange Valenti's favorite cousins. He'll hunt your bloodfevered ass down and snap you in half."

"Iridium did Fabian. And you killed Sonny, not me."

"Ange doesn't know that. You think Diamond gives a damn which of us he gets first?"

Vincent chuckles, mad. "Whatever. I seen what you done to Mina. Can't help going serpent on her, can you?"

"Keep her the fuck out of it." The vehemence of his own words snaps Joey cold.

"She practically pukes at the sight of you. But girls like a bit of vampire cock. You think she's not ripe for the taking? You think if I get her on my side, the others won't follow?"

Joey's tailbone twitches, and he longs to slash out his spiked serpent tail and rip Vincent's eyeballs out. But he can't kill Vincent for a few insults. He won't.

He forces a sarcastic laugh. "The fever's turned your mind. It happens. Ever watched someone die of bloodfever, Vincent? Blood fills up your eyeballs. Runs from your ears. Dribbles out your ass. You shit rotten flesh and vomit up your own melted guts. Hurts like a motherfucker, so I've heard."

Vincent's infant fangs glint, a bloody grin. "I ain't dying. Mina's already tempted. Don't close your eyes, Joey. Don't turn your back. Not for an instant."

Her name's sweet chime on Vincent's lips swells Joey's sinuses alive with envy and rage.

But it's not worth his conscience. Nothing is. Not even her.

He grips his elbows, wrapping cold snakeflesh tight, and lets Vincent limp away.

14

I didn't stop running until I reached Docklands, where the football stadium's white saddle roof loomed cold and dark and saltwater stink gave way to warm summer city smells of smoke, parched concrete, dust. Beyond, the sweeping neon arch of the Westgate Bridge gleamed, dotted scarlet with late-night traffic, headed for distant suburbs and the coast, where three million people didn't give a rat's ass about gang wars or murders or dockside ambushes gone awry.

I crumpled against a poster-ripped wall, choking for breath beneath a glaring orange streetlight, and my legs buckled. My muscles screamed for rest, but the stretching confusion and agony in my mind swallowed all my attention.

He was too strong. Too forceful. Too iron-willed. Without my magic, I'd never overpower him. Until I purged this sick yearning for his regard—and yeah, okay, his body—I'd never be able to go through with my plan.

And until I killed him, I'd never be free.

I leaned forward, hands on knees, dragging in big gulps of hot midnight air.

Never mind that I liked it when he touched me. That I could still feel him now, his tongue demanding in my mouth, the creature fighting beneath his skin, the way he offered himself to me like I'd left him no other choice.

A hotted-up muscle car cruised past, paintwork shining black, and a crude wolf whistle sailed out amidst drunk male laughter. I wailed a skin-rotting curse at them, but my voice came out scratchy and sore, and no magic thrilled my blood.

I struggled upright, my galloping heart easing at last, and I dragged my hair from my face and breathed deep. I'd fucked up. Joey had caught me off guard, I could admit that. I hadn't thought my plan through, and I'd jumped in before I was ready.

But I hadn't given myself away. Right?

He might realize all wasn't right with my magic, but he'd no reason to suspect my motives. If that fight with Diamond was a test, I'd surely passed it.

But I needed my magic back. My voice, my reflexes, my strength. And I needed to distance myself, remember his lies, forget how I'd craved him. Even find another guy, who I could tease into courting me like I mattered. Get seriously laid, and erase Joey from my dreams forever.

I snickered, trying to recover my reluctant sense of humor. Vincent was up for it. Maybe I'd give him a call.

But the idea just made me shudder.

Resolve pulled my spine straight, and I unzipped my phone and called Cobalt again. The rings buzzed dully in my ear, four, five, six, but he didn't answer.

I frowned as I ended the call, and glanced at the time on my glowing white screen. Just before one. Early for him. Maybe he was in the club and couldn't hear the phone. Maybe I'd embarrassed him last night, and he was ignoring me.

Maybe something else.

I swallowed, dry. I couldn't deny it. Something weird happened last night, beyond sly fairy nuance or memory magic's unpredictability. Maybe Cobalt wasn't okay.

My pulse clanged in alarm, and I couldn't shut it up. I really needed him to be okay. To explain what the fuck had happened, and get me my voice back before I lost everything.

I tucked my phone away. I knew where he lived, a dirty apartment block in the city. It wasn't far. I'd start there, and if he wasn't home, I'd search the clubs until I found him, and I wouldn't rest until he'd told me what was going on.

The solid comfort of a plan settled in my stomach like a good meal, and I stretched my aching calves and started walking.

Twenty minutes later, I reached his broken apartment block, jammed in between a shining new glass-fronted skyscraper and an Irish pub. I ducked down the alley, where empty silver kegs stacked three high against the spraypainted wall in the stink of stale beer and vomit. The pub was still open, and a creaky hillbilly song drifted from the open windows onto the street, something involving manic banjos, a wailing violin, and a rusty-voiced singer harping on about his poor ole yellow dog.

Next to the rows of green garbage bins, a drunken fairy sprawled on his tummy, pointy yellow feet kicked up and blue dragonfly wings fluttering lazy eddies in the dust. He warbled happily along with the music and tied knots in his long white hair with dirty fingers. He saw me and waved grandly, dust smudging his curled yellow nose. "No pumpkins left, sweetie. Come back tomorrow."

"Right. Thanks for the tip." I skipped up two floors, my boots clanging on the rusty fire stairs. Hamburger wrappers and crushed drink cans littered the metalmesh landing, and it shed dirt and rust under my feet. In the corner, a smelly black spriggan in a trench coat pissed crooked shapes onto the wall, swaying on drunken feet, and the bright puddle dripped through the slats onto the ground. Sourness wrinkled my nose. Charming. If Cobalt made much cash in his trade, he sure wasn't spending it on rent.

I rapped on his heat-warped plywood door, the chipped paint long faded, brighter where the number had fallen off. "Get up, ya lazyfae sod—"

Creak.

The door swung ajar. Too far for the chain to be on.

Inside, it lay dark.

Cold insect feet crawled over my skin. I glanced left and right. Doors sat silent and dark. No lightcracks leaked onto the landing to betray someone awake inside. Dead vinestalks hung limply on the rusted balcony in breezeless heat. Some-where a possum snorted and rustled. No stairwell lighting. No security. No CCTV.

Slowly, I pushed the door open. No sound, bar the ragged brush of wood on carpet. I reached around the doorframe. Fumbled for the switch. Flipped on the light.

The shadow-thing in the doorway leapt.

My stomach tumbled. I tripped, jumping for my weapon, and the shadow did, too.

Fuck. What kind of faux-sadistic fairy idiot plasters a mirror to the wall opposite the door?

I choked a laugh and sucked in a breath to ease my racing pulse as I slipped the knife back into its case. "Jesus, C, you scared me shitless."

No answer.

I stepped into the room. Roasted coffee teased my nose, reminding me how hungry I was, and my mouth watered. Orange light shed dimly from a single bulb. Television, pile of blue suede beanbags, ripped magazines piled waist high in the corner. Carpet threadbare and dusty. Empty glass vials scattered on the table amongst chocolate bar wrappers, rain-bow sparkle remnants catching the light.

I walked in farther. "Cobalt? It's me. Sorry to barge in, but I—"

Behind the beanbags, long midnightblue hair curled onto the carpet.

I scrambled to my knees at his side, turning his pale face toward me. His limbs lay limp, his black velvet wings crushed beneath him. I stroked his cold cheek, his pointy chin sharp in my palm. "C? You good?"

But he wasn't.

His head lolled in my hands at a crazy angle, his pretty mouth slack. He still wore the same inkstained shirt and jeans, but those deep blue eyes stared, glazed gray. I pressed my ear to his chest. No breath. I sniffed, searching. No lem-onscent of sparkle on his lips. I felt under his chin for pulse. Gone. Cold.

Dead.

I swallowed, my eyes burning. Gently, I laid his cheek on the carpet. Arranged that wonderful blue hair in a knot the way he liked it. Closed his dulled eyes, those lashes feather-light on my fingertips for the last time. I couldn't get his head to lie straight. My hands shook in his hair. Already his bright faecolors faded, drained. His indigo essence smeared dull and dusty on my hands, and his earthy smell accused me.

No blood. No bruises. He didn't look like it hurt. Just dead. And I never had the chance to tell him I was sorry.

Tears muddied my vision, and I wiped them viciously away. Like he gave a damn about that now, after someone broke his fucking neck.

Softly, I stroked his hair back one more time and let him be. *Sorry, C. I liked you more than you'll know.*

I stretched to my feet, guilt gnawing at my bones. Cobalt wasn't a good boy. Dozens of people would want a piece of him. But I couldn't kill the itch that his death was somehow my fault.

A lot of eyes had watched me last night. Joey, Vincent, Diamond, who the fuck knew who else. I'd taken Cobalt home in full public view. Everyone saw us leave together. And less than a day later . . .

I flushed. Sure. Like I was that important. *Get over yourself, Mina. No one gives a rotting spit what you do, or who you do it with.*

But no time to gawk and wonder. Anyone could've seen me come in here. If there'd been a fight, someone might've called the cops already, and I could no longer count on Joey's influence to extract me from a jam.

Swiftly, I rummaged through the glassware on the bench. All empty, crusted with crystals like coral, blue and green and yellow. I bent to search his pockets, trying not to look at his face. My crumpled cash—all he had—his phone showing four missed calls, a smudged makeup mirror still dusted with golden glitter. Nothing else. A quick search of the kitchen and the bedroom revealed the same. Nothing. Not a dealing quantity of illicit substance in sight. Even the cops couldn't bust this place.

If Cobalt had stolen my magic, he'd already gotten rid of it.

I strode out into the lounge room, frustrated. Something crunched beneath my boot, and I looked down.

Glass.

Colored shards, wickedly sharp, glinting purple and green and yellow like oil on water.

I leaned over and plucked one up. It glittered as I turned it, and puffed a faint pink halo. The dust settled on my hand, glimmering, and rich rosescent drifted.

I glanced around, my skin cold with the memory of smooth fairy fingers, the crisp shatter of wings. Window intact, dirty ashtray on the dresser in one piece. Nothing broken. And the shards were too big to be sparkleglass.

I let the fragment drop, and it pricked my finger as it fell. Crimson oozed, and I shook it away.

I grabbed Cobalt's phone and scrolled through the missed calls. All four from me. I flicked to the call records, his garish pink background glaring in my eyes, and my heart flipped a tiny somersault.

He'd called Diamond last night. At 3:47 A.M. Right after I'd passed out.

Probably from my fucking living room, while I lay there unconscious.

Diamond's words from last night floated back to me, and suddenly the entire evening made a lot more sense. Cobalt, texting as I walked up. Diamond's little taunts. *Actu-mally, I was looking for you. Just a pinch more rat-icality.*

Damn it. Cobalt had sold me out. Stolen my magic and handed it over so Diamond could blackmail me. *Hope it was fucking worth it, C, you dumb fairy twit.*

Unwilling tears prickled my eyes, and I forced them back, digging into my focusing mantra. *Cold. Iron. No fear. No sympathy. Don't let them get to your heart.*

Icy calm threaded my veins, and I set my teeth deliberately. The stinky glass-ass prick wanted my attention. Well, now he had it. As for what else he wanted . . . well, last night betraying Joey had been out of the question.

But things had changed.

My belly warmed. I'd do whatever it took. Tell Diamond whatever he wanted. Make him give me my magic back, and then Joey's tricky serpent ass would be mine. And just before I killed him, I'd tell him I'd turned. Twist the knife further. Chew just one more bleeding piece out of his heart.

I'd work for Diamond if he asked me to. What the fuck did I care? Nothing left for me with DiLuca anymore.

I stabbed the number and called, and as it rang, my stomach crawled cold, but I ignored the discomfort. Nothing Joey hated worse than a traitor.

I'd always hated liars, too. Too late to get precious about it now.

Diamond's giggle sparkled on the line. "Zombie-phone. Back from the dead. Uncanny. Who's this? No, no, let me guess—"

"Cut the shit." I clutched the phone tightly, struggling to even my voice. "I know you've got my spell. Tell me what you want."

Craftiness slicked into his tone like silver. "Ooh, I love it when you talk dirty. Better we discussify in person, doncha think?"

My spine tickled. I wanted to spin around, scan for enemies, put my back to the wall. "When?"

"Now, of course. You got something better to do?"

"Where?"

Claws slithered into my hair.

I jerked back, dropping the handset, and collided with warm glass.

Muscled arms folded around me, pressing me against his body, and his hot crystal chuckle teased my shoulder. "Hello, bluebell."

Bumps needled my skin. My breath squeezed tight. His rosy scent filtered strong and thick, and I cursed. Why didn't I notice him coming? My ears were shot, but that didn't mean I couldn't pay attention. I could even see us in the mirror now, muscles bulging and veins glittering scarlet in his crystalline arms, his glowing wings pulsing nectarine shadows on the floor, the wicked strawberry glint of his eyes, his sharp roseglass chin on my shoulder.

I sucked in a breath, forced my voice even. My pulse thumped, steadying me. I shrugged in his embrace, loosening my arms. "What, did you follow me from the docks?"

"Didn't need to. Anyone ever mention you feel great?"

"Pretty fucking clever, aren't you?" I twisted my elbow in tight to my side. Slowly eased my hand toward my knife.

Diamond cuddled me against him, his fiberoptic hair glittering over my shoulder. His hard body slid warm against my back. "Glad you think so. Smell great, too, when you're frightened. All salty and delicio-mous. You're a sexy lady."

I twisted the blade free and jabbed it threateningly against his hip. "Gee, thanks. What say you get your clever ass off me before I cut your dick off?"

He sucked in air between his teeth at the sting, but I could feel he was grinning. "Ooh. You got me. Girls in mourning all over town. I'll play nice."

I jabbed harder, twisting. "Who's playing?"

"Ah, ah, watch it. Okay. Keep your face on." He released me, giggling.

I spun around, my weapon bared before me. "Don't you ever touch me again."

"Whatever, bluebell. I win, you lose. You can't sing-ify any cracks in me now." His long hair sparkled as he nonchalantly flicked his wings tidy. His shirt still had blood on it from the fight, dried red stains not his own, the fabric claw-torn over ripped glass muscles.

He hopped lightly over Cobalt's body and flopped on his belly into the beanbag, tangling his feet up behind him like a kid and draping his chin on his hands. He rubbed glassy wings together softly. Veins pulsed like violet neon inside them, shedding glitterbright halos in the dim orange glow. "So. What can you do me for?"

I clenched my fingers tighter around the knife. "My spells. Cobalt took them. Where are they?"

Diamond clicked his tongue. "You first. Tell me how I can kill Joey."

I laughed, harsh. "You've used up your ammo for that one, Diamond. You promised you'd tell me about my mother—"

"And now you know." His glittery smile chilled me.

I shivered. I hadn't forgotten his threat to turn me into rat meat. "But not from you."

"Irrelev-a-ment. How?"

More laughter choked me, sick. "You've got to be kidding. No deal. Sorry. I'll figure it out for myself." And I spun away, frustration hacking at my nerves.

With a scythe of wings, he darted over my head. The door slammed shut. My hair dragged back in warm rosy breeze, and I toppled, my back thudding into the wall. My knife jerked from my grip and dropped, useless.

He plastered his hand over my mouth, holding me in place with strong thighs.

My muscles juddered in protest. I struggled, but he was too strong, and frustration gabbled uselessly in my limbs. Damn it. Without my magic, I was helpless. Again.

I shivered. Was this how human women felt? Afraid all the time? Overpowered, vulnerable, surrounded by men who could do whatever they wanted to you?

Well, it fucking sucked. Not me. I'd get my magic back if it killed me. This was no way to live.

His hand tasted sweet and warm, so smooth. His hips ground into mine, and he slammed my head back into the wall, doubling my vision for a second. His glittering glass gaze bored into me like hot needles, and all his charming fairy levity drained away. "I don't like this, okay? This is not my thing. I am not fun-ifying right now. But I want what you've got pretty bad, and don't think I won't do what's needified. I'm not afraid to be unfair. I'm stronger than you now, and I will hurt you like you've never hurt before, Mina."

I wriggled, but he held me. He nipped my earlobe and ground it between his teeth for a second, threatening. The sting shot through into my throat, and his hot whisper made it twinge harder. "Cut you. Bite you. Fuck you. Make you come. Make you scream. Whatever. All same-same to me.

But I will start liking it, Mina, once you scream." His tone softened, and his forehead pressed against mine, almost like he was pleading with me. His eyes glinted richer red. "Neither of us want that. Don't let it come to that. Please."

Ice crackled down my spine, and my blood burned cold. I didn't disbelieve him for an instant.

I'd seen Joey threaten unspeakable things to get his way, his promised acts of cruelty somehow more shocking in that smooth gentle voice, and the unfortunate victims could never be certain he didn't mean every word. Diamond was just as convincing. All the more because he wasn't excited. I could feel his cock against my belly, a warm swelling in his jeans, and he wasn't hard. Well, maybe a little. His breath felt light and even, his heartbeat against my chest only slightly elevated. He didn't get off on threatening me. All business, for the moment. In many ways, he and Joey were alike.

I nodded, barely daring to move.

His grip on my mouth loosened a little. "Your next words help, or I begin. Get it?"

"Mmm-hmm."

He removed his fingers, but didn't release me. "Get-um in his house. How?"

I licked sticky lips, swallowing. I didn't know details. "There's security. He's paranoid. You can't—"

"He live alone?"

I nodded. I'd only ever been in the front room at Joey's place, and never alone with him. I remembered it as dark, warm, glimpses of glass and metal in the shadows. I didn't even know what he did in his spare time. For all I knew, he kept a harem in there.

"Alarm?"

"Yeah."

"What's the code?"

"Jesus, Diamond, I can't—"

"Tell me the fucking code, Mina."

"I don't know it! He doesn't trust me." My face stung warm.

Diamond grinned. "Smart guy."

"Fuck you."

"When you seeing him next?"

"I dunno. Tomorrow."

"What's the plannification? Sneakem-up on me with an elephant gun? Lay a line of birdseed? Drop an anvil on my head?"

"Don't flatter yourself."

"Not helpful like I'd wishified, Mina." He shrugged lightly, wings flashing, and turned away. "I can't give you tasty helpings for nothing."

My hands trembled. Without him, I'd never get my magic back. I grabbed his arm, swiveling him back to me, desperation creeping deep in my bones. "What more d'you want? Huh? I can't see inside his head—"

"Then tell me his secreticality," Diamond hissed, his claws slashing my wrist. "Give me something I can use-ify, Mina. You know him bestest of anyone. Don't pretend you haven't sneakyplotted what you'd do in a fight."

I flushed. Of course I had. Largely eclipsed by what I'd do if I ever had him under me naked. But I'd watched him when he wasn't looking, figured out his secrets. We all did it, in gangland.

Diamond shook me against him. "How do I beat him, Mina? How do I deadify a sneaky black serpent who shifty-heals every wound and clawdrips nasty nerve agent? Tell!"

His claws dug in hard, mincing my flesh where Joey had already cut me. Hot blood trickled over my hand. If I told, I'd be a traitor. A liar. The thing he despised most of all.

Scorn hardened my resolve. He should have thought of that before he tore my heart out and spat on it. Once, I'd have sacrificed anything to protect Joey. But those days were over.

My pulse thudded cold, and I clenched my sticky palm. Grabbed Diamond's hair and dragged him close. Put my lips to his glistening glass ear.

"Salt," I whispered.

Diamond licked his lips, like he tasted my guilt. "Salt?"

The black revenge-beast in my guts licked me warm and slick inside. "Yeah. It clogs his skin, gets in the way. If he can't shift, he can't heal. That's how you kill him."

Hot relish poured over my skin, and pleasure shivered me darkly to imagine Joey's despair when he found out.

But tears burned the back of my nose, and deep in my heart, something warm and tender froze over.

15

Diamond squeezed my arm tighter. "Bullshit. How the fuck does he ever sweat, then?"

"I don't fucking know. Some weird chemical thing. You've seen him glow in the dark. All I know is, it works." Guilt mushroomed sickly in my stomach, and I hated it. Joey had hurt me more than I could ever hurt him. I shouldn't care.

But I did.

Diamond's arm tightened around my waist, and he smiled his warm dark smile. His claws slid from my flesh, and he stroked the cuts absently like he was sorry. "Good girl."

Bile salted my mouth. On the floor, Cobalt's body lay still. One eyelid drooped open, and his glazed eye stared at me, the chilldark accusation of the dead.

My skin shrank cold, and I shoved Diamond away. "I gave you what you wanted. Now give me mine."

Diamond stared at me, accusing. "What you wanna know?"

I couldn't meet his eyes. "Two things. Give me my spell. And how did you know about my mother?"

"I don't have your spell. It's already gone."

My stomach sank. "Where?"

He shrugged. "Your problem. Look for a scarfaced dealer named Ivy. That's all I know."

Memories flashed warm, a golden earthfae lady with a scarred cheek, who kissed my breasts and offered me sparkle.

I gritted my teeth. I'd missed that point totally. "And my mother?"

"No mystificality. Glassfae. Sometimes I see through."

Despair stung my heart. He hadn't really known anything. Just a flash of insight, a fairy trick.

I wiped my eyes and scraped back filthy hair. My body shook with frustration and rage and blind need for punishment. I needed a shower and a long night's sleep. "Fine. Thanks so much. Now get the fuck out." I scowled at him and turned away.

But he folded gentle fingers around my wrist, wrapping me tight. "Mina—"

"I said get off me." My knife was lost. I had no weapon. I couldn't even break his grip.

But he didn't hurt me. He just tilted his head, glittery, his eyes strangely soft. "Look. It doesn't have to be this way. Let's not fight."

"Don't give me th—"

"I meant my speakings at the club. We can use you. I can fixify you something better."

I laughed, my mouth sour. "Oh, sure. This is the 'we can be on the same side' speech? You've got to be kidding me." But chill stung my bones. I'd cut myself off from Joey, my friends, everything I'd ever known. I didn't have anywhere else to go.

Diamond's nose twitched. "So watcha gonna do? Stand there and hate yourself until you bleed?"

My face burned. I yanked my hand back and whirled away, fury rippling my lungs uselessly. "What the hell do you know about it, okay?"

"I know because I've been there." He touched my shoulder, and I resisted, but he forced me back around, gentle but insistent. "I know about self-hatings. About making yourself suffer. Don't stay there too long. It gets . . . ugly."

Sincerity? Jesus. This was getting awkward. But my nerves tickled warm, and I tossed sticky hair from my neck, sweating. "Yeah? Well, maybe you shoulda thought of that before we did our little deal. What the fuck do you care—?"

"My lover broke my heart for a vampire." He fixed me in his berry stare, unforgiving.

I squirmed. "I'm sorry, what?"

"She was beautiful. Outrageous. Got boredified with me, wanted something exotic. I saw the marks, and I hit her. Hard. More than once."

His gaze flickered away, and I realized that for once, he wasn't taunting me. I licked nervous lips. Where was he going with this? "Umm. Okay. That's . . . not real good—"

"How could she? All I'd done was love her, and she betrayed me. With a sickfilthy vampire." He dropped his gaze, and his hair fell over his cheek in a glimmering strawberry halo. His voice died to a glassy whisper. "That made it okay, right? That I punished her? Even made it okay that I liked it? She deservamated it. She's the monster. Not me. Never me."

His words resonated, uncomfortable. "Diamond—"

"I lost her. She's a vampire now. With him. That's what the fuck I care."

I swallowed, dangerous sympathy scraping under my skin. "I'm sorry to hear that. Look—"

"You have to forget it, Mina." He stroked a stray blue lock back over my shoulder. His touch lingered, startling, and his eyes glowed. "Don't let guilt chewify you up. You're better than that."

My throat seized, but somehow I forced a sound. "I . . . I don't know how."

"Then let me helpify." He took my hand and kissed it.

I held a shuddering breath. Just a brush of rosy lips over my palm, but it warmed my heart with a strange mixture of longing and shame. I didn't want to understand him. I'd thought him careless, shallow, cold, just because we weren't on the same side.

But sides meant nothing now.

Awkwardly, I slid my fingers between his. His knuckles were long and too numerous, his skin smooth like warm glass. "How?"

"New friends. New family." His whisper chimed like distant bells, almost nothing. "And me."

Need pulsed inside me, a deep-running current. I didn't have to bear my guilt alone. And I was done with DiLuca. No going back. Might as well start job-hunting now. "No tricks."

"Trickem off. Promise."

For a moment, neither of us moved. Neither spoke.

Slowly, Diamond took my hand. Pushed me gently backwards. Flicked off the light.

My pulse throbbed hard in my throat. Only his silhouette remained, the pulsing glow of fairy veins and the faint pink outline of wings.

We found the bedroom by touch. Dark there, too, warm and scented with dust, the only light Diamond's raspberry aura. I swallowed, nervous. This wasn't right. What was I doing here?

But ugly tension crippled me. My head ached. My heart stung raw with guilt. Maybe this was what I needed.

I took a deep breath and pulled his hands onto my bodice.

He lingered, tracing my curves, and bent to sniff my skin, trailing his mouth over my collarbone, the tops of my breasts. "You taste good, jasmine girl."

His beautiful shining hair trailed featherlight across my shoulder. I inhaled, shivering, my nipples stiff and eager for punishment. "You gonna hurt me?"

"Only if you want." He stroked my hair back and kissed my throat, maddeningly light.

But I could feel him shuddering, holding back. I tugged at his hands, frustrated. "Do it. I want it. Show me how it feels."

His breath tightened. "Mina—"

"You can call me by her name if you want. Show me what you want to do to her. Help me."

His eyes glassed over, hard and rubyred, and he shoved me backwards.

I landed on the rumpled bed, Cobalt's dusty scent a curse. Diamond hopped astride me and yanked my zipper down, spilling my breasts out. I wriggled free of my top and tossed it away. He traced sharp thumbs around my nipples, making them hard. His luminous wings shed pink neon over my damp skin, and I sparkled.

"You're a bad, beautiful girl. But you know that." He planted a hand on either side of my head, his shining hair hiding us. "No wonder your serpent lover hates you. All your kisswanting skin and needing eyes and dirtyred lips and you're bad inside like poison. It's not *shouldn't* want you. *Shouldn't* is such a wormsick excuse. He *can't*. It's against every right thing. He can't, but he does, and it shatters his world. That make you feel good?"

Guilt stung my veins. I wriggled, but he grabbed my hair to hold me still and forced his mouth down to mine.

For a moment I tasted him, strawberries and roses, his tongue tempting on my lips.

Poison spilled into my mouth, weak and watery. Acid remorse burned my insides raw, and I wormed my head aside, flushing. I didn't want intimate. I deserved hard, rough, careless. "Not on the mouth."

"Whatever." He slid downward, raking his mouth over my breasts, and made a throaty warble of desire as he sucked my stiff nipple deep into his mouth.

Sensation dragged along my nerves, sliding deep inside. Flesh swelled hard between my legs, arousal without emotion. He tortured my breasts, sucking them too hard, tingling the tight nubs between sharp teeth and letting them slip from his lips over and over until I moaned and writhed with brute sensory overload. It hurt. I didn't care. My mind was empty, my heart sore and seeking redemption.

I pushed against his mouth, and clawed at his shirt, ripping it open. I dragged my palms over hard-packed fae muscles, so long and smooth and wet with his glittery sweat, down over his waist into his lap. Slowly, I coaxed him hard, stroking, undoing his jeans to slip my hand inside. He felt smooth and warm, like hot glass, molding and swelling in my hand.

Swiftly he found my buttons and jerked my pants down. My boots stopped them coming off, so he dragged those off, too. He pulled into the air on urgent wings and flipped me over onto my knees, raking his claws over my bare back. The sting felt right, my skin afire. He attacked me with sharp wet teeth, nipping the tops of my thighs. "Say yes, bluebell. I don't force."

I trembled. I didn't want it. But I did. "Yes. Do it."

He bit me, hard. The shock tingled deep inside. I groaned, my juice at last seeping out to soothe my rough aching flesh. He parted my thighs and licked my wetness, and my body shuddered and wept in sympathy. My breasts swelled heavy. Tears squeezed from my eyes, and I let them burn.

"That's it. Let it hurt. You'll feel better." His rough whisper was almost tender. He pulled me back onto him, claws stabbing my hips, and pushed his long glassy cock deep inside.

I shuddered and groaned. So hot and hard. I was swollen, aroused for all the wrong reasons, and it felt just like the violation I wanted it to be. Black satisfaction squirmed hot in my belly. He thrust in again, harder, and sensation rippled inside me, desperate for closure. I swallowed, and lifted my head. "That all you got?"

He snarled and gripped my hair, yanking my head back. I gasped. It hurt. I wanted it. I pressed back against him, letting him use me like I used him. He bent over me, molding himself against my back, and forced even deeper inside me, his fairystrange shape not quite right. It bruised, and I cried out, but he squirmed his arm around my hips and did it again.

He scratched my ear with his teeth, blood stinging hot, and when I moaned, he bit me harder. "Like it? This is what you do to him. Shut up and take it."

And I did. Sensation speared inside me, not agonizing but desperate, and my flesh reacted with a rippling shudder. He pressed powerfully into me, harder, faster, and my muscles cramped tighter, stiffer, more unbearable.

My whole body ached. Sweat slid hot over my skin, dripping on the sheet. I couldn't get there. I gasped, my breath swollen and difficult. "Harder. Please. Help me."

He slid hot fairy fingers over my belly and slid them into

my hot folds, pinching my aching clit, pleasure mixed with pain. The tension built, twisting like evil springs inside me. Cramp speared my belly, agonizing. I whimpered, every thrust just winding me tighter. "More, god, more. I can't . . ."

He rubbed me harder and yanked my hair tighter.

I shrieked, and finally something snapped.

Desperate relief ripped through me. Not pleasure. Just release, my muscles screaming tight until I shuddered and groaned, and then the tension shattering away.

Diamond bit the back of my neck with a possessive growl, and followed me.

I felt the heat wash over his body, radiating from his skin to mine, the swell inside me, the hot sharp burst of his liquid. It didn't disgust me. I welcomed it.

When he was done, he licked the back of my neck, once. Blood seeped, tiny trickles teasing my skin. My belly hurt, the shock of my release still fading. He'd bruised me inside. My eyes stung. My lungs burned, parched. But it was nothing compared to the empty black ache in my heart.

I felt even worse now. Like I'd been saving my virginity for someone special, and squandered it on a whim.

Bad idea.

Diamond let me crawl away. Our fluid spilled down my legs, and I gripped the pillow and buried my face in it. It creased against my burning cheek, soaking up my stray tears. The cotton smelled of Cobalt, dry and sweet, but now it smelled of blood and roses, too.

Fabric whispered as Diamond cleaned up, dressed himself, the pink light from his wings wavering like eerie candle-flame. His light touch on my shoulder made me jump. "You okay?"

That he wasn't laughing at me only made it worse. My enemy had acted more honorably in this than I.

I curled up, my legs shaking, and the ache in my throat cracked my voice to a whisper. "Just fuck off, okay? You got what you wanted."

"Mina—"

"Just go!"

"Fine. Have it your way." His lips settled on my temple, a warm sweet kiss, and iridescent glitter showered in a faint breath of poison. "Get it now? It never feels better. It's not about you and the serpent, Mina. It's about you forgivifying yourself for abandoning her. Feed the monster, and it'll eat you." Warm raspberry breeze tickled my hair as he flitted away, and his ruby glow faded, leaving me in darkness.

Abandoning her.

In my mind, I cowered once again behind that dusty sofa, fear paralyzing my reason while my mother gurgled and died.

Bristly hatred crawled up my throat like a spider, and I screamed.

Nothing shattered. Nothing cracked or wilted. Not even an echo. Just dead, useless sound.

My throat tore. I tasted blood. My hands curled tight, quivering, and I screamed again, this time brimming with tears and rage and bitter hatred. Hunger ripped my stomach hollow, and I knew nothing I ate would ever fill it.

I'd lost my magic. Squandered my honor. The only person who ever had my loyalty was now my enemy. Nothing could make me whole.

Except revenge.

Unwilled, Joey filtered into my mind, image and scent and sound, hot and delicious against that metal wall. My shiver at his voice, his fresh menthol kiss. His fingers demanding and unflinching on my wrists as he whispered those horridsweet words. His body, strong and lithe on mine, snakeflesh's fevered shift underneath. The hot hard press of his need for me, his gasp when I touched him, just as I'd always wanted.

It hadn't seemed a lie. Too real, that trapped emotion flooding between us, the urgency and desperation in our kiss.

If he knew what I'd just done, he'd turn from me now.

I squeezed my eyes shut on tears and banged my fists on my thighs, bruising. No. I was in too far to stop this now. He had to die. Even if it meant no one ever cared for me again.

Not that Joey cared. Not for real. He just wanted to fuck

me, use me, work some frustrated lust from his system. The
bastard lied to me. He deserved everything he got.

And so did I. I wanted to punish myself, smack my head
into the floor, make my ears ring. Crunch my knife into my
palm, pain's rapid release, watch the guilty blood flow.

Disgust spewed sick into my guts. A black chasm creaked
open in my soul, and I wanted to dive in and drown. I wanted
to curl up in that dusty bed forever and cry.

But I dragged my aching body up from the sweaty sheets
and stumbled into the bathroom, my legs trembling but holding. My eyes stinging hot, but dry. My face tried to crumple,
and I pulled it straight.

If I'd learned anything in gangland, it was this: There's
no use sobbing over what's done.

Just get up, and get on with making it right.

My reflection in the mirror glared at me when I flicked on
the light, and I wrenched my gaze away. Blindly, I pawed the
shower on, leaning my forehead against cracked white tiles.
The pipes groaned, and cold gritty water sluiced through my
hair, over my clammy skin, down my legs, washing the mess
away. Slowly, the water warmed, and fairy shit and blood and
Diamond's fading pink glitterfluid swirled down the rusty
plughole.

As I soaked in the steaming water, Diamond's words
echoed like shattered glass in my heart. He was right. I hadn't
forgiven or forgotten my mother's death. But now I was act-
ing on it, wasn't I? Chasing her killer down? Making things
right?

I inhaled the steam, soothing the ragged hole in my lungs
where my magic used to be.

Or was I just holding on grimly to a past that was gone
forever?

I swallowed, and untangled the sponge from its wire hook.
I soaked it in fragrant golden soap and scrubbed, raking the
rough plastic curls over my body until I was clean, at least on
the outside. The familiar scent of Cobalt's dusky cinnamon
body wash strengthened me. I shampooed my hair twice,

raking my nails over my scalp, lathering out smells and touches and vibrations, and with each soapy slide of bubbles down my body, my anger grew.

By the time I'd finished, my hands shook with indignation, and I flipped off the water and squeezed out my hair with a vicious jerk.

Screw feeling sorry for myself. And screw Diamond and his brittle lies. He didn't know me. He wasn't on my side. He cared only about himself. I should've known better.

Ice steeled my nerves. A scarfaced fairy named Ivy. A vague recollection of her face was all I had to go on. It'd have to be enough. I'd start at the club, with the sparkle-brains, the spacers, the bloodsniffers. Maybe she'd even be there. I'd find her, explain the situation, get my spell back one way or another.

Relish set my teeth on edge, and my limbs flexed in anticipation as I toweled myself off.

And then Joey would die, and I'd be healed. And nothing he could say or do—no mesmerizing green glance or heartbroken whisper or dizzying mindfuck kiss—would stop me.

16

Delilah squirms her thighs on the velvet seat, and her shimmering silver dress sticks even though the air is chilled rigid. Around her, low couches and tables hide guests in seclusion, couples and more hidden amongst tall green plants and sculpture art. Rich, gullible soulflesh tantalizes her nostrils. Her mouth waters. Casinos are such ripe places for soulslaughter.

The sepia window beside her glimmers, reflecting chandeliers, caramel carpet, the trickling water in the black marble fountain, and twenty-nine floors below, the lights of Melbourne sparkle and dance in shimmering summer heat. Across the river, skyscrapers glitter, the stars fading overhead in orange cityglow. A magnificent view.

The view across the table's better.

Kane sits, eye-shattering elegance in his charcoal suit, diamonds glinting in his flawless white cuffs, his tie knotted perfectly symmetrical. His golden hair sparks, a faint green halo. A tiny frown lines his brow, and he pokes at a sautéed prawn on his plate with a silver fork. "I like fish," he remarks, his voice soft. "Swimming things taste good."

Pleasure shimmers along her nerves at his smile. He pops the prawn into his mouth, and the crunch of that roasted pink flesh between his teeth makes her want to squirm. His shiny black gaze fixes on her, gentle but relentless, and his face betrays nothing but polite interest. At his most urbane and charming.

But Delilah imagines the ashen fire of his kiss, the power lurking just beneath the surface, and lust spills deep into her belly. She's no aristocrat, and the demon courtiers sneer at her, laugh at her ambition, kick her aside like vermin, even though all she ever wanted was to be one of them. To dance in their candlelit halls, laugh and drink bloody wine at their soirees, play their heady power games with souls and black eternity. Instead of eking out a dirty, unseen existence in the serving classes, a starving dog begging for scraps from their table.

In hell, Kane was untouchable, a distant, haughty prince to fantasize about. Here, he's all too near. All too real. She can barely believe she's finally made it. And it makes her long for more than combat, more than the heady bloodrush of rivalry. His body fascinates her, his slightest movement a temptation.

A worthy adversary. Tricking him will be most satisfying.

Under the table, she clutches the vial Ivy gave her, the sparkles tingling sweet invitation in her palm. She sips her champagne—French, of course, not the local imitation—and smiles back, gritting her teeth. "Are you always this weird?"

He dabs his lips neatly with a napkin. "Apparently."

Her covetous nature purrs. Fuck, his mouth is beautiful, his altarboy lips a seduction, those strong white teeth a sensual promise. Delilah laughs, charm littering ash from her hair. "Rubbish. Who told you that? Don't pretend mortals don't fall at your feet by the dozen."

The promise of black demonic compulsion sizzles from his golden lashes, threatening. "That's not the same thing."

Claws prick and shudder inside her fingertips, longing to erupt, and she wraps her hands tight under the white table-cloth. "Really. You're telling me you've never been on a date?"

"Not for a long time." He folds the napkin away on the table. The silent black-suited waiter offers more champagne, but Kane waves it off, his rings glinting. When the man leans forward to whisper something in Kane's ear, Kane turns away to listen, and deftly Delilah snakes forward and tips the sparkle into his red wine.

The spell glimmers softly and dissolves, mournful song's faint echo lingering.

Swiftly, she tucks the vial safely away under the cushions. A tempting waft of sweet banshee sadness tickles her nose and evaporates.

Kane turns back. Her clotted heart beats faster, warmer. Did he notice anything? She forces a sultry smile. "Then what's so special about tonight?"

Kane leans his chin on sparking hands, golden hair tumbling on his cheek, and fixes her in his hot stare. "You tell me."

"Wh-what do you mean?" The press of his red tongue against his teeth makes her weak. Her skin shivers, tightening. Her silvery evening dress barely covers her breasts as it is, the narrow twin front panels slanting down to meet somewhere just below her navel. Surely he can see her nipples, thrusting out eagerly into the silk. She wants to touch them, stimulate herself, put an end to waiting.

Fuck, this is embarrassing. He can't have cast a hex on her. She'd smelled no threat. He's just a man, even if he is powerful, snarling and graceful like a tiger. If she'd realized she was this horny, she'd have downed an appetizer before she arrived.

A moan of frustrated desire wells in her throat, and she tries to swallow it. She's tried mortal men. It's not the same.

Kane shrugs. Reaches for his glass. Sips. Lets the tainted wine spread on his tongue. "I mean, you tell me. Why you follow me, watch me. Why you're so desperate to be nice to me that you'll risk a flaying."

"Surely you've figured that out." She drinks more champagne and watches, her breath catching. *Drink up, pretty. Then we'll see who's desperate.*

He swallows again, deep, and sighs, a faint dark stain sliding on his lips. "Mmm. I like this. Your choice?"

"Of course." She fingers her glass's rim. His gaze follows, and triumph bubbles rich in her blood. She gives a playful, naughty smile, the one that brings mortal men to their knees. "Kane, are you staring at me?"

His lips drift apart, and he licks them, candid. "Yes, I think I am."

She wants to purr. *Here, kitty kitty.* "Why, you naughty prince, whatever for?"

"Because you're pretty." He drains his drink. The spelled wine stains the glass dark as he tips the last of it between those sulky red lips. He savors it and swallows, and slides the glass away with two fingers, leaning forward to sniff the air in her direction.

She wriggles closer, folding her arms on the table so he's only lazy inches away. "Am I? What are you going to do about it?"

His smile quirks, wicked. "Maybe I'm imagining that flaying we talked about."

Her own lips curl in response. She can smell his ashen lust. Hellflames spring alive in her hair, and she doesn't puff them out. "Why don't I believe you?"

He reaches over scattered scarlet roses and brings her hand to his lips, and the shock of his kiss burns. "Because we're both from hell, honeychild. You'd be stupid to believe a word I said."

In the shadows behind tall green foliage, Ivy stares, and a single hot tear slides down her newly perfect cheek.

Shining golden hair. That perfect face, those mesmerizing lips and hot black gaze she'll never forget. So elegant, every movement a seductive melody, his rich stormy scent filling the room even though no one else can smell it.

She clutches soft greenery, crushing it in a faint chlorophyll tang. It's him. Her beautiful golden lover. So long ago, those sultry nights in . . . where? Her memory mists over, like a love scene veiled in gossamer, and all she can remember is his kiss, his hot smooth hardness inside her, her body awakening to ecstasy beneath his skilled fingers.

Her golden skin swells, sticking tight to her flowing dress. Her heart thuds, rocking her body with a strong pulse of desire she can't ignore.

He said he loved her, and she knew it was true, in the way he looked at her, touched her, made her feel.

And now here's that nasty wine-haired demon girl, with her dirty fingers and slutty half dress and flaunty female curves, using Ivy's own slinky songspell and those big pretentious near-naked breasts to seduce him.

Her guts twist tight. *No no no.* It just won't do. Kane is hers. When he sees her, he'll know. He'll remember, and his jaded heart will melt and he'll never look at another woman again.

Her gaze clings to him like a magnet. Her body thrums. Already she can smell him, his ashen hair, his rich charcoal skin. And now Delilah rises, throws him a red hellharlot's smile, and sways away toward the ladies' room.

He's alone. Now is her chance. Ivy's nerves bubble with excitement, and she tidies her flowing silver hair and flutters over.

Kane's velvety black gaze flicks over her. Her heart seizes with love, her breath stolen.

He glances away, and doesn't look back.

Ivy swallows, and summons her courage, her voice shaking. "Umm. Excuse me. Don't you remember me?"

Kane looks up again, sparking fingers toying with his wineglass. His face so perfect, young, his gentle cheekbones a temptation. Golden hair falls over his cheek—so endearing, she wants to weep. He sips, showing pouty scarlet lips. Danger glints like fire in his eyes. "Should I?"

Ivy smiles, bright as she can. "It was a long time ago. Somewhere. We danced. You kissed me. We made love."

Kane shrugs, elegant. "If you say so."

"You must remember." Doubt seeps into her blood, sour and unwanted.

Ash puffs from his hair, and he tosses his head impatiently, his neat nails flushing blue. "Lady, I've had a thousand like you. Hardly surprising if you didn't stand out."

"But you said you loved me!"

He grips the glass tighter, claws springing sharp, and the

liquid boils inside, angry steam wisping. "To shut you the
fuck up? Very likely."

Ivy's heart wrenches painfully, tears scorching. "But—"

The air shimmers and shifts, and suddenly she's pressed
against his powerful body, his arm crushing her wings flat
and trapping her immobile. His lips burn her skin, still an
inch from hers, and his hair flushes angry blue. He whispers,
and rich thunderscent sears her lips. "Want to try it again,
fairy? Want to fuck? I'll rip your wings off with my teeth
and drink your blood from the hole. I'll tear your soul screaming from your stupid heart and chew it to shreds before it
even gets a whiff of sulfur. Suggest you leave me alone, whoever you are."

And he's back in his seat, suit fresh and elegant, not a
blond wisp out of place. Like he never moved.

She staggers, her tender wings a splash of abused bones.
Her vulnerable mind sloshes sideways and backwards, time
spinning in meaningless gray froth. He never loved her.
Didn't recognize her. Doesn't even remember touching her.

And here's Delilah again, approaching behind, sharp
heels tapping across the floor.

Swiftly, Ivy ducks back behind the ferns before Delilah
sees her, hot doubt piercing her guts. Delilah takes her seat
with a flourish, long brown legs on show.

Ivy studies them together, squinting with cunning. Kane
is fixated on the demon slut, his smoldering eyes dark with
intent. The horrid woman laughs, fiddling with one purple
spiral curl, and Kane laughs with her.

Ivy's palms tingle, and hot sparkle remnants fly on her
breath. Of course. Delilah is bewitching him, with the very
spell Ivy sold her. He didn't recognize her, because Delilah
won't let him.

Well, two can play at that. Frustration grips her ribs like a
vise, and she gnaws her knuckles bloody on sharp anxious
teeth. At least she knows the spell's working. So she'll make
an even stronger one, thwart that hellcow hussy at her own
dirty tricks, and Kane will fall in love with Ivy all over again.

But where to get the spell? Where to get more pretty blue banshee juice?

Ivy giggles, and covers her mouth. That particular toy isn't dead yet. The pinkjewelly fairy boy was most certain about that. His cute little scheme to trap her depended on it.

Grab her. Hold her tight. Squeeze out that last, strongest bit of magic, the elusive golden spark that makes the banshee's heart beat and her breath rise and fall. Add lashings of stolen sympathy. A drop of intrigue. A sparkling splash of desire. And then Kane will be Ivy's.

Simple. But how to lure a tricksy little banshee?

Crafty shadow fingers stroke Ivy's cheek. *Why, with a snake for bait, of course.*

Ivy laughs, tosses silver hair over her slender shoulder, and skips to the elevator, tiny daisies of happiness shedding a flowery trail from her wings.

Delilah pours more wine, and rich scarlet grapescent intoxicates her. "Might I suggest dessert?"

But Kane's eyes are fixed on her lips. "Suggest whatever you like."

Her power over him sends a thrill deep into her belly. She anticipated fear, but she's not afraid. She smiles, triumphant. "Well, we do have a little business to discuss. The matter of that flaying, for example—"

"Never mind that. I was hasty. Forgive me if I'm wary, after . . ." He trails off, reluctant even through the haze of songspell.

"After?" she prompts gently, twirling a saucy finger in her hair.

"Well, you know. Phoebus and I fought. My mother left. I'm alone, you understand. The court accepts me for now, but—" He flashes a charming smile. "I can't be seen to be weak. To tolerate intruders." For a moment, his gaze shines hard, so swift, she might have imagined it. And then he smiles again. "That sort of stuff. You do have a way of making me look soft, sweet thing."

Delilah laughs, secret delight licking her veins. He's talking like he's drunk. "Get your hand off it, Kane. You're a full-blood prince of hell. Far as I can see, you own this town. You're raking in souls by the thousands. Do you really give a moldy ratfuck what the demon court thinks?"

Kane grins, wickedly seductive. "Not for an instant. Bunch of jealous limpwits. But—" He tapped blue-streaked nails on the table. "—they have their uses. And for now, I must comply." His eyes glinted angry green. "Play their protocol games. Ask their *permission*. Me. Can you imagine?"

She purses her lips in sympathy. "Oh, I know. Poor baby. Humiliating, isn't it? But . . . maybe if we could be seen to form some kind of . . . relationship . . . the court might be more impressed?"

Ash coats his nails, and he flicks it off, lazy. Promise glows molten in his eyes. "Tell me more."

She savors a delicious shiver. "We can play their game, make them think we're enemies. Lure them in and crush them all when the time is right. Make them bleed, watch them scream, you know the sort of thing. And then, we can rule—" She sucks the strawberry from her champagne between her lips and crunches it, slowly, so he can watch. "—together."

Scarlet flames flicker along his fingers. "Interesting idea. Do you think you can play nice with me?"

She purrs, and licks strawberry juice from her lips to tempt him. "With you, baby, I can play real nice."

"Mmm. What did you have in mind?"

"Oh, honey. No short answer. You got all night?"

"Yes." His gaze doesn't falter.

Her nipples tighten, painful. Now or never. She leans forward to whisper, her skin thrumming tight. "Well . . . it'd involve you tearing my clothes off and telling me what you'd like me to do. Maybe you could tie me up. I imagine I'll moan and scream quite a bit. There'll be licking, and sucking. Maybe a spanking or two. What do you think?"

Blue sparks crackle in Kane's hair, and hot darkness descends like death.

A burning black gale whirls around her, the dizzy sensa-

tion of falling. Charcoal stings her nose, and her ears ring
with buffeting wind. Her hair swirls. And then she lands with
a cosmic thump with velvety soft carpet beneath her feet.

Her head steadies. She gulps a breath and opens her eyes
to golden light, dimmed sultry. A dark-tinted window over-
looks the city beyond shadowed furniture, a vase of lilies,
some sterile gray room. A mirror glitters before her, showing her wide green eyes, tangled hair, shimmering silver-
clad body. But then he's behind her, his golden hair falling
on her collarbone, his lips hungry as he swipes hot kisses
on her throat. He glances up at her, his shining black eyes
reflected in the mirror. His fingers slide on her shoulders,
his strong-muscled body a threat, his thunderstorm scent making her drunk.

Excitement licks hot down her spine. "Where are we?"

"Do you care?" He grips her dress's narrow shoulder
straps and yanks them apart. The fabric tears down the front,
and he lets it fall. Sparkling silver pools around her ankles.
She's naked underneath.

Kane surveys her reflection. Scarlet flame wraps lustful
fingers in his hair, and his black eyes glitter hard. He pulls
the comb from her hair and tosses it away. Redwine curls
tumble on her bare shoulders, and her skin burns.

Delilah shivers, nerves twitching her limbs. In the mirror, the purple curls between her legs glisten wet. She feels
like a virgin, unbroken, inexperienced. Afraid. Everything
depends on this. Should she move on him? Let him lead her?
Play the whore, or the nun?

But she doesn't have time to decide. The black wind
swirls again, tilting the world like orbit out of control, and
next thing she knows, he's dragging her onto him on scarlet
sheets, her naked body covering him.

Greedy flame licks her skin. Dizziness can't hide the hot
male shape of his hips between her thighs, the hard thrust of
his cock pressing up against her through his clothing. He
grips her wrists cruelly, and his growing claws rake deep.
The sting and her own bloodscent excite her, and slickness
slides between her legs, making a mess on his lap.

She slides his jacket off, rips his shirt apart to feel his chest under her hands. His skin is golden, perfect, fragrant muscles packed tight, beautiful demonflesh sliding hard and irresistible under her palms. Lust ripples through her for this magnificent body, the power she can feel barely restrained beneath his skin.

But it's not only that. She's so lonely for home, her heart's breaking, and now that the demon court has cast her out, she's alone, an exile, never to have this again. Humans, fae, they can't make up for it. Not the same. Never the same.

Hateful tears swell her eyes. She can feel the foolishness welling up in her throat, but she can't stop it. She growls, her teeth springing sharp, and sinks her mouth onto his nipple. He tastes of ash, of burnt human flesh and writhing soulblood. The stormy scent of his power fills her mouth, and she aches. *Yes. Oh, yes.*

Kane hisses and pulls her closer, and thunder rumbles in the distance, a hellish echo of his lust. She tears at his clothes, ravenous, and in the tiny scrap of her mind that isn't fixated on fucking his sexy demon brains out, she wonders faintly if she might not be losing control.

Soon, they're both naked. Mirrors line the walls here, too, and their bodies look beautiful together, golden and brown like melting sugar. His hair spreads like a golden halo on the scarlet satin. He cups her big breasts in his hands, twisting her stiff nipples until they plead with pain and desire, and when he lifts himself up to suck one into his mesmerizing red mouth, pleasure such as she barely remembers arrows deep into her body, and her thighs tremble with need.

He rasps his tongue over her puckered flesh, making her moan. "Say it, minion."

"Not so fast." She rubs herself on his big hard cock, her slick wet flesh slipping oh so easily, and he sighs and reaches for her, his strong fingers finding her clit and torturing it, sliding a dangerous claw inside her. Fuck, he feels good. Her weeping flesh tightens around his finger, begging for more, harder, deeper.

He grins. "Say it."

"No." She'd imagined teasing him, making him tremble and sigh and beg her to finish it, but there's no time for that now. She shudders, and lifts herself up to find his cock and press him into her.

In a dizzy flash, she's on her back under him, his weight light but somehow immovable. He pins her wrists to the sheet, biceps bulging in light demon bloodsweat. He brushes his cock over her wet flesh, teasing her clit until she's breathless and shuddering, nudging her entrance, pressing oh so lightly but not pushing inside. Her pulse thuds with frustration, and wantonly she thrusts her hips against him, desperate to get him inside her.

Golden hair falls in his face, tickling her cheek as his lips burn hers in a throaty whisper that echoes in hell. "My game. My way. Say it."

Her throat clutches tight. He's capable of denying her. "I want you in me. Do it. Now."

"Didn't catch that."

She knows what he wants, and the words chafe her dignity raw, but she doesn't care. "Take me, prince. Fuck me. Please, just fuck me."

His rich, cruel laugh teases her ears cold, and suddenly, he vanishes.

Dizziness hits her like a bloodstained hurricane, and her muscles cramp. Lightning blinds her, the ashen air sparkling with ozone.

Cruel brass daggers spike her wrists, driving through her flesh, twisting between the bones to pin her to what a moment ago was soft cotton but is now rough, unforgiving rock that scars her back raw like burning iron.

Agony racks her body where a moment before she'd drowned in insane pleasure. Her own blood splashes her hair, musky with lust, and she screams.

Scarlet hellsun scorches her eyeballs. Superheated air burns her like a furnace. She squeezes her eyelids shut, only to have them wrenched open again by some black compulsion she can't fight. Deathblue sky burns. Carrion birds squawk and scream, their shadows flitting. Her body shakes uncontrollably, and cold terror pierces her veins like steel. She's a child of hell, and it still scares her rigid.

Kane's shadow looms over her, a dark slash of relief from the raging sunlight. He's still naked, his human form still smeared with her sweat. Fury slashes bright blue lightning from his hair, his fingertips, the tip of his still-hard cock. Thunder cracks, echoing, lost in distant canyons. "Did you really think to trick me, you scumsucking little maggot?"

Defiance rattles in her heart, though all she wants to do is scream and beg and plead with him to fuck her, touch her, finish her off. "Worked, didn't it?"

He wrinkles his perfect nose, distaste a golden gleam in his eyes. "Not totally. I'd thought you smarter. A stupid fairy spell? On me? Are you serious? Pay attention, insect. I could smell your lies from across the table. Why do you think you've been so horny all night?"

Realization pierces her skin like molten wire. He didn't touch his champagne. All that time she'd tried to drug him, and he'd drugged *her*.

All her lust, false? The way he made her nipples hurt and her body ache for belonging, a lie? It felt so real. Coalblack hatred bubbles in her heart.

Kane nods, grinning like a playful child. "That's right. Same trick I used on Phoebus, and he was much more talented than you. Being in the family and all, I'd hope so. You're so weak, you're not even funny."

She struggles, the blades slicing deep into her wrists. "What do you want?"

Kane gives another hellscarred laugh, scattering obsidian shards. "From you? Don't make me puke. Maybe I'll just let you bleed for a few hundred years."

She shakes her head, desperate. "No. You'd not go to all this trouble for nothing. What do you want?" She licks sunburnt lips, nervous. "I can still be good to you. Let me."

"What, are you offering to suck my cock? Charming."

"If that's what it takes."

"What rotten ethics you have, you shitty slut." He bends closer, until she can smell that gorgeous demon skin. His finger slips out and runs circles around her nipple, pinching it, sparking horrid pleasure once more in her still-quivering sex. "Maybe I'll take you up on that. First, you'll tell me all about you and Shadow."

"What? I don't know what the fuck you're—"

"Don't lie. I know all about your imbecilic plan."

Her pulse thrums. "What plan? I told you, I haven't seen Shadow. I never even talked to that feather-ass bitch—"

"Then why are there filthy sugarstink imps in my city?" Kane snaps needle teeth within an inch of her lips, smoke hissing. "Shitting in my gutters. Bleeding on my pavements. Getting their fucking bones stuck between my teeth. 'Fess up, shitlicker, before I rip your skin off with a blunt hacksaw and feed it to you on toast."

"I don't know!" Terror pierces her limbs, worse than the knives. She's got no idea what he means about Shadow. But Kane will kill her anyway. Rend her limb from limb under hell's bloody sun and feast on her steaming flesh. It's what she'd do, in his place. "It's the truth. I swear on . . . on a thousand years of servitude. Two thousand. Whatever you want."

"You're already mine." He licks blood and spit from her lips, and his tongue makes her squirm. "For now. After a thousand years, even torturing you would get boring."

Despair polishes her cockiness bright. Either he'll believe her, or he won't. "Cut the crap, Kane. You're the prince. You can tell if I'm lying. Do it if you dare."

His eyes glint with invitation. He forces her lips apart for a kiss, his ashen tongue delving deep into her mouth, and the surface of her mind rips apart under his compulsion like wet paper.

She screams into his mouth, the pain is so intense. Like an axe through her skull, rending it apart so he can see inside.

Grimly, she holds on. She's suffered worse rape than this. The court banished her, but not before they'd had their way.

Kane pulls back, panting, her blood streaming down his chin, and the agony subsides.

Surprise and fury burn like rubies in his eyes. "It's your

cursed defiance, bitch," he snarls. "You're so fucking naïve. Why do you think I insist on obedience? The stink of your arrogance burns holes in the air. You're letting him in whether you mean to or not."

Delilah chokes, her breath wet and sore, and her heart quails. It could be true. Maybe her thoughts are more powerful than she knew. To dent even Kane's ironcast authority . . .

The idea should delight her, but her stomach writhes. She hates Kane, desires him, covets his position, rank, privileges. But she hates those honey-licking feathered freaks more.

"I didn't mean it. Please. You have to . . . I'm begging you. Forgive me." Her bowels water, humiliated. She struggles, the knives slashing her wrists bloody once again.

Flames erupt from Kane's fingers, singeing her hair, but his lips purse, sulky. "You're lucky I don't drag your skanky traitor's ass before the demon court and suck the marrow from your bones."

"Just do it, then, you bastard." Fury shudders the words from her lips. He's already decided her fate. He's playing with her.

Kane shrugs, careless, and snaps sharp teeth on her nipple, forcing a cry. He licks blood off and grins. "I still might, if you don't do as I say. First, you'll beg a little more. I like that. Then, I think . . . yes. You'll suck my cock. Long and slow and hard. If I come hard enough—and you swallow like a good girl—maybe I'll help you out. Hmm? Yes or no?"

She grits her teeth and forces a nod.

His scarlet lips curl, cruel and hot like chili against her ear. "Yes or no, Delilah?"

Humiliation froths sour in her throat. "Yes, my prince."

Kane's laugh crackles like hellfire. "Actually, never mind. I just wanted to hear you say it."

And in a smoking flash of light, he's gone.

She's alone.

The scarletbleed sky shudders and threatens, clouds boiling. Already, the hellred sun scorches, sizzling her skin to blisters. Cackling carrion birds swoop and dive closer. She struggles, blood splashing, but the wicked blades that shackle her hold fast, grinding agony between her bones.

A bird settles beside her, talons clicking on hot rock, its hungry black eyes staring. She spits and hisses, sparks flashing from her hair. The bird just blinks, and hops closer.

Her guts spike cold. Kane's left her here, at the mercy of vultures and pitiless heat.

But not to die. Demons don't die that easily. He'll let her suffer until he thinks she's had enough. And when the sun has roasted her to a crisp over and over, and the birds have torn every shred of flesh from her bones enough times, he'll come for her, and she'll scream and beg and plead with him to set her free.

That's what he thinks.

Delilah grits her teeth, sweat dripping in her eyes. News flash, shitball. She'll not give him the satisfaction. She'll come back stronger, craftier, with more and better tricks, and next time, he'll not seduce her so easily.

No one humiliates her like that. Not even a prince. Damned if she'll ever beg him for anything again.

Another bird lights screeching by her elbow. Delilah squeezes her eyes shut, and as cruel curving beaks rip her belly bloody, she clenches slashed fists and swallows her screams.

17

I checked my weapons to a tall green troll girl at the scarred black desk and strode into Unseelie Court. Coarse sound hammered my ears, stuffing my head with gibberish, the complex weave of vibrations that had once been so musical now just noise. My lungs shuddered in the powerful bass, the screech of electric violin scraping my teeth on razors.

The floor was packed, colorlit smoke drifting down amongst a sea of sweat-damp limbs, writhing bodies, shimmering fairy wings. My tight pants stuck in sweat on my thighs, my corset stifling. If it didn't reek of smoke and bodies and bloodstained perfume in here, I'd smell myself, stale fearsweat and sex and fading fairy glitter. I needed fresh clothes, but I'd no time to go home and change.

My muscles ached, bereft of magic, and I struggled for breath as I stumbled awkwardly between some giggling fairies slamdancing and a pair of luscious troll boys in tight jeans, studiously adhering to the naked-to-the-waist-if-you're-hot rule, long black hair plastered wet to muscle-packed shoulders as they kissed like they hadn't eaten for a week.

A pretty blue airfae girl teetered into me on tall heels, powdery wings gracefully sweeping her upright. Her big green eyes shone wide and wet with telltale sparklesheen. "Sorry. Didn't mean it. Oranges."

Her words lost themselves in the din, but I saw her lips move. My skin tightened. I couldn't filter the sounds apart anymore, and I resisted the compulsion to dart my glance left and right, plaster my back against a wall with no windows. How would I hear an attack coming? What if someone crept up on me? I was used to being untouchable. Now, I was weaponless. Weak. Fair game. I didn't know how to protect myself.

"S'okay!" I yelled over the music. "You know an earthfae lady called Ivy?"

But she'd already scuttled away in a twist of applefresh breeze.

Awesome. Now that I couldn't coat my voice in persuasion, even little fairy girls ignored me. The sooner I had my spells back, the better.

I spied Vincent and Iridium at the bar, and gratefully pushed my way over. I shouldered aside some drunk human guys in leather and chains, who were hitting on some tiny spriggan girls with short skirts and goggling eyes, obviously underage but glamoured up as sultry teenage vixens who knew what went where. One already had some guy's hand up her skirt as they danced, his spit shining around her mouth. My sympathy didn't rise. *You make your bed, you fuck in it, ladies. Welcome to Unseelie Court.*

Vincent smiled tightly at me as I took the stool beside him. He wore a fresh shirt, no longer coated in blood and puke, but his dark jagged hair still ran with sweat, his handsome face flushed. A yellowing bruise already faded around one eye, where someone had caught him a good one in the fight, the scraped scarlet clawmarks already half-healed.

Was he still pissed at me? I couldn't tell from his expression. Wet woolly confusion wrapped my brain. Iridium licked his slobbering lips at me over a tall scarlet drink, and I ignored him. I wanted a drink, but I didn't wave at the barboy. I needed all my wits. "Hey, Vincent. Where's the boss?"

If Joey was here, I was leaving. But Vincent just shrugged, tense, and his scabbed knuckles shook as he dragged on his cigarette. He wouldn't meet my eyes.

"I'm looking for Ivy. Fairy dealer, not one of ours. Sort of a goldy color, scars on her face. Know her?"

Again Vincent shrugged, swallowed, sucked in a draft of

smoke. His body shuddered, and he exhaled hard. "Don't think so."

My stomach coiled. He was my friend, after all, even if we'd argued. "Are you okay? I mean, be shitty with me if you want, god knows I'm pissed as hell at you. But you look like crap."

Iridium giggled and slurped his Bloody Mary through a straw. Freak.

"Hungry," Vincent muttered, and tossed his cigarette away, glowing ash spilling to the floor. He looked up at me, and his glassy brown eyes burned. "Wanna dance?" And before I could react, he slipped his hand around my waist and twirled me onto the floor.

Pressing bodies consumed us, fleshy and hot, and the sugary smell of fairy sweat ran thick. Vincent pulled me in tight. He could dance, all right, his body pressed up against mine and moving just right, his fingers stroking my spine beneath my hair. He had a hard-on, and his breath was ragged, but that was okay. He smelled of cigarettes, sweat and perfume, and something darker, saltier, more thrilling.

What he didn't smell of was alcohol. My skin prickled. "Vincent—"

"Shhh." His hot breath licked my ear.

After a confused moment, I slid my arms around his neck and sighed. Maybe this was his way of apologizing, saying it was okay that I'd dredged up the most hurtful insults I could think of and thrown them in his face. I'd deserved what he'd said to me. If he wanted to forget it, that was fine with me.

But his fever burned me, the tight thrum of his heartbeat against my breasts swift and skittery like a bird's. He buried his face in the curve between my neck and shoulder, and his wet lips scorched like desire. "God, I'm starving. You smell so good. So fresh."

I didn't mind him touching me. It felt sorta nice. But I knew for a fact I didn't smell fresh. My instincts sliced sharp like glass, and I laughed to hide my shiver. "Vinny, I'm so not sleeping with you in this lifetime, okay? It'd be like screwing my gay little brother—Jesus fucking Christ, Vincent!"

He bit me.

Sank his teeth into the curve of my throat and crunched them, hard.

Pain stabbed. I struggled, but he pinned me close. Blood and spit trickled over my collarbone, hot and sticky, but he didn't let go. He murmured, and lapped it up with a hot wet tongue, and bit me again.

My shoulder cramped, agonizing, and truth tore in like a bullet in the guts.

Bloodfever.

That's why he shivered and sweated and puked gore. Why the cuts on his face already faded to nothing. He'd caught the bloodfever from some manky bloodsucker, sometime last night after I'd told him to fuck off. And now, he was hungry.

Once they were hungry, and keeping down what they ate, it was over. They'd beaten the fever, and they wouldn't die. Ever. At least, not of natural causes.

And Vincent—my charming, confused little Vincent, with his girly diamond earrings and ruffled shirts and sulky hot-chocolate eyes—was a vampire.

A vampire, gorging himself on my blood.

Dizziness swamped me. I felt him suckle, my skin stretching around his teeth, his tongue licking me lovingly, hot liquid gushing out into his mouth. . . .

My body jerked awake, and I grabbed his hair, trying to pull him away, but his arms trapped me, immovable, stronger than he'd ever been before. "Christ, that hurts! Get the fuck off me."

Finally he tore away, and I stumbled, clutching the cuts he'd made. Blood squelched warm under my palm.

His breath rasped, his lips dripping crimson. His gaze tracked to my bleeding throat and jerked away again. "Shit. Sorry. I didn't mean . . . I'm just . . . my gut aches, and I'm so fucking hungry, I can't . . . it's all I can think about."

"Don't ever do that again." My neck ached like a vise clamped down on the muscle. Blood ran down my chest, dripping between my breasts, smearing my skin with gore. I wiped it off, but it kept dripping. I pressed my hand to the gash and covered my disgust with a shaky laugh. "What the hell happened? You're not gonna go all sparkly in the sun on me, are ya?"

Vincent spluttered, but kept it down. "What?"

"Never mind. Does Joey know?"

He licked his lips clean, and his eyes glinted wickedly at me as he panted for breath. "Who gives a fuck? He doesn't own me."

My guts twisted. "Oh, fuck a peacock. You didn't—"

"Damn right I did. Iridium's already in. You coming?"

I backed off a few steps, dread filling my chest like water and stopping my breath. I didn't know who I was afraid for. "No, wait a minute, think about it—"

"I've thought. We can beat him, if you're on our side."

That "we" smelled of Iridium, sly and vicious, and it made me shiver. I forced a laugh. "Don't be daft. No one gives a damn what I do."

"Bullshit. They all look up to you. They know you're his best girl. If they see you with me, they'll follow." He slipped his arm around my waist again, and the smell of my own blood sparkled my tongue from his breath. "Come on, Mina. It's the chance we've been waiting for."

I shook my head, holding him off. "For what?"

"To get rid of Joey, of course. It can be quick, if you want. I know you got a thing for him. He don't have to suffer. And then it'll be you and me, on top of the world."

My bones spiked cold. I'd already betrayed Joey to Diamond, but this sounded so . . . mercenary. To murder our boss, for what?

Power? Such a fleeting thing in gangland, where even your best girl wanted to kill you.

Money? Don't give a shit. It can't buy me safety.

The chance to make ourselves a target for every jealous

underling or bored Valenti thug who thought it was his lucky night?

It didn't seem right.

My thoughts tumbled. Sure, I wanted Joey dead. But I had good reason.

Didn't I?

I imagined him, bled out in some grimy alley somewhere, his snakeflesh torn in multiple ragged fangwounds, dark snakeblood splashing over and over again until he stopped shifting.

It didn't make me feel good. Sordid, somehow.

But he'd still be dead. The creeping black voice inside me whispered cold and rough like a lizard in my ear. *How it happens doesn't matter. You'd still win.*

It didn't seem like a victory. The idea of killing him for cash or advancement just made me squirm.

So how was that any different from killing him for revenge?

My guts watered, sick. Was I changing my mind? Losing my nerve? Fuck. Shoulda known that kissing thing was a bad idea.

Vincent must have mistaken my silence for acquiescence, because he glided closer, seductive. A dark smile revealed sharp white teeth still stained with my blood. "Thought so. You won't regret it."

My sluggish reflexes screamed at me to run, but my mind raced for answers, solutions, a plan: (1) Talk Vincent out of it. Didn't seem like an option. (2) Pretend to go along with him, and get caught up in whatever sick mess Iridium was cooking up. Nope. (3) Elbow him in the guts and walk away, and make an enemy of him just when I needed all the friends or at least all the people who didn't want to kill me—I could get?

Or . . . (4) Stall. Good one. I licked dry lips, my throat parched. "I dunno. It could be tough. Can I have time to think about it?"

"Sure. Whatever." Vincent pressed into me, sighing and sniffing my chest for bloodscent. Spit ran on his teeth, glinting purple in the nightclub lights, and his whisper hissed like fever as he trailed his lips over my collarbone. "I know you and Diamond got it on, Mina. I can smell his filthy fairy come inside you. You got off, didn't you? I can smell that, too. He fucked you, and you came on his cock like a bitch. So don't get precious about your fucking honor with me."

I stiffened, and his grip tightened painfully on my arms. He laughed, dark and wet and rich with copper, and regret sickened my stomach cold. He wasn't my Vincent anymore. He was sick, ravenous, twisted by the virus, some infected monster wearing Vincent's skin. Always hungry, always needing. It happened to them all. Any shred of humanity still clinging to life would soon be gone, torn up, eaten away.

My eyelids burned. Maybe, if I'd gone with him that night, eased his loneliness along with my own, this wouldn't have happened. But now I'd never get my friend back.

And now, true fear hacked ice into my spine. He might really hurt me. "Vincent, please—"

He nuzzled bloodsticky hair away from my throat and sniffed at me greedily. He kissed me, hungry fangs stinging. "Just a little more," he whispered, that dark wheedling tone crawling shivers into my scalp. "God, you taste fantastic. So delicious. And I'm so fucking starving. I could touch you while I do it. It won't hurt, I swear."

And I'd so heard that before.

My muscles stung tight, and I jerked my knee up, connecting with a sick crunch.

That's gotta hurt when your dick's hard.

He yelped and folded, his breath knocked away, and before he could recover, I bolted.

My heart thudded as I pushed my way through the cavorting crowd. I wasn't afraid he'd follow me. No, he knew what I thought of him now, and infected didn't mean psychotic or irrational. More likely, he'd find some other succulent girl or boy to quench his fevered thirst.

Great. My conscience really needed another kick in the guts.

I headed for the ladies' room, trying to catch my tortured

breath. My neck ached like someone had punched me, pain grabbing all the way down my chest.

My legs shook, and I stumbled. Great night. Joey kissed me. Cobalt died. Diamond . . . I flushed. Well, Diamond fucking used me. And now this.

Dizziness swirled in my skull, the world tilting upside down, and I thudded into the smeared metal door and staggered into the bathroom.

Cracked white tiles, gleaming purple under ultraviolet junkie lights. Rusted metal mirrors, the row of steel sinks a mess of makeup and hair and vomit. The blue lights fuzzed every edge, and my eyes ached trying to focus. In a stall, someone warbled and groaned.

I caught myself on the sink's edge and stared my reflection down, breathing long and deep and willing my pulse to slow.

My eyes stared back, dark and wide. I looked gaunt, frightened, a crease splitting my brow. Blood and vampire spit splashed my arm, my bodice, the tops of my breasts. Blood, thick and lumpy and disgusting, gleaming a sickly blue in the distorted light. I swallowed, my guts worming hot. Diamond's blood. Vincent's. Joey's. But most of all, my own.

I dragged my hair away with a squelch, and my skin ripped, fresh blood welling. Ouch. My wound gaped, stinging where his teeth had cut me. Already the skin tried to clot and knit together. Vampire bites heal fast, dying bloodfever remnants ramping up metabolism and healing. That's why vampires don't die. And why I was probably going to be sick.

Horrid salty stink hung thick in my nostrils, and my stomach somersaulted. I turned the slimy tap and scooped some water into my mouth. It didn't help. I splashed myself. The blood just spread. My nerves screeched, and I did it over and over, frantically trying to rinse the blood clean.

Hot fairy fingers folded over my wrist.

I wriggled, water spilling, and only slowly did my strained eyes tell me the truth.

Yellow fingers. Broken blue claws. Brittle applegreen hair crinkling over skinny fae shoulders.

Violet fluttered, torn white wings wafting blessedly cool air over my face. Her breathy voice soothed my buzzing ears. "Hey, where's the fire? S'okay." And she actually scrunched up a handful of paper towel and blotted the blood from my chest.

I swallowed, my throat swollen. Her fingers felt smooth and comforting as she wiped me clean, dabbing the wet paper carefully around my cuts. Her reflection gave me a tired smile, her long yellow face gleaming, and my guts clenched at the fresh blue bruises around her eyes, the angry welt at her throat. She'd suffered for my selfishness last night, and no doubt those marks weren't the worst of it.

When I was her, I'd despised people like me. Rich, cold, complacent, too self-important to pay me any attention. All she'd asked for was a little cash, and I hadn't even blinked as I brushed her off.

Useless guilt prickled my heart with hot needles, and into the tiny holes seeped anger. I couldn't change my callousness now, only make some pissweak apology. Sorry wouldn't stop her hurting.

I covered her hand with mine, halting her, and prised the paper free. "Thanks. It's all right."

She hovered anxiously on quivering wings, slender feet trailing behind her. She wore the same smeared skirt and flimsy top, her skinny legs bare. "Who bled you? Them skanky Sunshine fangboys? You wanna be careful, they say no rabies in Melbourne, but ya never know with them ratty ones, right, they—"

"No, Vi. It's okay. Just an accident. Really." I tossed the paper at the overflowing bin and surveyed my masterpiece. Clotting, torn, Vincent's telltale blunt teethmarks swollen, but clean. I glanced at her in the mirror. Still she hovered, touching my hair with hesitant fingers.

I swallowed again. "Look, sorry I brushed you off last night."

Violet shrugged, her gaze slipping. "S'no problem."

"No, listen. I . . . I got a lot on my mind, I didn't realize . . ." I sighed, turning to face her. "Fuck. It's no excuse,

Vi. I was a bitch, and I'm sorry for . . . whatever he did to you."

"It ain't your cactus pie." She forced a weak smile. "He ain't so bad. Gets a little nippy, but his dick's about as big as his brain, if ya know what I mean. I got him fooled real good. I'm like, *Ohmigod, that hurts!* but in truth, I can't feel a fucking thing." She snickered, pleased.

After a moment, I snickered, too. Gotta be glad for small mercies. No pun intended. "Hey, listen, if I can still help you out—"

"Nah. S'okay. He's drinkin' with the troll kids. On his scrawny black ass in five minutes. I got me the night off," she announced proudly, and eyed me with shy admiration glimmering in her wide blue eyes. "So. That boss o' yours. He treat you right?"

"Not so bad." Inwardly, I winced. Now she asks me for a job, and I get to score a few more bitch points for telling her no.

"Bet he's a real firecracker, huh? Edgy guy like him? Shit, I bet he's got ya tied to the bed every night."

Stupidly, I blushed. "It ain't like that. Listen, can I ask a favor?" Okay, now I felt really shitty. But I needed any help I could get.

She beamed. "Oh, sure. Watermelons. For you, any time."

"You ever hear of Ivy? Earthfae lady, runs sparkle outta someplace in town?"

She twiddled yellow fingers loftily. "Maybe."

My heart thrummed faster. "You know her?"

"Hair like starlight? Knows all the cute boys? Kind of a white messy thing on her face, like a scar or something?" She tossed her hair over her cheek and did a perfect facsimile of Ivy's haughty face-hiding maneuver.

My excitement ignited. "Yeah, that's her."

"Never heard of her." A nervous glint surfaced in Violet's grin.

Afraid? Unsure? Grasping for money? "Come on, Vi. I really need this."

"You ain't scratchin' for a hit, are ya? 'Cause if I hadda

heard of her, I'da heard her stuff is raw. It'll fuck you up real good. Let me put you on to some propersweet glimmer—"

"I'm not scoring. I just need to find her. Come on, I'll make it worth it." Soon as the words left my lips, I was sorry. I squirmed, sure she'd give me the big old Violet middle finger.

But she just shrugged, uneasy. "Got no time. Sorry."

"Thought you had the night off." Instinctively, I grabbed her shoulder, stopped her from turning away.

She tried to shake me off, and at last, hurt washed over into her eyes. "Don't push me around. Thought you was better than that."

I gritted my teeth and forced my grip to relax. She was right. Gangland had hardened me, made me jumpy. I overreacted a lot. Good thing I couldn't sing, or she'd be on the floor. "I'm sorry, okay? I'm a little wound up."

Her eyes shimmered, her bottom lip trembling like a little girl's. "Fuck you, Mina. All fuckin' superior on me 'cause some weird gang monster wants to screw you. You as bad as the rest of 'em."

Embarrassment whipped my nerves to a tense pitch, and words spilled out before I could swallow them. "That so? News flash, sweetheart. Unlike you, I don't have to screw anyone to get what I want anymore."

Her face drained sallow, and her mouth quivered.

My face burned. "Shit. I didn't mean that. Sorry, Vi."

But airfae anger swirled cold around my legs, buffeting my hair tight, and Violet's lips peeled back to bare jagged black teeth. "Piss on you, bitch. You was always too high and mighty. I even had to show ya how to suck cock without choking. Lucky some trick didn't claw your stuck-up bloody face off."

"Vi—"

"You know what? I'm done watchin' out for you. You ain't my problem no more." She yanked back brittle green hair, angry tears shining golden on her cheeks. "There's an empty train tunnel a couple blocks off the line near Flagstaff Station. Some old platform half-built. That's where Ivy hangs."

Violet knuckled her eyes dry and fluttered haughtily toward the door. "You can keep your filthy money for her poison. Hope it burns your eyes out."

I stuffed my hand into my pocket and flung the bundle of cash after her, limp plastic notes spilling orange and yellow on the sticky floor as the door slammed behind her.

I'd gotten what I wanted. But it didn't feel good.

A wet blue fairy wriggled on her back from under the cubicle door, giggling drunkenly at me. Her soggy gray wings smeared brown in the muck, tangling with gritty blue hair, and her torn dress slid off one shoulder to reveal a small round breast with a hard dark blue nipple.

I scowled. "What the fuck you looking at?"

She tugged her nipple thoughtfully, sucking a finger between ripe inky lips before sliding it between her legs to touch herself. Her eyes glazed, sparklebright. "Nice bitchfight. Want me to eat your pussy, gorgeous? Make you feel g—"

"Piss off." My stomach bubbled warm, and I nearly slammed the door off its hinges getting out of there.

18

Streetlights shone through silent tree branches, casting eerie yellow shapes onto the summerparched lawns of Flagstaff Gardens. The deathly still plane trees overhanging LaTrobe Street blanketed me in shadow as I walked, my heels clipping dusty asphalt and echoing in the empty street. No wind breathed; no leaves rustled. Somewhere, fighting cats yowled. Bats flapped and circled above, their rotten fruit-stink souring the dense air. Across the street, beyond twin tram tracks, concrete office buildings loomed gray and forbidding.

On the corner, a snoring water fairy curled up on the lawn, wrapped up like a baby in dripping green wings with his thumb tucked safely in his mouth. I ducked beneath the blue Flagstaff Station sign—it also helpfully directed me to the tramstop across the street, presumably in case I had no change and wanted to bum a free ride, which, as every Melbournite knows, is what trams are for since they put those stupid ticket machines in—and hopped down the grimy stairs.

A steel concertina gate greeted me, locked fast. I peered through, the hinged steel bars cool on my fingers. The last train was long gone, the next not until at least 5 A.M., and no one was around. But security lights still burned. Yellow corridor, low ceiling, more stairs around a sharp corner.

No rent-a-cop in evidence. No camera.

I flipped out my knife and jammed it into the lock with a twist of my wrist, and the tumblers split with a satisfying crunch. One side remained bolted to the floor, but the other sagged open an inch, inviting. I winced at the scratchmark on my blade as I slipped it away, but what choice did I have? I couldn't sing a hole in a wet paper bag, let alone shatter a lock or sonicbend a steel bar.

I grabbed the door's loose edge and shoved. The criss-crossed iron folded aside with a groan of rusted joints, and I turned sideways and squeezed in. The grimy metal scratched my leather, the zip between my breasts catching until I shook it free.

Down the stairs, around the corner, into the station proper. I vaulted over the yellow plastic entry gates, my heels echoing in dry silence. White lights sliced the ceiling and glared on the orange-tiled floor. A drink dispenser hummed, glowing with garish advertising. The light over the ticket machine flickered, and shadows flitted across the wall, long and sharp like knives. I jerked around, blood throbbing.

No one. Just my nerves, tricking me.

The downward escalators lay still, dead. It looked dark down there. I shivered. I didn't like it underground. The hot darkness, the dank dusty smell. The feeling of being trapped, the loss of control. All those tons of rock teetering above my head, longing to crush me.

I took a calming breath and stepped onto the silent stairway.

Ribbed metal clicked under my boots as I descended. The black rubber handrail stuck clammy to my palm, and the ceiling loomed frighteningly close. Already that musty traintunnel odor dried my mouth.

The wide island platform lay deserted, the tracks empty. Yellow metal walls and bench seats gleamed under blank blue television screens. Along the far wall on each side, shiny letters spelling FLAGSTAFF repeated over and over, leading off into the gloom to die.

I peered up and down the tunnel, and walked over to do the same thing on the other side, straining my useless ears

out of habit. Of course, I heard nothing, only wet cotton silence and my own pulse gurgling. I should have detected
water dripping and rats chewing cables all the way down to
Southern Cross.

Frustration nibbled my toes at my ineptitude. Flagstaff
had four tracks on two levels. Which one did Violet mean?
In which direction?

I hopped down into the ditch, careful not to trip on the
tracks. If she'd tricked me, I deserved it. And if I'd been
nicer to her, she might've given me more clues. No point
wishing. I'd just have to go hunting.

I slipped out my phone and switched it to flashlight. The
screen glowed white, casting cool light in a fading cone a
few feet before me. I checked my knives and strode toward
the black tunnel mouth.

Darkness loomed, the illuminated letters reaching only a
few feet into the tunnel. My nose wrinkled in metal death-
stink, and something wriggled and crunched flat under my
boot. My nerves jerked, the old fear wriggling out like a black
worm from deep in my soul.

Sweat trickled from my hair down the side of my neck.
My ears rang, deaf. Already the walls shuddered and closed
in on me.

Beyond my hallowed light, the train tracks disappeared
into murky blackness. Somewhere, another rat—or
something—scuttled, a dry sound like newspaper that
could've come from any direction. I swallowed rising panic.
I couldn't hear a damn thing. Christ, it was like being blind.

I forced my fingers steady, and slipped out a knife. The
warm hilt comforted me, smooth and curving in my palm,
such a close fit. I adjusted my grip backhanded for swift-
ness, held the phone out like a glowing shield, and took another step.

"You'll never find her like that."

My heart hit the roof of my mouth. I whirled, blind and
deaf, slashing uselessly at black air. My phone clattered to
the ground, light lurching crazily.

But I knew it was him.

Even before he slinked like a serpentine shadow into the light, I knew it was him.

And even though I was half-deaf and straining to see, I hadn't totally lost my situational awareness. I knew exactly where the wall was.

So I slammed my forearm across his throat and rammed him back into it.

19

My hips crunched into his as I fought for a hold, forcing my quivering knifeblade up under his chin.

His heartbeat matched mine, swift and steady. My nerves tingled. Was he following me? Stalking me? Maybe he'd figured out my plans and had come to kill me before I killed him.

Fury whetted my dulled reflexes. Good luck.

I fought the tremor from my voice with stubbornness. "What the fuck you doing here?"

"Same as you, I guess." Joey didn't flinch. His eyes glinted neongreen in my phone's harsh glow. He lifted his hands carefully out of my reach, but his fingertips narrowed and blackened, and wicked green-tipped claws like thorns snicked out, a venombright threat.

I jammed the knife in tighter, cutting his flesh for the first time in my life.

Hot blood slicked. The sight of it, shining black in the dimness, made my body burn, and the vengeance-beast roared at me to finish it once and for all. My voice quaked. "I don't think so. God, I should just kill you right here."

He nodded slowly, just a tiny movement, and distant pain washed his eyes paler. "I don't get it. I've never hurt you. What did I do?"

"You know!" Absurd guilt stung my lips. My skin still crawled with Diamond's clinical caress. Could Joey smell it?

Did he even care? Anger clenched my teeth until they hurt. "Stop playing with me. You've known from the st— Ow!"

My hipbone exploded in a brief but distracting burst of pain.

Blinding fast. Deadly accurate. Unyielding. Christ, he could move when he wanted to.

Rough concrete crunched my shoulder blades. Steely fingers wrapped my wrist and jammed it against the wall, twisting my elbow cruelly.

Pain speared. He'd shifted and snaked his arm backwards, an impossibly double-jointed move, and now it was me trapped between the wall and his body, his grip immovable.

Shit.

He stroked one venomswelled fingertip over my bottom lip, threat or promise. "Bad girl."

Venom's honey sweetness seeped between my lips, laced with something bitter and intriguing, and my skin shrank, in fear or anticipation, I couldn't tell. Horrid truth gnawed once again at my nerves. I'd given myself away. Without my magic, I was just a girl. And Joey was a freak of nature, both faster and stronger than me. One swipe of poisoned claws, and I'd die frothing at the mouth.

No more pain, no more guilt. No more desperate nightmares. No more sick disgust at my own fear.

It'd almost be a relief.

I set my trembling mouth tight and tried not to close my eyes. Gangland was tough. I'd known it'd kill me, one way or another. Damned if I'd hide now. I wanted to see it coming.

But he just stared at me, confusion clouding his eyes. "What's on your mind, Mina? You're smarter than this. You've lied so beautifully, Christ, I've believed every word and invented a few more myself."

"Dunno what you mean." If he was faking his bewilderment, he was very, very good. My fingers numbed, and my knife slipped. I struggled against him, trying to twist my arm free.

He just pressed tighter, harder. "And the way you kissed

me last night? That was brilliant. You had me. If you hadn't pulled a switch, I'd have done whatever you wanted. But coming after me when your spells are shot? That's just fucking sloppy."

"I'm doing fine, thanks."

Urgency thickened his voice. "I hate it when you lie to me. I can feel you're weaker. You sound different. You don't move right. You can't hear anything, can you?"

I wriggled, and fought to control my knife. If he wouldn't do it, I'd damn well make him. "So finish me off," I taunted. "I'm useless to you now. What the fuck do you care? You'll just find another gullible little girl to do your dirty jobs."

He laughed, serpentine and bitter. "Yeah. You know what? I don't give a shit." He wrenched the blade easily from my hand, tossed it point first into the gravel at my feet.

And let me go.

I swept it up, dropping into a fighting crouch. I balanced the glinting blade before me, and my bruised forearm twitched. *Come on. Try it.*

But he just looked at me. "You can't go in there alone, Mina. Not like this. She'll tear your heart out."

My phone lit his face eerily from beneath, casting a compelling gleam into his eyes. It made me think of mint, and his fresh cool hair on my face while he was kissing me, and I swallowed, venom remnants cold on my lips.

Part of me longed for us to be like we were before. We'd worked well together, he and I. A good team. He always knew exactly what to do and how far to go, and I did it without question or hesitation. I wanted to take his hand, take comfort in his cool skin on mine, slink into the dark and fight off our enemies together.

My knife hand quivered. If he came an inch closer, I'd slice him up right here. "That's my problem, not yours. I'm handling it."

"Mina, for once don't be rash."

"You used to want me rash."

That unnerving smile. "You think Ivy doesn't know you're coming? Think she'll return your spells without a fight?"

My stomach prickled like a cactus. "How the hell do you know about Ivy?"

"What do you care? You gonna let me help you or not?"

"You know her, don't you?" A hot splash of suspicion sickened me. "You and her. You knew she could do this. Did you put her up to it?"

Even as I spoke, I knew it was ridiculous, and Joey laughed darkly. "You wouldn't say that if you knew."

I didn't even ask. I just looked at him.

He shrugged. "Let's just say she and I have reason not to like each other. And it'll be my pleasure to hunt her down with you."

My belly warmed. Not such a dumb idea. Truth be told, I needed all the help I could get. And it'd be a fine joke, right? He helps me get my magic back, and then I use it to kill him.

I tossed my hair back haughtily. "Fine. Do what you want. I'm going this way." And I bent to retrieve my still-glowing phone and strode away up the tunnel.

His hand warmed my shoulder.

I spun, shaking, and backed off in a hurry. "Don't touch me, okay? Last night . . . That thing that happened? It was a mistake. I c— Just don't touch me, all right?" My voice trembled, and I didn't even believe myself.

But Joey just tasted the air, a light snakerattle vibrating his tongue, and exhaled with a snakeweird hiss that tingled my skin afresh. He jerked his head in the opposite direction. "Actually, it's thisss way."

God, that lisp still made me quiver. I nodded stiffly, warm with embarrassment and stupid gratitude. "If you say so. After you."

He showered me with that disarming smile. "With you behind me? Not on your sweet life."

And he gestured me ahead, and as always, I could do nothing but obey.

The tunnel enclosed us, dim and spooky, the train tracks gleaming like rust-flecked rivers for a only a few feet ahead before trickling away into the dark. The platforms on either side gave way to narrow maintenance walkways, only sparse inches across, and the walls loomed close and impenetrable.

I wristed cool sweat from my forehead, and the light bobbled and jerked. Joey stalked a few feet to my right, silent, his lean shadow slinking along the wall. I could smell him, fresh and warm, that minty taste a thornsharp threat amid the soft metal stink of concrete and rat dirt.

If he wanted to kill me, I'd be a corpse by now. Right?

The close heat clogged my throat like glue. I tried to breathe slowly, but I longed for light and space and fresh air, and my treacherous pulse tightened in my chest, cramping my lungs until I could force in only a tiny volume of air. I swallowed, trying to suck breath through my nose and calm down.

Joey touched my elbow, cautious. "There."

"Where?" I shone my flashlight and squinted in the direction he pointed, but darkness formed a thick wall.

He melted into the blackness, and I followed, my boots crunching carefully on chunky gravel. Gradually, the wall emerged, rough concrete daubed in blue and yellow spraypaint. Joey grabbed the rail and swung himself up onto the walkway. Between two carbon-blackened bulkheads, a ragged crack gaped, only a few feet wide.

He offered me his hand. I ignored it and squirmed under the rail and up.

I stretched out my light and peered into the crack. Dark, musty, the faint telltale smell of burnt sugar. My tongue tingled. Fairies lived here.

But narrow. Cruelly, scarily narrow, the other end out of sight.

My skin rippled. "You smelled that from back there?"

"Like a chocolate shop." Automatically he lowered his voice to a murmur, as I had. "Get rid of that light, or they'll see. Want me to go first?"

"Nope. I'll go." I spoke before I could change my mind. With him behind me, no way could I chicken out and turn back.

Steeling myself, I switched the flashlight off.

Blackness closed in, complete. My eyes strained for one tiny mote of light, but there was nothing. I closed my eyes and opened them again. No change.

My skin shrank cold. My chest heaved, and my ragged breath ripped my ears, amplified. The air hung heavy like soaked wool. I couldn't breathe. In my mind, massive rocks tumbled, crushing me. Cold sweat dribbled between my breasts, and I wanted to swat it away, but my muscles froze. I couldn't move. I was helpless. I gasped. "Joey—"

"Peace. You're okay." His smooth hand took possession of mine, and soon I felt concrete under my palm, guiding me, repositioning me in a stifling black velvet world where up, down, left, right meant nothing.

Gratefully, I clutched the rift's edge, my breath calming. I wasn't crushed. He hadn't slit my throat in the dark. My swimming head righted itself, and gradually, my straining eyes detected a faint greenish halo in the distance. Light, spilling in the other end.

I sheathed my knife and shoved my hip into the crack, squirming in past a concrete lump. The sooner I escaped this benighted hellcave, the better.

Rock scraped my breasts, squishing them tight. *Don't panic. Stay calm.* I thrust my hips forward to get my bum out of the way and forced myself in farther. Damn skinny fairies. My nipples protested, smarting against my leather. Good thing I was so slim, but no amount of sucking in your breath makes your boobs smaller. I tried to breathe shallowly and shuffled along, heels catching on broken shards. The floor wasn't even, and more than once I had to twist my ankles painfully to get through.

Light flared closer, a dim green haze in the corner of my eye. I heard Joey ease in beside me, swift, silent but for a tiny scrape or two. I was about to force a laugh, tell him he was crazy, he'd never fit, but the soft squelch of shifting flesh stopped my throat.

My imagination scuttled, wild like a trapped fly. How much had he shifted? Just enough to compress his bones, or . . . My mouth dried. What did he look like? How did it feel, that warm rough rock sliding against smooth snake-skin? . . .

Concrete smacked into the side of my head, and I dragged my concentration back.

Shuffle, stretch, wriggle. Nasty sugarplum stink thickened already heavy air, my sweat tweaking bitter with anxiety. The light shone brighter, if I wrenched my eyeballs as far as I could to the right. I detected faint shadows, lumpy rock-shapes inches from my nose.

I jerked a quick glance at Joey, my curiosity burning. Still couldn't see. He'd never shown me. Too cautious, too in control. Me trying to kill him wasn't likely to change his mind. But some prickly part of me still longed to see, touch, taste, caress that smooth reptile skin with my cheek. . . .

I squeezed my hip past one last rocky lump, and popped out.

I sucked in a deep, grateful breath. My lungs inflated sweetly, and ripe oxygen relief cooled my muscles, soothing my heartbeat to a rapid thrum. I blinked, straining my vision in dim green glow.

Another stifling hot tunnel, rough and unfinished. A few feet to my left, work had ceased, leaving a ragged rock wall slashed with drillmarks and broken chalky slate. To my right, the tunnel stretched into darkness. Rubble littered the empty floor, no tracks, no wires, nothing.

Behind me, Joey squirmed out, and the wet fleshsound told me he'd reshifted. I sneaked a look, trying to keep it casual. No change. Neat, unruffled, breathing only slightly hard. Glowing faintly green with neon sweat, pale hair plastered to his cheek, shirt wet like my own clothes and sticking to his perfect skin.

Dark curiosity warmed me again. What happened when he bugged out? His creature was an accident of faebirth, not a magic trick. Nothing so convenient. He'd have to slither out of his clothes, and . . .

"Okay now?" His smooth hand touched mine, and I jumped. Damn it.

"Uh-huh." I dragged dusty wet locks from my face and turned away.

The cavern's ceiling faded into darkness. Opposite, they'd installed a few platform sections, and on the flat concrete, creatures snored and wriggled, a somnolent pile of warm wet wings, entangled limbs, dusty colored hair. I wrinkled my nose at rotten food and stale fairy sweat. This place needed one big shower.

On the platform's tiled edge, a skinny waterfairy gurgled and muttered, his insensible limbs thrashing in some nightmare's greedy grip. His translucent wings flopped over the edge like wet plastic, and his eyeballs rolled, glazed bloody with bad drugs. In the corner, a hunchbacked green troll with rotted black horns gnashed his teeth and rocked on his heels, slamming his forehead into the wall over and over.

I shivered, and Joey and I shared a glance. If this was where Ivy sourced her ingredients, no wonder her sparkle was lethal. It made sense of Diamond's containerload of fairies, though I didn't get why he needed to import any when we had enough broken, hopeless fae in this town already to stock a hundred nasty underground pharmacies. Maybe they were special orders. And as for why she wanted my song . . .

My stomach clenched hard, and I gritted my teeth to stop the bile leaking out. If she'd already put me in some cheap-and-dirty pick-me-up, I'd kill the murdering hellbitch right here.

Joey tasted the air, tonguepoints flickering, and touched a finger to his ear. *Listen.*

I strained, but heard nothing bar snoring fae and my own gluggy heartbeat. Frustration spiked me raw. If the boss, who didn't even have ears half the time, could hear better than me, it really was time to shoot myself.

I steadied my breath and blocked out the mess of noises one by one. . . .

Singing. A breathy, high-pitched fairy voice, warbling inane melody. And everyone on the platform was either asleep or dead.

My throat tightened. Joey touched my hand and pointed, but I'd already seen it. On the platform, beyond the crush of bodies, a narrow doorway led into greenlit darkness.

I stole forward. My boots scraped minutely on uneven ground, and I winced. A rusty ladder led up to the chest-high platform. Beneath it curled a nest of fat little baby spriggans, sleeping in the nude with their chubby thumbs tucked in each others' mouths and their little green babytails knotted together. Their turned-up noses twitched as they burbled happily, blowing bubbles in their sleep. Cute little things. Pity they'd grow into monsters. But still my indignation sparked. What kind of parents left their kids in this place?

I couldn't climb the ladder without waking them, and a baby spriggan's screech is the soundtrack of nightmares. So I flexed my thighs and vaulted up, the tiles warm under my palm. My heels clicked quietly as I landed beside a paralytic firefairy, his long graceful limbs wasted. His pretty flame guttered, almost extinguished, smoke wisping weakly from slack fingers.

I froze in a crouch, my thighs tense, my muffled senses as alert as I could make them for sound and motion. No echo. No one awoke. The singing didn't stop.

From the doorway, broken glass clinked, a muffled female curse.

I straightened, and behind me Joey hopped up, lighting gracefully to his feet. I hadn't noticed that he didn't have his cane. I knew he didn't need it to walk. But seeing him without it was strange. Like he was undressed. Or disarmed.

Inwardly I snorted. Not likely. If he wanted to kill me, he had all the weapons he needed, right there under his skin.

But we'd a common enemy now. I didn't know why he hated her so much. I didn't care. It'd serve me well, and when we'd beaten her, the game would be back on.

My pulse quickened. Just for now, it was like it used to be. I couldn't resist the ghost of a smile, and just for an instant, warmth glimmered golden in his eyes.

A fraction later, it was gone.

My heart ached. Damn it if I didn't miss the way we

moved together, thought together like two halves of the same person. How could a man who was the other half of me be my mother's murderer? I'd refuse to believe it, if I hadn't seen it with my own eyes.

But I had. Even if I was drunk and sparkleblind and screaming with my mind ripped open at the time. I'd seen it. It had to be true. Right?

I swallowed and silently unsheathed my knife. Joey eased out wicked wet claws. And step by careful step, we advanced.

Over a fat naked goblin, my foot sliding in wet snot trickling from his nose. Around a muttering vampire boy who crawled in circles in his sleep, yanking his own hair out string by greasy black string and stuffing it in his pockets. The smell thickened. The troll kept banging his head, blood gushing down his twisted green face. Creatures muttered and groaned, dribbling and quivering and writhing like worms, all lost in their own psychotic worlds, their minds erased, ruined, muddled beyond recognition.

Images washed, my mother moaning incoherent sounds, clawing at her face, bloody spit dribbling from those pretty lips that sang me spellsweet lullabies when I was a baby. The day she died, she wasn't herself, her mind erased, too, her body's shell housing some vacant monster that wailed in pain.

I cracked my jaw tight, and kept moving.

My toe caught a furry faeborn thing's long deformed hand, and I recoiled, anticipating a hiss and a bleary-eyed challenge. But she merely licked catlike teeth with a coiled sandpaper tongue and went back to sleep. I tiptoed over her mismatched limbs, one leg with the elbow backwards, a mutant mix of paws and flippers. Sympathy mixed with wariness to sicken my stomach. Any faeborn kid who survived to adulthood was lucky, but some were luckier than others.

At last, we reached the doorway. I adjusted my knife grip, breathing to relax my jumping nerves. Sneak in. Jump her. Pin her down, demand she return what she'd stolen. And if that didn't work . . . well, Joey and I had a creative imagination for threats. We'd think of something.

I rolled my shoulders loose, muscles crunching, and stepped toward the door.

Joey's hand slipped warm into mine, and he tugged me back.

Jesus, don't get all protective on me now. I glared and shook my head.

He flickered his eyebrows at me, deceptively calm. Joey-speak for *Do as you're fucking told, girl. Don't make me tell you twice.*

My fight. I mouthed the words, deliberate so he could see.

He just put that infuriatingly calm finger to my lips again. For a moment he let it linger, his claw smooth and temptingly sharp. And then he coiled his forearm swiftly around mine and pulled me behind him.

For an instant, all my attention zoomed in on that shifting flesh. Warm, slick, so very smooth, sliding muscles wrapping me tight. Bumps tingled my skin, and I shivered.

I wrenched my concentration back, flushing, but stupid admiration still teased my blood. Gutsy move for a guy convinced I'm gonna kill him.

Sure. Or maybe just cold, calculating, biding his time.

My guts writhed. Even now that I knew the sordid truth about him, some timid little girl inside me still longed so badly to believe in him, she determinedly covered her eyes. Christ, what did he have to do before I'd hate him like I should? Slit my throat with his own hands?

Angrily, I tugged my hand away, but it only left me bereft and cold.

He gestured me to his right. I moved over as far as I could, only a few feet. I glanced around, my mouth dry. One entrance, too narrow to enter side by side. No light. Maybe no other exit.

Not a smart place for an ambush.

My foot crunched on broken glass, and abruptly the singing stopped.

I froze, and held my breath. Shit. She heard me. Without my hearing, I was blind. Should I wait, or strike?

In a flash, the light flared bright in a verdant halo, silhouetting a pair of long ragged wings.

Too slow.

Slanting silver eyes glinted evilly from the dark, and a crusty cackle drifted out. "Oh, lookie, serpent. You brought her. Just like you said."

I tensed to flee, but hot despair flooded. The bastard tricked me. Again. My muscles refused to obey, and rampant chemicals in my blood screamed uselessly at me to move, run, fight.

A long yellow arm lashed from the dark. I snarled and jerked back, but too late.

Bitterstinging claws fastened cruelly around my shoulder and yanked me inside.

20

I hurtled forward, my knife slipping from numb fingers and clattering on the ground.

I grappled for her wrist, trying to lever her off me. Fairy fingers dug into my bare shoulder, drawing blood, and the pain spiked my struggling nerves alive.

I wrenched my shoulder tight and spun, using my grip on her wrist as leverage. My body cartwheeled. My boots smacked the floor, hard and stable, and my momentum yanked her off her feet. Blindly, I pulled as hard as I could, and let go, flinging her fairylight body across the room. She hit some wall or shelf with a satisfying crunch of shattered glass.

I panted, the world fading slowly into sight. Dark cavern walls melting into the distance, benches cluttered with dirty glassware, shelves of sparkling rainbow vials. My mouth watered, the dark velvety habit igniting longing in my blood. My palms itched. Hunger flowered darkly inside, that snitchy little voice whispering, *Kill her and take the sparkle. Forget all this. You know you want it.*

I bit my lip and forced myself to think of shy, deceived Cobalt, midnight hair tumbling, breathing my stolen magic into a vial just like those. Did one of them hold my song? What color would it be? Surely, I'd recognize my own essence? Surely there'd be some lingering sound, some remnant?

I strained my ears, searching, but caught nothing.

Some swirling crystal sphere thing sat on the bench, eerie green light glittering inside like sticky faedrenched goo, and when I looked at it, my hair sprang and sparked with weird static, hypnotic images of strangers and unknown places skidding through my mind. I shivered and tore my gaze away. What the hell was that?

But no time for sightseeing. Already Ivy launched into the air, torn wings flapping like stretched white sheets. Broken glass splattered with spilled spells glittered scarlet and blue in her wild silver hair. Chartreuse blood dripped onto her dusty gown, and she snarled, her golden hands clawing. A bloodstained sleeping beauty, pissed to hell that we'd woken her up.

She hovered just out of my reach, and laughed, her pretty face twisted. In the eerie light, her cheek shone flawless, the scars gone. "So you're still strong. Good, good. Hate to think I'd ruined you already. Now come over here and drink this." She ducked to the bench and plucked up a dirty glass tube. Inside, brown sludge bubbled and steamed, stinking of rotting skin and foul sweat. Just like Cobalt's memoryjuice, only a hundred times worse.

Beside her, the green sphere swam brighter. Static rattled in my hair, and my vision swirled dim.

I hissed, baring my teeth, angry spellcraft clouding my mind. My blood boiled toxic with hatred. She'd ruined my life to give some whacked-out sparkle freak a cheap high, and she was cackling about it like some crazyfairywitchbitch.

Black deathfury clotted my heart, and evil energy slashed urgently into my limbs. I gasped and exulted, my bones wrapped deep in pleasure. Better than sparklewash. Better than sex. Just like having my song back, only more delicious, more malevolent. *Now let's see who's stronger, bitch.*

My fists clenched tight, and I lurched forward, intent on tearing her throat out with my teeth.

In my scarlet mist, I barely registered Joey sliding his arm around my shoulders, whispering tightly in my ear. "Don't, Mina. She's spellfucking you. Keep it real."

I ignored him. My fingers clawed like talons. This was no spell. I felt fine. I felt great. She'd ripped my heart out, and she deserved no less from me.

He persisted, his body warm against my side, fighting for my questing arm. I shook him off. Ivy grinned and curled her finger, beckoning.

My rage exploded. I wanted to gouge her heart out. Claw her face off and eat it. Smash her into her stinking rainbow-glass wall over and over until the flesh shredded from her mutated fairy bones.

Sharp fangs sliced my ear, and the hot shock slammed me back to reality.

Like breath on a mirror, my fury evaporated, and dirty fairy spellcraft crystallized like diamonds in midair and tinkled to the floor.

My limbs weakened. Dizziness spun my head in circles. My knees buckled. I stumbled, and Joey caught me.

Scarlet drops spattered warm on my shoulder, and chill racked my skin tight. My heartbeat warmed to his, steady, comforting. His arms felt safe around me, a living version of my tight leather. Nothing could hurt me in there. I wanted to huddle into his embrace and let him protect me.

Not a fucking chance.

Steadily, I pushed him away and lifted my chin. Attacking her wasn't an option. Bargaining would have to do, at least until I could catch her off guard. "What do you want?"

Ivy folded her wings in a puff of golden dust and picked up a glittering glass wand to twirl. "Cleverthing like you? You know what I want."

"I know Diamond gave you my song. What's your price?"

Ivy mimed dabbing at her eyes. "So sad. Already gone, my love. Lost like breath on the wind." She cackled, her eyes glinting golden with wicked delight. "Got a good price for you, too. Love and deliciousness. You make a delightful lovespell. But it's not quite paid for yet."

My heart glugged. "Gone? It can't be."

"Mmm. My thoughts exactly. Gone? Already?" She waved her arms, indignant. "How'm I supposed to make my pretty

hellangel love me when it's all *gone*? I want *more*!" Crimson
treachery ignited in her gaze, and she lifted her skinny golden
arm and hurled the sparkling wand to the floor.

Glass shattered, and a sweet pink cloud puffed like ethe-
real smoke.

Joey cursed and flung himself at her, a sleek black arrow
in the air. Telltale bitterness stung my nose, the rotting stink
of glassfae magic turned sour, and I stumbled back.

But too late.

Time jerked like a braking train, and slowed.

Air screeched to a halt in my ears, skidding like car tires.
The mist motes danced slower, slower, until their sparkle
shimmered and froze in midair. Joey's swift dive hit insolu-
ble friction, and his black shape smeared to a stop, caught in
midflight. Ivy leapt into the air and hung there, her gown
billowing in swelling pink fog.

My lungs jerked in panic, drowning me. My arms waved,
desperately slow, and I tumbled backwards in slow motion,
my momentum sucking away into some black void until I
hung suspended on my back, my limbs flung out like a
weird ritual sacrifice. My tangled hair spread motionless
in a stained-glass azure snapshot, and blood dripping from
my torn ear froze halfway to the ground.

I struggled, willing my muscles to work, but nothing happened. I couldn't move. I couldn't breathe. Joey was stuck in
midair, blurred like a jolted photograph. The world had frozen in time.

Ivy giggled and fluttered to her feet. Unaffected. Free.

My head throbbed. My lungs ached for air. A scream
brewed in my throat, but I'd no breath to make it.

Dread chewed my guts ragged. Surely this was it. I'd die.
Not a rotten sparkle hit, not a bloody gunshot in the dark or
beaten to death in some stupid gangfight. Tricked by a mad,
magicdrunk, lovesick fairy. Great.

I couldn't move my eyeballs. Her soft footsteps rang uncannily loud in the crisp magical silence. She loomed into
my vision and peered down at me, and her smile lifted her
face to another level of strange fae beauty. Delicately dusted

golden skin, liquid silver eyes with sweeping white lashes, small coquettish lips, cheekbones translucent like crystal. Even scarred, she was beautiful. Now, she was exquisite. This reluctant lover of hers must be blind.

Not that it mattered now, lying here at the mercy of her strange whims. Even if I could tell her I'd no voice left, that I'd never in my life sung a love spell anyway.

Her eyes glowed hot. "Ready to feed me, prettyblue?"

My blood lurched, cold. I struggled, but my nerves sparked uselessly in limbs that just couldn't move, no matter how I coaxed.

She tweaked my nose fondly, brandishing the crusted glass tube so the memorysauce sloshed, brown and sloppy like runny shit. "I'll need everything you've got left. So no shygirl, okay?" And she forced a cold finger between my lips and poured the sour brown froth in.

Cold, viscous, disgusting. Stinking grit fouled my tongue, coated my teeth, dribbled down my throat. I gagged, and she forced one hand under my chin and the other over my lips. My teeth crunched, and the feral stuff crawled down my gullet like a rodent.

Already my head swam, colors reeling, shapes hurtling like earthquake debris. Christ, the stuff was strong. Much stronger than Cobalt's. It tore my mind open and whipped the insides to pulp. My face burned. My eyes stung and watered, and I couldn't blink to clear them. My nose scorched inside, acid fumes ripping at my nostrils.

The gunk hit my stomach, and my guts heaved. Acid splashed my throat, splurting out my nose like horrid drunken vomit, but she wasn't letting go. She tapped my larynx with impatient knuckles, and my treacherous muscles convulsed in a painful swallow.

Down it went, frothing foully in my stomach. Sickness choked me. My vision flared scarlet, and cramp rammed my guts like an iron fist, and then everything scrunched up and sucked away into a swirling black vortex of pain.

Somewhere, Ivy cackled and sliced cold grasping talons into my brain.

Images slashed, razorsweet. Tumbling like spinning blades, colors crashing discordant, the brassy shapes of melody and memory mingling. My skin crawled with ants. Pieces of my brain tore away and slopped onto the floor, pink and shining like gristle.

I choked a scream. Bile splashed my mouth, and with that bright salty shock, I realized I was still alive.

Alive, and hovering on silent wings in a dusty gray room, where moonlight slashed like blades between the cracks of drawn blinds to carve bright furrows on the grimy floor.

My mother's house. My mother's room. And there she lay, crying on the floor with blood smearing her face.

Inside my snap-frozen body, I wriggled and thrashed and wailed in horror.

But I couldn't move, couldn't speak, couldn't escape Ivy's crawling invasion. Vicious agony stabbed my skull, deeper, harder. In her search for the nonexistent remnant of my song, she was ripping the carcass of my memories raw.

Here we go again.

21

The dusty floor glitters in flitting moonbeams. My mother groans, a horrid multilayered chord of agony and despair. A window shatters, and hot breeze gusts in. I breathe in, pollen and sweet moonlight sparkling on my tongue.

This is new.

The angle is different, the colors strange. I can see my mother's hands clawing at the rug, her ripped nails painted blue, the bloodstained jewel in her ring. Everything is splattered with an eerie metallic light I've never seen before, shadows tarnishing the shapes with gold. Terror no longer constricts my chest. My limbs no longer cramp and shake. Strange lightness fills my body, like my bones are hollow and my flesh less dense. Breeze blows my hair back, and I smile.

The images struck me dizzy. This wasn't right. I'd never felt this before. What was Ivy doing to me? What feral lies did she feed me?

The banshee's pewter gaze rolls, sweeping the room, and it lights on me.

Dread pierced my bones like hot needles, agonizing. No, Mother. Don't see me. Don't see how I failed you.

Her mouth gapes ugly in terror. Her nails rake the floor, grasping for a hold as she tries to crawl away from me, but her legs crumple and she wails in frustration.

I giggle, rage and mirth rolled into a prickly black ball in my throat, and look down.

I'm six feet off the floor. Hovering on glitterlight wings that trail past my feet. Sparkles dance in my breeze and flow from my long silver hair. And below me, crouched in a shivering mess behind a dusty black sofa, hides a skinny blue-haired banshee girl in a tight black T-shirt and lacy jeans. High-heeled feet blistered. Smeared eyeliner bleeding onto her face in a wash of terrorblack tears.

I wanted to wail and kick. Ivy was there. Ivy saw it all.

And everything I'd seen while I sweated and writhed in Cobalt's reluctant embrace, I'd seen through Ivy's hate-twisted eyes.

Fourteen-year-old me hadn't really seen the killer at all. They weren't my memories. They were hers.

And whatever Joey was hiding from me just got a whole lot bigger.

My blood iced, but I couldn't close my eyes. I couldn't stop watching. As her spellsharp fingers wormed deeper into my brain, ripping me apart in search of whatever elusive spark brought my song to life, her brimming thoughts bubbled over, splashing like bright raindrops into my memory.

And like a bodysnatcher's unwilling victim, I became her.

Footsteps whisper in the silence. I dart back into shadow, flick, flutter, fly. It's Joey, dark and slender in the long coat and neat black suit he wears to hide himself. With that longish blond hair and deathpale skin, he almost looks human. But he can't hide his aliengreen eyes, so deep and shining and unblinking like a snake's.

My bleeding cheek twitches in memory of his nasty slashing claws, and hatred bubbles like tar in my throat. Inwardly I giggle. Everyone knows what you are, DiLuca. I'll make sure of that.

He tastes the air, spears his cold green gaze left and right, and with a smooth wristflick pulls his pistol from under his coat.

The banshee woman moans and gazes up at him. No fear in her tarnished silver eyes. Only pleading, deep and desperate and heartbroken, tears rolling down her cheeks in black and bloody streams. "Please. Help me."

A nasty cackle rises in my throat, and I swallow it before he hears. He doesn't know her, the crying banshee. I don't know her. She was just in the way. See what happens when you cross me, serpent? People get hurt. And hurt. And hurt, over and over until you say you're sorry for what you did to me. Until I scar you the way you've scarred me.

Joey kneels beside her, black coat flaring on the dirty floor. His free hand goes to her forehead, her throat, her chin, and his whisper comes out ripe with sympathy and disgust. "Christ, lady. You're a mess. C'mon, before she comes back." And he slides his arm under hers, tries to help her up.

"Nooo!" A drawn-out moan, empty, her magical voice a parched husk. Her hands flap, beating away invisible bats, and her lips stretch around silent, heart-ripped words she can no longer make the sounds for. "Please. Just finish it. The monsters . . . get them off me . . . ahh!" And she surrenders to helpless squeals and thrashes, her mind gibbering insane. She claws the air, her spine distorting. Her eyes roll, blind and bloodshot, her pretty mouth froths pink, her breath rattles with phlegm and blood like plague-rotted death.

She's lost.

Joey's fist clenches, and slowly he lets her go. Stands. Sights. Fires.

The shot shatters the brittle air, and the echoing tingle along my arms makes me jump.

His head twitches up, his senses uncannily accurate.

I freeze, my glamour slim and silent, making me invisible. I hold my breath, wrath twisting my mouth tight. Oh, no you don't, snakefreak. I'm not finished with your sorrow yet.

He stares right at me, but vision isn't his forte. He can't see me. I smile, triumphant. And with an angry snap of wet fingerwebs, he flicks the weapon away and stalks out.

I howled inside, my body shaking. It was all true. Joey shot my mother. There, in front of me, clear as ice. He'd taken her life, right there on the floor in our dusty living room, and in all these years, he'd never said a word to me. He'd lied to me, just as I'd feared.

But he hadn't murdered her out of spite, oh no. I should've

figured it wasn't that simple. He killed her out of mercy. To spare her agony and dribbling madness.

To save her from Ivy, who'd already killed her with memory magic. Torn out her song and her mind and her soul, squeezed them mercilessly like tortured rats until sparkling banshee-juice dripped out, and poured it still screaming into a tiny glass prison.

Like she'd surely do to me, if I couldn't break free.

Ivy giggled and capered about, rubbing multijointed hands together. Foul memorysauce bubbled and roiled with delight in my guts, grabbing my mind's edges with eager talons and wrenching them apart. My consciousness stretched, distorted like melting plastic, a blazing pain deep in my skull that wouldn't ease.

Mindless noise filled my throat. I couldn't open my mouth. Ivy hit me again with her spell's full force, a hurricane buffeting through my mind, hurling everything in its path to the winds. Pressure squeezed tighter, like a metal band around my skull, and something inside my head tore free.

Agony ripped fresh current through my nerves. A spasm thrashed my body like a whip. My jaw ripped free at last, and I howled.

Broken. Torn. Empty. No magic in my voice. A forlorn, desperately human sound that made no echo.

Ivy screeched, her hair streaming back in eldritch breeze. "Give it to me!"

My spine whiplashed again. Cosmic glass shattered, and I thudded to the ground, my breath knocked away.

With a metallic groan, time started.

Glass tinkled. Discarded paper whipped in the wind. Joey's body broke from its prison and speared through the air to the place where Ivy had been, and he tumbled and rolled to his feet with serpentine grace. Still human, his claws twitching, shiny black snakeskin creeping up his forearm.

I struggled to scramble up, my spine shrieking in pain. My wits clogged. Had everything happened in the space of a blink?

I tried to talk, to make sense of it all, but my jaw wouldn't move. My tongue numbed. I pushed myself up, and my arm buckled like rubber under my weight.

Panic frothed my blood to bubbles. But all I could do was flop like a beached eel.

Ivy loomed over me, wings spread threateningly, her face a mask of fury. Joey swiped at her with bared claws, venom splashing, but she snarled and blasted him back against the wall with a handful of swirling wind.

Joey hissed and slashed, and she pointed a threatening finger at him, sparkstrewn wind whipping her hair wild. "Away, serpent, or your pretty banshee dies. Just like her mother."

And her squealing magical shade dived at me like a transparent bat, fangs bared, those invisible talons clawing deep into my brain once more. My ears screeched and exploded, wetness pouring down my face. Pain rocketed through my bones. Flesh tore inside my head, hot blood spraying the walls like some homicidal madwoman's padded cell.

But I could still see. I could still feel, every scrape and munch and vicious slash in my brain, a petrified patient awake on the operating table. And somewhere inside, the little iron ball of my will swelled shiny with the last ragged scraps of my pride, and I held on to my sanity with grim, determined fingers.

No. Fuck you. You can't have me.

But terror bloomed bloody in my heart, and I sobbed, my dignity drowning in crimson agony.

Screw not showing my pain. I don't care if he sees me weeping. God, please, if you're there, don't let me live much longer. I don't wanna die like her, slobbering and insane.

Please, just let me pass out.

But I didn't.

22

Mina screams, and it's the worst sound Joey's ever heard.

His bones jangle, worse than claws raking a blackboard. More horrible than a dying scream, because she's still alive. The awful ripped melody of her horror shatters through his sinuses, and cold reptile blood seeps into his throat. Broken, terrified, raw with agony and despair.

Just like her mother.

Ivy's revelation pierced him cold, like a bullet to some bright nerve center deep in his heart.

Mina, that dead banshee's daughter.

He staggers against the wall, trapped by Ivy's magical cage, his mind reeling with misunderstanding and cross purposes and all the fucking stupid things he's said and done.

He never knew. Never picked it up. Never saw the resemblance in Mina's sharp little nose, the delicate feminine line of her chin.

Crazy images spin and flee, memories, conversations, the intoxicating heaven of her kiss. All adding up to the crushing conclusion that she never meant any of it. Never wanted him. Never felt anything for him but hatred, when all along his feelings for her have been . . . unfathomable. Frightening. Impossible.

How long has she known? Has she been waiting all these years simply for him to drop his guard?

But no time to reflect on his foolishness. Ivy looms over

her like some appalling albino bat, screeching in delight at her misery. The magical green ball casts their shadows on the wall, eerie neon silhouettes with a life of their own, and green shadow-Ivy's claws hack a jagged crack in shadow-Mina's skull and wrench it apart in a splash of shadow-blood.

The real Mina groans, her body jerking in some magic-whipped fit. Her face shines deathly pale. She chokes, and blood coats her delicate lips even redder. She can't move, can't fight. Can't free herself.

Invisible enchanted fists pound Joey's body into the wall. A bone crushes in his hip, excruciating, and he bites back a yell. Instinctively he shifts the joint, a fluid motion of sinew and bone and muscle from human to snake and back again, and the break mends, but it doesn't stop fucking hurting.

Bits of green shadow-brain splatter the wall, and shadow-Ivy cackles and delves for more, poking inside shadow-Mina's spreadeagled skull like a mad fairy surgeon. Mina's head falls to the side in a beautiful spill of bloody blue hair, and she gazes directly into Joey's eyes.

For a moment, his heartbeat strangles.

Sparkling static crackles between them, furious fairy magic and everything that's gone unspoken. Her throat jerks, but no sound comes out. Tears spill from her terrified ruby eyes. Her mouth quivers, and she stretches painful lips around words that fire like guilt-drenched arrows straight to his snakeblack soul.

Help me. Please.

His guts twist with rage, and he thrashes against his magical bonds, the force smashing into his body over and over, squashing his breath away. A rib breaks, stabbing like hot wire into his lung, but he can't care.

If he can't help her, she'll die.

But he can't get free. Can't save himself, let alone this woman, who for some insane reason, he would risk everything for.

This woman who's trying to kill him. The woman he's obsessed with beyond reason and common sense and every clever and cautious thing he's ever learned.

His vision blurs, and the stubborn reason-creature in his mind kicks and thrashes in denial. He can't love her. It's impossible. It's foolish. It'll get him killed.

But it's real. Might as well call it what it is.

The wall carves into his shifting shoulder blades, infuriating. Snakeflesh writhes dark and hot just beneath his skin, itching to burst forth, snap tight, escape. The serpent might be too narrow and sinuous to be caught in Ivy's magical web. He'd get free in a swift thrash of tail and fin. Maybe. Unless the spellwrought threads snap his spine in half.

Acid frustration sears his blood. He can't. Not the hideous creature, not in front of her. She'll shrink away, turn from him, never let him help her once she sees what he really is.

Never let him love her.

Ivy knows too well his ugly self-loathing. It's what she's betting on.

He can't. But he must. Better Mina lives and despises him, than the alternative. Either way, he'd better get used to being without her.

Besides, if she dies . . .

The black mist fogging his brain to midnight clears in a warm flash of jasmine-scented sunlight.

If she dies, none of it fucking matters anyway.

Pungent facestruck chemicals spurt into his blood, and he shifts.

His bones creak in protest for a millisecond, and then they sigh in aching relief, and stretch. His skin warms, exothermic energy spilling to the air. Scales erupt, tighten, flex, his new skin drying rapidly in the heat. His spine crackles, subsuming limbs, sprouting fins and tailspike, twisting and growing ribs, pulling guts into shape.

His vision dims, colors bleeding out, and shapes sharpen and wobble as his eyelids recede and his lenses snap tighter. Nerves lengthen and flare alive in his flesh. His pulse quickens and cools. His sinuses stretch and snap into shape, the vibrating air a sharpsweet glory on his tongue, in his mouth, over his elongated throat. Fangs erupt from his gums and bleed bitter venom.

An intoxicating wash of scents dizzies him. So beautiful, this fresh sensory banquet. So soothing and satisfying, the cool shift of elongated muscle and bone.

So much like home.

Sweet resignation floods his snakecold heart. Let her see. It's the truth, after all. Might as well call it what it is.

Mina chokes, and stares.

Blood clogged my throat, rich and thick like salty chocolate, making me wheeze for breath. My head ached like a thousand scorpions threw a wriggling stingfuck party in there.

But I didn't care.

Because through the dizzy haze of my agony, I saw something I never thought I'd see.

Black, so black and delicious like midnight velvet, but smooth, gleaming, sleek. His long body curved gracefully, twice the length of a human or more, the razor fin along his back sparkling with broken glass and venomsplashed fairy glitter. Glossy webbed fins folded neatly along his flanks, tipped with delicate claws that glimmered like tiny green jewels.

He flexed lithe muscles along his spine, his elegant head rearing back, and his tapering tail curled into view, topped with a wickedly sharp spike. His underside shone an even deeper, softer black. The exquisite line of his jaw gleamed narrow and perfect, his fangs shining clean and sharp and lovelier than any vampire's cruel weapon. His eyes glowed, the deepest green I'd ever seen, stripped of their human defenses and burning with pure and powerful emotion.

And his primal, honest beauty broke my heart.

My ravaged brain managed a splash of awestruck incredulity, sprinkled with wonder.

This was what he hid from me? This astonishing, perfect, magical creature?

Delight swirled crazily in my chest. I couldn't deny this anymore. He didn't want to share, didn't want me close to him. But he'd exposed his worst secrets, shown me his deepest, blackest heart, and I still didn't want to look away. I couldn't bear to look away.

I knew the truth now. About my mother. About Joey. About what lurked beneath his human form. And about what he meant to me.

He was part of me, and for better or worse, I couldn't live without him.

Tears flooded my eyes, a burning mist. Maybe because I was already crying. It didn't matter.

Nothing mattered anymore.

I let my eyelids flutter closed and waited to die.

23

Her eyes close, blocking out the sight of him, and Joey swivels away. He coils his long serpent body tight, muscles bulging, and flicks free from the tangle of fabric he was wearing and onto the concrete floor. It's rough and delicious under his belly, broken edges sliding like a gritty caress.

Ivy shrieks, vibrating his body with sensation. "Stay back, serpent, or watch her die." She flings another cosmic punch, but he's too swift and darts away. The force slams into the wall behind him, thrashing itself to nothing.

His forked tongue flickers, tasting, hunting his adversary on spelldrunk air. His constricted reptile brain thinks in compartments, detached, analytical. One thing at a time. Mina struggles only weakly now. Ivy's killing her, knifing deeper and deeper into her soul, searching for something that isn't there.

Cold reptile hatred needles into his blood, and ragevenom seeps from his clawed fins. He hisses, and it feels good. Ivy should die, for himself and Mina both. Swipe his tongue along her cooling skin, taste her dying sweat, feel the breath rattle in her throat as she expires.

But his hungry tongue can sense a vile memoryspell connection between them. It stretches the air, taut like a glassy spiderweb, thrumming with every vibration. If he breaks it, Mina's mind might shatter forever.

On the wall, a distorted black shadow-Ivy drags another

hunk of bleeding flesh from shadow-Mina's skull, stuffs it into her mouth and chews, smacking her shadow-lips with glee.

Fury and fear ripple Joey's spine. Venom swells his fangs tight, and he rears up to strike.

Shadow-Ivy cackles, and the real Ivy grins, yanking Mina's limp hair. "Kill me, and you kill her. I win."

Joey doesn't think. He just thrashes his wickedspiked tail and swipes the shimmering green globe off the desk.

Ivy and her shadow howl as one, and dive for it.

But too late. The sphere hits concrete and shatters into sparkling dust, and the light shrieks like a skinned rat and snuffs out.

Darkness, lit only by a single sputtering candle. Shadows smother, huge and threatening.

Joey coils under the table, muscles rippling, and hisses delicious pleasure. Serpent likes the dark. Reptile eyes drag in the tiniest particles of light. Tongue licks the air clean. Sweet vibrations tingle his belly, his spine, his nerves afire, and he sees everything.

Mina jerks, her back arching impossibly high. Sweat and blood run rivulets on her gothicwhite skin, trickling scarlet on her chin, her shoulders, her spreadeagled arms. Candlelight gleams on her torn black leather, her rich azure hair quivering vertical. A stark, beautiful death scene. Fit for an angel. But he won't let her go.

Deadly swift, Joey strikes for Ivy's throat.

Ivy screeches, flapping her arms to ward him off. His fangs slash fresh scars that hiss green across her eyes as the venom sinks rapidly in. She howls in agony, her skin bubbling.

The air groans and shudders, and something invisible shatters like thunder.

The spell's broken.

Mina slumps to the floor, groaning. Rolls onto her side, wriggles weakly, trying to sit up. She's alive.

Hot relief washes Joey's blood, and with a thrash and a crackle of protesting flesh, he shifts back.

Disorienting, as usual. Blackness thickens like treacle, the air cool and useless and bereft of sensation. His bones snap into place, and he gasps on the floor, his lungs expanded too fast. He crawls blindly toward her on shaking limbs, his human eyes only slowly adjusting.

In the corner, Ivy yells and thrashes, hands plastered over her eyes. He can't care. Just let Mina be conscious, and not a charred shell, her brain gutted, wailing in animal pain and confusion.

He'll kill her if he must. He won't let her live like that. The least he can do, after all she's endured for him.

And then, maybe he'll just let Ivy kill him, too.

He grips Mina's cold hand and searches for his voice, his larynx still dry and growing. "Mina, talk to me. Wake up."

Mina groans again and blinks bloodshot ruby eyes. Her syllables slur together like she's drunk. "Joey . . . Whatthefuck . . ."

Invisible sunshine lightens his heart. *Thank you.*

I blinked through a melting haze of bloody scars. Agony still raped my skull, my vision tumbling black. My throat pinched raw like I'd screamed too much. My stomach convulsed, trying to purge that ghastly memorysauce, but nothing came up. I tried to talk, but only incoherent syllables came out.

With a final shimmer, my vision cleared. Candlelight. Sparkling vials. Blood on the dusty floor. Ivy's screams pierced my head like needles, and it all came back. Serpent. Me screaming. Ivy eating my brain with a fork. She'd stolen my voice, chewed it up like mincemeat. My exhausted nerves sparked in fury. I wanted to twist her neck until it snapped.

Joey gripped my forearm. "Come on, princess. Let's go."

Right as usual. We were in no shape to fight. Ivy would have to keep. I struggled to stand, pain stabbing my limbs and cramping my guts tight. Not a scrap of scale or fin left on him, just flawless human skin, iridescent with his strange sweat. It didn't escape me that he was naked, either, and my body chemistry screeched with hormones and endorphins and all the prehistoric megapanic overkill your brain spurts out when it thinks you're dying.

Flame raged in my veins, and my reason melted away, ragged like burning film. I wanted to curl my neck and howl like a werewolf at the moon, swivel my face to the wind and sprint until my leg muscles melted in a lactic acid tide.

Most of all, I wanted to peel off my wet leather pants and pin him to the floor and fuck, over and over and again and again, until we made babies or died trying.

Ivy howled, her wings scything, and I dragged my fatigued mind from the gutter. No time for weirdness now.

Did he just call me 'princess'?

I stumbled and scraped my wet hair back, averting my gaze. "I'm okay," I mumbled. "Let's get outta here."

Ivy flapped aloft and dived for us with a hideous screech, blood streaming from her eyes.

Joey scooped up his coat. I fumbled for my knife, and as I turned to run, seductive glitter from the gadget-cluttered desk caught my gaze. Spells, all wrapped up in glassy suits. On impulse, I scooped up a handful of Ivy's tricks and stuffed them inside the broken zipper of my top. And we ran.

Leaving any chance of retrieving my magic behind us for now.

On the platform, creatures barely stirred, safe in their drugnumbed dreamings and unawakened by the din we'd made.

But not all. As I sprinted past, a slimy tentacle flopped around my ankle like a wet tongue. Yuck.

I kicked the evil thing off, but my skin crawled, and a few meters short of the platform's edge, I leapt.

Right into a snoring pile of baby spriggans.

Flesh crushed under my heel, and an almighty screech split my head.

And everyone in the cavern woke up.

24

I staggered onto the tracks, my head clanging like I'd slept in a belltower. Yells rent the air as creatures stumbled, wriggled to their feet, launched crazily into the air to fill the place like a drunken locust swarm, tangling limbs, glowing eyes, thrashing fairy wings.

Oops.

A metal wing sliced at my eyes. I ducked, the sharp edge barely missing my face. Claws poked my ears, raked at my arms, pulled my hair. Bodies crushed me, wrapping around my limbs, dragging me down. Sugarstink sloughed vilely in my nostrils, and I fought a painful retch, my guts already abused.

My knees scraped the gravel, and I whiplashed and kicked to get free. A baby spriggan squawked and chewed at my toe with his sharp little gapped teeth, and I wriggled him off. I struggled to turn my head, to spy our exit, but the way was blocked with gibbering, capering fairies. We'd have to find another way out.

I glimpsed Joey, a dark shadow in rainbow chaos, and I flexed my thighs and cartwheeled, kicking a slavering needle-toothed monster in the face on my way to grab his outstretched hand.

"This way," I gasped, but he already dragged me toward the abandoned tunnel.

Needle jaws munched my calf. Pain lanced. Blood spattered on the long grinning snout of some faehorn crocodile-thing. Her hair hung in wispy clumps from a half-bald head striped in rough scales. Her face hung lopsided, distorted, a black gaping hole where her ears should be, her jaw distended huge and skinny.

Teeth grated on my shinbone. I yelled and struggled, shock crawling my nerves tight. She let go and munched again, a bigger bite. Joey cursed and slashed at her skinny chest, but she held on grimly, blindly. Wings brushed my face, leaving hasty smears of panic in their wake. I fumbled in my vest. My fingers closed around a smooth glass marble, and I flung it at the creature, hoping it was something that'd hurt.

Glass cracked, and caustic smoke erupted in a rich blue cloud.

My lungs burned, and I choked on gristly envy. Some hapless creature's jealousy, sucked from their brain with Ivy-spell and stuffed into glass. The crocodile-thing shrieked, greenish scales bubbling as the foul acid ate in. She tore away, bloody leather shreds hanging from shark-hooked teeth.

I staggered into Joey's shoulder, my calf afire. He gripped my hip, pulled me upright against him, and we ran for the inkblack tunnel. Behind us, the mad fairy zoo cavorted and squealed, the cacophony reaching new heights. I heard teeth clashing, and flesh ripping. I didn't look back.

Joey wore nothing but his long coat, but he didn't limp on the sharp gravel. He tugged me into the dark tunnel, and gradually my harsh breathing and the ragged pump of my heart soothed my ears over the chaos.

Darkness hemmed us in, and I had only our footsteps crunching on the gravel and Joey's featherlight touch on my fingertips to rely on. I fumbled in my pocket, but my phone was lost. Behind us, the fairy circus scaled a threatening crescendo.

The blackness thickened, and tension curled my nerves like wire. And then metal snapped on flint, and a faint orange glow lit train tracks half-buried in rubble, ragged heaps of twisted metal and debris, rough-drilled walls. Flame stretched and flickered in his elegant hand. Cigarette lighter, rescued from his coat pocket.

He dragged me to a halt, his breath short, and gestured with the flame. "Look."

But I'd already seen it, and together we staggered over. Funny how our eyes go the same places, he and I.

In a rough crevice, a rusted ladder stretched upward. I squinted. At the top loomed a dark round shape, maybe a grating or sewer cover.

He wiped sweaty hair from his eyes, leaving a faint neon streak. "Think you can climb that?"

"Guess we'll see." My bleeding calf ached, but already I stretched on my toes, grasping for the lowest rung.

The metal cut my hands, old and corroded. I swung myself up, biceps throbbing, hauling up rung by rung until I found my feet, and then I scrambled up that ladder as fast as my shaking legs would move. The walls cocooned me tight like a horrid silkworm, and I longed for the sky, stars, dry breeze on my face. Beyond that, I didn't want to think.

My arms threatened to buckle as I climbed, and one or two rungs snapped in my grip, just rust and dirt. Joey slipped up behind me—Jesus, that man can move silently when he wants to.

I reached a heavy grate clogged with dirt. I shoved at it with the heel of my hand. No movement. I hit it harder. It screeched aside an inch, and pale golden light knifed in.

I smelled fresh air, blessedly sweet like an ice cream head-ache on my palate, and relief spiked hard in my chemical-rich blood.

The street. Part of the station. The doorway to hell. I didn't care. I braced my back against the wall and shoved again, and inch by inch the grate squealed away.

I climbed out, my knee crunching on gritty sidewalk. Weak streetlight flickered over a narrow alley, tall tenements so close together, I could reach a hand out to either side and touch them. Early morning, still dark. Traffic's distant hum greeted me like a friend. I embraced a deep lungful of stinking night air, and the glittering city never tasted so good. I wobbled around and held out my hand for Joey.

Purple light blossomed in my eyes, dazzling, and a horrid glassy chuckle tinkled in my ears.

My pulse jerked up and sideways, but too late. Nowhere I could go.

My back thudded against the wall. I squinted through shielding fingers, and the purple flash faded to a fragrant strawberry glow.

Diamond sniffed and tossed his hair back over glowing pink wings in a prismed fiberoptic flash. "Ashamified of you, bluebell. So predictamable."

Joey erupted from the rusted rungs like an angry djinn. Swift and silent, he landed between us on soft bare feet with uncannily elegant balance, searching behind him with one hand to make sure I was safe.

Strange warmth spilled into my heart. Shielding me with his body. Him, protecting me. He hadn't always done that. Something had changed.

Joey shifted his left hand with a threatening squelch and flexed venom-dripping black webs before Diamond's eyes. "I'm already having a shitty day, glassfae. One chance. Back off. Now."

But sick memory kicked me in the kidneys, almost knocking me to the ground. I'd almost forgotten. Joey didn't know what I'd done. Didn't know what I'd said, what I'd given away.

"Joey, for fucksake." Wildly, I grabbed, trying to get him behind me, away.

He shook me off. I yowled, but I was helpless, my voice a parched, empty shadow.

Diamond wrinkled his pointy nose at me in a smile and flung out his hand.

Joey didn't flinch. He just struck, a shiny black blur.

Venom splashed. Diamond darted away on swift glass wings. Joey swerved in midair and flipped around, still human, but his fangs dripped green poison and his eyes glowed icy with reptilian fury.

Soft white crystals splattered his skin, and as I watched, frozen in icewalled dread, Diamond threw more.

Salt.

A fat white handful, sticking like a paintsplash to Joey's neonbright skin where his coat slipped away from his chest.

Joey's head snapped up, and he glared at Diamond with feral serpent hatred scorching in his eyes.

Diamond just leapt back and upward on a flash of wings. He twitched out a gleaming pearly pistol, hurtling backwards in midair like some fucking Tarantino film, and fired.

The shot jangled my ears, and blood flowered scarlet on Joey's chest. Right in the salty splatter, beneath where his collarbone met his shoulder.

Joey blinked.

Swallowed.

Choked.

Diamond swooped, cackling like glass on broken brick. "Shiftify that, serpentbrain."

25

I stared, breathless, my heart plugging my throat like a hot slug.

Joey coughed, bright blood coating his lips. A round scarlet stain blossomed on his chest, soaking the salt. Only a nine-millimeter, not a high-velocity weapon.

But enough to kill.

He staggered, doubling over as his body contorted, human and serpent fighting like snarling beasts under his skin. Glossy black snakeskin erupted on his shoulder, and his bones lurched and shifted, dragging his collarbone long and angular.

The salt didn't burn. It didn't rot or froth like acid. It just clung there, to every slide and crunch and shiny black ripple his flesh made. He swatted it off, but too late. He couldn't shift back. The salt-drenched bullet lodged in his misshapen chest—his lung, the way his breath splashed crimson—and not a damn thing he could do about it.

And now Diamond could polish him off at will.

All I had to do was nothing, and Joey would die.

I'd thought that was what I wanted. My only reservation would have been that I wanted to pull the trigger.

Diamond clinked to the ground in a glassy pink breeze and leveled his weapon at Joey with a crystalline snicker. "Didn't think so. Sorry. Fun while it lastified, and all that." And he curled his sparkling claw lovingly around the trigger.

I didn't stop. I didn't think. I just launched myself at Diamond and clawed for his eyes.

I thudded into him, my nails bared, and we crunched against the wall. He snarled and fended me off with a translucent forearm, but he didn't drop the pistol. I kicked wildly at his shins.

He gripped my wrist, that brittle strength I remembered, and held me away. His lips shone like pink sparklegloss, his heightened color shining berrybright. "Stop pretending, bluebell. Let's finish what we startified."

I wrenched away and leapt backwards to land between Joey and Diamond. My thighs tensed to jump, and I cracked a parched laugh. "We never started. Don't fucking flatter yourself. Get away from him."

Diamond sighed, ruffled his hair, and leveled his pistol again. Aiming right through me, steady as steel. "I never held anything against you, Mina. Hell, I like you. But I'll shoot through you if I mustify." His eyes shone hard and brittle, cold gemstones, all soft remnants erased. If there'd ever really been any.

Behind me, Joey spluttered, "Move, Mina. It's too late."

"Shut the fuck up, Joey!" Tension shook my body rigid, and my heart clenched tight.

Diamond didn't budge. Wings flared for balance, pistol steady as steel. "Last chance, bluebell. Him or us."

My thoughts raced. Either way, Joey was screwed. I could still save myself.

Yeah. I could live, as the traitor who'd torn the heart from the only man who gave a damn about me.

Live, when I knew he'd died despising me.

Live without him.

I'd rather die.

I heaved in a breath to answer, and glass clinked in my bodice.

My fingers tingled. I'd forgotten Ivy's spells. My teeth clicked shut, and hope flickered warm over my heart.

My pulse quickened, sour. It savaged my conscience to

use stolen magic. What if the poor creatures were alive, and searching, like me?

But I wasn't the only one who needed saving, and I'd be damned if I let Joey go out this way.

I let my fingers drift to my throat like I was nervous. Better hope something here can smash faeglass. My fingertips brushed my torn zipper and slipped inside, searching for bodywarm glass.

I'd no time to choose. I just grabbed the lot and flung them to the dirty concrete at Diamond's feet.

Glass shattered, and fragments speared, a glittering shrapnel starburst. The backs of my hands stung. Green steam puffed weakly, melting away, and I smelled bitter fairy heartache.

Diamond jerked backwards. "Whatthef—"

Brutal force rammed me sideways into the wall, and my ears split like a rotten orange under an iron hammer of thunder.

Sonic boom.

My skull vibrated like a hellstruck bell, dizzying. The ozone tang of some creature's blinding rage stung my nose. Joey tumbled into the juddering bricks, vibration flattening him onto me like an oyster on a rock. His fevered blood slicked my skin, his painful breath crushing. Air ripped from my lungs, and my vision darkened as blood rushed away from my head.

As abruptly as it had conjured, the boom dissipated.

I shook my head, blinking. Joey stirred against me, a living sigh of pain and stiff misshapen muscles. My vision cleared. Discarded litter eddied in the dying breeze. Broken brick scattered the concrete, and opposite, a jagged crack two hands wide now split the wall in two.

Dust swirled, clearing, and streetlight twinkled on rosy faeglass shards.

Diamond curled against the wall, clawing the bricks under a jagged rainbow of broken wings. Ragged holes gaped in his beautiful glasspanes, sharp edges stained green and blue like hellish church windows, and glittering fairy blood ran, flushed golden with pain. He howled, broken, and his cracklined claws snapped off as he tried to haul himself up.

In no shape to chase us anywhere.

No time to gloat. Or think.

I wobbled up on unsteady ankles, heaving Joey with me. "C'mon, let's get outta here."

His bloody hand slid sticky in my grip. Too much blood. I could smell it, rich and warm. It coated his chest, smeared his arm, stained the ends of his hair, and still more bubbled from that ragged salt-drenched hole.

He sucked in a tight breath, his misshapen body still writhing in a futile effort to shift, and his voice choked wet with blood and sarcasm. "Change your mind? Or lose your nerve?"

I glared, my mouth dry and my face burning. He knew. He always knew when he had me cold. "Don't argue, or I swear I'll fucking leave you to bleed."

Unsettlingly, that brilliant smile shadowed his crimson-wet lips. "Yes, ma'am."

And together we stumbled down the alley, the traitor and the murderer, hand in bloodstreaked hand.

26

Deep in the glowdark cavern, Ivy rolls and moans, water pouring from her swollen eye. Venom still stings her half-blind, and her torn cheek burns like a cruel lick of demonfire, but it's cold compared to the scorching black hate in her heart.

The serpent's scarred her again. Her beautiful face a ruin. Her wings torn and bruised. And all for his useless blue shygirl who wouldn't give up her spells.

Ivy almost had it. Almost wrapped her fingers around the elusive songbird essence, that golden melody that sparked the girl alive. Still in there, though the girl's voice had long faded. But now it will never be hers. And pretty Kane will never love her.

Ivy howls, her heart bleeding, and her anger flares the candle into blinding light that hurts her one good eye. Broken glass glares malevolent rainbows, the spilled sparkle garish and unforgiving. Around her, creatures still caper and flit, screeching and moaning and spending their energy. She knows she should rise, clean up, think of a plan, but unwieldy emotion smothers her in loss and sadness, and she curls tighter, hiding her slashed face with trembling wings.

Eventually, the voices muffle and fail, silence broken only by wet fae breathing.

Ivy sobs, and the candles burn lower. Maybe she's meant for this. Hunger, sorrow, aching loneliness. Maybe she deserves it, for all the horrid things she's done.

Dream images flit, beautiful and grotesque, hell's harsh red landscape, her lover's golden skin. A leering shadow looms over her in a nightmare, malice wrapping scarlet around its reaching fingers. *You wrecked it, Ivy. They're gone.*

Ivy whimpers and scrapes her ruined cheek on the coarse floor. "They got away! The snake and the pretty blue song. They got awaaayyy!"

You let them get away. Shadow-Ivy lurches forward, swelling into a misshapen monster. *You're weak, Ivy. Useless. No wonder he doesn't love us.*

"Wasn't my fault," Ivy mutters, fingering her mouth.

It is your fault. Shadow-Ivy pokes her swollen eye with a sharp black claw, and Ivy howls and grabs her face. *Stand up for yourself, if you ever want him to look at us again. You do want his love, don't you?*

Ivy nods, frightened, golden images of her lover slipping from her grasp. "Yes yes yes. Lovely golden boy. Mine . . . that is, ours. Yes. Ours."

Shadow-Ivy wraps Ivy's hair around her fist, threatening. *And you're not gonna let that slimy snake get the better of us, are you?*

"No!" Ivy wails and flaps her wings, but to no avail. "Not my fault! Stupid blue girl wouldn't sing. Nasty snake, nasty black slimy nasty slippery nasty . . ."

Then you know what to do. Shadow-Ivy releases her and flickers away, lurching on the wall like a lunatic, and her gloating fingers slide lovingly over Ivy's sparklecrusted glassware.

Dusty cogs whir in Ivy's brain, and she smiles, crafty. Tasties, yes. Magickings, sweet or evil, stolen from fairies and distilled to dazzling power by her meddlings. A firefairy's flame, a hungry vampire's rage. Just an added splash of enchantment to make her stronger.

Mmm. Swallow them all, lickety snap, and the spells will be hers, at least for a while.

Yes. She'll hunt them down again, Joey and his sweet siren. Use her souped-up powers to trap them, rip out the sky-girl's singsong properly this time. Then Kane will be hers, and she can torture the snake man all she wants later.

Clever girl. Shadow-Ivy grins, deathblack teeth glittering.

Ivy grins back. And then she digs a handful of colored spell-crusted vials from the rubble and tips them down her throat, trick by sparkling fairy trick.

27

Broken windowglass glinted on the black pavement, staring at me like accusing eyes as we stumbled along. It must have been 5 A.M., dawn not yet fading the sky, and black heat still clawed the air dry. Blood clotted on my skin, Joey's and my own, and sweat trickled sticky and rank inside my clothes.

He staggered. I propped him up awkwardly against my hip. His body chilled my skin through my torn leather. God, he was cold. Clammy. Shaking. His breath rasped, hyperventilating. Shock. Hypoxia. Wet exothermic death. If I didn't find him someplace to mend soon, he'd . . .

No, he couldn't. Not yet. Not like this.

I knew the truth about my mother, but I still didn't know the why. Why Joey had held this back from me all these years. Why he let me dig for the truth when he knew it all along.

We rounded the corner into the street, where tiny terrace houses cuddled behind iron fences, brick-edged flower beds, painted lacework verandas. North Melbourne, maybe, blocks away from the station. Who knew how far we'd come underground, or in which direction?

Soft streetlights shone on the leafy shoulder, and lamps popped on in front windows, all those happysleeping people blinking, wondering what all that blasted noise was about.

I hauled him one more step, another, farther. Here, this one, painted ivory with green trimmings. No lights here. I peered over the fence and through the uncovered window.

Bedroom empty, bed made, rich white quilt smooth under a pale silken canopy. Lamps off. No activity. No one home.

I creaked the tall iron gate open and dragged Joey up the steps. Blood spattered in our trail, fat spots gleaming black in the dim light. I rattled the brassy handle. Locked. I rang the doorbell. No answer. No lights sprang on. I checked for wires. No alarm. Perfect.

I slammed my elbow into the doorglass. Smash. Sting. Ouch. Sharp edges scraped my wrist as I twisted my hand around, fumbling for the button. The lock sprang open, and I extricated myself and dragged us in, pulling the door shut behind me.

Cool still air greeted us. I flipped the switch, and soft downlights welled on overpolished floorboards. I fumbled the chain into the slot on the door, so at least we'd hear them coming.

White stairs curved upward, and underneath, a corridor led to a sparkling steel kitchen. To the left, a pale lounge lay shadowed, golden-tasseled cushions, shag rug, brass-edged mirror above a tiled fireplace, the works.

I dragged him across the plush bedroom carpet into the bathroom. White tiles sparkled like a fake smile when I flicked on the light. The mirror showed us dusty, bleeding, pale like ghosts. An ivory bathtub sat polished and smug in the corner, spotless like no one had ever used it.

Pity it was all about to get plastered in dirt and snake-blood.

I yanked open the glass shower door, dragged him in with me, and spun the taps on. Warm water sprayed, soft and clean, the rushing droplets so welcoming. My body ached. My heart ached harder. I yearned for a long hot shower, a soft fluffy towel, a warm bed. But this wasn't for me.

I yanked Joey under the spray. His legs buckled. I hauled him up, glassy flecks still stinging in the backs of my hands. Bloody water splashed my face as I struggled to wash that ugly salt away, let his skin breathe and shift. I pinned him against the wall with my thigh and tried to peel the sticky coat away. "Stand up. I can't do this without you."

He struggled to stand, breaking out in chilly luminescent sweat. His breath gurgled wet. Blond hair plastered to his face, stained tawny by blood and water. His eyes glittered, feverish.

I couldn't get the coat off his contorted shoulder, so I ripped it apart with a few savage tugs. It plopped in the corner, bloody water swirling down the drain.

The sight of him shocked me cold. His human skin gleamed deadly pale, blood like a stark crimson aberration on a corpse. Even the snake's skin was dull, that vital shine lost. The wound was neat and round, crusted with clotted salt and soot and rosy flecks of broken Diamond.

Drenched hair dripped in my eyes. I wiped it back with my forearm, and pulled his naked body under the spray. Water splashed in crimson rivers, and I scrubbed the crusted gunk off with my fingers, trying not to look at his chest's strange curves, the long black twist of serpent muscle along his stretched collarbone.

The way he was, well, totally naked. And wet. And in the shower, with me.

I fumbled. He bit back a grunt of agony and swatted me away, his touch frighteningly weak. "I can—"

"No, you can't. Shut up and let me help you."

Finally, the corruption was gone. The bleeding slowed to a sticky seep, on the outside at least. But the clotted hole already flamed with infection. I reached over his shoulder, dreading what I'd find. But his curving mottled flesh was clean. No exit wound ripping his rib cage apart. The mess was all inside.

He pressed my hand to his chest, murmuring.

Under my palm, something rippled, serpentine, and my nerves jerked tight. "What?"

He whispered again, his hair sticking to my cheek. "Make it . . . make it bleed. I still can't . . ."

I swallowed, and pressed harder.

Blood gushed scarlet, washing the salt away, and this time he hissed, his fangs popping, eyes glassy with pain. He hunched over, a growling shriek tearing from his broken lung. Blood spattered the floor, the glass, my legs. Sinew stretched and popped across his chest. His mutated shoulder crunched like grating bone, and with an agonizing wrench of muscles, he pulled the joints into place.

Shiny black skin erupted on his chest. Spines crackled. Bones crunched, muscles writhing and stretching, and the ruined flesh paled, reshaped, healed. Ragged scarlet edges seeped away, and his skin reformed, smooth and white.

He cracked his vertebrae, one after the other, and rolled his shoulder with one final vicious crunch. He sucked in a ragged breath and spat out a dirty mouthful.

A tiny flattened blob of steel clinked onto the tiles.

I stared.

He straightened, panting. Water streamed over his shoulders, down his chest, his legs, washing the dirt and blood away. Perfect. Flawless. Human. Just his corpsewhite skin and the pain crimping tight around his mouth to show he'd been shot.

He fixed those slanted green eyes on mine, and his gaze stripped me bare. "Thanks."

I flushed. Distantly, I recalled I was showering fully dressed. Drenched, my hair glued to my shoulders and matting my face. My boots filled with water, blistering my feet.

My tight leather swelled even tighter, constricting my chest. My pulse raced. I didn't know what to do. Run. Kiss him. Cry.

He slicked a wet blue curl from my shoulder with one finger, and sensation shivered hot in my bones. I felt it along my skin, deep in my breasts, between my legs. Nerves jerked me stiff, and I swiped fingerprints on the clouded glass door, trying to push it open and get away from him.

He yanked it shut with a resounding clang. "Not so quick. You're bleeding."

"S'okay." I scrabbled at the glass, fright clawing in my stomach.

"It's not fucking okay. You've got glass in your face, and god knows what else. Come here." He grabbed my wrist and pulled me close.

Blood squelched between us, and this time it was mine. His fingertips whispered over my cheek. My cheekbone stung, and he held up a wickedly sharp twist of pinkstained faeglass.

Shocked, I touched my face. Blood slicked, but I couldn't find a wound. Must be a fine cut. I hadn't felt a thing.

He dropped the splinter and turned my face up to the spray. So gentle. Unwilling, I closed my eyes, sighing, letting the warm flow cleanse me. Water caressed my lashes, my cheek, my mouth, washing off blood and dirt and painful memory.

He slicked his fingers through my hair, stroking it back, and tension eased across my temples. My head still ached. My body still complained, my muscles stressed and overtired. My pulse still jumbled with mixed emotions and distant panic, but somehow the sweet tenderness of his touch made it bearable.

I stretched my neck, letting the water soak me again. Bumps shivered my skin, warm comfort welling up from deep inside. God, I wanted to stay and let him care for me. It made me sick. It made me melt. It made me quiver with all the starbright longing I'd ever kept inside, all the times I'd avoided his gaze or halted an inch from reaching for him. Every night I'd spent cold and alone, wishing that for one dazzling moment, he'd see me for what I am.

His caress slid to my shoulders, and distantly I tried to focus, think, reason, but my tired mind just sank further into this warm, comforting mist of oblivion.

Shoulda run while I had the chance.

Hypnotic, shivery bliss washed over me, so beautiful, I sighed. Stupid to think it'd happen any other way. He'd always owned me. He just hadn't claimed me yet.

I swallowed, my mouth sticky. "Feeling better?"

He let his touch linger, that unspoken arrogance that maddened me. His finger traced my collarbone, teasing, and my nipples sprang tight, rubbing painfully against my waterlogged leather, longing for his touch. Fresh moisture soaked between my legs, and I ached.

His gaze followed his fingertip. Idly, he drifted his touch lower. "Much."

"Good." I stepped closer, and at last our bodies touched. He felt lithe and warm, his strange minty scent tempting me. His heartbeat echoed in my chest, perfect counterpoint to my own. I reached around him, and the delicious fresh texture of his skin tempted me to pull him into my arms and get this over with.

Instead, I grabbed the taps and twisted them off.

He'd shot my mother out of compassion, not malice. That didn't make it okay that I'd lost her. It didn't make it right that he'd lied to me about it for five years.

It certainly didn't make it okay that I'd fallen for him like a stupid little girl. That he'd toyed with my affection all these years. Given me just enough to keep me waiting for him, and then pushed me away, time after time.

He never gave me a chance to get over him, or to find someone else. Always just keeping alive a flicker of hope that, one day, he'd love me like I loved him.

And now he never would. I'd helped him heal tonight, but it didn't matter. I'd betrayed him, and Joey never forgot. Never forgave.

Self-loathing boiled like hellbrew in my heart, and I swallowed angry tears. He might not be a vicious murderer. But he'd still ruined my life. And I wasn't about to let him keep doing it.

My chin trembled, my throat stinging raw with all the things I'd never had the courage to say until now. I folded my arms across my wet chest and planted my back against the dripping glass door so he couldn't get away, and my ruined voice crisped sharp like a blade. "You wanna play with me? Fine. Let's play. You killed my mother, you lying son of a worm."

28

Joey swallowed. "Did Ivy tell you that?"

I gripped my elbows tight. "Tell me? She showed me! I was standing there. I saw everything!"

"Then you know how it happened." He was breathing hard, unknowable emotion glittering in his eyes like drugshine. But he didn't touch me, or try to get away.

"I want to hear it from you. Tell me what you d—"

"She was dying in agony with her mind torn out!" Blood blossomed on his lips, and he didn't lick it off. "She begged me to end it. What the fuck else was I supposed to do?"

"I don't care about your reasons! Why did you lie to me about it?"

"I never lied to you. I didn't realize that woman w—"

"Aveline, Joey. Her name was Aveline."

"Fine. Aveline. I didn't know Aveline was your mother. I didn't even know anyone else was there. I'm a fucking idiot, okay? Doesn't make me a liar."

I laughed, bitter. "You're one stubborn prick, you know that?"

He just stared at me. Steadfast. Ineluctable. So honest, it ripped my heart raw.

I squirmed. He'd always acted honorably. "Whatever. Don't believe you."

"I don't give a damn what you believe. It's true."

"Yeah? Then why the hell did you help me? Huh? Why'd

you drag a dirty sparkleblind slut out of the mud and spend the next five years not fucking her? Because you bloody well felt guilty, that's why."

His gaze slipped. "That's not what happened."

My fingers itched, infuriated. "Really. Then go on, astonish me. You've got about ten seconds before I end this conversation and get as far from you as possible, so you'd better make it good."

"You needed help!" He licked his lips, his voice strained. "I felt for you. Is that so hard to believe?"

My lungs constricted, and I gritted aching teeth. "You're the worst goddamn liar. You never gave a fuck about me!"

"Right. That'll be why I followed you into a psychotic witch's trap, then. Because I don't give a sh—"

"Save it, okay? You always pretend you're protecting me, but you're not. You're just protecting yourself, you and your precious family."

His eyes burned eerie scarlet. "Fuck you, Jasmina. You wanna talk about pretending? Fine. I trusted you, and you lied to me. You told that pinkglass prick everything, and it damn near got us both killed. Did you get what you wanted out of it? Huh? Did you get off? Did he pay you, or fuck you?"

My blood flamed hot, tearing burning shreds from my skin. I wanted to claw my eyes out, rip the skin off my face and hide forever. I'd never felt more like a whore, and rash hatred salted my heart.

His mouth twisted, his disgust jagged like a blade in my guts. "Uh-huh. That's what I thought."

God, I hated this hold he had over me. I felt like screaming, and my hands shook. I wrapped my arms tighter around my chest. "Don't you dare put the guilts on me. What the hell do you care, anyway? You treat me like a slut. Why shouldn't I act like one?"

"What the fuck is that supposed to mean? I've never abused you, or taken advantage of you. I'm always professional. What else do you want from me?"

Laughter rippled me sick. "You just don't get it, do you?"

"Whatever. I trusted you and you spat on it. If you were

anyone else, I'd kill you right now." His eyes glinted, a savage promise. His muscles flexed, threatening to shift, and danger vibrated like a scream down my spinal cord, as fierce and immediate as if he'd wrestled me to the wall. "Go on. Leave. Why the hell should I care?"

I clenched my teeth on a burst of fresh tears. "Don't you judge me. I thought you killed her. I thought you took my safety, my childhood, my reason for living. What else was I supposed to do?"

"How about stop and fucking think? I've always done everything I could to keep you safe, Mina. Give you a place in this world and look out for you. You should have known that."

My heart wrenched painfully tight, deep inside where I hid my blackest secrets and desires. I longed to croon bloody submission and silence, to shut him up before he said something I couldn't take. But my voice growled like grit on glass, groping desperately for my missing spells and finding only empty air.

Frustration and fury bubbled in my gullet, and everything I held back spilled out on a boiling tide. "Don't make me laugh. You despise me! Ever since we met, I've ripped my insides out to please you and you just shove me away."

"What? I never meant—"

"Shut up. You treat me like I'm nothing. All I ever wanted was your respect. Just one little sign you didn't think I was trash, but no matter what I do, I'm never good enough for you."

Unbelievably, he laughed. "*You're* not good enough for *me*? Are you insane? You think I want it like this? You think I get off on forever holding you away from me?"

My cheeks burned. "I don't wanna hear it."

"I don't care. Christ, you broke my fucking heart and I still can't keep away from y—"

"Shut up!" My voice ripped ragged. "Just stop it! You stole my life, Joey. I can't forgive you!"

"I don't need your forgiveness. You do. When you gonna forgive yourself?"

Too sharp. Too deadly accurate. My heart stung, poisoned like he'd slashed me open inside. "That's not your fucking concern."

"Fine. Screw talking. If you're gonna do it, do it." And he snaked a swift hand into my jacket and grabbed my knife.

I jerked back, my pulse thudding tight. My back hit the glass. Hair splashed in my eyes, and my heart swelled to choke me. This was it. He'd slit my throat.

But he just caught my fingers and wrapped them around the knife handle, squeezing tight so I couldn't let go, and tugged the blade to his throat.

I struggled. "What the fuck are you doing?"

He yanked tighter, baring his throat to the knife. The sharp edge sliced his skin, blood and water trickling down his collarbone. "Go on. Kill me. See how it feels."

"Joey—"

"Face the truth, Mina. Yeah, I shot your mother. She begged me to finish her, and I shot her point-blank in the skull, and it made me sick. I puked my guts up in the gutter outside. That make you feel better?"

My voice erupted in a scream. "Stop it!"

"The hell I will." He grabbed me and shoved me harder against the glass. My blade sliced his shoulder crimson, but he didn't care. My skull clanged, and clarity rang cruel in my head like hellstung bells.

I couldn't do it. I couldn't cut him from my heart. Any more than I could kill him with this knife.

Joey meant too much to me. He'd crawled deep into my flesh like a cancer, and if I hacked him out, I'd bleed to death.

He released my wrist, and the knife clattered on the tiles. He wrenched my arm behind my back, forcing me against the steamy glass wall, and now his hot body covered mine, tense and tight and dangerous, tumbling my emotions and my desire wild like a storm-tossed ocean.

Acid tears skinned my eyes raw, and sickness twisted tight and sore in my guts.

I'd failed.

Seven years wasted.

All those nights I'd dreamed of what I'd do and say when I faced my mother's killer, and here I was. Scared. Sobbing.

Now I was exposed, helpless in the grip of the one man whose insight always stripped me bare.

His words came out stained with pain and blood. "You want the sordid truth? I want you. I've always wanted you."

I sucked in a wet breath, tears aching my throat full. "Don't. Please, just let me go."

"No, Mina. Just listen." He twisted my arm tighter, sweet tension straining my wrist, and I couldn't help but listen as he tore me apart word by horrid word, his bottomless gaze drilling into mine and sucking out the last of my resistance. "It's true. Nothing honorable about it. I took you from that filthy spriggan's den because you were beautiful and I couldn't bear to watch you bleed. Do you remember?"

"No." I knew I shouldn't listen. Shouldn't succumb. He'd only push me away again. I struggled in his grip, but it was useless.

I remembered everything.

Swift, elegant, his gentle hand on mine, the way he stroked my hair and cleaned my bruises and touched that soothing finger to my lips, my first intoxicating taste of mint. I was smitten, a slave girl rescued by a dark and dangerous prince. I'd wanted him to kiss me, but he'd just thrown me that unnerving smile and looked away.

"I wanted to take you home and bathe you and dress you in silk like a doll. I took you outside and cleaned you up as best I could, and the whole time I chastised myself for getting a hard-on for this poor bleeding little girl. Back then I wasn't very . . . I didn't like to be touched, get me? But everything about you enthralled me. You gazed up at me with those pretty red eyes full of pain, and I nearly lost my mind and had you up against the wall."

My breath caught, a treacherous thrill. He made the crudest things sound passionate. "So why didn't you?"

"You think I liked that about myself? A scared little girl covered in bruises and spriggan bites, and all I could think about was spreading your legs and licking you until you moaned. Like I wasn't enough of a monster already."

His words spiked sharp desire into my belly, and I nearly whimpered. I could already feel his tongue on me, doing exactly what he described. His hair brushing my thigh, his skin's glossy slide on mine.

His grip slid to my waist, and I didn't pull away.

He inhaled, scenting me. "I tried to scare you off, show you what I really was. But you turned out to be smart and talented and perfect, and I only got more obsessed."

"But you were so cold to me." The words slipped out before I could stop them. "I begged and you gave me nothing. I thought I was broken."

Surprise brightened his eyes. "No. Never. Never believe that."

Dizzy emotion swamped me. I wanted to sob. He'd finally admitted he wanted me, and I'd just blown the biggest job of my life. If he saw my weakness, he'd abandon me.

My trembling mouth parched. "I'm so afraid all the time. I couldn't even kill you when I had the chance. How can you even look at me?"

He brushed warm kisses on my forehead, breathless. "I love looking at you. You're strong and brave and beautiful and so far above me, it stings my eyes. Looking at you is like . . . it's like praying. You let me believe there's more."

I closed my eyes, stunned. He made no sense. He made the most perfect sense in the world.

His lips lingered warm on my cheekbone. "And you broke what's left of my heart when you betrayed me, and I should tear your pretty throat out, and if anything ever hurts you because of me, I'll never forgive myself."

His conflicted words dazzled me. Warm menthol mixed with blood's coppery tang on my tongue, and it made me damp and needy. He didn't have to say those things. He'd already disarmed me.

He glided his cheek against mine, and his whisper slid seductive and warm in my ear. "See? I should cut you loose. I can't need you. I can't possibly want you."

His rich minty scent lit my skin, spilling warmth through my tired muscles. "Not possible," I murmured, mesmerized. "Doesn't make sense."

"Exactly. I can't kiss you or hold you or make love to you, because you're a soulless, lying witch who betrayed me and nearly killed me. And you know what?"

I swallowed, warm. "What?"

"If anyone ever finds out how helplessly I adore you, they'll take you and bruise you and cut your beautiful skin just to hurt me. And when that happens, I won't care about protocol or demon court rules or saving my own ass. I'll just lose my mind and fucking kill them all."

Dark velvet desire shivered all the way to my toes.

He sniffed his way up my neck and sank sharp teeth possessively into my earlobe. His whisper burned my ear, dark and exciting. "Is that besotted enough for you, princess?"

Exhaustion screamed brutal agony in my soul. He was the last thing I wanted. He was everything I'd ever longed for. And I was weary to my core of figuring out which.

Rich inevitability wrapped me like warm chocolate. I didn't struggle. I just let it flow.

Truth was, he was both. And no matter what I did, I was lost.

His lips brushed my cheekbone, and he tasted my blood, a seductive flicker of serpent tongue that dragged my breath away. Sweet surrender thrilled in my veins like magical melody, and with a tortured sigh, I tilted my mouth upward for his kiss.

Slow, deep, dangerous. As hot and delicious as I remembered, a dark temptation that scarred my soul. My tongue brushed his lips, and he groaned and slid his hands possessively into my hair, and any control I'd imagined slipped away like a fleeting moonlit shadow.

Helpless, I parted my lips and let him taste me, explore my mouth and my tongue. God, he kissed like I felt, desperate and ripped raw with tension and hurt, everything that last time I'd been too shocked to recognize, and the force of the feeling between us ripped an insatiable croon from my throat.

His lips slid hot on mine, demanding my desire, and tingles crept from deep in my spine to coat me in sparking need. The poison sacs under my tongue stung weakly, but I couldn't even make a drop to give him pause. Surely, he was a demon in disguise, bent on corrupting my soul and dragging me bleeding to hell, because I couldn't resist him, not now, not ever.

My knees buckled, and he caught my waist and held me against him, never breaking the kiss or letting me have a moment's respite or thought. Dimly I remembered I'd shut off the water, that the scorching heat rippling over me was all my own, that the only things caressing me were his hands and his mouth and his naked, tight-muscled body. "Mina," he whispered into my mouth, his strange tongue flickering so sweetly against mine. "You're so perfect. I swear you'll kill me, one way or another."

Longing sparked my skin alive, and I ached so hard inside, I wanted to cry. I couldn't forgive the way I felt. I couldn't deny it, either. I just sank my hands into his dripping hair and kissed him harder.

He trapped me against the wall with his hands busy on the front of my bodice. His smile curved breathlessly against my lips. "Wanna know a secret?"

"Uh-huh." Somehow my hands got distracted on his body, his shoulder's smooth curve, the perfect shape of his chest. I loved the feel of him, so hot and tense, quivering under my palm.

He stole another kiss. "I don't even care what you told him."

My mind raced. Surely he teased me. "What?"

He broke my zip open and my breasts popped out, free at last. His burning gaze raked over me, hungry, and a dangerous shiver swept my spine. He nudged my chin up, kissed my throat, my shoulders, my chest, his strange minty lips trailing ribbons of hot sensation behind them. He savored my scent with a throaty sigh. My nipples were already tight, and under the scorching heat of his breath, they sprang so hard, I gasped. His wet hair dragged hot sparkles from my skin as he nuzzled me, inhaled me, tested the texture of my skin on his. "Diamond, I mean. I want to care. I want to so bad. But . . . Fuck, you're amazing."

He wrapped his tongue around my nipple, sucking it into his hot minty mouth. Flame blossomed along my nerves, and it felt so good, I shuddered and gripped his hair and pulled him closer. "But what?"

"But I want this more." He teased me, licked me, bit me gently with burning serpent teeth, and desire melted deep into my belly. He knew just how much I could take, exactly how much sting felt good, precisely where pain tipped over the edge into pleasure. Not fair.

Something hot and sticky tingled over my breast, warmth sinking deep. He hadn't broken my skin. The venom wouldn't hurt me. But the danger spiked excitement deep into my bones. He sucked me, teasing with his tongue, and I arched, straining for more, my nerves sparking alive.

He swept me up like I was weightless and carried me from the shower to sit me on the vanity. He slid my sodden boots off one by one and dropped them with a wet squelch. Then his fingers crept to my buttons, and he started undoing them, the swollen leather popping apart.

I shivered under his gaze as he revealed more and more. He dropped to his knees and trailed mintburning kisses down my ribs. "I can't think about anything but you. I can't breathe when you're close to me. Nothing makes sense anymore, and I don't know what the fuck I want. Except this."

He moved lower, dark and sultry with intent, and his hot mouth injected liquid fire under my skin. He nibbled my hipbone, tasted the swelling curve at the junction of my thighs, and sweet tingles swept my skin there. God, I loved it when he bit me. Maybe I was sick. I didn't care.

He peeled my wet pants over my butt and off onto the floor. My skin scorched under his hungry gaze. He'd already seen me naked. But this time it was different. I felt like a teenager, first time undressed in front of a man. Nervous, unsure, hopelessly naïve. Afraid he'd hurt me. Terrified he wouldn't.

I wore little black satiny shorts for underwear, and he

scraped them away, too. The faint blue hair between my legs sparkled with moisture, and my inner muscles clenched tight, longing for his touch. He nuzzled me with a soft sigh, inhaling the wet scent of my arousal, and when he traced gentle fingertips up my thigh, hot pleasure slipped deep inside me in anticipation. "I know you hate me. I know I should kill you for your lies. But I can't help it. I want you close, Mina. I want you to be all mine. Can you understand that? What fucking sense does that make?"

It made so much sense, I wanted to scream, beg him to take me.

He didn't ask, or hesitate. He just slid his tongue right between my soft, wet folds.

Oh dear god. Hot, deft, delicious, so deadly accurate, I groaned, a luscious menthol burn that made me shiver and melt all over. Sensation seared along my nerves, frightening. Just the feel of his strange, succulent tongue on my flesh dragged me dangerously close to the edge. When he found my clit and lovingly tasted it with a soft groan of desire, delight bolted deep into my belly and quivered me weak. The strong forks of his tongue squeezed me, wrapping around my most sensitive place and stroking until it swelled tight and hard and the sensation melted me to mush.

Pleasure wrapped me tight, hot and sweet and so wonderfully real. My fingers clenched on the sharp marble edge, and the tiny scrap of my reason that wasn't a quivering mess of delight glowed hot with golden wonder. He was actually going down on me.

Him. On me.

I'd dreamed this a hundred times, with other guys or on my own when I touched myself, dull and frustrating. This was better than any of them. And not just because he was talented, but also because I actually felt that he wanted to.

He licked me, stroked me, swallowed my juices as if he liked how I tasted, and hot spasms rippled my limbs. God, he felt good. Better than good. He felt like he cared whether I liked it or not, and tears pressed unwanted behind my eyelids.

Tension crippled me, months of denial and humiliation and tears all building up in one massive, beautiful crescendo. My clit flowered unbearably tight, my pleasure centering too fast, and I banged my head back against the mirror, trying not to embarrass myself. "You feel too good. Stop it."

But he'd trapped me, with his will as much as with his body. He eased my thighs farther apart and licked me slowly, deliberately, from my center up to the very tip of my sex, and by the time he reached that ultrasensitive bud and teased it, I was nearly sobbing. *Don't beg, Mina. Don't say it. He'll only make you wait.* "Ohmygod. Harder. More. Please . . . ahh!"

He sucked me deep into his mintscorched mouth, and I lost it.

Heavenly flashburn ignited in my sex, scorched up to my breasts and sizzled out my fingertips. My nipples stung. My muscles ached and shook with pleasure that just wouldn't let me go. He wouldn't let me go, sucking that hard little bit of flesh between his lips over and over until I panted and groaned, my vision blurring with delight, and deep in my broken ears, I heard the distant chime of my long-lost melody.

Hot tears swelled my eyelids. He knew exactly how to please me. He always had. Only now he was giving it, without demanding anything in return. Surely, it didn't get any better than this.

And then, his tongue shifted. Long, sinuous muscle, sliding deep between my legs, the twin forks caressing me in the most intimate of places. Before I'd even finished coming, he thrust his tongue deep inside me, curling around my sensitive shapes, stroking me so hot and delicious that my pleasure exploded again. It hit me from nowhere out of the dark, all hot and rippling and perfect, and I cried out, helpless to stop him manipulating my body.

I struggled to breathe as my pleasure spent itself. I felt faint, dizzy, all the blood dragged away from my head to chase his intoxicating touch. He withdrew and licked me softly, not for pleasure but for comfort, so warm and tender and passionate, I wanted to curl up and let him wrap his arms around me and soothe me to sleep.

Distant protest sparked along my nerves. This wasn't right. I wasn't supposed to feel like this. What we'd done wasn't sex, right? I could still get away, pretend it hadn't happened, rescue my heart before he pushed me away again.

But he slid up my body, so warm, covering me in burning neon kisses, tasting every curve, every muscle, igniting another slow burn deep in my belly, and by the time his hot green gaze swept mine again, I was gasping, my nerves on fire. He tangled his hands in my wet hair and dragged my lips to his for the most desperate kiss yet, raw and barely restrained like he couldn't get enough of me.

I closed my eyes. His lips bruised mine, mint igniting my mouth. I slid my arms around his neck and pulled him in. I could feel the rapid beating of his heart, the hard press of his cock tempting between my legs. Losing all that blood hadn't hurt him any. If I wrapped my leg around his hips, I could take him right here.

Fresh desire pulsed between my legs, the bench already slick with my lust and getting slicker. Tension rippled deep, making me moan. I wanted to feel him inside me, deep and hard and close, just once before we realized this was a bad idea and slunk away into the dark.

Temptation wilted my wits. Just a fuck, right? It'd feel so good. So easy to pretend he cared. I might hate myself afterwards, but I'd get over it. I always did.

I wrapped my thigh around his hip, pulling him closer, and his hardness slid in my wet folds, making me quiver and ache. Oh, god, I could feel the tip of him pressing against me. Desire slashed my reason bloody, and like a whore, I thrust forward, desperate, begging him to bury himself deep.

"Mina, don't." He pulled back, breathing hard.

"Please," I whispered. "I want you." *Use me, break me, fuck me so it hurts. Just sex. Just hot dirty release.*

And then his besotted green gaze trapped mine, and the bottom dropped out of my world.

Reality slammed into my guts, warm and fatal. This was not *just* anything. I wasn't pretending he cared. I was pretending I didn't.

He wasn't just some crush or lingering infatuation. He was an addiction, raw and relentless, worse than any sparkleburn. Being without him didn't just hurt. It emptied my soul.

Resignation burned my throat like a dirty sparkle hit. I understood addiction. Sometimes your best intentions just aren't enough, and no matter how hard you try, there you are again, picking scabs off your arms and spewing on your own ankles.

Sometimes, fighting the need is pointless.

You just have to indulge, and hope like hell it doesn't kill you.

Something hard and mirrorbright in my heart cracked apart, and I grabbed his hand, hopped off the bench, and led him to the bedroom.

My feet left sodden dents in the thick carpet. Light spilled in from the bathroom and the corridor, and bronze velvet curtains lay open over the window, exposing us to the night. I didn't care. I pushed him backwards onto the bed, beneath a silken canopy dappled with silver thread shimmering like starlight.

His dripping hair stained the creamy coverlet pink, shadows outlining his lean shapes in black. My pulse quickened. God, he was beautiful, his body all wet and slick and packed with muscle and bone, serpentflesh a dark promise beneath his skin.

I shrugged my heavy wet leather top off my shoulders and climbed onto him, planting my hands beside his head. My hair fell over him, damp and blue, his luminous sweat lighting it from beneath like a weird green halo. His body felt warm and delicious between my shaking thighs. I was hungry, desperate, starving for him.

I ducked and kissed him, and his hands sliding over my waist, my hips, made me shiver and groan. Anticipation rippled my muscles deep inside. I wanted to take that delicious cock and slide it into me, feel him inside me at last, move with him and come with him and never let him go.

But not yet.

He started to speak, but I pressed my finger to his lips.

"Nuh-uh. Don't say a fucking word." I couldn't resist a smug smile as I crept lower. He'd teased me for too long. I'd make him suffer for this, oh yes. When I was through, I wouldn't be the one begging.

I traced my lips along his collarbone and inhaled, and his minty flavor made me drunk, the texture so smooth on my tongue, his curving muscles so perfect. My mouth watered for him. I curled my tongue over his nipple, and underneath, something lithe and muscular shifted.

My heart skipped.

He slid tense hands into my hair, gripping tight. "Mina, you really shouldn't—"

"Shut up." I twisted my head to free myself, and rubbed my cheek on his hard belly, luxuriating in the velvety steel of his body. Just as I'd imagined. Nothing wasted. All sinew, toughened muscle, tension. I tasted his hipbone, tested it with my teeth, licked my way across his belly. He shivered, and delicious harmonics tingled my tongue. My sex ached. Oh, for my music, to hear every serpentine shudder. The strange hot sweetness of his shimmering sweat intoxicated me. I moved lower, hungry, and at last claimed his hard length in my mouth.

Mmm. Like the rest of him, fresh, burning, strange. His taste sparkled hot on my lips and shivered urgent warmth through my belly. His breath caught as I stroked him with my tongue, and at that tortured sound my body ached and hungered like fever. God, I needed him. I needed him to want me like I wanted him.

I tilted my head and slid him deeper, sucking, and he sighed and shuddered at my touch, his fingers curling in the sheet. But still he tried to pull away from me. "Mina, don't."

I grinned, and teased him with my tongue. "Why? Got somewhere to be?"

He snaked up and pulled me off him, grabbing my wrists. I fought, excitement aching deep, but he pinned me effortlessly to the soft bed, his body lithe and easy on mine, and dear god, his strong grip wrapping my wrists spurted sweet flame into my blood. It made me all slick and hot and shivery inside, and my flesh he'd just so elegantly teased to orgasm yearned for him all over again. My clit ached, and deep inside me, my pulse throbbed hot with longing.

I struggled, but he just held me tighter, catching my bottom lip between his teeth with a wicked smile and a tempted groan.

A frustrated croon of desire bubbled in my ruined throat. Christ, I hated how he always had to win. But I loved it, too.

He closed his eyes, inhaled the scent of my hair, let his mouth drift down to my throat, up over my chin to my lips. "No," he whispered, "I just don't want to miss this," and I swear my knees went weak.

I shivered in his embrace. So close, I could taste his lips. His damp hair glowed neon green, curling at the ends, lending him a softer edge that tore fresh wounds in my heart.

His glorious scent disarmed me, his closeness a rich temptation I couldn't fight. He could do whatever he wanted with me. I'd always known it, ever since that very first day in the spriggan's filthy den. Anything that had passed between us since then couldn't change that.

I quivered and melted, and with my resistance dissolving in unsteady emotion, I surrendered and let him make love to me.

He nuzzled my chin up to taste my throat, his fingers still tight around my wrists, not painful but safe, protective, reassuring. His minty lips burned me, savored me, lingered on the soft place where my pulse beat strong and rapid against his tongue. My desire responded, soaking me like that hot steaming shower only sweeter, darker, more desperate. I wrapped one leg around his hip, urging him closer, sweat and my wetness sliding on our skin. My hair spilled on my shoulders, and he brushed it aside with his mouth to kiss my collarbone, the hollow of my throat, the curve between my breasts. Hot sensation flooded me, fresh, perfect, like the ripple of music on my skin.

I arched my back, willing his mouth onto my breasts, but he took his own sweet time, teasing me with the tiniest kisses and licks like sparkling fairydust over my skin before he sucked my eager nipple into his mouth.

Yes. My body flushed with pleasure, enough to make me moan and struggle against his hands. God, I loved what he did to my breasts. His teeth stung me, just the way I wanted, and his lips dragged such pleasure from my nipple that I thought I'd melt in scorching harmony. He released me to slide his hand between my legs, and caressed my clit, so light and gentle, I moaned. And then he did something swift and sharp inside his mouth, and I exploded.

The sting ripped straight down a hot wire from my breast to my sex. My nipple flowered rapidly between his lips, hard and big and so sensitive that one flick of his tongue was enough. I gasped and shuddered and came, the flesh between my legs swelling too fast, too hard. My pulse throbbed with rich chemical pleasure. Through a dizzy haze, I realized he'd bitten me, poisoned me just enough to make it feel good, and dark deliciousness made me shudder and jerk all over again.

I groaned in delight as the shocks faded and he slid his body up over mine to kiss me again. His cock slipped against my wet flesh, a sweet tease. The bittersweet taste on his tongue swelled a lump in my throat, and it wasn't from the venom. He'd let me see, back in Ivy's cavern, that smooth succulent serpent he'd always kept hidden. And now he'd let me feel him, taste him, be with him. Finally, he was letting me close.

Tears welled, hot and sparkling with desperate gratitude. I swallowed in our kiss, trying to get more of him, all of him. Venom smeared between us from my aching breast, warm and secret, like nothing could ever touch us. He curled his fingers between mine, pinning my hands on either side of my head, and I pressed against his grip, light-headed, wanting to tangle my hands in his hair, slide my hands over his smooth flank and drag him onto me, into me.

He murmured in satisfaction and kissed my lips, first the top one, then the bottom, sucking them tantalizingly between his teeth. "You liked that?"

"God, yes. Do it more. Show me. Please—"

"Shh." He just gazed deep into my eyes so I couldn't look away, and slid inside me.

Slow, delicious, totally in control. His sweet menthol freshness filled me, mingling with the sultry heat of his flesh. My muscles rippled and clenched as his cock slipped deeper. God, it felt all the better for how tight I was. My swollen glands protested, sore, but I didn't care. I moved my thigh up along his hip, opening myself. He thrust even deeper, harder, his fingers tightening around mine. "Jasmina," he breathed into a kiss, "you're so beautiful."

Oh, sweet lord. If I wasn't crying before, I surely was now. I didn't just feel it where his flesh slid into mine, that glorious friction, the shape of him caressing sweet hidden places inside me. I felt it in my heart. He filled me, both in flesh and in soul, an empty place inside me now hollow and cold no longer, the missing notes in my melody slotting perfectly into place. And it hurt, deep inside where I'd always imagined myself a whole person.

I had nothing. Nothing but this, him, now. I belonged with him, to him, completely and inescapably. And it didn't shame me. It just made me feel at home.

He moved so sweetly inside me, like everything he did, so precise and elegant and deliberate. I pushed against him, moving with him, and a whole new symphony of sensation built slowly inside, chord by perfect chord. Satisfaction drowned me deep, led me breathless to pleasure I'd never imagined, sparkling inside me like hot crystal. I'd wanted him so long, this was like a misty-eyed dream.

I bit my lip, and my own salty tears ran into my mouth.

He held me, kissed me, tasted my tears away. His whisper fell like warm rain on my lips. "I know, princess. I'm sorry. Just don't talk." And then he thrust harder, and all words and reason fled.

My muscles stretched and rippled, so good. I tilted my hips upward to accept him, offering my parted lips for another kiss. He took it, sliding his shifting mouth on mine, tasting my tongue until I swallowed and gasped for breath.

I clutched his hands tightly, tears spilling on my cheeks. Of course, he knew just what I liked, thrusting deep and slow and hard, until pleasure deep inside me shuddered and threatened to break. His hands on mine, pressing me into the bed, felt safe, warm, protective, like he'd never let me hurt again. He slid hot kisses onto my throat, and I tilted my head back, arching against him, lost in perfect bliss.

I'd had sex with who knew how many guys, sometimes conscious and indifferent, other times drunk or insensible on sick fairy drugs. Most were ashes on the breeze. A few stuck in my memory, for good reasons or bad. But this was different. This felt—oh, god, *he* felt—like it meant something more than mindless sensation or distraction or punishment. My body thrilled like dark and dangerous melody to our shared heat, our kiss, the luscious slide of his weird skin on mine, the secret way his breath caught as he found the deepest place inside me he could manage. My nipples slid on his chest, tight and hard and so sensitive, the pleasure stabbed deep. I'd barely dreamed it would be this good.

But I'd also dreamed of more.

I shivered and moaned under him, the relentless pleasure of him inside me too much. I needed to come. I needed to stop this right now before I lost my heart. His will was iron. He'd break me before I broke him. Unless . . . Desperate, I licked into his mouth, searching for serpent fangs, that secret fluid, that sharp twinge of pain.

He dragged his head away, gasping. His shining fangs sprang out, and he bit them away with a groan. "Fuck, no. Not in the mouth. You'll choke."

So beautiful, slick and curved and wicked. So deadly. The sight made me quiver inside, glowing beginnings of orgasm taunting me. "Just a little bit. I want it."

"No." But his hands shifted in mine, and that slick skin enfolded me, so hot and smooth and delicious, I shivered.

Oh, god. I arched, the sweet friction inside me scorching my pleasure harder, higher, closer. But his neck muscles corded, and he gritted his teeth and shifted back, sweat glowing on his face.

"Please, Joey. I want all of you. Show me." Little cries forced from my throat, and I curled my legs around his hips, pulling him harder, deeper, searching for that elusive melody. His muscles strained against me, his bright neon scent of changing already tingling my nose. The strange lithe flesh moving and swelling under his skin felt so perfect. So natural.

But he fought it. He averted his face, stained hair falling over his cheek. Despair leaked scorching into my pleasure. He wanted to shift. I knew he did. Wanted to taste me with those enhanced senses, feel our bodies entwined and molding together, skin to glossy skin.

Harmonics shivered me, tuning me to higher pitch. God, I wanted him to. Even a little. That rich dark serpent flesh against mine, his minty neon scent, the hiss of his gentle claws as they teased my skin to ecstasy. Tension built inside me, twisting tighter and hotter and more urgent. I tilted breathless on the edge of mindless orgasm, and I wanted him to show me so bad, I moaned it aloud. "Do it. Just do it. Please."

But he wouldn't. Wouldn't look at me.

Wouldn't let himself be.

Even after all we'd survived, he was still holding back from me.

And just as I was about to shatter like a crystal glass in perfect harmony, he ripped himself away.

29

My body convulsed, discordant. Delirious, I reached for him, but he scrambled away, muscles shining pearlescent in the dim light. My wetness gleamed on his skin, my sweat and spit and juice mingling with his.

He cursed and crunched shuddering claws in the bedspread, leaving ragged holes. "Fuck. I can't. I'm sorry."

"You can. You have to. I don't care. Please." My words choked, breathless, my throat sore and crackling. I sat up, shaking, my hair falling in wet blue tangles. My sex ached. My nerves jangled like an unresolved, broken chord. I wanted to scream, to roll him under me and impale myself on him and finish what we started.

Don't let me ruin this now. Don't let the spell between us break. Not when we've just begun.

"No, Mina! You don't know what you're saying. It's my fault. Just let it be." And he curled himself up, dark muscle roiling under his skin, and rolled away from me so I wouldn't see.

Sweat glistened on his taut body in the dim light, and my fingers ached to touch him, comfort him. But I didn't know how. Nothing more I could say.

Even after everything we'd done—all the times we'd drawn inexorably together, magnetized despite our best efforts to hate each other—even after all the walls had crumbled between us, he still wouldn't let me in.

Sorrow hacked a blunt axe into my heart, severing my infant melody like rusty piano strings, and inside I screamed.

Even after everything we'd just been through, Joey was back to business as usual—pushing me away and making it impossible to get through. Even after I'd opened myself completely to him, he couldn't drop his guard and do the same for me.

The man was a lost cause. When would I ever learn?

My own stupidity crashed in, and I wobbled. What he'd said to me meant nothing. He didn't care about me, not enough to give something back. He just thought I was hot, like every other fucking freak I'd ever met.

Just too squeamish about shifting to go through with it.

Sickness blotted my stomach like clotted blood. Stupid to think he'd ever trust me again after what I'd done.

Tears blotted my vision. My heart still thudded. My skin still tingled from his touch, and inside, my muscles still trembled in anticipation. I wanted to cover my face, sob until my guts ached, spring over there and claw his eyes out for preying on my naïveté.

But no use crying over what's done.

I grabbed my top and pulled it on, snagging my damp skin in the zipper, and stumbled into the bathroom. The tiles still shone with water and blood, and the light glared crimson accusation like a punch in the guts. I dragged my soaked pants on, fumbling my feet in wet leather. My bitten ankle stung. My boots were too sodden to wear. I grabbed them and scrambled out, tripping over my ankles, trying not to run. I had to get out of here.

My feet slipped in wet carpet, his gaze hissing holes in my skin. I didn't look. Didn't speak. Just stumbled blindly into the hall and out the door.

Outside, the relentless heat slammed into my chest. Red fingers of dawn twisted in the sky, and brutally cheerful magpies chortled in weeping green foliage over traffic's distant screech.

The sound clanged like hellscreams in my ruined ears. Tart

eucalyptus mocked me, an unwanted echo of his minty flavor. I ran down the steps and out into the street, where our blood still splashed the pavement like a murderer's crimson trail. Stones stung my bare feet. I didn't care. I had to get away.

Not until I'd turned the corner did I slow down, staggering to a stop in a narrow side street, bricks warm and rough against my back. My lungs ached for air, and the dusty heat stifled me. A stitch chewed my side. I dropped my boots and bent over, massaging my ribs, my thoughts flogging in crazy circles until I didn't know which way was up.

But I finally understood: I'd lost him. I couldn't ever have him, and he'd haunt me forever.

My heart howled like a wounded animal, and remnants of Ivy's memoryspell scraped my wits raw and vulnerable. Confusion and grief dragged my mind in six different directions at once, and with a tortured groan, the fabric started to rip.

I gritted my teeth and hung on.

I'd lost Joey. I'd lost Vincent. I'd even lost Violet. Add to the list Diamond, who'd likely kill me next time he laid his dirtyberry eyes on me, and Iridium the psychofairy, whom Vincent had likely poisoned against me. Oh, and not to mention the entire Valenti family from Angelo on down, after I'd knifed their favorite cousin to death.

Excellent. My chances of living out the day slimmed by the moment.

I had no job. No magic. No strength. Even my revenge had given up on me in disgust. And without my song, I was helpless.

Headache stung my eyes crossed. I coughed, and a few broken notes grated, sliding around the pitch like a drunken melody but never hitting the spot. A few wispy curls of magic floated on the air, but they dissolved without a trace.

I wasn't silenced. But I was gagged, truly as if they'd cut my tongue out. I couldn't fight off a sparkleblind fairy like this.

Finally, the ache in my ribs softened, and I crunched my waist in with sore hands and sucked in grateful breaths. The sun rose rapidly, melting the sky bright. I stared at my bare feet. Blood seeped between my toes, staining the concrete, and the only choice I had left coalesced in my mind like a clot, deadly and inevitable.

Wait for them to come and kill me.

Or get my magic back.

At least if I could sing, I'd have a fighting chance.

I straightened, determination hardening like ice in my chest, and the chill sparked energy through my tired muscles. One last effort. Back to Ivy's. Give her whatever she wanted. Beg if I must. Buy some other poor creature's magic if I had to. It was me or them. And I wasn't ready to die.

Oh, no. Not yet. Even just to spite them all, I'd stay alive.

My mother would never be avenged. But I'd just have to learn to live with my fear.

I don't need your forgiveness. You do. When you gonna forgive yourself?

Joey's words boiled in my chest like rich acid reflux, and I choked and spat them away.

And then, who knew? Maybe a change of venue. The gang scene in Sydney might use a hard young thing like me. Outside Kane's dominion, new enemies, new friends, Darling Harbor glowing neonbright with fairy glitter, golden casino chips at Star City, breakfast by the ferry wharf at Circular Quay by the blinding white Opera House, sweet frangipani drifting on sultry sea breeze.

Sydney traffic sucked, and it was a bit grungy compared to cosmopolitan Melbourne, but liveable. And no one there knew what a miserable coward I was. I'd been there once, backup for Dante and Joey on some dodgy import deal, and the demon lord painted my ass with his greedy eyes the whole time. I didn't mind working my way up. Maybe I'd get lucky.

Joey hated Sydney. Too much goddamn salt in the air.

Suits me.

I yanked my sticky hair back, sweat already dripping down my neck. I could do worse than demon's arm candy, right? At least I'd be someone's idea of a good time. Distaste rumbled my stomach, but I swallowed it down.

Face it: I wasn't much good for anything else. No skills, no references. I'd never had a real job. What could I do, be a waitress? I didn't even know how to make coffee.

It was decided, then. Beg my song back. Go home, pick up my stuff, avoid getting killed. And then hit the highway north, hitch a ride with some horny truck driver and wheedle him to my will with a glimpse of cleavage and a sultry suggestive song.

I wiped one stinging foot on the opposite calf and bent to pick up my boot.

And something cold and hard thudded into my skull.

Pain lanced, and my legs buckled. A rich fairy chuckle caressed my ringing ears. I tried to turn, to fight back, but dizziness disoriented me. I couldn't see. I couldn't feel my knife. My kneecaps smacked into concrete, and the world shimmied through silver to black.

30

In the bedroom, Joey rakes shuddering claws in the fabric until he hears the door slam. And then, with an irresistible thrash of aching muscle, he shifts.

Too fast. Too hard. It hurts, his snakeflesh swelled tight with the delicious memory of her touch. The faint fragrant salt of her sweat burns his changing skin. His spine drags long and tight, tendons squealing with effort, and he writhes, ripping out his frustration. Blood and venom splash the walls. Fabric rips, his furious spines catching on silk and velvet, the blind destruction of an angry beast. Viciously he thrashes his tail, snakes onto the floor, and whiplashes in fury, and somewhere glass smashes, a lamp or a window. He doesn't feel it. All he can feel is her, not here. Gone. Lost.

Desperate frustration hisses in his long throat. He couldn't do it. Couldn't bear her revulsion. Couldn't get it into his stupid thick head that maybe she really didn't care.

Sure. She thinks that now. Wait until she realizes she's opened her body to a scaly black monster.

Venom swells his mouth tight and angry, desperate for release, worse than any pent-up orgasm. He coils, and strikes like black lightning at the wall. Fangs crush and spurt. Venom splashes, and relief washes through him like horrid pleasure, a nasty parody of loving her. He strikes again, and again, until his jaw aches and the wall's a sodden mess of torn plaster. His muscles shudder and spend themselves.

He thrashes onto his back, spines crushing in the carpet, and shifts back, panting.

Colors flash to life and sting his eyes wet. His human body aches, his limbs sore and flushed with weakness. Broken glass prickles his back. His gums sting. He crawls to his knees, coughing bloody green clots onto the carpet.

The stain soaks in. Nice. Whoever lives here is gonna be so confused.

A smile twists, but no humor softens his thoughts. Nothing about this fucking creature is funny anymore.

He stretches, crunching the last few muscles back into place. Venom and sweat coat his hair, his skin, his fingers, still the faint sweet tingle of jasmine.

Fuck it if he can't still smell her. He'll never stop smelling her, feeling her, tasting her rich female skin, the way her flesh trembled and swelled under his touch.

If she were here, would he apologize? Try to make it up to her? Say, *"It's not you, it's me?"*

Wetness chokes him, a real laugh this time. Jesus. If she were still here, he'd do whatever the fuck it took.

But the mistake's made. She's gone. What's he gonna do, chase after her? Beg her to forgive him? Tell her he loves her?

Fuck yes.

He drags himself up and walks to the wardrobe on unsteady legs. He needs another shower. He doesn't care. Slide the door open, fumble through a crush of hanging clothing, find something he can wear. He grabs a black shirt, some jeans, a pair of random boots. Whatever.

Urgency itches his blood as he dresses. Go after her. Make sure she's safe. For all he knows, Diamond is still alive. Iridium could be stalking them both. And as for Ivy . . .

He nearly trips, darting into the bathroom. His phone sits lifeless in a reddish puddle. Might still be okay. No time to think. He scoops it up and stalks out the door, raking tense hands through his hair to shake out the worst of the mess. Wasted venom tingles and smears on his palms, a snide accusation.

She's left the front door open in her haste. Morning light hurts his eyes, glaring golden in the heat like hellish sunrise. He scans the street, lines of parked cars, weeping eucalypts on crisp green grass. She's not there.

His fingers twitch for the safety of his lost cane. He sniffs, testing the air, letting his tongue flicker and fill in the sensory picture in four dimensions. Pollen, dust, the fresh tar of warming asphalt. Across the road, a tart oilsplash from a passing car, the fumes bright and green, only a few minutes old. Skin and sweat, distant echoes from hours ago. Last night's cat piss, a sour splash on the lawn. And there, below, the fleshy taste of fresh blood.

He squats. Clots spatter the pavement, old and dry, but here's a new spot, scarlet in the dust. She's gone this way. His bones shudder, hungry, and he can't help but slide his finger through the stain, sniff it, bring it to his lips. Her delicate taste sparkles his mouth, and sweet lightness lifts his heart. Goddamn it.

He switches his wet phone on as he walks. It flickers and lights. She hasn't called. A text message pops up from Vincent. Then another one. He doesn't read them. No time for Vincent. For any of it, except her.

Morning shadows ooze pale beneath cars and lamp posts. The stink of car exhaust grows stronger. Already, the heat dries his hair sticky and foul, plastering hot clumps to his cheek. A skinny girl pushing a pram eyes him doubtfully, and circles around him as far as the gutter will allow. He flicks her a sharp smile. *Chill, lady. It's rats, not babies.*

On the pavement ahead, he spies a shinyblack shape, and his heart tilts. He scrambles to his knees to cradle it, and her poisonflower fragrance hits him full in the face.

Her boot.

Boots, in fact.

Both of them, abandoned in a narrow alley between two back fences. Leather drying crisp in the sun. He remembers sliding them off her pretty feet, her long smooth muscle at last revealed, her ankle's sweet curve watering his mouth. He never got to kiss her there. Not enough, anyway.

His pulse swells, threatening to drown him, and grimly he keeps it down. Unlikely she left them on purpose. More likely, she got no warning. Swiftly he scans the ground, the walls, smelling and tasting, hunting with sharp serpent senses. Dust, ancient rain, insects' sharp acidburn. No glass. No blood. Nothing to show who took her. Only jasmine, and the lingering sharp scent of her sorrow.

Fuck.

Fear for her life wrenches his spine into serpentine shapes, and his old self-preservation instinct kicks in, cautious chemicals leaching into his blood. It's daylight. He can't shift here. His glamour is weak, a flickering faeborn disease he can't control. Someone might see.

It's still early morning, the summerlit street deserted. No one's around. Surely it's safe. He crouches in full sun, slides his cheek onto rough concrete, and shifts.

Just a little. Just enough to liberate his senses, let his sinuses stretch. The sun shines gloriously warm, the ground crunching so rough and wonderful under his smooth scales. Vibrations shiver his elongated neck, the lost echo of footsteps and wingbreeze and a stifled yell, roughened by sorrow and cracked melody. He inhales a heated mouthful, and his forked tongue sizzles on that familiar, loathsome taste.

Certainty ignites crimson fury along his nerves, and his human hands crunch tight on loose gravel. He knows where Mina is, and who has her.

And in the jagged haze of his overwrought senses, he doesn't sense the footstep behind him until it's too late.

"What the fuck you doing, freak?" The voice rips like claws along Joey's bones, and a boot slams into his throat.

Joey flexes, and strikes for Vincent's mouth.

Fangs clash, a brutal kiss. His gums rip, venom and virusrich blood splashing like hot honey in his mouth. The impact jolts his spine alive. He's clumsy, while he's still got limbs, but it's enough to make the fucker back off.

Vincent lurches backwards with a curse-ridden snarl.

Joey whirls and snapshifts back, his hair crackling with

static in sudden freedom. He backs off along the wall, his human skin burning with acid and snakeshiver, and crude urgency pumps brittle cold blood into his heart. Mina could be dying already. "No time for your shit, kid. Go kill yourself a schoolgirl, or something."

And he turns away.

Vincent grabs his shoulder and flings him back around. His dark hair shimmers with sweat. Blood drips from his lips, staining his jeans, washing the venom away. "Don't walk away from me."

"Not very original." Joey crunches out warning claws, venombright. He can't poison a vampire. But Vincent might not know that. Already, his serpent mind snaps awake, measuring strength, testing reflexes, weighing up moves.

Sun in his eyes. Should turn the fight around. Breeze on his face, an advantage for smell and taste.

Rust twinges his palate, and his gaze snaps over Vincent's shoulder. Iridium, grinning at him with that mad razortoothed smile. Crazy metal-ass fuck.

Vincent's chocolate eyes glint, but there's no fever, no virusmad confusion. Just hatred. "It's time we finished this."

Joey should feel elated, confident, darkly excited. All he feels is frustration, and fear for her. "I don't have fucking time f—"

"You want this family? Fight me for it."

And there they are. The goddamn magic words.

Joey's mind somersaults. Kill Vincent. Own the family once and for all. Delilah won't care, so long as she can taunt Kane. And Iridium's a follower, the gang scene just an outlet for his twisted urges. If Joey can kill Vincent, Iridium will fall into line. The rest of them are nothing. Winner takes all.

He waits for ice to burn cold in his blood, the everreliable instinct for survival and victory that's kept him alive through years of threats and gangfighting and mutinous fairy minions. Sometimes, killing is the only way.

But a rational whisper stings, blocking out the black killing rage he's come to rely on. *Even a two-day-old vampire is close to unkillable. It won't be a quick fight. Precious min-*

*utes that Mina doesn't have, not with a vengeful fairy head-
case sucking out her life force. If you stay here, she'll die.*

Vincent gives a fangsharp grin. "What's the matter?
Mina screw your brains out at last?"

Anger spikes, and his fangs snap tight. He knows Vincent is provoking him. Doesn't make it any easier not to
slash his face off. "Don't dirty her name in your fangslut
mouth."

"She feel good? Fuck, yeah. I bet she did. I bet she's got a
cunt like a hot velvet glove." Vincent's crafty eyes narrow,
and his smile twists nastily. "'Course, I'll have to fuck her
once I kill you. Clean her out. Get rid of your feral stink,
y'know. Makes the blood taste like crap." He cocks an eye-
brow over his shoulder. "Whaddaya say, Iridium? Might
take a few times until she's ripe. Think she'll mind?"

"Shouldn't think so." Iridium picks at his claws with a
wicked razorblade. "Not with the proper persuasion."

Icy shards rip Joey's blood cold. Inside him, snakeflesh
writhes and aches, screeching at him to let it burst out and
rip that filthy tongue from Vincent's throat. His fangs stretch
and swell so hard, it hurts, chewing at his gums to strike,
slash into Vincent's sneering face and stab the sick little shit
so full of venom, his eyeballs pop green. Drag that razor
across Iridium's skinny throat and watch the blood spurt.

But he hesitates. Mina's life is worth more than his jealousy. If she lives through this, she can screw whoever the
fuck she wants and he'll be grateful.

His claws quiver cold. Well, maybe not whoever. He
draws the line at metalfae psychos and scumsucking vampire assholes who can't find their own fangs with two hands
and a toothbrush. The thought spikes hot human jealousy
hard into his balls, and his skin itches for a fight.

"Save it, shitworm," he spits, rainbow green in the flashing sun. "She's in danger. If we do this now, she'll d—"

"Shut the fuck up." Vincent snarls, and steps closer, his
hot vampire eyes glowing scarlet. "Don't use your bitch as
an excuse. You scared, that it?"

Vincent's coarse challenge jabs into Joey's blood like icy

needles, and spines spring harder along his back, ripping his stolen shirt open. His thoughts tumble. This is insane. Already she's bleeding in his mind, pleading with him to help her while her last drop of life splashes out on cold stone.

But is her life worth more than the family? More than safety, the cool sense of security that comes with power, the soothing knowledge that no one will stab you in the back tonight because the sniveling fuckers just won't dare?

If he runs from this fight, he'll never be safe again. She'll never be safe.

Vincent licks hungry teeth. "Thought as much. Fucking coward. Last chance. You or me. Now or never."

And Joey knows what he must do.

Hot contentment floods his sinuses, and he flexes shifting hands in a shock of delicious snakenerve. The words boil up in his hissing throat, and nothing he's ever said has felt so right.

Crazy laughter bursts strange berries in his mouth, and he jolts Vincent still with the full force of his eerie smile. "You know what? Take it all. I don't give a shit."

And with a hot snap of eager flesh, he shifts.

Vincent curses and stumbles, but too late. Joey hits the sunwarmed pavement, roughness delicious under his smooth black skin, and slithers away.

Snake over grass and gravel, pollen and dust and sweet vibration slicking his body tight with excitement. Sun burns, blinding monochrome, colors faded dim but sharp in his cold serpent eyes. Vincent's voice is crisp, thrown into high definition by the delicate mesh of touch and sensation, and the jagged scythe of Iridium's rusted wings through the air sends bright shivers along Joey's nerve-ripe spine.

Flash into the gutter, spines rippling, where leaves crackle under his belly on the stained concrete. The vibration of Vincent's steps soaks into his body like a threat matrix, directional, quantitative. Sniff, taste, slice the air with tongue and ultra-sensitive fins. Water's echo fills his sinuses, liquid trickling across rock somewhere far beneath, and he dives unerringly for the uncovered drain without having to rely on vision.

Slither down into warm thick darkness, bricks scraping. Splash into smooth cool water, his fins shivering in the freshness. His nightbright senses flash with shapes, edges, the soft glitter of trickling fluid. His mouth stings brilliant with dirt and tasty refuse. Yes.

Satisfaction slides thick and black into his cold snakeblood. Let Vincent and Diamond and Iridium kill each other. He doesn't care. Somewhere down here, he'll find her. A chink, a crack, some narrow rock-scraping entrance to the railway tunnel, and he'll find her.

And if Ivy's so much as chipped his deathpretty princess's sweet blue nails, he'll sink venomswelled fangs into her skinny fairy throat until she stops wriggling, and swallow her whole.

31

It wasn't dark anymore.

And my head hurt, like I'd scraped acidsoaked steel wool in there.

Situation normal.

My pulse thudded, sluggish. Light flickered, blurry at my vision's edge, and I groaned and forced my eyes fully open.

Ivy leaned over me, grinning, her face a swollen mess of purpling cuts. Candlelight lurched grim shadows across her face, the cavern's ceiling looming. "Awake, naughtyblue?"

I scrambled to sit up, to get away from her, but I couldn't move my limbs. I opened my mouth, and cold magic like cobwebs clogged my throat. I struggled, my muscles jerking. My chest heaved. I could breathe okay. My heart still beat, my blood still warm. But she'd enspelled me, or drugged me with some tragic fairy compulsion that cast me in invisible glass. I couldn't move.

The grimy floor pressed cold into my back, and bile frothed in my throat, the sick memory of grasping spriggan fingers. I choked, straining to speak. "What you doing to me?"

"You stupid or something? Need the rest of your song. Making a spell."

Laughter spasmed my lungs. "There's none left, Ivy. You already took it. Calm down and we can talk about th—"

"Oh, but there is. Some left, y'know." She placed a clammy finger over my lips, her silver eyes swimming molten with giddy fae magic that hadn't been there before. "No nasty snakething to save you this time, skyhair. Open up to me."

Ozone stank in my nose, the rich thunder of her twisted spells. Tears blurred my vision, and my headache flared to full-scale agony. But tiny hope flared in my heart. Was she telling the truth? Did some remnant of my song remain?

Horrid memories of her sharp shadowy fingers ripping my brain to shreds piqued my dread, and I gritted my teeth on a sick stomach. "No, Ivy, listen. You'll kill me. I need it—ah!" A cry ripped from my lips, the first sickly crunch of her invisible teeth into my mind.

I struggled furiously, and my muscles twitched wildly like electric shock, but I was helpless. I screamed, my spine afire, and she scrambled around in my head like an angry child in a toybasket, tossing images and memories and tortured emotions left and right.

In the deepest, safest corner of my brain, a tiny golden seed stirred, and murmured a forgotten snatch of symphony.

I jerked, surprise searing my nerves bright like arcweld.

The golden kernel sighed and sparkled, and I grabbed at it, desperate, hope hacking sharp teeth at my veins. If something did remain of my song, she wasn't getting her grubby hands on it. I'd die first.

Or second.

Either way, I wasn't giving up.

"Caterpillar!" The real Ivy slapped my cheek, her anger flaring green in a filthy aura. "Stop wriggling. You're spoiling it!"

"Wait," I gasped, stalling. "One question. One question and I'll go quietly. I promise."

"Question, schmestion," she muttered, sniffing at my lips. But she did pull back a little inside my head, her shadowy claws not digging quite so deep.

I sucked in a grateful breath, girding my strength as best I could, and blurted out the first thing that came to mind. "Why'd you hurt my mother?"

She tapped her claws on my teeth. "You *are* stupid. To tease the serpent man, of course. Now sit still."

My lips writhed back from her creeping touch. "But Joey didn't know her. Why torture an innocent woman?"

"Because he cut my face and laughed about it!" Her spit flecked, splashing my face. "He tortured *me*! Pretends he's got honor and conscience and never does anything wrong, but he's an evil nasty horrible snake and he hurt me and I'll hurt him back over and over and again until he says he's sorry!" Her face crumpled in tears, and she pecked me cruelly with her nails like a mocking raven's beak, stabbing my arms, my breasts, my face.

I struggled to avoid her, to save my eyes. It wasn't right. The Joey I knew didn't delight in torture. "But why?" I gasped. "Why did he cut your face?"

Ivy gnashed her tiny teeth at me, and laughed.

And behind her, emerald serpent eyes glinted at me from the dark.

My heart leapt. I tried not to look. Not to give him away. But my throat caught tight, my lungs straining for air, and I let out a helpless little gasp.

Ivy whirled, wings scything, and dived for him, and in the dark his eyes winked out.

My heart gabbled cold, and inside my head the golden kernel wailed an ear-shattering warning. I couldn't see. Where was he? What was she doing?

Invisible sounds tortured me. Glass broke. Skin scraped on concrete. Teeth grated like a scratched blackboard. And Ivy lumbered into the light, dragging my beautiful, thrashing black serpent by his long spiked tail.

Icy razors ripped into my heart, and I didn't know if it was terror or rage. Had he followed me? She wasn't strong enough to hold him before. What the fuck was he doing, getting himself caught like that? If he'd come for my sake, I'd really kill him this time.

Joey squirmed and scythed, raking the glass-strewn floor, his sharp tailfins slicing into Ivy's flesh. Bright greenish blood gushed from her slashed palm, dripping hot and thick over the snake's tail. But she didn't let go, dragging him across the floor to dump him in a slithering black pile at my feet.

He writhed and fought, slashing at her with sharp fins, curling in on himself to strike with those long glossy fangs I loved. But she spat a spell-sparked curse at him, green smoke hissing from her teeth to curl around him in a sticky magical web. "Be still," she snarled, and though venom dripped hellgreen from his mouth and his fins quivered with frustrated rage, his spine shuddered like a seizure and he couldn't strike.

Couldn't shift. Couldn't move. Like me. Trapped.

Ivy giggled, and shoved his shining black flank with her pointed foot. "So tell her, snakypet— Oh, I forgot. Can't talk, can you?"

"Let him be." My voice vibrated steelsharp, errant harmonics twanging like broken piano wire. Her malicious smile poured dread into my heart. My bones clanged cold. I wanted to block my ears, shout out so I couldn't hear what she'd say.

"It was because I tricked you, snaky, didn't I?" Ivy grinned in triumph. "Yes indeedy, I did. Tricksy old me. Told you I could cure you of this *slimy. Pukeworthy. Monster.*" With each word, she poked a vicious claw into his quivering black nose. "And you believed me! What a laugh! And you did frightful things, didn't you, pet? You hurt and stole and killed so I'd give you your poxy cure. And I lied all along! Ha! Good joke, eh?"

Joey's eyes flooded dark with unknowable serpent emotion. Ivy's sticky web still trapped him from throat to tail, but he struggled to turn his head, look away from me with eyes that couldn't swivel or close to block me out.

Suddenly, I couldn't breathe.

Ivy giggled and smiled at me brightly, but then her face crunched in a deadly scowl. "But *he* didn't think it was funny. Oh no. He had to go and hurt me. But it was just a trick!" She clawed at her ruined face, rage staining her eyes black. "Just a stupid giggly trick and you cut my face *again,*

you nasty nasty nasty . . . Ohh, I'm gonna make you hurt."
Her wings flailed in windy rage, drowning out her words.
She dived on me, talons outstretched like an evil goldplated
angel, and plastered her sugarsweet lips over mine.

Her teeth banged in, bursting my lips. Pain spiked, but I
barely felt it. I was too numb.

I'd been so fucking stupid.

All those months of circling each other like hungry pan-
thers abruptly made sense. He wasn't standoffish for ego's
sake. He didn't hide his serpent for caution, or because he
was too in control to care.

He loathed the very idea of himself. He couldn't bear me
to see, to feel, to touch him.

And I'd demanded he show me, right when his defenses
were weakest.

No wonder he'd shoved me away.

Ivyjuice flooded my mouth, angry, bitter like dead grass.
Cruel shadow-knives slashed into my head again, slicing
into my deepest consciousness, and the tiny golden music in
my mind shrieked and twisted like a cat-gnawed mouse, trying to get away.

Ivy thrust her tongue into my mouth, raping, hunting for the
elusive magical spark that made me who I was. I didn't care.
Torrid guilt crushed me breathless, and weakly my limbs
shook, the last remnants of fight shocked out of me.

My stomach churned, sick with bile and fairy spit and my
own acid selfishness. God, I'd so blindly misused him. He'd
told me all the truth he could, bled his heart out on the floor
at my feet, and I'd been too wrapped up in my own self-
inflicted misery to listen.

He'd given me everything he had. And like a needy,
spoiled little princess, I'd thrown it back at him.

If I died now, he'd never know how much I regretted it.

Fresh fire lit in my muscles, and I clamped my jagged
teeth around Ivy's tongue and bit down.

Poison squirted, my swollen sacs emptying into her
mouth. She screeched, a wild ululating cry that split my ears
like ripe pumpkins, and tore herself away.

Rich fairy blood spurted over my face, sweet like nectar with her madness. The invisible steel bands that pressed me down dissolved, and I whiplashed my screaming limbs and landed shakily on hot bare feet.

She wailed, clutching her bleeding mouth, and a melody-sharp cackle erupted from my throat. Now she had two wounds. One from me. One from him. Seemed only fair.

I crouched, flexing my aching thighs for shaky balance, and beckoned to her with two bloodspattered fingers. "Like that? Want some more? Kiss me again. I dare you."

Ivy wiped frothing blood from her toxin-swelled lip, her face contorted in pain and fury. "You nasthy liffle rath. Why you gottha be tho mean?" And she dived for her table, where rainbowglass scattered jewelbright in a tumble of rusted metal forks and broken containers. She scrabbled through the wreckage and came up with a bubbling green vial, which she uncorked and upended into her mouth.

Her throat bobbed, swallowing. Emerald fire glazed her eyes, the stolen spellcraft glittering like stars.

Stocking up on powers. Next time she kissed me, I might not be able to hold her off.

I flung myself at her, rage flowering in my muscles, a pale shadow of my old strength but invigorating still.

My body crashed into hers, flinging her off balance. I rolled clumsily to the floor, missing petrified Joey by inches. Ivy flared her wings and caught herself, and before I could react, she grabbed another spell and swallowed that, too. Her wingbones quivered scarlet, rage or lust or some other stolen emotion, and between her fingers, eerie flame crackled.

My skin bubbled cold. What new threat did we face? What strange power did Ivy harbor now?

On the floor, Joey shuddered and tried to shift. Muscles pulled along his side, scales writhing and melding with white human skin, and I glimpsed a faint flash of his hair, silhouetted jagged against flickering candlelight. But Ivy's woolly green webspell held him fast, and with a final thrash and an evil greensplashed hiss, he gave up.

Ivy cackled and threw the empty glass tube away. It smashed on the floor, and she dived for me, her wings' ragged holes swiftly repairing themselves on some blackhearted enchantment.

I dodged, but she was too quick. She grabbed my throat, stinging claws digging, and rammed my back into the wall, squeezing my breath away.

I gasped, trying to kick my way free, but I couldn't connect. She was too agile, balancing on her wings and a seething updraft of hate. Her swollen cheek deflated as I watched, infection's red veins vanishing, leaving only angry cuts still bubbling fresh with snakerot. Her gaze swirled violet, boring into mine, and the shock dizzied me like vampire hypnosis, sick and hot and terrifyingly welcome. Her voice glided into my ears, seductive like fairysweet honey with the new magic she'd swallowed, making love to me like flesh on flesh. "No more fighting. Give me your songs, pretty."

Hot fleshscent rolled on my tongue, and those insidious shadow-fingers forced one last time through the cracks into my skull. Her foul hypnosis swirled ugly in my aching brain, and my belly filtered warm and sensual with the crushing need to obey.

I choked and struggled, straining until my throat bled for those last lost chords, but they crumbled to ashenbright dust in my mouth.

Despair crippled me. I couldn't fight this. I didn't want to. It hurt too much.

Grimly, I squeezed my eyelids shut, trying to break her hold, but horrid compulsion sprang them open again and her gaze ripped into mine, inescapable, unstoppable.

An appalling pulling sensation gripped my blood, like all my body fluids dragged toward her on invisible clamps. My heart galloped, unable to compensate, and my feet flushed cold without blood. Sweat sprang. Tears leaked from my eyes and sucked across the air toward her. Spit spilled from my glands and flowed onto my chin. My stomach juices churned and climbed my gullet, eager to get out, and between my legs wetness flowered, a cold slimy splat that crawled and spread and disgusted me.

My head throbbed, dehydrated. Blood trickled warm from my nose, and I gasped out my last wet defiant breath. "Fuck you."

Ivy's mad golden eyes swirled with dangerous inspiration. "Don't think so, pretty. Give up already, or I'll snap your precious boyfriend's snaky neck."

Joey thrashed and spat, glossy skin quivering over muscle ripped tight. The spell's relentless grip contorted his spine into unmakeable shapes, but he couldn't break free.

"No!" Horror clawed my guts with iron. Ivy flung me aside, tittering with glee, and I fought like a maddened wasp to break free of her spell, to run to him, but too late.

She'd already grabbed him. Two hands, smoking with spellcraft and caustic hatred.

Joey wriggled and snapped bloodbright jaws, his spiked tail quivering, but her claws dug in, cutting his tough black skin like paper.

I watched, helpless, as she shoved her slender knee beneath his middle. And with a sick crunch of bone and sinew that ripped my ears bloody, she cracked his spine in two

32

Joey's eyes glazed cold, like frost crackling on a window.

My guts spasmed, fear-iced air forcing down my throat.

Bloody flecks hissed from his tongue. His fins quivered, shedding venomdrops like rain, and the whole back end of him flopped limp.

"Oops. Silly me. Did I break something?" Ivy giggled, and dropped him, her greedy shadow-fingers reaching for my soul. Pain slashed, melting my bones, scouring my muscles to gunge. Her claws dug deep, grabbed at last the glowing golden melody like evil metal pincers and started to rip it free.

But Joey's angry, helpless gaze burning my skin thrust cold determination worthy of a serpent deep into my heart. My abused nerves sparked alive with indignation and bloody stubbornness.

He wouldn't die for me. Enough people had died for my cowardice already.

After all that had happened, the least I could do for him was fight her for a moment longer.

Long-suppressed emotion shook like quartz crystal in my heart, and shattered.

My lonely melody sputtered and flared brighter like a hungry candle. I opened my mouth, spellcharged air sucking deep into my lungs, and I sang.

A deep, pure, shattering glissando of rage.

It swelled and rolled, filling my lungs and mouth and ears with sweet exultation, and my blood caught fire.

My golden melodyseed burst in dazzling supernova, scorching Ivy's fingers to the bone. She screamed, a deathly howl of agony and surprise that was totally drowned out by my stunning harmony.

Victory and long-lost vibration stroked delight deep into my blood. Oxygen rushed to my spellslashed brain, better than any spell or faesweet drug. Instinctively, I stretched my rusty vocal cords, and for the first time in so long, the note rippled and broke into a perfect, awful, hellish chord, relentless multiplication building a ladder of destructive frequencies, climbing octave after octave in a shining cascade of spelldrenched death.

Yes. Warm honey gratitude spilled into my belly, and my nerves responded, electric wonder sparkling along my limbs, jerking my tendons tight and my reflexes ever sharper. And the sounds, oh god, the sounds, full and swelling and beautiful in my ears, every breath and twitch and tiny mote of movement pinpointed in three dimensions for me to consume.

But it wasn't only music that filled my senses. My skin sparkled with alien spells, all the drugmagic that had been sprinting around in Ivy's blood pouring into me, mine to exploit. Flame rippled along my forearm, some fairy's stolen baublefire, and green envy zinged sparks between my fingers.

My deep undulating vibrato stretched the unearthly sound to the finest quality. Louder, louder until the concrete above our heads shuddered and cracked with a deafening rumble. Clattering footsteps and fairy wails filtered in as Ivy's creatures panicked and fled, or rolled over, too out of it to care.

Rocky shards rained, and Ivy swooped at me, ragged wings flapping, her sharp fairy teeth gnashing for my throat. "Look what you've done!"

I just twitched away—Christ, it felt so good to *move*— and pitched my rage higher.

Harmonics blazed like gunfire, raking the air raw, and she thumped squawking into my shimmering wall of sound and fell back.

I laughed, music dripping with poison from my tongue, and the metal table shuddered and warped. God, it felt good, this sinister melody surging through my veins, my muscles at knife-edge response, this warm dark feeling of *me*.

I'd missed her, my beautiful dark muse. And she'd missed me. I could feel it, the way she caressed me inside, stroked my eager flesh, vibrated in my fluids like a lover's tempting touch.

I whirled, my balance light and perfect. Ivy perched over Joey on the desk's twisted edge like a dusty golden bird, gripping with broken claws, her wings curled menacingly. "You want him? Come get him."

I longed to let Ivy have it, open my lungs all the way and sing spine-crackling retribution until my throat bled and the treacherous fairy cow melted into a quiver of bleeding jelly.

But I'd no time for useless vengeance. Not while the ceiling was about to cave in on us. Not while my heart lay broken and nerveless on the glass-tinkled floor.

More rock showered, a dark crack splitting apart in the ceiling, the smell of dust and ancient bones. I risked a glance at Joey, who lay quivering like a long black coil of hate. He tilted his elegant chin up at me, just a fraction, and the tiny movement stroked thick in my ears, fragrant from his warm menthol skin.

I danced in slow motion across the shuddering floor, edging toward Ivy. Glass crunched under my bare feet, the sound of my skin slicing a sweet harplike ripple. Rock cracking, dust clouding in my eyes. Another step closer, feeling with my ears for Joey's hissing breath. "We need to get the fuck outta here before it falls in, lady, and I'm not leaving him."

Her gaze darted to the cracking ceiling. "And I won't let him go. Not without your spell! Stalemate, pretty. What ya gonna do?"

Despairing, I stared at him, his sleek black body thick with dust and rocky shards. He flashed me a glance that shone like starlight with apology and rich minty memory, and my heart sputtered.

So green, his gaze. Normally so cold, hard, unknowable.

Only now, it wasn't. He'd let me through. His compassion slashed my bruised soul like sweet razor melody, and I knew.

The normal world, where people chatted and laughed and acted nice to each other? It wasn't for me. I lived in a darker, richer place, where danger coiled in the gutters and dripped like bloody scarlet sunset through dusty windows.

But that didn't mean I'd sacrificed my honor. I didn't have to become a murderer, a liar, lose the last scrap of conscience that made me whole.

He'd taught me well. Never break your promises. Always follow through on your threats. And sometimes, when what's at stake is big enough, risk everything to prove your point.

No matter how deeply you fear you won't measure up.

Some things are just worth dying for.

I stalked one last dancer's step closer, crude vibration swelling threat in my throat. The ceiling cracked wider, and a jagged rocky chunk shuddered and gave way. It thudded onto the desk, crushing it effortlessly to crumpled metal in a rain of dirt and pebbles.

Ivy screeched and darted backwards on hovering wings. "Shush, you silly blue thing. You're making a mess!"

Wild conviction sparkled goldenblack rivers on my breath. I hit another shrill high note, sliding up the octave on warm oily confidence so long lost. Magic thrilled in my throat, rippling the air with ineluctable vibration, and the rock above her gave an almighty groan, and fell.

The earth shuddered. Thunder tore my ears. Dust exploded, pebbles and rockshards flying, and Ivy disappeared under a rain of dirt and tumbling debris.

The air hummed, evil fairy magic writhing in protest at its absent mistress. Green light glimmered and popped, and with a sick crack and a puff of sugar-stinking smoke, Ivy's spell broke.

In a shiny black flash, Joey shifted.

I tumbled to my knees in the rockpile at his side, my destructive song's echo fading. My feet stung and bled, and jagged broken glass sliced painful welts into my knees, but I didn't care.

His eyelids fluttered closed, dust caking his pale lashes. Raw scarlet bruises mottled his spine, and furious snakeflesh writhed under the skin over his ribs, his spine curling in pain or the last useless jerk of paralysis.

I cradled his head in my dusty lap, brushing rocky shards from pale hair. Guilty tears throttled my vision gray. I shook them away, and my throat crackled, dry from misuse and fear. "Joey, talk to me. C'mon."

Around us, rock still shuddered and threatened. I'd done some real damage, and now it was too late to stop it. I didn't care. If I'd let Ivy break the only person I cared about, I'd just stay here and die.

I buried my face in his hair, that wonderful minty scent dusty and wet with my tears. His skin felt cold, clammy, no warmth in his blood.

My heart quailed. I couldn't be without him, not now. I didn't know what else to do. I'd lied to myself about going to Sydney. Working for anyone else felt like treason, and I'd done enough of that already.

"C'mon. Wake up. Shift. Do what you need. I don't know how to help you." Frantically, I tried to recall what he'd done in the shower, how he'd healed himself. But I couldn't remember anything but the way he'd felt against me, inside me, the soul-rotting despair in my heart when he'd pushed me away.

His chest heaved, but no air sucked into his lungs. Blood spilled from his mouth, dark and oxygen-starved. He still didn't move. Just convulsed like a sparkle overdose, his limbs jerking on random electric shock.

I tried to sing bright summer into his ear, a tingling magical melody to strengthen and revive him, but my voice quavered and broke, the spell flying apart like smashed glass to tinkle on the shuddering floor.

Despair glutted my stomach cold. I gripped his hair under a thickening rain of dirt and rocky shards, and pressed my cheek to his, his skin's sweet friction on mine no longer a pleasure, but a dark threat of loss. Tears leaked onto my face, smearing in the dust. "I didn't mean what I said. I didn't get it. Please, don't fucking give up. God knows I deserve it, Joey, but don't give up on me."

My voice shimmered, crystalline with unspoken emotion, and golden glitter tumbled like sparkle on my breath.

I blinked. What the hell?

Strange, heartbreaking melody pealed in my throat, rich with honey and mint. It warmed my soul, that song, like a hot bubblebath or a crackling fire on a deep winter's midnight. And as I watched, a tiny spellwarm halo shimmered and brightened around us, glowing like golden fairylight.

His skin sprang alive with sudden sweat, heat rolling off him in a wave. His body jerked in my arms, and his spine made a sickening crack that ricocheted like a gunshot.

A bloody, tortured groan ripped from his lips, and I choked on a howl. Surely, I'd failed him. Poisoned him. Drained him to death with my fear, just like I'd done to my mother.

He gave one final bone-shaking shudder, and air rushed hard into his lungs.

Spellshine dazzled, golden. Glossy snakeflesh rippled in his back, mingling in a blur with glowing white human skin. Ribs contorted. Sharp black spines grew and subsided. Tendons twisted and stretched and contracted, pulling his muscles into grotesque and alien shapes. His limbs flexed, impossibly lithe and jointed, and with a final twist and tortured heave, he slammed back into his human body.

He coughed, venom-tinged blood splattering my thighs, and his eyelids fluttered open.

Slowly, he focused on me, his lovely fierce-green eyes bloodshot, and warmth glowed in my heart like long-lost sunshine.

The dust made him blink, and something foolish and wonderful caught in my throat. I didn't say anything. I didn't have to. I just stroked dusty hair from his face and grinned like a lovesick idiot.

He swallowed. "Ceiling's falling, Mina. Can I get up?"

"Sure, boss." The words stuck, strange in my mouth.

And we pulled each other up, clinging hands and entwined limbs and warmth.

The rock surrounding us rumbled, and I choked on dirt, the old fear of dark spaces closing in on me like water.

He tugged me toward the main tunnel. "Outta here."

But glimmerwhite caught my eye, and I turned. In the corner, something groaned and struggled under a rockpile, and a long dustcaked hand emerged, fairy claws raking the air for freedom.

I hesitated, my heart thudding in the thick air. Ivy lied to me, tricked me, tried to kill us both. Stupid to let her live.

But I was done with blind revenge. I couldn't just leave her here.

"Wait." I slipped my hand from Joey's and crawled into the dust, gritty pebbles scraping my palms.

Ivy stared, her pretty face caked in bloody dust and blood. Bleak despair shone dully in her gaze, and her wings jerked weakly. "Pumpkins," she mumbled, drowsy. "Tasty. Where's the ketchup?"

A big hunk of concrete crushed her straining belly. I shoved it aside with a flex of magic-ripped biceps. Rocks tumbled, revealing her battered body.

I waited for her to heave in a dust-choked breath, flap her wings, get up.

But she didn't. I touched her chin, and her golden head flopped limp, her breath hissing away. Dead.

The ground tilted, splitting beneath me with a deafening crack like gunfire. I staggered, off balance, teetering toward the darkness. Joey caught my hand, and together we dived out onto the platform.

Behind us, the ceiling thundered down, shaking the floor like world's end.

The crash echoed, rolling up and down the empty tunnel like a storm, and faded to silence.

Dust clouded. A single electric light flickered and buzzed. I coughed and rolled onto my back, my eyes stinging. My lungs ached like I'd held my breath for days. Which, in a way, I had.

Joey crawled up and offered me his hand, his lean naked shape in golden silhouette. My magicsharp gaze trailed over the lines of his muscles, that pale perfect skin. Even coated in dust and blood and broken glass, he was magnificent.

My skin warmed. *Even?* Who was I kidding? *Especially.*

I took his hand and levered upright. My bloody footprints scarred the dust.

Joey arched his eyebrows, an elegant dusty smear. "You okay?"

He'd only just started asking me that. I didn't know what to say. "What? I mean . . . yeah. Thanks."

"Good. You got plans this afternoon?"

"What?" My brain couldn't keep up. Not with him standing so close, naked, his hand in mine.

"This afternoon. Now, in fact. You doing anything?"

I flushed. I'd imagined being far away from here, and remembering my gutlessness stung me raw. But now I was stronger. Now, I knew what I wanted, and I wasn't afraid. I loaded a half smile and aimed it at him. "Didn't have much lined up."

"You do now. My place, an hour. You know where it is. Two four eleven."

"Huh?"

"The alarm code. It's two four eleven. Let yourself in." He slid his hands along my jaw and kissed me, for a few precious, dizzying, far-too-short seconds. And then he whirled and dived for the tracks, his body slipping smoothly into its glossy black skin before he hit the ground and whiplashed away.

I stared after him, stunned. Two four eleven. Twenty-fourth November. The day he'd found me.

God, I had so much to learn.

33

I didn't shower or change my clothes, though I badly needed both. I didn't even go home. I just crawled up that rusty ladder, out of that dusty wreck of a tunnel into an abandoned pile of pinkglass shards, and hauled my dirty, bruised ass to Southbank as fast as my trembling knees would take me.

Two tram rides and a few blocks walk in the roasting sun later, and I walked through the glass lobby, sweat crinkling my hair as it dried in air-conditioned chill. The security guy followed me with his beady black gaze as I passed, his green forehead crinkling beneath polished white horns, but he didn't say anything or stop me.

The elevator mirrors showed me smeared in dust, my lips bloody, my arms crisscrossed with angry scratches. My bare feet ached on cold steel. My nerves sprung like steel wire, and I quivered, reflexes prickling, clutching the metal handrail tight.

When the lift halted, my throat swelled. I half wished the door had welded shut, so it wouldn't let me out into his scrutiny's harsh light, where I might burn.

The door slid aside. I swallowed, and stepped out.

His heavy door clicked softly open when I pressed # to finish the code. Inviting blue-filtered light welled inside, the air dry and warm the way he liked it, his intoxicating minty scent permeating everything. Soft carpet caressed my feet as I stepped past glass bookshelves, sparse slategrey furniture, a white flowering lily. I heard soft air-conditioning, the breath of breeze on covered windows, somewhere the faint cool hum of a fridge. Everything spotless, fresh, tidy. Not a mote of dust on the floor. Perfect.

I found him in the lounge, quiescent and easy on soft cushions, waiting for me. He wore black, but soft, silken, absent his usual sharp edges. He'd showered, and his damp blond hair curled at the ends the way I remembered. I could hear the crisp edges curling. I wanted to twist it over my fingers, sink my lips into it.

I lingered on the steps under the archway, ultraconscious of my own dirty blue hair, my smeared face and ripped pants, the blood and dirt I was smudging all over his carpet. "Umm . . . Hi."

He stood and glided over to me, cooling my tingling hand between his. "You're early."

"Yeah. Look, I shoulda cleaned up, I'm sorry—"

"Stop it." Effortless, how he silenced me with a word and a stunning smile. "You're perfect. I . . . please, allow me." And with a gentle but inescapable tug, he led me along the softlit corridor to the bathroom.

Candlelight shone warm on black marble, the scent of bubbles like lilies. My reflection shone dimly in the glass shower door, a halo of blue like a frosted angel. Cool black tiles soothed my feet. He'd filled the sloping bathtub for me, and the delicious lap of warm water on porcelain licked my ears.

He touched my shoulder, turning me to face him, and slid one slow easy finger down between my breasts, easing my zipper open, click by sensual metallic click.

Already my breasts ached for his touch, the pressure only growing as my tight leather loosened. My nipples twinged in anticipation. But I was sweaty and dirty and smelled nasty, and I flushed and halted his hand with mine. "I can do it."

"I can do it better." He slid the zipper to the bottom and slid my top off my shoulders, raking his hot gaze over my naked chest. His fingertips whispered around my throat as he unclipped my choker and drew it away. Then he turned his attention lower, coaxing my torn pants off with gentle hands. I'd lost my underwear back at the last place, and the sweaty leather peeled from my skin to leave me naked.

I fidgeted, flushing, and he wrapped me in lithe strong arms and turned me to face the mirror, his warmth luscious against my back. My pale skin stood out against his black silk, the dark marble, my dirty sapphire hair mixing with his blond. "Look at you," he whispered, his touch fairylight on my belly, and his gaze flamed with such passion and dark intent that I trembled.

His intake of breath at my shudder spoke volumes. Silently, he took my hand and helped me into the bath.

Hot water softened with soap slid velvety over my skin as I slipped deeper, the warmth caressing my legs, my sex, my belly. I laid my head back on the contoured edge, the water licking up my neck, into my hair. Soap bubbles popped in harmony, sliding soft and warm over my skin. He slipped his shirt off, revealing that eerily flawless skin I loved, and knelt beside the bath, dipping a sea sponge into the water.

I closed my eyes, tension washing away, only to be replaced by a deeper, more pleasurable ache as he slid the soft sponge over my body. He cleansed my feet, my torn ankle, blood slipping cool into the steaming water. He trailed the warm softness over my thighs, lingering, up to my belly, my breasts, my arms, my bruised palms, until my own wetness slid hot between my legs and I ached for his kiss and his skin on mine. He washed my hair, dipping hot water and sliding fresh soap through the tangled mess until it sifted like silk, and I couldn't help but moan at the tingles sweeping my scalp, shivering all the way to my toes. "Joey—"

"Shh." His fingertips swept down my flank, eliciting a gasp. He slipped his palm over my thigh, tracing the sharp tendon, my tight muscles. Sleepy pleasure drifted in my blood, and I eased my legs apart, exposing my sensitive inner thigh. He stroked me gently there, teasing in circles, creeping upward until his fingertips brushed my fine wet hair and parted it, slipping inside.

I sighed in lazy delight, my moisture flooding warm into the water. He stroked me, caressing my secret shapes, finding the hidden places that gave me the most pleasure. I opened up and let him explore me, play with me, tease me to slow tension that swelled and heated inside me until I moaned sweet ecstatic melody and arched my back, soap bubbles spilling warm tingles over my stiff nipples.

Surely I couldn't come like this. Too gentle, too easy. I needed force, pressure, violence. But the rich elegance of his touch was too much. Pleasure grew and flowered, the harmony building inside me ever more intricate and beautiful until I moaned and shuddered and let go, sweet release spilling breathlessly through my belly, my tension dissolving into ripples in the water like a perfectly pitched chord.

When at last I came down, he silently helped me from the bath and dried me in a warm fluffy towel. He caressed me softly, soaking up the last of the bubbles and the water. I leaned against him on wobbly legs and for once let him take care of me, and when he squeezed the last drips from my hair and led me to his bed, I didn't protest. My time would come later, my demands, my way. For now, I owed him this. I'd accept whatever he wanted to give and ask for no more.

His room lay dim and warm, soft downlights dimmed almost to nothing. He laid me down in warm mint-scented sheets the color of slate, and stretched out beside me, leaning on one elbow, blond locks tumbling over his hand.

I rubbed my shoulders in the silkiness and reached for him, glossing my palms over his hard-muscled chest. I wanted to feel him against me, press my breasts against his chest, wrap my legs around him and hold him close.

But he caught my hand, holding it gently away from him. Mortification seized me, and I pulled back. "Sorry, I didn't mean—"

He hushed me, a soft finger on my lips, and reached over to turn the lights down.

Warm darkness enfolded me. No light, only his faint green gleam. His breathing, my heartbeat, his crisp hair falling, the soft slide of skin on silk. And then another sound that twinged my nerves tight: the sweet crackle of shifting flesh.

A faint hiss tickled my ears, a rasp of breath. Thrumming vibration, a quicker, different heartbeat, a slicker, crisper friction of skin. Liquid's minute green glow, reflecting in the fresh glint of beautiful shiny eyes.

My lips trembled, and I held my breath.

I felt it first on the side of my thigh, the brush of smooth skin, so warm and soft. Delicate, hesitant, afraid I might break.

My nerves glittered. I didn't pull away.

Up to my hip, a little more insistent, trailing sweet warmth behind. Daring, I reached out in the dark, and my fingertips brushed a tight warm curve.

My skin tingled, and I let my touch roam.

So sleek and lovely, slight roughness when I stroked one way, perfect smoothness the other. The harder ridge of fins, tucked neatly away so he wouldn't hurt me. I ran my finger along them, savoring the tiny sharpness, seeking out the softness of his flank once more. His muscles rippled alive under my touch. He rubbed lightly against my hand for a moment, and then bumped me gently away. *Don't. Let me.*

He curled lovingly over my hip, his body's sensual stretch and glide so perfect, I shivered. So slow and luxuriant, savoring my every curve. I slid my hand along his skin and pressed him closer, so warm and beautiful.

Something hot and wet flickered over my belly, a lithe caress that tingled darksweet melody under my skin, and when he did it again, I had to moan, it felt so deliciously right. He took his time, tasting me, searching for my pulse and feeling it against his tongue, first in one place and then another until my whole body sprang alive with hot, sultry sensation.

I shuddered as he slipped up over my ribs, so strong yet light, his long muscles stroking me from hip to breast, and when his curling tongue licked my aching nipple, the sensation burned deep down inside me like molten fire. I arched my back, and my music responded, lilting my breathy sing-song desire into the dark. The silken sound of his skin on mine thrust a hot ache between my legs. I wanted to wrap my leg around him, pull him between my thighs and press tight.

He coiled amorously over my breasts and slid down my flank, the rest of his body still climbing over my opposite hip, wrapping me in his hot silkiness. My flesh molded to him, accepted him, begged for more. I bent one knee for him, and he coiled over my hip, under and around my quivering thigh, licking my skin lovingly. Warm shivers spread my desire deep like fever. And then he softly constricted his muscles, all the way up and over my body, and *squeezed*.

Oh, god. I forced my eyes shut on a scarlet wash of brute need. Pulse thudded between my legs, a desperate pleasure-pain, and wetness spilled from me onto the sheet, the breath forced from my lungs for more reasons than one. So safe, so secure. So needed. I wanted to cry. To be wrapped like that in his body, so raw and exposed. All barriers stripped away, no more lies or façades or deliberately hurtful words between us. I'd dreamed of it for so long, it didn't feel real.

But it was real. Shudderingly, deliciously real.

His tongue teased the crease at the top of my thigh, cramping my belly with delicious anticipation. When he nuzzled his way into my lap, I groaned and dragged my legs apart, releasing my aching clit from its hiding place to beg for attention. I was so swollen there, it hurt, the very air an unbearable stimulation on my exposed bud, and only one thing could cure me. "I need you. Please, touch me."

He curled possessively around my mound, squeezing me tightly, as if I didn't already understand that he owned me body and soul. He inched closer, feeling for my throbbing pulse in the warm crevices. When he flickered his long hot tongue along my slit, tasting me, my flesh nearly burst with the sheer force of sensation.

He teased me now, stroking me lightly, soft tantalizing licks stopping short of where I needed it most. He slipped his tongue deeper into my folds, searching, pushing inside

me and out again, and I moaned and pressed into him, incoherent. He hissed, the vibration exquisite, and at last he drove
his tongue against my clit.

Pleasure stabbed me deep. He licked me hard, fast, just
how I needed it. I spread my legs wider, pushing into him,
and a few more skillful flicks over that hard little burning
point and I exploded.

Even better than before, hard and fast and intoxicating,
my body igniting with fierce delight. Rainbow chimes spilled
from my lips, my magical voice exulting with a wild trill. I
was probably breaking glass in the next room. I didn't care.
He'd given me everything I'd ever wanted. Trust. Affection.
Respect. If I didn't know better, I'd say I was in love.

I flopped, catching my breath, my muscles still limp with
pleasure. He glided off me, nestling in my warm flank with
a serpentine quiver of satisfaction. With a gasp of delight I
felt him shift, and then his mouth captured mine, breathless,
a desperately human kiss that tasted of mint and my sweat. I
wrapped my legs around his hips and drew him onto me, his
hair sifting like raw silk in my fingers, his taut muscles so
hot and lithe against mine. His cock slid so easily into my
wet folds, his lovely shapes so good against me.

He groaned into my mouth. "Mina, you're so precious.
Don't let me hurt you."

Baffled laughter spilled from my lips on glittering soprano song. "You can't, not anymore."

He gripped my hip to hold me open and thrust in all the
way.

Hot, hard, as good as I remembered. God, he was so hard
for me, I felt every curve and ripple, his minty heat delicious
as he pushed deeper, and this time his control was slipping.
He took me strong and deep, in a flood of kisses and hot
shared breath, his relentless green eyes ablaze with desire.

I tilted my hips up, moving with him, and my pleasure rose
with his, so many months of tension finally resolving. Our
bodies shared, worshipped, pleasured. His muscles slicked
under my hands, his strange neon sweat tingling like mint-

candy. He buried his face in my hair, nuzzled my throat, sank possessive teeth into my ear, and hot dark shivers shook my spine all over again. His thrusts hit that hardening sweet spot deep inside me, over and over, dragging me closer and closer to glorious resolution, and when he arched to suck my nipple deep into his mouth, I shuddered and cried out his name and melted all over him in a wild exultation of crazy, perfect melody.

My pleasured song danced and rippled over us, tingling his hair with wild green sparks, and he bent his mouth to mine and mashed our lips together and let himself come, his body buried as deep in mine as he could make it.

We juddered and gasped together, sweat mingling, his blond hair stuck to my forehead and my fingernails clutched tight in his hips. Our heartbeats matched each other, our limbs molded together, and we lay there kissing again and again until our mouths were raw and our lips numb, but we didn't care. He pulled me with him onto his side, our bodies still joined, and I wrapped my arms around his neck with my aching thigh around his hips and we kissed some more.

At last, his lovely cock slipped out of me, and I crooned in protest, my legs heavy and limp. He stroked my tender lips with his thumb, his body still warm and alive against me.

I snapped playfully at him, and even in the faint luminescence of his skin, I saw that dazzling icewarm smile. My heart somersaulted. God, I loved his smile.

I smiled back sleepily, fatigue washing happy and warm through my body. "You're okay, Joey."

"And you, Miss Mina, are trouble. But I like it." He kissed me, one more time. I didn't want him to stop. But my eyelids slid closed, and in my warm sweet dark lullaby I felt him shift against my side. I slipped my thigh over him, and we slept, with his sleek black body wrapped around mine and his narrow head nestled tight in the crook of my shoulder.

When I woke, he leaned beside me, his blond head resting on his hand. He twirled a lock of my hair around one finger, letting it catch the soft light in a sparkling blue halo. "Evening, princess."

I smiled, sleepy, and stretched up for a kiss. I loved the smooth hardness of his body against mine. "What time is it?"

He caught my bottom lip in his teeth, provocative, and the kiss lingered, his hot menthol taste shocking me awake. "Time you went home."

"Oh." I fidgeted, awkward. Was he sick of me already? "Okay."

"To change. I'm taking you out to dinner."

"You are?"

"Said I would, didn't I? I know just the place. I'd say wear something sexy, but you always do. And bring something sharp. We've got work to do first."

My smile curled, delicious. "Okay."

"Fuck, don't smile like that unless you want the consequences." His mouth captured mine, and he pulled me on top of him, and my flesh opened so easily for him, sliding him inside me like we'd never been apart.

A breathless hour of kissing and stroking and sighing later, I reluctantly wriggled from his arms and went home to change.

In hot velvet evening, my place loomed dark and silent without him. I popped the harsh lights on, and for the first time I noticed how sparse the place was, how empty and heartless, the stark gray furniture unrelieved. A chill shivered my heart. I'd been so empty and alone. But for the past few hours, I'd felt at home. Safe. Alive.

Contentment gleamed like sunshine. I fumbled for my pocket to call him, hear him say my name, prove it wasn't a dream. But my fingers brushed empty leather. My phone was lost. I'd just have to take it on trust.

For once, that didn't seem a bad thing.

I stripped, tossed my wrecked clothes into the corner and took a quick shower, his scent on my skin steaming up the glass, faint iridescence washing away. I put on my shiniest black corset, my tightest, smoothest pants, the sharpest heels I could find. I slipped fresh knives under my jacket and painted my makeup sharp and bright. I steamed my hair ruler-straight, jagged blue ends glinting like razors, and swapped my ripped choker for a fresh one with ruby studs to match my eyes.

And Joey and I went to work.

34

In a dark, hidden corner at Unseelie Court, where music soaks like a distant bloodstain through red velvet curtains and fragrant drugsmoke hangs low, Iridium slouches on a plush scarlet sofa and watches Vincent work his sultry vampire magic.

In the booths around them, couples and threesomes sigh and snort sparkle and fuck, too drunk or high to pay attention. Opposite him, Vincent is clean and handsome tonight in white linen and pale jeans, soft brown hair in artful disarray.

The girl he's playing with smiles and blushes, flattered by his attention, blissfully unaware. He looks boyish, charming, harmless. The perfect gentleman, the perfect killer.

Iridium's cock stiffens just watching him. Only a beginner, it's true, but the relish Vincent puts into his work is better than rape. This is the second masterpiece he's created tonight, the new vampire always hungry, no amount of blood and pain and breathless surrender enough.

A bleached white earthfae girl nuzzles Iridium's lap, her forest fragrance swimming in his head, her slow eager fingers exploring his aching cock through his jeans. For a moment, it eases the torture in his warped bones. He's paid her well enough to adore his misshapen body. Maybe he'll choke her with his hard-on. No point in wasting good cash.

Then again, who gives a fuck? Now the snake is gone, he's free to practice and refine his art. Maybe he'll take this one home and show her his toys. She'll give him a fine blow job hung upside down by her ankles, the blood seeping from her throat.

Vincent's canvas is beautiful, long dark locks lush on her pale shoulders, pouty lips painted yet another shade of Iridium's favorite red. She sits primly on the couch's edge, dark skirt covering her shapely legs to the knee, and Vincent clinks champagne glasses with her, favoring her with that killer smile. She's already mesmerized, her deep brown eyes glazed with mutant hypnosis and the blood he's slyly fed her, and she answers Vincent's inane questions with a helpless quaver of desire in her voice.

Iridium nods, intent. "Good. Now ease her into it. She's yours."

Vincent grins and leans over to whisper dark suggestion in her ear, and as Iridium watches, she relaxes, her trim posture leaching into a wanton slouch.

The white fairy burbles happily and unzips Iridium's jeans with her pointy teeth. Iridium stares, hypnotized by the helpless look in the dark-haired thing's eyes, and absently pushes the fairy's mouth onto his cock, her hair tangling loosely in his crookedsharp fingers. "Take it slow. I want to watch."

He means Vincent, not her.

Vincent takes the glass from the toy's limp hand and puts it aside. "Undress for me, darlin'."

Dreamily, she obeys, unhooking her dress at the back, baring small white breasts with stiff nipples. Vincent dives and bites one with a heady crunch, and the girl smears the blood on her palm with a rich cry of spell-drenched pleasure, painting her torso red like pomegranate juice, writhing her body and moaning.

Vincent groans and swallows, blood gushing over her breast to stain the cushion.

Iridium sighs and shudders, sweet pain thrumming in his muscles like whipcord. He likes this part. Watching them surrender, demean themselves, crush their dignity to dirty shreds. His cock swells, and the fairy murmurs and sucks him harder, deeper, the scrape of her tiny teeth adding to the sensation. Her sugary fairy tongue sliding along his misshapen length makes him *want*. Unquantifiable, indescribable, that tortured mix of frustration, envy, and hatred for the world that made him like this. "More," he demands, breathless. "Make her work."

"Touch yourself, baby. Make it feel good." Vincent rubs his face in scarlet trickles, his fangs making swift shallow cuts in her skin as he nibbles.

The dark-haired girl pulls her skirt up, her flimsy underwear easy to peel away. She smears her own blood between her legs, moaning as she strokes herself. Her legs are spread wide, and Iridium savors the view. She's got pretty girlflesh, all swollen and tight like a weeping red rosebud. He'd like to lick it, and for a dim, confused instant he wonders what it'd be like to make her come, not with torture but with a gentle caress.

His head aches. Whatever. She'd feel good on his rusted teeth, the sweet slice of skin and nerve, blood spurting as he tears the pulsing shred of flesh free. Pretty, luscious, desirable, everything he's not.

The fairy girl swallows, taking him deep in her throat. He reaches for an empty bottle and cracks the lip hard against the table's metal rim. Glass shatters, cruel shards glinting sharp. He pushes the jagged bottle across the table.

Vincent catches his eye, and licks hungry lips, his breath quickening. He doesn't need to be told what to do. Softly, he folds the girl's fingers around the bottle and whispers with a feral smile.

The girl's eyes glint, and she grips the glass tight. Spreads her legs. Brings the bottle closer.

Iridium's broken toes curl in anticipation, a sweet spike of agony, and hot liquid metal rushes painfully up his cock, nearly, almost . . .

A freezing iron point jabs against the vein in his throat, and a wicked spellsong voice cuts his pleasure cold. "Suck it back in, metalfreak, or I let it out this end."

I yanked Iridium's slick bronze hair back in the stink of blood and metal sweat, and sang bitter harmonics that rattled his iron bones cold. My song felt rusty, unskilled, like I'd not used her in a while. And I'd changed while she'd been gone. We'd spend a while getting to know each other again, my cruelwitch song and I. But damn, she felt good.

Iridium grunted and spasmed, and the poor little girl with his cock in her mouth choked, spit and dirty quicksilver dripping thick from her rawburned lips. I shoved her with my pointed toe. "Outta here, darlin'. Fix you up later. Go wash that out with soap, ya hear?"

She licked her lips hungrily, sparkle-stung eyes wet, and scuttled away.

Vincent jerked up from his feasting, crimson trickles sluicing from his chin. His gaze shone blank, hungry like a trapped beast's.

The girl with the broken bottle in her hand jerked and blinked, color flooding her cheeks. "Huh? Wh— Ahh!" She screamed and dropped the bottle, hands flailing to cover herself, get away, hide.

Joey strode up, black suit immaculate, cane in hand, soft blond hair tidy beneath his hat. He swept the room with cold green eyes. "The rest of you. Out."

Even the three naked fairies screwing in the corner scrambled to obey, a flurry of rainbow limbs and lust-drenched green wings. Joey offered a hand to the half-naked girl, but she cowered under the table with wide eyes, hyperventilating and clutching her bloody dress to her breasts.

Iridium rolled crazy two-tone eyeballs up toward me and threw me a rusty, unhinged grin. His weird cock still twitched in his lap, semi-hard and growing. "Wanna sing like that on me?"

"Shut it, psychofae." I jabbed the knifepoint tighter into his neck. Blood spurted cold onto my hand, a dirty steelgray smear, and disgust shook me rotten to my guts.

It was simple, in the end, to baffle club security with a few sly seductive notes, and they hadn't objected when the metal detectors went off. And this monster was our own family. No Valenti asshole could complain we were breaking the peace. Just taking out the garbage. Cleaning up our act.

Vincent snarled, righteous, clawing the couch like an evil house cat woken from a nap. "None of your fucking business, Joey. You gave up your right to complain. Fuck off." He tried to slink away, a blur of vampire-spelled movement, but Joey flashed out a blackscaled hand and caught him by the throat. The brass head of Joey's cane smacked him in the balls, and he crumpled to his knees easy as you please.

Vampires. They ain't so tough.

Joey leaned over him, a lean black shadow, and slid glinting claws sharper into the soft skin around Vincent's windpipe. "A fine mess. What shall we do with them, Mina?"

I shrugged, Iridium's rustfoul breath shuddering my blood. "I vote we waste them both."

Did I mean it? Right this moment, I didn't know. I've never been the thinker in this outfit. Iridium was scum of the earth and deserved to be put out of his misery. On the other hand, it wasn't Vincent's fault he was sick. But did that mean we should set him free?

Vincent gurgled, venom already swelling the cuts, his vampire flesh quivering as it tried to heal itself. Fever shone wild in those precious brown eyes I'd been so fond of. "You mouthy fucking bitch. I thought we were friends."

"My friends don't eat people, Vinny." My hands shook, Iridium's sharp hair slicing into my fingers. "They don't trick girls into fucking themselves with broken glass. They don't hurt people for f—"

"Peace, Mina." Joey's cool voice soothed my nerves. He dragged Vincent's face within an inch of his, glistening fangs popping out coated in neon venom. "Last warning, kid. And only because once she liked you. Cross me again and I'll kill you. Insult her once more and I'll kill you slower. I understand that you need to eat. But play these filthy games again with anyone—anyone, scumsucker—and I'll skin you alive and swallow you raw, piece by stinking piece. Get me?"

Iridium giggled, metal on glass, shivering my spine. I cut his skin deeper, but he didn't care. "Tasty," he commented, and licked his twisted lips.

A glowing venomdrop plinked onto Vincent's cheek and

carved down his bloody chin. He cursed, trying to flick it off. "Gct off mc, ya sick motherf—"

"Yes or no?" Joey shook him harder, blood spurting from his claws.

"Okay, yeah, whatever. Just get your greasy claws off me."

"Fine. Get the fuck out." Joey shoved him aside in a green and crimson spray, and turned to me, claws twitching.

I swallowed, sick, and deep in my chest, my magic flickered. I didn't want to be a killer. But someone had to do it.

Joey's cold eyes softened. "Go get us a drink. I'll take it from here."

Iridium's scalp slicked cold on my fingers. I trembled. Did Joey think I was afraid? "It's okay. I can—"

"I know you can, Mina. Go get us a drink. Please."

Warm gratitude seeped into my limbs, and I sheathed my knife and walked out. Vincent snarled at me from the floor as I passed, and with a sweet twinge of regret, I ignored him.

Around me, the crowd seethed and danced, heavy music rich with electric harmonics, wonderful in my starved ears. The place was going off tonight, the fragrant full moon firing spellmagic in the air and lust in the blood. Fairies and trolls and spriggans danced sinuously in the crush, green and blue and scarlet, wings and limbs entwining in fresh sweat, lips shining with kisses, eyes glazed with pleasure.

Excitement rippled the air. Movement, breath, sparkling attraction, skin's rich slide on skin. I shouldered through to the bar, enjoying the feast of color and light, but I couldn't help reaching back with my ultrasharp ears.

Clotting bloodstains, velvet's rich rustle, the cold rasp of Iridium's breath. I didn't hear Joey speak. Only a razor swipe of claws, and a rich metallic death gurgle.

My boss is a killer. No question. But he doesn't deal out death lightly, and in this dark shadowy world, that makes it okay with me.

The sexy blond barboy grinned at me, he of the scars and leather. His blue eyes glinted sharper tonight, bright with moonlust and sly come-on. "It's a beautiful night to be alive."

"It is that." I winked and ordered Joey's scotch, along with a plain vodka tonic for me, and waited.

On the stool next to me, a blue fairy girl inhaled a sparkling green line from a shiny mirror. My stomach twisted, mixing unnerving disgust and need.

I gulped my vodka whole and put the glass down. I'd learned my lesson with that stuff. Hadn't I?

Joey's arms slid around my waist from behind, his hands smooth and clean, delicious lips warm on my ear. "Done. Forget about it. Let's have the night off."

It didn't seem right. At the same time, it was right. This was gangland. No time for regrets or false sympathy. I turned, enjoying his embrace, sure he'd pull away too soon.

But he kissed me. In front of everyone, hungry and fresh with excitement. He'd always gotten off on danger.

I flushed, pushing away. "You shouldn't do that. What if someone sees?"

"We'll deal. Who gives a fuck what they think? I won't let them hurt you, Mina." And he kissed me again. Not just a tease or a provocation. A proper lovers' kiss, tongues mingling, his glorious minty taste almost washing out my need for anything and everything except him.

Almost. When he released me, my treacherous gaze slipped, eyeing off that lucky fairy girl and her score.

He licked his lip, tasting me. "I want you to give it up."

I tried a smile, but it broke. "But—"

"But nothing. You work for me, and I need you in control."

"Okay." My voice strained, cold. I couldn't get used to this weird new dynamic between us. How was I supposed to know what was work and what was . . . the other thing? "Fine. It's all just business for you, right?"

"Let me finish. You're also my friend, and I care if you get hurt. And you're my lover, so long as you want to be. I want to know it's you I'm making love to, not some wild fairy glitter that makes you horny."

I stared, my jaw dropping.

His gaze slipped, and then fixed back on mine. "Call it vanity. I just need to know it's me you want."

If I didn't know better, I'd call that smile bashful. I felt like giggling. "I'm sorry, I think you've got the wrong girl. My guy never says goofy romantic shit like that."

"Give him time. He only just worked up the courage to say anything." He took my hand and whirled me into his arms, easing into the anonymous crowd on the dance floor.

Warm sound and fragrance drifted over us, the comforting press of invisibility. My leather encased me, safe and dark, and his arms around me felt the same way. Sweet melody filled my heart with sunshine, and the sparklehungry rodent in my guts sniffed and scuttled for cover.

A smile crept over my lips. For nights like this, I could kick anything. "I'll see what I can do. I might need some help. Y'know, to calm me down. Help me relax. Distract me when I get the urge." I arched against him, purring like a cat, my body tingling with fresh longing.

"Princess, you can consider your urges my personal responsibility."

"Good. Because I've got one right now. See to it." I offered my mouth up for a kiss.

"Yes, ma'am." He brushed a kiss on my lips, and another, and we lingered, deaf to everything but each other, until the lights went up.

Epilogue

Behind the bar, Akash inhales the sultry fragrances of lust and movement, and fresh tears of gratitude spring to his aching eyes. Glorious. So diverse, these myriad tastes and smells, so earthy and fleshy and hot. His skin flushes for the hundredth time, his own salty sweat a temptation. He wants to run his tongue along his forearm's curving muscles, lick it up, feel it slide down his throat.

A shining white fairy girl orders a drink he's never heard of, and he lets Rainbow's skilled fingers do the work, tipping in ice, measuring the heady liquor, filling the glass with a squirt of fizzy brown liquid. He flashes her a smile, the air a sweet thrill on his teeth, and she blushes and lowers her eyes. Rainbow's body has that effect on people, and it makes Akash burn inside with anticipation and memory.

Sex as a woman felt so wonderful, he thought he'd died and gone to hell. All that tension, building up inside as Rainbow caressed him, kissed him, thrust inside him, found such sweet spots in his stolen flesh as he'd never known existed. The smell of flesh on flesh, the sweet sound of caresses, touching's rich friction blinded him with raw sensation. And then the unbearable stress broke deep inside him, tearing such pleasure from his limbs and his belly and his heart, he cried, and Rainbow had to kiss his tears away.

Akash wipes the glowing neon bench with a warm wet cloth. It's already clean. He just likes the feel of it, smooth warmth sliding like skin under his palm.

His sharp eyes scan the crowd, fairies, glamour-blind humans, vampires with glinting sharp teeth. He'd almost been sorry to give up the woman's body. But Rainbow was his only safe hideout. If he wants to stay here, he'll have to be careful.

And here comes the first test. Kane, immaculate in his soft dark suit, golden hair sparking bright and fluffy around his face, scarlet lips twisted with rage.

Nerves tighten in Akash's stolen body, and he grips the glasses tight to still shaking hands. All depends on this. Last time, Kane let him off with a warning. He'll not show mercy a second time.

Kane flings himself onto a stool, ash raining from his hair. His claws rake smoking dents in the glass bar. "Give me absinthe and cognac, three and one. No ice. Now."

The demon's voice shivers Akash's stolen spine. So soft, so tempting. Brimming with promise and vice. Makes him burn to scream his true name, fall to his knees, and beg for mercy.

Shaking, he forces himself to relax, to let Rainbow's talents take over. Short glass, three shots green, one brown. He slides the drink across the counter, his breath stuffed tight.

Kane grabs the glass and drinks deep. Akash's eye hungrily follows the line of the demon's strong male throat, the curve where his pulse nestles, throbbing hot and black. . . .

Kane looks up, green sparks flashing. "What the fuck are you looking at? Not getting enough from your pretty-eyed girl?"

Akash swallows on a heady bloodrush. He's got the hard-on of his life standing here, so thick and aching, he wants to howl to starry midnight and satisfy it in anything that'll come close enough. This place is wonderful. If Shadow thinks Akash will meekly return home when this is over, Shadow can think again.

Unconsciously he mimics Rainbow's learned human

speech, clipped words and fragments that mean nothing. "Nothing. No worries. All good."

Kane eyes him hotly, plonking the empty glass down. "Get me another one, then, and keep your honey-licking fingers to yourself."

No suspicion in his gaze. No seething demonic compulsion on the air.

Kane hasn't noticed a thing.

Secret delight courses through Akash's veins. It worked. He's safe. He should call Shadow, tell him everything is ready to go.

Maybe later. After all, Shadow isn't the only one who can steal souls back from Kane. And now that Akash is here, he understands how Kane's winning.

Sensation. Pleasure. Temptation. This beautiful, agonizing, exquisitely addictive world.

They like what Kane's doing to them.

And two can play at that game.

Akash smiles Rainbow's best ladykiller smile and grabs another glass. "Coming up."

Read on for a preview of the next book

in *The Shadowfae Chronicles*

BLOOD CURSED

Coming soon from St. Martin's Paperbacks

"Where do you want it?"

Hot vampire lips caressed my shoulder in a fall of sweaty nightblack hair, and his salty breath burned.

I swallowed, sick. Smoke and hot nightclub lights dizzied me. Bass vibrated my lungs, guitars, and a screeching electric violin, the raw melody of fairy desperation. Around us, bodies writhed and danced, rainbow limbs and wings and glazed faestruck eyes, the scent of flesh and kisses a sweet temptation.

The vampire licked sweat from my collarbone, searching with his iron-pierced tongue for my pulse, and my stomach clenched. He wore black leather and lace, diamonds flashing neon, and behind ragged sable-dyed hair his eyes glinted, drunken sapphire blue.

His white shirt lay half-open, glowing purple in ultraviolet rain, and on his chest a fat scarlet gemstone glowed on a chain, shot through blue and green by wicked nightclub lasers.

My pulse quickened, and the veins in my wings swelled. There it was. My prize. All I had to do was say yes.

Just one bite, and the gem would be mine.

I grabbed his coarse locks and tugged his kisses onto my throat. He groaned and crushed me against the mirrored wall, licking a warm wet trail up to my chin. The glass slicked my wings, warm and clammy, offering no comfort. My guts squirmed tight, but I didn't wriggle away.

It'll be easy, Emmy, Jasper had whispered. *Show him some flesh, tease him a little, give him a quick taste and he's yours. Just get me my gemstone.*

I didn't want to. Not vampire bait, not me. No matter how Jasper charmed or persuaded or disarmed me with that dazzling fairy smile.

But saying no to Jasper was a trick I'd never quite gotten the hang of.

The vampire nipped at my bottom lip, fangs stinging. He tasted of meat and bourbon, fleshy and sweet. "I said, where do you want it?"

I let my lips part, my dusky breasts heave and swell. My long crimson hair tumbled invitingly, showering him in my spell-lured scent. I'd dressed for the occasion in silver stilettos and a glittery dress with a tight skirt, a scooping neckline and no midriff. Plenty of succulent bloodfae flesh on show, my dark skin beading with scarlet-tinged sweat.

Vampires love bloodfairy juice, see. To them, it's like the smoothest, slickest drug, heady and fragrant, sliding down their throats like hot opiumsweet honey. The near-full moon that lit the sky outside only made me tastier, throbbing like a tide in my pulse, igniting my blood with excitement and intoxicating fleshy flavor. Vampires can't resist.

And, unless they've survived long enough for their bloodfever to reach equilibrium, they're always hungry.

Always.

Which made me perfect bait. This guy—whatever his name was, kinda cute if you liked emotrash bloodsuckers—didn't stand a chance.

I gave him a sultry whore's smile, my nerves thrumming tight with danger. *Look, vampire. Candy. Come get it.* "Anywhere you like it, baby."

He growled, deep like a hungry beast, and drove hot fangs in hard.

Pain clawed deep into my throat. I squealed, but no one

heard. Lights flashed, uncaring, and deafening music rolled onwards, wire grating on steel. My blood splashed the mirrors, running in a sticky ruby glow. No one cared. Just another bloodfae slut, taking her medicine.

God, it hurt. My own bloodscent made me retch, my senses squealing peril, but I couldn't break free. Couldn't squirm away from his steely grip around my waist, his hot tongue pressing my skin, his crunching teeth forcing ever deeper into my throat.

He sucked, and faintness washed my head bright. My skin tore off in his mouth, agonizing. He groaned and rubbed against me, his lean body tense and hard, a gruesome parody of sex. He swallowed, sucking harder, dragging the blood out against the current, a horrible suction that pulled all the way down to my guts.

My limbs folded, watery. My wings slackened. Dizziness blurred my skull like cotton wool. His heartbeat thudded through my chest, alien, stealing my body's rhythm until we throbbed together as one. He gave a helpless shudder and drove deeper, swallowed faster, a tortured groan spilling out like he couldn't take any more.

My rubyshine blood gushed from his mouth, over my breasts in a hot sticky mess. His body jerked against mine in release—okay, that was gross—and I fought crippling dizziness and forced cramping fingers under his neckchain.

His fangs scraped bone, resounding though me like claws on a blackboard, and pain jerked me stiff. His hot wet body sickened me, the guttural growl in his throat as he came disgusting. I fumbled harder, desperate. At last I found the little metal knot, and I flicked the spring open and pulled the chain free.

Got it.

He didn't care. Didn't even notice I'd ripped him off. He'd gotten what he wanted, and he slumped panting against the bloodspattered couch with a groan of pure pleasure. Sweaty black hair fell in his face. His eyelids flittered closed, and glowing fairy blood—my blood, hot and fresh—splashed scarlet down his chin. He'd orgasmed sharp and hard just from my spellsweet taste, and his leatherclad thighs gleamed black and shining from the feverpink mess we'd made.

My head swam. I stumbled, and hid the bloody chain behind my back in a trembling wet hand. Blood trickled between my breasts and clotted there. Drowsiness tugged my eyelids, but I fought it and gave my glamour a clumsy kick. Whiteblue spellsparks glittered the air between us, invisible to anyone but me, my innate fairy magic messing with his mind. *Don't see me, scumbag. Don't see what I did. Only the blood, rich, hot, rubysweet . . .*

Spellwrought confusion swirled green in his eyes, and he threw me a dripping crimson grin. Panting, he fumbled in his pocket and tossed me a folded wad of cash, hair tumbling in bloodstained black knots over his chest. "Thanks, darling."

"Any time." I fumbled the catch, shaking. The money stung foul in my hand. I wanted to throw it back, scream, claw his face off.

But I forced myself to fake a whore's smile, wink at him, turn. *Don't let him see. Never show them how they've hurt you.*

I pushed through the shimmying dancefloor crowd, disgust still surging an evil tide in my blood. Heat choked me, thick with sweat and the smell of blood and sex. My guts squirmed like an angry snakepit, and I burned to scrub angry claws over my skin, rip away the horrid feeling of being fed upon like a dumb beast.

Shaking, I dug a handful of tissues from my bag and dabbed at the blood, wiping myself over and over until my hands were a wet red mess. A hot lump crawled up my throat to choke me. I could still taste the vampire's fleshsweet breath. Still feel his lips crawling on my throat, his teeth slashing my muscle, blood's dizzy surge away from my head.

The ragged hole he'd made in my throat burned. Soon it'd be healed, his virusrich spit already thickening my blood like sticky acid. But the humiliation mushrooming in my guts flamed hotter.

God, I hated this. I'd sworn I'd never stoop this low. I'd

seen firsthand what selling your blood did to you. Always
light-headed, always sick and dizzy like a permanent black-
sparkle comedown. Desiccated skin, brittle hair snapping,
rabid thirst that never ceases, hallucinations, waking nightmares, gnawing on your own fingers for protein. It's an
addiction, cruel and sweet and deathless, and eventually, it
kills you.

Once, I'd had a friend who bloodwhored. Now he was
dead. I should know better.

Yet here I was, prostituting myself on my dark fairyboy's
say-so.

Rage stung my eyelids wet, and I flung the stinking money
aside. The notes spilled on the floor, and colored fairy hands
scrabbled for them, claws scraping, voices squealing their
delight. Sickness bloated my stomach like rotten food. They
were welcome to it. After all, I had Jasper, didn't I? To keep
me, feed me, dress me in nice clothes. All I had to do was
say *yes* to everything.

You liked it, Em. The unseen moon's warm whisper
pierced my heart. *You liked that vampire's kiss. You wanted
his mouth on your skin, those slick fangs digging in, splitting
your delicate flesh, tearing you open, sinking deep inside. It
felt good to be wanted. So dreamy and free. So right. Isn't
this what you're meant to be, bloodfairy girl?*

My stomach heaved, and I covered my mouth and ran.

Music cackled accusation like a witch's laughter. Lights
glared, flashing on my luminous ruby bloodstains, showing
me up for everyone to see, and though I was lost in a perfumed
crush of bodies and wings, I'd never felt more exposed. *Look
at me, everyone. Look at the worthless bloodwhore.*

I stumbled on shaking legs. I felt hot and sick inside, like
a scolded little girl. I needed to pee. I wanted a shower, to
take a scrubbing brush to my filthy wet hide and scrape
those greasy vampire fingerprints off my skin forever.

Not yet. Jasper first. I clenched my fists, determined, and
the vampire's chain sliced my knuckles. I shook the stinging
chain free, and the crimson gemstone flared, as if coals ignited within.

I eyed it warily. It dangled from its chain, strobes flashing blue and yellow, but something definitely glowed inside.

A trick of the light? Surely.

I leaned closer, the light attracting my covetous fairy eye. Pretty, all shiny and glowing and sugarynice. Jasper and his mates were businessmen—selling fairy drugs and collecting protection money is business, see, and you don't say the word *gangster* around here, we're all businessmen or entertainment professionals or security consultants—and part of Jasper's business was getting things that didn't belong to him. He and his boss, a cocky glassfairy freak called Diamond, ran all sorts of shit in and out of all sorts of places. But I didn't know why he wanted this. My stomach warmed with childish envy. Maybe, once he'd finished, Jasper would let me keep it.

I peered into the gem's center, mesmerized by the tiny dancing flame. An eerie whisper slid into my head, ghostly and cold like mist. *Free meee . . . ssspare meee . . . take mee awayyy . . .*

Mmm. Pretty thing. I hummed softly to it, and the light flared brighter.

The air juddered, and erupted with a jagged scream of agony.

I yelped, and jerked backwards.

The vile thing clattered away, and the scream slashed to silence.

Shit. I scrambled for the gem on the dirty floor, dodging high heels and bare clawed toes and boots. At last, my clawtips brushed cold facets. I grabbed the chain and hopped to my feet, glaring at the dangling gem with suspicion licking my nerves cold. "Shush, nasty."

It sparkled at me, dark and threatening, and something black and forbidding swirled deep inside.

I glanced around. No one was looking at me. They hadn't heard a thing.

I sniffed, doubtful. I'd hallucinated that. Jewels don't scream. Or light up by themselves. Right? Just because I'm a fairy doesn't mean I believe in ghosts and woo-woo.

A dry murmur wormed into my ears, cold like rustling leaves. The glow inside swirled, flaring like a firestorm, and swiftly I stuffed the nasty thing into my bag before it could scream at me again.

A cold hand clamped my aching shoulder and spun me around.

My wings sprang taut. I stumbled, pierced by pale green eyes shaped with golden glitterliner.

A tall blond woman smiled, fangs sharp on scarlet lips. "You for sale, pretty?" She wore a short red dress over long pale legs, her faded blue eyes hard. Beside her, a dark-eyed fangboy in leather pants and no shirt winked at me, his tangled dreadlocks a shock of dusty blue. Sharp studs glinted in the collar that chained him to her wrist, and he sniffed in my direction like a hungry dog.

Great. Paris Hiltonvamp and Tinkerfang the Chihuahua. More horny vampires out for bloodfae sweets. Story of my life.

But I was alone, with no Jasper to protect me, and unease shriveled my throat.

I cocked my hand on my hip, faking nonchalance. "I'm sorry, do I know you?"

"You smell nice." Tinkerfang ghosted his damp palm up my cheek, a feverwarm caress. He smelled sour, of meat and sweat.

"Look, don't touch me, okay? I'm not selling."

"No need to be shy." Paris grinned, and grabbed my elbow.

I struggled, but she was too strong. Vampires were all too strong. "Let g—"

"We watched you feeding our friend," cut in Tinker. His black-smudged gaze draped over me, relishing the bloodstains, the sweat, the clotting fangwounds, and he leaned over and licked a hot slick trail up my cheek.

Yuck. I squirmed, dread thrumming my wings tight. His whisper burned my ear, bittersweet with cigarettes and lemon-drenched sparkle. "You were so fucking hot. I wanna drink you dry, baby. I wanna slice you all over and lick it up. Come play?"

I shrank back, disgusted, but Paris held me, and suddenly I was trapped in a cage of hot vampire limbs and invading fingers. Tinker stroked me, licked me, nuzzled my neck where the blood still trickled. Fleshscent stuffed my nostrils, and my blood warmed, thickened, pumped harder. Unseen moonlight tempted me, dragging on my fluids like a swelling tide, drawing me to wild fairyspelled desire. Blood throbbed sweet desire between my legs. Let them feed on me, eat me, suck me dry . . .

I jerked away and ran, horrid vampire laughter scraping in my ears like sandpaper.

I forced my way through the packed crowd on the dance floor, where fragrant sweat slicked on rainbow muscles and wingdust sweetened the air like candy. Glamours clashed and sparked, the air alight with the dazzling fairy magic that made us look normal to humans. Lights glinted on diamond earrings, shining wet fangs, glowing fairy eyes smeared blue and green with sharp glitterpaint.

Sweat slid down my neck, stinging. My hair stuck to my bloody chest. I glanced over my shoulder, my pulse burning. Couldn't see them following. Didn't mean I was safe. The sooner I found Jasper the better.

Above, the mezzanine loomed, dark and backlit in ultra-violet. Pounding music shimmered the air like heat haze as I forced beneath the iron railing into the shadows. A drooling blue fairy sprawled head downwards on the stairs, violet curls dangling, eyes gleaming dully like dead orbs from too much cheap sparkle. Telltale green dust still sprinkled his face, and a scrawny green spriggan girl licked it up eagerly, slurping her long black tongue over his nose, his lips, his pointed blue chin.

Drugsmoke shone in eerie purple light, green lasers flashing shadows from bodies, crawling wingbones, limbs contorted in pain or delight. Back here, the floor lay littered with crunched foil, dusty mirror shards, the sickly gleam of broken syringes smeared with greenmetal fluid. My sharp fairy ears twitched, and even in the crunching din I heard pulses, heartbeats, wet rasping breath, weaving around me and into the darkness like a throbbing web of life.

I sidled into flashing blue dark, stretching onto my tiptoes to look for Jasper. The tip of my nose whiffled, searching for his distinctive honeycomb scent amongst cologne and candy and the dark flowery cream of fairydust.

And there he was. Lounging against the iron wall, a long lean shadow sparking with static charge, the heavy glamour that turned him ordinary if you didn't know how to look. Long lean legs in his habitual black, his pale arms and face a bitter contrast. Wild, crisp black hair, fresh with glitter and perfume, golden rings flashing in his ears. His velvet-dark butterfly wings shed dust that glimmered and swirled in purple-shot lights.

I swallowed, and walked in his direction.

He leaned one steel-bangled forearm against the metal, muscles roped tight. Talking to someone, one of his sleazy friends or a mark. I couldn't see. And then his wings swept back, and his long hair tumbled forward over a narrow green shoulder slick with blue waterfae sweat. Lavender lips, wet neongreen wings, a slow tempting smile.

I halted, my heart thumping.

A female smile.

Her green arm slipped around his waist, and he tugged her rippling golden hair back and kissed her.

My skin burned cold. I didn't want to look. But horrid steel spikes jabbed my muscles, pinning me in place, and I could only stand and stare.

Kissing another girl. Not just a hello-sweetheart-wanna-buy-my-drugs kiss. A slow, deep, wet, tongue-on-tongue, let's-get-naked kiss. Bodies rubbing together, his thumb pressing her chin upwards the way he liked, holding her so she couldn't escape even if she wanted to. And she already melted in his arms. I could tell by the way her eyes closed, her head fell back, her glossy wingveins glowed brighter. I knew that hot, helpless dizziness, how he made you feel wanted, beautiful, the sexiest woman in the world. His hand crept up her skirt, between her thighs, caressing, and she moaned and pulled him closer.

Numb, I turned away, that old clockwork denial wound creaking its springs tight in my heart. It was okay, wasn't it? Just kissing. Stupid to be upset. I knew Jasper wasn't a saint. Hell, he sold drugs and stole stuff for a living. What did I expect? And I wasn't exactly blameless, right? I'd just been kissing another guy. It didn't mean anything.

Crazy laughter burst from my lips. Tick, tock, wind the clock, pretend it isn't happening. Only I could come up with an excuse like that. They weren't just kissing. The fucker was cheating on me. After everything I'd done for him.

Music throbbed in my guts, stirring them like worms in a mudpile. I felt hot and sick, impotent anger chewing my stomach raw. I'd sold my blood. Whored my dignity. Let some horny bloodsick beast chew on my throat and come in my lap with my blood running down his throat. I'd humiliated myself for him, and he didn't care.

I swallowed, sniffling, but my throat cramped hot, and the tears just flowed faster. Not because Jasper lied to me. Not because he'd treated me like an idiot and it hurt deep inside like a poisoned blade.

Because I knew. I'd always known. I'd just never seen with my own eyes before.

I was besotted, but I wasn't dumb, and fear and puppy love hadn't dulled my sense of smell. Sometimes he reeked of cheap perfume and sex, fruity kisses in his mouth that weren't mine, and like an obedient little wifey, I never complained. Only smiled and did my best to forget about it, and cried later in the bathroom where he wouldn't see.

I only had myself to blame. Too pathetic and weak to do anything about it.

Well, not anymore.

Blindly, I walked off, fisting my tears with blood smearing neonbright. My sharp heels scraped welts in my ankles as I stumbled. I didn't care. This was the last time Jasper would humiliate me like this. If he wanted to screw other women, fine. He could do it without me to come home to.

I plonked my ass onto a bar stool and swallowed, my bruised throat aching in dizzy alcohol scent. The neonglass bar glowed blue, vibrating under my palms as the music throbbed, and my blood invigorated, strength flowering in my muscles. Conviction hardened like steel in my heart. Yes. He could have his precious gemstone—whatever the horrid thing was for—and then I was dumping his dusty fairy ass.

But the cowardly worm in my stomach quailed and shivered, chewing its tail in mocking fright. *But you've got no cash, Emmy. No stuff. Nowhere to go. Whatcha gonna do, get a job? You're just a useless bloodfae bitch. Who'll protect you? How will you ever survive in that big old nasty world?*

I clenched hot fists on the glass, sparking my courage. "Shut up. Screw him. I'll get by somehow."

But that sniveling fearworm just coiled there, a greasy smile on its fat face. *Sure, Emmy. You keep telling yourself that.*

I ordered a vodka and lime, and as I sipped the tart chill through a straw, determination ebbed uneasy in my heart. I could do it, right? I wouldn't let him charm me this time. I'd forget his absent tenderness, the heady flavor of his kiss, the safety I felt in his arms. Instead I'd remember all the times he'd hurt me, all the thoughtless assumptions, harsh asides, and jokes at my expense, and I'd give him his gemstone and take off before he could work his sultry spell on me.

Get your hand off it, Emmy. One glance from those sultry hellviolet eyes and you'll melt. You really think you can stand up to him? Remember what happens when you piss him off.

My courage wavered, the twin tangs of vodka and dread sour on my tongue. I still had aches from the last time he'd taught me a lesson, and the old fear crept comfortably into my stomach, warm and oily from constant use. I should just forget about it, the way I forgot all the fights and slaps and nasty words. Most of the time it was okay between us. Maybe this'd be the time he'd change, stop snorting so much of his own product, treat me better . . .

Yeah. And we'd all get ice-skating lessons in hell.

No, it was over. I was leaving him. I'd give him his lousy gemstone and walk away.

Uh-huh.

In a minute.

I gulped my drink, trying to suck confidence from alcohol and sweat-drenched air.

"Ember? You okay?"

That crystalchime voice rang sweet alarm in my head. The smell of roses rolled warm and tempting over my skin, and on the blue glass before me, my shadow's edge glowed pink.

Shit.

Not Jasper. Worse.

My heart sank.